MARRYING MISS MARSHAL

LACY WILLIAMS

This book is dedicated to Luke and Laney for their endless patience.
Love you two.

CHAPTER 1

*T*he report of a rifle echoed through the red-walled canyon, ringing in Marshal Danna Carpenter's chest. A second report sounded soon after the first.

She reined in her mount and pushed back her Stetson, instantly alert and scanning the area for trouble.

The shots could've been someone hunting game, although there wasn't much of it to be found in these washed-out ravines southwest of town. Or it could've been someone discharging their weapon for a more nefarious purpose. As town marshal, she had to be prepared for both possibilities.

Danna's horse shifted beneath her, its movements telling her it sensed something wrong, as well. But what?

Then, in the last rays of sunlight slipping over the canyon's edge, she saw him. A man staggering along the canyon floor, booted feet dragging in the sandy soil. He carried some kind of luggage over his shoulder. From this distance, she couldn't see a rifle...

Too far away to determine his identity, Danna guessed she didn't know him. His clothes were too fine for these parts— dark pants, vest, jacket, and a bright white shirt. Most folks around here wore woolen trousers or denims and plain cotton shirts.

What was he doing so far from town? And on foot? Any halfway-intelligent person knew you didn't traipse around the unforgiving Wyoming landscape without a horse, or a mule at the very least.

Before she could decide whether to waste the last of the sunlight to check on the stranger or to head out of the canyon toward home, her horse's ears flicked back and his shoulder quivered beneath her gloved hand. The ground trembled.

From around a natural bend in the canyon, a cloud of dust rose like steam from a kettle and sent fear skittering down Danna's spine.

The terrible sound she was hearing began to make sense: hundreds of pounding hooves, getting closer every second.

Stampede. She couldn't leave an injured man to be trampled to death. Danna kicked King's flank and gave a shouted "Hiyah!" The horse rocketed toward the figure still too far away.

Peripherally aware of the canyon walls racing by, Danna watched the greenhorn pause and looked up toward the sky. What was he doing?

A few hundred yards behind him, cattle rounded a bend in the canyon. The beasts bellowed, and that must've jarred the tenderfoot from his stupor, because he turned and faced the approaching wall of horns and hooves. He froze. The item he carried slid to the ground.

Words rose in Danna's throat, but she had no breath to call out, not when all her concentration centered on reaching him in time. He wouldn't be able to hear anyway.

As the cattle closed in, the man's sense of self-preservation

2

seemed to kick in. He turned to flee, caught sight of Danna, and ran in her direction.

Danna fisted her mount's mane with both hands, leaning forward until her torso rested against his foam-flecked neck as she pushed the animal even faster.

The man looked up and, for a moment, time seemed to suspend itself. His eyes—a bright, clear blue—met Danna's, and she saw his fear and surprise.

A solid wall of cattle closed in behind the man. Too close.

Clinging to the saddle horn with her right hand and gripping her mount with her knees, she caught hold of the tenderfoot under one arm and used her horse's forward momentum to sweep him up behind her.

"Hold on!" she cried. The man's arm slung tight around her waist, Danna pulled the horse into a tight turn and fought to keep the stallion from unseating them both. She knew the fear of death in that moment, her twenty-four years playing out before her eyes. So many mistakes made...mistakes she desperately wanted a chance to rectify.

They weren't going to make it. A squeeze of Danna's legs sent the horse into a smooth canter, but it was too late. Several cattle overtook them, one bumping the horse's flank. The animal stumbled but somehow managed to keep its feet.

Fear stealing her breath, gasping, Danna clung to the horse's neck as it sped forward, outrunning the cattle and their thundering hooves.

Thank God. What had the fool man been thinking?

* * *

"Do you have a death wish?" the woman—woman—who'd saved Chas O'Grady's hide shouted over her shoulder. He barely heard the words over the din of the cattle still surging around them.

3

Her glossy black braid flopped over one shoulder and thwapped him in the chin. "Didn't you hear the stampede?"

Chas sucked in breath after breath of wonderful, fresh air before he could force any words—like, *I thought the racket was distant thunder*—out of his frozen jaw. "You're a woman!"

His arms still around her, he felt her stiffen. But the pounding adrenaline and building anger in his system kept his words flowing. "Are you entirely out of your head? You could have been killed riding straight into a stampede."

"Perhaps you'd rather I hadn't rescued you? Because you would've been trampled if I hadn't scooped you out of there." He felt her inhale deeply, then she blasted him again. "And I certainly didn't see any men around to do the job properly."

The woman's fiery retort stymied him for the moment, because it was true. There hadn't been anyone else in the canyon, and he would never have been able to outrun the cattle.

She'd risked her life. The realization brought bitter memories to the surface. Chas blinked away the images of another woman falling, her blood spilling.

This woman wasn't dead, though. Even though she'd put herself in danger for him. Memories and self-loathing churned in his gut until his rescuer turned her horse up the canyon wall, nearly unseating him with the sudden movement. Chas clung to the woman's waist, eliciting a huff from her.

Her faded denims and wide-brimmed hat had caused him to assume she was a man from a distance, but with his arms wrapped around the curve of her waist, there was no mistaking his rescuer was pure female.

He couldn't get a good look at her features from behind, but she must be nearly as tall as his six-foot stature; the brim of her hat rested inches in front of his nose. Several dark strands of hair escaped from her braid and curled along the nape of her long, slender neck. Her head was in constant motion, darting left to right, and it gave Chas fleeting glimpses of her cheek-bones, the soft bow of her lips, the dark sweep of her lashes. She was beautiful. And she guided the horse as if she and the animal were one.

In any other circumstance, she would have turned his head, trousers notwithstanding.

They pulled ahead of the cattle and edged toward the canyon wall. The cattle veered away and he felt the first stir-rings of relief. The woman slowed her horse to a walk as it went quiet around them.

With his detective's nose for curiosity already piqued, his mind swirled with questions. Why was she riding alone in this rough part of the country? And dressed as a man? Could she possibly work for one of the ranching outfits in the area? What rancher or foreman would hire a woman to work on their range? "What are you doing out here alone, anyway?" he demanded, trying to force back his darker emotions. "It's dangerous."

"I could ask you the same," she returned sharply. "You're obviously from a big city. How'd you get lost out here? What happened to your horse?"

Her questions sparked his irritation.

"I'm not lost." That statement was a bit of an untruth, but Chas wasn't about to admit that his sense of direction had been compromised by the winding canyon. He'd been operating as a private detective for several years. Being a little out of place was not the worst situation he'd ever managed to escape from. He would've found shelter eventually, if this female cowpoke hadn't come along. Probably.

"And if you must know, I had a horse. I bought her in Cheyenne, but...well, let's say the man who sold her to me may have exaggerated her condition."

He thought he heard a chuckle from his unusual compan-ion, but he couldn't be sure. He should end this conversation immediately, but his curiosity got the better of him. "Tell me, do all women in the Wyoming Territory dress the way you do? Or are you attempting to pass yourself off as a young man?"

"No," came the sharp retort.

"No to which question?"

She didn't answer, but he felt her draw back on the reins, and the horse slowed.

"Are we stopping?" he asked. "Why?" They hadn't even attained the canyon's rim yet. He'd hoped to make it to the small town of Calvin before evening set in.

"It's getting hard to see." The woman's words were clipped and terse. "I won't risk my horse or our lives trying to climb this shale in the dark."

Chas glanced at the purpling sky and realized how long the shadows had gotten along the canyon walls. He was no outdoorsman, but even he could tell it would be full dark in minutes.

"We can't just stop, can we?" Chas brought to mind the hotel room he'd hoped to find tonight. With a bed. A chance to wash away the trail grime he'd accumulated since leaving Cheyenne two days ago.

"It looks like there's a level patch up ahead." She nodded, though he couldn't see what she was talking about. It all looked the same to him. An uphill climb. "We'll stop until the moon comes up."

"Are you sure it wouldn't be better to keep going?"

She ignored him. As the last of the sunlight faded into pitch-black, the woman pulled up her horse on a somewhat flat piece of land.

If they were going to spend the next few hours trapped together in the dark, perhaps he should apologize. Certainly, it wasn't her fault her actions had touched on a sensitive memory he spent most of his time trying to suppress.

Best get it out of the way quickly. "Miss, I'm sorry—"

She interrupted him by pulling out of his loose grasp and sliding off the horse's back.

A bit miffed at her dismissal, he followed. And misjudged her closeness, thanks to the darkness. His momentum nearly knocked both of them to the ground, but he steadied her with hands on her forearms.

Her breath fanned his chin, her warmth tangible as the night cooled around them. Chas's heart thundered in his chest, much like those hooves that had been so close to taking his life. This time for a different reason.

"Miss, I meant no offense by my earlier words. I was..." He paused, looking for the right thing to say, knowing he couldn't tell her about Julia's death. "I was simply expressing my surprise to find my rescuer a woman."

She pulled away, but he still sensed her nearness. Her movements as she slid something from the saddle seemed jerky and stiff. It was clear she'd rejected his apology.

He went on. "I am grateful for your fancy riding. I'd rather not meet my Maker today, and I've no doubt those beasts would've stomped all over me if not for you."

"I would've done it for anyone."

Her voice sounded muffled, and he wished for a candle or a beam of moonlight so he might see her face.

"Stay here."

She disappeared into the darkness. Only the muted sounds of boots scraping against stone told him she was still nearby.

Stay here. He mimicked her curt command silently. What did she think? He would wander off in the dark and get lost? She'd already made it clear what she thought of his abilities traversing this very canyon. Agitation and impatience made him restless, and he paced away from her horse.

And stepped right off the edge into nothing.

* * *

DANNA HEARD AN INDISTINCT SHOUT, the scrabble of falling rocks, and then silence.

"Hello?" she called, not bothering to disguise her annoyance.

She kept moving toward the small stand of bushes she'd spotted as darkness fell. Where there were bushes, there would be dried twigs to light a fire. If she had to wait until the moon came up, she wanted to be able to see the man she was stuck with.

She tried again. "Mister?"

He'd flustered her with his nearness after he'd landed on top of her while attempting to dismount the horse. She hadn't been so close to a man since her husband's death. And even during their brief courtship and the early days of their marriage, Fred Carpenter hadn't caused turmoil in her gut like the warmth from this man's hands did. What was wrong with her? Fred had only been gone a few months. And she didn't even know the stranger's name.

Irritated with herself, she spoke once more. "Tenderfoot?"

No answer. Her extended boot met some resistance, and she knelt to gather the dry undergrowth from the bushes. Using the flint and steel she'd retrieved from her saddlebags, she had a small fire burning quickly. She turned toward her horse, standing right where she'd left it, but the man was nowhere to be seen. She resisted the urge to groan. After making sure the fire had enough fuel to burn for a few minutes unattended, she returned to where she'd left the tenderfoot just moments before.

Past her placid mount, the rocks on the edge of the slope had been disturbed. She frowned and walked over, noting this area had a bit of a drop-off instead of a gentle slope. It was hard to see in the dark away from the fire, but by leaning over the edge and squinting into the darkness, Danna was able to catch sight of the tenderfoot several yards away. He lay still, one shoulder cocked in an awkward position.

"Oh, no," she breathed. Louder, she called out to him, "Mister, can you hear me?"

A soft moan erupted from his lips, but he didn't move other than to roll his head toward her.

Forcing calm she didn't feel, Danna retrieved her rope from its tie behind the saddle and looped it around the saddle horn before tossing the length to where her unlikely companion lay.

"Mister? Can you reach the rope?" She didn't expect a reply, so she wasn't too surprised when none came. Keeping one hand on the rope, she scrambled down the steep incline as best she could. She slipped twice, and rocks bit into her palms as she fought to keep from joining the tenderfoot in a tumble. She wouldn't do him any good if she injured herself, too.

When she reached him, Danna knelt at his head and studied the man.

His hat had slipped to one side, and his sweat-matted hair was dark next to his fair skin. "Mister, you've sure got a way of getting into scrapes," she muttered. She probed his scalp and neck gently with her fingertips, searching for injury. Though obscured by a few days' growth of stubble, he had a strong jawline. He gasped when her palm brushed his right shoulder. Keeping her touch as light as she could, Danna ran her fingers over the arm and shoulder, and he moaned again.

"Hurts."

"I know. Looks like you've knocked it out of place." She prodded his torso and legs but found no additional trauma. She did find a gun belt and weapon at his hip. She ignored those for now. "I can reset it for you. But we need to get you up the hill, so I can see what I'm doing."

"I'll try." He clenched his teeth as he rolled onto his good side.

She helped him to his hands and knees, but he shook his

head and collapsed onto the rocky soil. "I can't..." he wheezed "...make it."

"All right." She smoothed a hand over his forehead as if she were comforting her almost-niece, Ellie. "Tell me your name."

"Chas." A breath. "O'Grady."

She filed the name away. O'Grady sounded Irish. She nodded absently and murmured, "I'm Danna Carpenter," as she considered the best way to get his shoulder back into the socket. "What brings you to Wyoming?"

"My job."

"Not cattle."

One corner of his mouth quirked upward. "How'd you know?"

"Lawyer?"

He snorted a laugh, then grimaced as if the movement pained him.

"Railroad surveyor?" she guessed, and gave a mighty tug.

O'Grady's upper arm and shoulder slid into place with an audible click. She was impressed when he didn't cry out, just rolled his head and looked at her with those blue eyes.

"Thanks. You're a doll."

Then he passed out. Danna sat next to his unconscious form in the darkness, willing away the blush that had flamed across her cheeks at his words. Stunned.

Something had happened inside her when he'd looked at her, when she'd heard the endearment he'd spoken.

Something inside her opened, like a flower unfurling. Attraction? Whatever it was, she didn't like it, not one bit.

CHAPTER 2

*C*has sat quietly near the small fire his rescuer had built. With nightfall a chill had fallen, and he was thankful for the warmth the crackling fire generated.

"How's your pain?" His companion asked as she propped herself against a barrel-sized boulder and removed her hat, loosing a spill of dark hair that had come out of its braid. She stretched her trouser-clad legs in front of her, eyes on her boots. Was that a blush on her cheeks? It was hard to tell in the dim, flickering firelight.

He rotated the shoulder, wincing a little. "Bearable. Better than before, thanks to you." He didn't want to think about what would have happened to him if he'd been left on his own in a haze of pain, shoulder dislocated.

He was grateful to Miss Carpenter for saving his hide, twice, but embarrassment was the primary emotion that registered.

He'd never had this much trouble with a case before, and he hadn't even made it to the town where he was supposed to scare up a group of cattle rustlers. It didn't matter that his cases usually took him to large cities like Chicago, St. Louis, or

Austin; he'd been a private detective long enough that he shouldn't have required help.

And his shoulder still ached, though not with the piercing pain he'd felt before she'd knocked it back into its socket. The pain was enough that he sat back while Danna Carpenter had spent several minutes scouting for more firewood. His mother would have had a conniption if she'd seen him allowing a lady to perform such a task without offering to do it himself. His mother had subjected him to extensive training during his youth, preparing him for a life as the second son of one of Boston's prominent Irish families. A life he would never live, not after the disaster he'd made of things.

"Do you live near here?" he asked, because he needed to keep his thoughts away from Boston and everything he'd lost.

"In town."

"Really? Hmm. How far?"

She grinned softly at his question. "Calvin is a few miles still. North, if you were wondering."

Her smile did funny things to his insides, left him feeling like he'd fallen off the edge of the cliff a second time.

"What's your business in Calvin?" she asked after a moment of quiet not long enough for Chas to gain his composure. "Are you visiting family?'

"You're a nosy one, aren't ya?" He didn't want to react to her. And his irritation that he couldn't seem to help himself made the words sharper than they ought to be.

Her eyebrows pinched, and she looked away from him, one side of her face falling into shadow, "Comes with the territory."

What did she mean? Chas didn't have time to consider the meaning behind her cryptic words. She looked back at him with unabashed curiosity, obviously waiting for him to answer.

"I don't have family here. I'm a businessman."

Her eyebrows pinched briefly before her face cleared. "What were you carrying with you? It looked like luggage."

He groaned. "A pair of saddlebags." With his letter of introduction for the local lawman inside. Passing his good hand over his face, he huffed a breath. "I don't suppose there's any way we could go back for them..." Then another thought occurred. "Do you think they could have survived being trampled?" How much more misfortune could befall him?

"I don't know if they'll still be intact. But to be honest, I wasn't too keen on climbing this hill in the dark." She motioned behind her. "Even after the moon comes up. We can wait until morning and try to find them."

"Thank you."

She stood and went to her horse, untied something from behind the saddle, and tossed it to him. A dugan—a bedroll, he'd heard them called.

"Sure you don't need this?" he asked as she pulled another object off the horse.

"I'm sure." She shook out a slicker, a large one that could have belonged to a man, or at least someone taller and broader than Danna. It made Chas wonder if she belonged to someone else. Was she married?

Returning to her seat against the taller rock, she swung the coat around her shoulders and tucked it underneath her chin. Her dark eyes met his, and he felt a spark sizzle between them before she looked into the fire.

What was this? He'd never felt this...connection with anyone else, not even with—

He spoke quickly to keep the thought from its finish. "Will your husband be out looking for you? I'd hate to fall asleep and wake with a gun in my back."

Something flickered across her face. Pain, maybe? "No."

"A father? Brother? Uncle?"

Now her mouth flattened into a grim line. She tossed the twig she'd been playing with into the fire and dusted her hands together. "No. No husband, no father. Not anymore."

13

Her words hinted she might've been married at one point, but her closed expression told him it would be best not to continue that line of inquiry. Suddenly, she straightened her shoulders and met his gaze head-on. "Where are you from? Back East?"

"My accent?" he asked with a rueful smile.

She nodded. "You're Irish?"

Intrigued, he leaned forward, resting his elbow on his bent knee. "How did you know?"

"A good guess." She shrugged, and he followed the motion of her hands as she folded them over one knee. "And I believe your hair is red as well, although I didn't get a good look in the dark."

"It is."

He wanted to keep talking to her, wanted to know why she dressed as she did, why she was alone out here. But he also wanted to protect himself from this tenuous tie they seemed to share. He who always pried for every piece of information from any person he came into contact with, feigned a yawn and rolled himself in the dugan.

"Thank you again, and goodnight."

* * *

"MISTER."

The sound of gunshots rang in his ears, blood covered his hands. Pain speared his right shoulder. Had he been hit?

"Tenderfoot." A boot nudged his ankle and drew Chas out of the nightmare. Memory.

He blinked, trying to dispel the images of the woman he'd loved dying under his hands. He rolled off his injured shoulder, shook his head to clear it, and took in his surroundings.

Muted gray light threw Danna Carpenter into silhouette as she knelt over the embers of last night's fire. The sight of her calmly going about her business quieted the raging maelstrom of emotion and memories bombarding him.

At least she had her back turned, so he could shake off the trembles his nightmare always left behind without an audience.

He couldn't help groaning as he pushed himself to his elbow. Danna turned back and helped him sit upright on the hard, cold earth. The dugan still covered his legs.

"Here, this should help with the stiffness in your shoulder."

Before he realized what she was doing, she'd opened his coat and unbuttoned the first two buttons on his shirt, exposing his injured shoulder. She hesitated—must've seen his gunshot scar—but then a welcome heat seeped into his skin. She'd warmed a folded square of wet cloth to make a compress.

Her eyes met and held his as she pressed the hot bundle against his abused muscles. He couldn't decipher her expression in the semidarkness, but a connection sparked between them. She was too close.

As if she'd had the same thought, she backed away.

He looked down to hide his confusion and immediately noticed his rumpled state. He was a mess. Needed a bath and a shave, and his clothes were covered in dust.

"Coffee." She pressed a tin into his hands and retreated again. "I'm not much of a cook. I think I scorched it."

A sip of the black sludge confirmed her words. He swallowed when what he wanted to do was spit it out. It did warm his insides.

"Thank you," he said, voice rusty.

"Thought your pain might be bad after a night out in the cold. You were moaning in your sleep."

His back teeth clenched. He often thrashed around because of the nightmare, but he wasn't about to admit to it. She'd probably ask questions, and he couldn't afford to share the answers. Not when he'd been responsible for the deaths of the two people he'd loved most in the world.

"Thanks," he muttered again, forcing himself out of the bedroll and into the bracing morning air. Taking a moment to stretch the kinks out, Chas absently rubbed a particularly twinge-worthy knot in his lower back while he watched his unusual companion as she used her boot to kick dirt over the graying embers of the campfire.

She looked up at him, this time with her hat pulled low over her brow. He couldn't read her eyes.

"If we find your things quickly, we can make it back to Calvin by breakfast."

His rumbling stomach thought that was a good idea.

"Your shoulder might act up a bit when we're jostling around on the horse's back, so you'll just have to tell me if you need to stop for a while."

He was ready to have some distance from this confusing woman and the draw he felt toward her.

"I'm sure I'll be fine. Let's go."

* * *

NEARLY TWO HOURS after the tenderfoot's declaration, Danna wasn't so sure his wounded arm was holding up. She'd kept her mount to a plodding pace, though both she and the animal wanted to move. Even this slowly, she felt Chas O'Grady's body grow progressively stiffer as the morning wore on.

The sun finally peeked over the canyon's rim, but finding anything in the torn-up ground left by the stampeding cattle was proving impossible.

The tenderfoot shifted in the saddle, a soft gasp making her turn her head for a glimpse of his face. A muscle ticked in his jaw. With her late husband, that had been a sure sign he was either mad or hurt. "You want to stop for a while?" she asked.

"No. I'm sure you need to get home."

She did, but she kept quiet.

"My saddlebags had some important documents in them. If they somehow survived, I'll need them."

"Fine." She knew he was hurting, but if the man wouldn't admit it, what could she do?

Danna kept her eyes on the chewed-up ground. Just looking at how the sandy canyon floor had been marked by the thousands of hooves, she doubted there'd be anything left to find. However, she understood his need to keep looking. She knew what it was like to lose something important and never get it back.

And what had those cattle been doing in the canyon anyway? She'd mulled it over all night, awake in the dark, while she'd tried to keep her gaze and her thoughts from straying to the man who'd slept just across the campfire.

She'd spent far too long staring at his broad shoulders, the only part of him not wrapped in the blanket, trying to pinpoint what it was about him that unsettled her.

For now, she chose to ignore that unruly flash of emotion last night. She couldn't be drawn to the near stranger. He made her uncomfortable. That was all.

It wasn't danger. She was well acquainted with the prickling at the back of her neck, beneath her hairline. No, this was more of an intensity. She'd been aware of his every movement, even after his breathing had settled, signifying he'd dozed off.

She almost thought those prickles of sensation were...attraction. But that couldn't be right. She'd never felt anything like this with Fred. Maybe she'd been too young when she married Fred, or maybe she had felt something similar at the beginning of their acquaintance, and she'd forgotten. She'd been married to Fred for eight years, after all.

The tenderfoot groaned, stifled it, and shifted again. "Maybe I should walk for a while. I might have a better chance at spotting my saddlebags that way."

He must be hurting something fierce by now. She

shrugged and reined in her mount. She'd have a better view from her horse's back, but if he wanted to walk, he could walk. The tenderfoot huffed softly when his shiny boots hit the ground.

"You sure you don't want to stop for a while?"

His only answer was a silent frown. The tenderfoot wore the same closed expression that Fred had worn when she'd asked too many questions. Fine. She wouldn't ask about his arm again, even if it fell off.

She forced her thoughts back to the cattle and what they'd been doing in this canyon. The roundups and cattle drives should have already been completed in this area. The ground above the canyon was dry, not terribly good for grazing. So what had that many animals been doing here?

It was a mystery. "Did you happen to see any brands on those cattle last night?"

"What?" The tenderfoot glanced up at her, focusing those intense blue eyes on her momentarily. "Oh. No, I didn't get a good look at any of their markings. Why? Did you recognize them?"

"No." Danna scanned the landscape, aware that his eyes remained on her, uncomfortable with his scrutiny.

"Why do you want to know?"

"It's a bit unusual for the cattle to be in this area this late in the year." And she thought she'd heard gunshots immediately before the cattle had stampeded. But in the confusion, she couldn't be sure. "Most have already been driven to Cheyenne for market. The vegetation starts to get scarce."

"Hmm..." He didn't sound terribly interested, but she supposed he wouldn't be.

Slowly, they drifted apart as they searched the ground.

She guessed he was a professional cardsharp, a gambler. He'd told her last night he was a businessman. Only, who would come to the tiny town of Calvin, Wyoming, to do business? And his fancy city clothes didn't fit in around here. It was a good thing she wasn't interested in him. A gambler.

Her thoughts distracting her, she almost missed the mangled piece of leather half-buried under the sandy dirt.

"I think this is it," she called out, and he joined her as she dismounted from her horse. He picked up the leather bags, juggling a pouch and canteen when they fell out of the hole torn in one side.

"I can't believe it. The saddlebags are ripped, but everything inside appears to be intact." There was wonder in his voice as he riffled through his belongings.

He took what looked like an envelope out and tucked it into his breast pocket beneath his vest. A second item quickly followed the first. Danna couldn't see what it was, something wrapped in leather and tied with a thong.

Were these two things important? If so, why hadn't he kept them closer in the first place?

"God must be watching out for you, Mr. O'Grady." The instant Danna spoke the words, his expression closed.

"I sincerely doubt God has spared any thoughts for me lately."

* * *

CHAS TRIED to ignore the pain that throbbed up his arm and through his shoulder with each movement the horse made as they headed to town, but it proved impossible, even when he closed his eyes against it. He knew his companion was trying to make the ride as smooth as possible. She held her horse to a walk and traversed more ground to avoid the gullies. He appreciated her efforts, but he still ached something fierce.

He just wanted to get to town and soak his aching joints in a tub of hot water. And find something to stop the growling in his stomach.

He and Miss Carpenter hadn't spoken since he'd gotten back on her horse. Her comment about God's favor had thrown up a wall between them, and he was glad for the distance. The sense of connection he'd felt with Danna since their chance meeting had him off-kilter.

After the horror of Julia's death and his part in it, he'd vowed not to allow another woman close. Not ever. Six years had gone by, and his vow hadn't been difficult to keep. He hadn't met any woman who'd compared to Julia.

Until now. And Danna Carpenter couldn't be more different from his first love. She was tall and slender, where Julia had been of average height and curved in all the pleasant places. Julia had been femininity personified, always dressed immaculately, with lace or jewels accenting her best physical attributes. Danna Carpenter dressed like a man and didn't seem to care about her appearance at all. Not that she had to, with her expressive brown eyes and that crown of long, black hair.

Julia had used her feminine wiles to manipulate him.

And it had cost her life, because he hadn't been able to resist.

Chas shook himself from his thoughts, noticing that the horse seemed to move faster now, although Danna held it in check. Chas locked his eyes on the horizon, hoping they were getting close to Calvin. A small speck appeared, then another and another, and finally they got close enough that he could make out the individual buildings.

His heart sank. The town was even smaller than he had imagined. It might pose a challenge to get the information he needed to make his case and find the rustlers. He wasn't likely to blend in.

Miss Carpenter's horse crossed one dusty street, passed the railroad tracks, and turned onto the second. He supposed this must be the main thoroughfare.

Perhaps the town did have some charm, though none of the buildings matched. About half were brick, the rest wooden. Most of them were unpainted, as if they'd been constructed hastily and occupied quickly. Likely they had.

Several houses had been built on the street behind the buildings, one larger than all the rest. A mansion, in this small town?

Danna reined in her horse in front of the second-to-last building on the street, the most unique one. Its first level was rock, but the second, constructed of wood, looked as if it had been added on later.

Unless he was mistaken, a dog bayed from inside. Strange. Perhaps it was a child playing.

Danna shifted toward him. "The livery is at the end of the street. I've got to go in and check—"

"Help! Marshal!" A high-pitched, female voice cried out.

Someone needed help. Chas jumped from Danna's horse, jarring one ankle and his injured shoulder when he landed. The horse shied at the unexpected movement.

"O'Grady!" Danna voice followed him, but he didn't have time to stand around and help her, and she was a good horse-woman anyway.

Chas darted across the street. His heart thudding in his ears made it hard to determine which direction the cry had come from, but he thought maybe from the left, so that's the direction he turned. He stalled at the first corner, where the boardwalk ended at an alleyway between buildings. Which way?

"Help" the voice warbled now, sounding a bit muffled.

"O'Grady." Danna clapped a hand on his forearm, her expression fierce under the brim of her hat. "Don't ever do a fool thing like that again. My horse could've—"

"I have to—"

"Marshal!" the distant woman shouted.

Danna stuck two fingers in her mouth and issued an ear-splitting whistle. Instantly, the shouting stopped.

While Chas gaped at Danna, a small nut-brown head popped up from behind a pile of crates on the boardwalk in front of the nearest building.

"Missy McCabe, come here," Danna ordered. The head turned into a pair of shoulders, and a little girl emerged from behind the stack of crates. She stood in front of Danna with her head down.

Chas calmed the chaos in his head, now that it became apparent that there wasn't a true emergency.

"What is going on?" Danna asked, her voice sharp.

"Sorry, Marshal," the girl said. Her shoulders slumped even more.

Marshal? A sick feeling stole over Chas.

"My brothers stole my dolly, and I thought—" her lips quivered "—thought you might put them in jail. Or help me get her back."

Danna knelt to the girl's level, gentling her voice. "Missy, you know I'm busy dealing with important business. I don't have time to chase down your doll."

Chas looked at the woman he'd spent the last twelve or so hours with. Really looked at her.

And was astonished he hadn't seen it before. The gun belt slung low on her shapely hips. The trousers and man's shirt. The flash of sunlight from a badge pinned to her shoulder, just visible inside the lapel of her jacket.

She was a marshal? She glanced at him, and he realized he must've spoken out loud.

"Why don't you see if your ma can help you?" Danna advised the girl.

"She won't," the girl mumbled to her bare feet. "They ain't gonna listen to her."

"Perhaps your brothers will tire of playing and bring your doll to you after a while."

The little girl sniffled, eyes pleading with Danna. Danna sighed. Pulled a penny out of her pocket, and held it out. "Why don't you buy some candy?"

The girl's eyes lit up.

"And no more screaming around town, all right? Mr. O'Grady thought you were really in trouble."

The girl ran off. Danna watched, wearing an expression he couldn't decipher. Maybe longing?

He couldn't contain the words inside him any longer. "You're a marshal?'

CHAPTER 3

*D*anna heard the disapproval in O'Grady's voice. After a night without sleep, plus the other troubles she'd been dealing with, her temper flared.

She hiked up her chin, pinned him with the same stare she'd used on what seemed like every male in town. "I haven't been hiding my badge."

His eyes flicked to the tin star at her collarbone, then away. "You didn't introduce yourself as a lawman."

She hated feeling defensive. Shouldn't have to feel that way. Tried to keep her voice calm. "If you recall the circumstances surrounding our introductions, it didn't come up. Good day, Mr. O'Grady."

Without a look back, Danna strode back to the boardwalk and down two doors to the combined jail and marshal's office and unlatched the door. A large blur of fur and teeth nearly knocked her onto her backside and took off down the street, howling at the top of his lungs. Fred's dog. She didn't bother to go after it, not as exhausted as she was. He'd come back when he got hungry. Unfortunately.

Dismay filled her as she stared at the chaos inside.

Wanted posters were strewn across the floor, some with muddy pawprints obscuring the writing on them. The desk chair had been knocked over. The desk itself appeared not to have suffered, and that was all Danna cared about. She hung her hat on a peg next to the door and slid her arms out of the sleeves of her coat.

The sound of firm bootsteps on the boardwalk just outside her door alerted her that Chas O'Grady had followed her. "Did someone put an animal in here? A prank, perhaps?"

She bristled at his insinuation that someone would play such a prank on her, and that she couldn't handle it if they did.

She crossed her arms over her middle. "It's my dog. Was there something else I could help you with?" She had to work at keeping her tone businesslike. Fred had always said her temper would get her in trouble. Now, as the marshal, she couldn't afford to let it get the better of her.

O'Grady stared at a spot on the floor for a long moment. So long that she wondered if he was going to say anything at all. Finally, he sighed and pulled something out of his shirt pocket. It was an envelope, the one he'd put there earlier when they'd located his saddlebags. He handed it to her, then waited as if he expected her to open it.

So she did, only to find a letter inside. Her mind spun, trying to figure a way out of this situation gracefully. After his earlier disdain at her profession, she had no intention of revealing to him that she couldn't read.

Fortunately, he seemed not to notice her hesitation but spoke quickly and quietly. "I'm a private detective hired by the Wyoming Stock Growers Association to look out for the interests of cattlemen in this area."

Danna looked over the top of the letter she couldn't read. O'Grady had half-turned and face the window to the street outside. Not much to see; the jail was one of the last buildings on the street. Most of the interesting happenings in town centered around Hyer's General Store or in the street in front of one of the three bars.

Not a gambler, then? "So, you're a Pinkerton? I didn't think they took jobs this far west."

His eyes remained on the window. He didn't crack a smile. "I'm on contract with a different agency, but yes, similar to a Pinkerton. There have been reports of cattle rustling in these parts, and I've been sent to find the criminals behind it."

Now she raised her brows. "I haven't heard anything like that." She thought back to the spring cattle drives, shaking her head to clear the pain of missing Fred as much as to stir her memories. "A few missing cattle earlier this year, but that could be explained by predators or natural causes. Wandering off. Nothing recent."

His eyes narrowed, but he still looked out the window. "My employers are concerned with more than a few missing cattle, Marshal. If there's something going on here, I'll find it. I'm very good at my job."

She didn't doubt it, but he seemed too citified for Calvin.

He turned, reaching out a palm. She slapped his letter into it, and he stuffed it back into the envelope.

"I've done my duty and notified the local law." She easily read the derision when he spoke the word. "And I'll expect you to stay out of my way."

Danna worked at curbing the anger that formed a tight knot in her chest. What would Fred have done when faced with a nuisance like Chas O'Grady? Probably turned the other cheek.

"If there's anything I can do to help..." she gritted the words out through clenched teeth.

Chas gestured to the mess covering the floor. "You appear to be plenty busy. I'm sure I can find my way around town. Good day."

With that, he strode out of the office. Danna slumped into

the chair behind Fred's old desk. For a moment, when he'd first stated he was a detective, she had hoped that Chas O'Grady might be her ticket to winning the townspeople over. If they saw a man working with her, would they start to trust her to take care of the town? They'd been remarkably cool toward her since she'd been appointed as marshal. But no, he wouldn't help her. It seemed by his abrupt dismissal, he'd be working against her.

Frustration boiling, she curled her hands into fists on top of the desk. She'd proved herself those first two years Fred had let her be his deputy. They'd accepted her in that position. Why was being marshal different? And why did it hurt so much to find that Chas's reaction was the same as everyone else's? She didn't feel anything for him. Wouldn't.

Weariness swamped her. All she wanted to do was go upstairs to her small room above the jail and sleep. Instead, she rounded the desk and picked up the loose papers strewn across the floor.

She'd moved the mess to the top of her desk but hadn't started sorting yet when a commotion outside had her rising from the desk chair.

"Marshal—"

"—that varmint—"

The door burst open, and Wrong Tree ran in with tail lowered and droopy ears, followed by Will Chittim, the young livery stable hand, and Martha Stoll, one of the crankiest women in town. Wrong Tree scooted behind Danna and underneath Fred's desk until just his tail was poking out.

"What's the trouble?"

The barber's wife pointed at Danna, face flushed and emotions running high. "Your dog. Your awful, no-good varmint of a dog, that's what the trouble is!" Her voice rose throughout the rant, and she ended with a screech.

"Danna—Marshal—" Young Will's voice cracked when he

rushed to speak. "I put the dog in your office last night to keep him from runnin' the streets, but someone must have let him out today."

"I did."

Martha drew in a deep breath. "He was digging up my prize rose bushes. That's the third time this week! One of them was completely ruined. Ruined!"

"Mrs. Stoll—"

"Don't offer me any more of your empty platitudes, young lady."

Danna bristled, both at being spoken to as if she were a child and at the childish title. "Mrs. Stoll, I apologize—"

"I don't accept it!" the other woman said with a stomp of her foot that would've suited little Missy McCabe more than it did the forty-something adult female. "I want that mongrel eliminated. If you won't do it, I'll make a complaint to the mayor. The dog is a menace to this town."

"I'll take care of it, Mrs. Stoll."

"You'd better." With those parting words, the woman stomped her way out the door and slammed it behind her.

Will ran a shaking hand down his face. "I'm sorry, Marshal. I saw the pup trot by, on up the boardwalk, but I was talkin' with a gent who wanted to rent a horse, and I couldn't go fetch him. By the time I got away, he was in Mrs. Stoll's garden. You're not really going to hurt him, are you?"

"Of course not." She didn't like the dog. They'd never gotten along in the eight years she'd been married to Fred, but she couldn't do a thing like that. She had too much respect for her husband's memory.

"Not because of you," she told the dog when he stuck his head out from under the desk, looking up at her with falsely innocent eyes.

"He hasn't been the same since Marshal Fred's been gone."

When the mutt approached him, Will obligingly knelt and scratched under its chin.

"Mmm..." Danna hummed, watching the two interact. None of them had been the same since Fred's death. The dog was the least of her worries. "I suppose I should try and find him a good home out in the country. With lots of space to roam."

"And a nice, big garden to dig up?" Will asked, attention still on the dog.

"We'll see."

* * *

CHAS STRODE DOWN THE BOARDWALK, ignoring the curious glances of passersby. He probably should stop into some of the stores and start making contact with the owners, but his thoughts were too chaotic and his shoulder ached miserably. Instead, he headed straight for the hotel.

What kind of town made a woman its marshal? It was a dangerous job. Dangerous for a man. How could a woman handle it?

All Chas could think about was Julia and how she'd died. And how her death had been his fault. He'd brought her into a situation fit for men only, and she'd been killed.

Being a lawman was a man's job. What was the town thinking?

He secured a room at the hotel. It wasn't as grand as he was used to, but it would do. He had a long soak in a hot tub that loosened his shoulder, and only then did Chas feel moderately better. Well enough to venture out and find something to eat.

The hotel clerk recommended the café down the street. This time when Chas walked down the boardwalk, he nodded and smiled at the men and tipped his hat to the ladies, soliciting giggles and smiles behind gloved hands from some of the younger women.

In the café, he was seated by a matronly woman and served a cup of coffee by a slender girl of about fifteen.

It was midafternoon, and the café was mostly empty. Only one other patron was seated across the room, an older gentleman dressed in denims and a clean light blue shirt. He had a white hat on the table at his elbow. A wealthy rancher? Chas nodded to the man but chose not to interrupt his meal. Perhaps he would introduce himself when his stomach wasn't so loud.

"Thank you," Chas said when a steaming plate of roast and potatoes was set in front of him.

"Anything else?" the girl asked.

"Mmm." Chas hurriedly swallowed the coffee he'd sipped. "I'm new in town and seeking employment. Do you know of anything?"

"Ma might." The girl went into a rear room, and the older woman appeared in her stead.

"Ya seekin' work?" She eyed him skeptically. "Not a cowpoke?"

He shook his head.

Chas's heart sunk as she frowned. "Don't know anyone in town needin' help." The café matron left with a shrug.

The door swung open, and another man entered, this one in a rumpled, untucked shirt and brown trousers. His fingers were stained with ink. A shopkeeper? The second man joined the first at his table.

Chas went back to his meal, trying to remember his manners. The food was delicious and he wanted to inhale it.

"Marshal's back in town," the new man said to the rancher, the low words piquing Chas's attention, though he kept his face downturned as if he hadn't heard.

The rancher grunted but didn't speak.

"Seems she didn't find no help for hire over in Cottonwood Creek. Still no deputies to work with her."

Danna Carpenter was marshal alone? She didn't have any deputies? Surely that couldn't be right.

"That's a shame," the rancher said. "A real shame." The grin on his face belied his statement.

The lunch Chas had consumed suddenly sat like a boulder in his gut.

* * *

Two days later, Chas was back at the café, this time during the lunch rush. Frustration over this case had cost him a sleepless night.

He'd hoped to find a temporary job. Working for someone local would lend him credibility and pave the way for his investigation.

But no one in town needed help. He'd avoided the dressmaker and the livery but spoken to every business in town that was a viable option. All he got were resounding "no's."

However, one suggestion he'd received over and over again was, "The marshal needs deputies."

It seemed to be a joke around town, though how anybody could think it funny that a woman was in charge of maintaining order, he couldn't comprehend.

He'd entertained the thought of working with Danna for scant moments before he'd rejected it. He couldn't work with a woman. Couldn't get close to one, even though she'd saved his life. It was too much of a risk.

His dreams of Julia's death had returned, as if the event had happened only yesterday, another reason he hadn't slept last night.

There was no way he could be a deputy for Marshal Carpenter.

But he didn't know how else to stay in the area, and he

needed a reason to stay in town, or folks might start getting suspicious.

He needed to gain the trust of at least a few of Calvin's citizens, get the lay of the land and find some clues to the missing cattle.

"We can't wait any longer..." Low but heated words from the table next to his floated to Chas's ears.

"We got our orders. The boss said wait."

Chas threw a casual glance over his shoulder, hand on his coffee mug as if he were looking for the waitress.

Three men at the next table over shoveled their meatloaf into their mouths. The layer of dust covering their denims and chambray shirts and the shaggy haircuts and scruffy facial hair marked them as cowboys, but these men had a look to them that was rougher than the typical cowboy.

Chas's senses went on alert. It might be nothing, but usually his instincts were good. He snuck glances out of his peripheral vision, trying to memorize their features without catching their notice.

Two had beards—brown and black—and the third a long, sand-colored mustache that trailed all the way down the sides of his face to his chin. The brown-haired man had a scar running down one side of his face, from temple to jaw. The man with the black beard and hair had dark stains on his trousers that appeared to be spittle from chewing tobacco. The sandy-haired man had unusual pale-blue eyes.

"The other boys'r getting restless. Ready to move on."

The first voice answered, "Boss says wait, we wait."

"But the grass is all dryin' up now."

The door opened, and Chas dared a glance at the other table, as if he were looking to see who'd just come in. The man with brown hair was speaking. "The cattle—"

A sharp grunt from the pale-eyed man silenced whatever

the speaker would have said. Chas's ears were attuned to every word now.

The blond-mustached man caught Chas's eye. Chas gave him a nod, hoping the other man wouldn't notice that he'd been listening in on their conversation.

"Afternoon." The man said, lifting his coffee cup in salutation. "Ya new in town?"

The other two men looked up. With all three pairs of eyes fixed on Chas, his discomfort grew, especially when he noted the gun belts on each man's waist.

He nodded. "My name is Chas O'Grady."

The man with black beard and hair curled his lips in what should've been a smile, but just looked as if he bared his teeth, two of which were missing in front. "Earl."

"I'm Big Tim," drawled the man with brown hair. He was big indeed, looming head and shoulders over Chas. Big Tim did not smile a greeting, just stared at Chas with an unwavering gaze.

"What brings you to our fine town?" the blond man asked. Chas couldn't help but notice he hadn't offered a name. "You sound like a city fella. You got family here?"

This was where things could get sticky. As a rule, Chas tried to keep to the truth as much as possible. That way, there was less chance of trapping himself in a lie.

"No, no family here," Chas said easily. He used what was left of his roll to sop up the red gravy on his plate. "I'm a businessman of sorts. Got bored in St. Louis and wanted to see some of the West. The horse I bought in Cheyenne expired in the badlands, just the other side of your town. So I'm here now until I find something new. You don't happen to know of any open jobs in town, do you?"

The two dark-haired men went back to their food as if they'd weighed Chas and found he wasn't dangerous, and wasn't of consequence. The blond man didn't seem convinced and watched Chas with narrowed eyes as Chas dug a coin out of his pocket to pay for the meal.

"'Fraid not," the blond said. "We're just local cowhands. Trying to make a buck of our own. About the only time we get to town is to find us a little female companionship, if ya know what I mean."

From his correspondence with the Wyoming Stock Growers Association, Chas knew there were two major outfits in the area. Most of the smaller ranches only hired cowboys during the spring and fall, when it was time to drive the cattle to market. "Do you work for Parrott or Brown?"

"Brown."

"Parrott—"

Big Tim and Earl spoke over each other.

The blond glared at both his companions. "We're between outfits right now," he said. "And dead broke. Sorry we cain't help ya."

Chas nodded at the obvious dismissal and rose to leave. As he walked away, he heard a hiss, "Ya idiots!"

Emerging into the sunshine outside the café, Chas crossed to the general store and waited for the three men to exit the eating establishment. If he could see which direction they headed, perhaps he could follow.

Of course, their hard appearances and conflicting answers didn't necessarily mean the men were involved with the cattle rustling, but something didn't ring true about them.

Problem was, how could he follow them without being noticed? Although the small town of Calvin had a bit of foot traffic on its dusty thoroughfare, it wasn't enough for Chas to disappear, should the need arise. Perhaps he could invent an errand in the same area of town, once he determined the men's intentions.

He didn't have to wait long. The three men stepped out

onto the boardwalk moments later, arguing. He was too far away to hear what about.

Chas pushed off the post under the general store's awning, intending to follow them. A commotion in the other direction pulled his attention away.

Two men tumbled out of the nearest saloon, dust flying as they rolled into the street. Shouts and men followed them out —wasn't it a bit early for the saloon to be so full?—and Chas spared a glance back toward Earl, Big Tim, and the blond man. They'd ignored the ruckus and continued down the street. He stepped off the boardwalk in that direction.

A new shout, this one in a different octave, met his ears. He stopped, watched in growing horror as a slender figure ran up to the fight. Marshal Danna Carpenter.

From the looks of things, she was going to jump right in.

And then he saw the glint of silver in one of the fighting men's hand.

"Knife!" The word ripped from his lips.

CHAPTER 4

*D*anna looked around at the faces lining the street outside the saloon. Most men watched the fight, but some watched her. Waiting to see what she'd do. Like always. Waiting for her to prove herself.

No one joined her just off the edge of the fracas created by the two drunks who'd burst from the saloon. She needed to separate them before they got hurt.

"Stop!" she shouted, but it didn't faze the men. "Ellery Hamilton. Stop fighting this instant!"

Nothing. She took a breath and waded into the conflict, getting an elbow in her shoulder as she broke the hold the men had on each other. She kept her feet, but barely, getting between the two men.

A flash of metal alerted her to the weapon, and she blocked the swipe of Ellery's knife with her forearm against his wrist. The blow hurt, but not as much as a stab wound would have.

"Put the knife down," she ordered. Still no reaction from either tussling man. It was as if she wasn't even here. Hamilton got one arm wrapped about her midsection, cutting off her air with a huff.

She had no choice.

Danna stomped on his instep.

When Hamilton's restraining arm went slack, she used all her strength in an uppercut against Ellery, who stood in front of her. Pain radiated through her fist and up her arm. Ellery slumped to the ground in a satisfying heap, though Danna could see he wasn't completely unconscious.

Using a move Fred had taught her, she gripped Hamilton's arm—still around her waist—spun around so she was behind him, and jerked his arm up tight against the center of his back, immobilizing it and hopefully letting him know she meant business. It was helpful she was almost as tall as he was—it gave her more leverage against his arm. Inebriation slowed the man's response, but he finally stiffened against her hold.

"Did you see that?" someone in the crowd asked.

"Not bad for a gal who put curtains up in the jail," a second voice called out.

"Blue, flowery curtains," came a hiss, followed by several snickers.

"You finished?" she asked the men in front of her, doing her best to ignore the onlookers. She hoped Hamilton couldn't feel her shaking. That swipe with the knife had been too close for her comfort.

"He shtarted it," Hamilton slurred.

Ellery groaned from the ground, stirring.

"I don't care. You're both coming down to the jail to sleep it off. Then I'll check with Billy Burns about any damages you'll have to pay."

"Whoossh gonna help ya drag both of us down there?" Hamilton's belligerent question resulted in chuckles from those nearby.

Ellery pushed to his hands and knees, still gripping the knife. He looked up at Hamilton, malice on his face.

Without warning, Hamilton jerked his arm free, bucking

against Danna's hold. His other elbow rammed backward, catching her in the shoulder. She lost her balance and stumbled. But she stepped between the two men once again, determined to end their fight. Meanwhile, Ellery lurched to his feet and lifted his knife.

Danna swung her arm out wildly, praying she wouldn't be cut, when someone close yelled, "Hey!"

The interruption was all she needed. She slammed an elbow into Hamilton's gut behind her, and he folded. From her peripheral vision, she could see someone knock down Ellery a second time.

Danna gritted her teeth. She'd had the situation under control.

Ellery tried to get up again. A shiny black boot came down on his back, sending him sprawling. A matching one kicked his knife away.

Danna looked up and straight into the unsmiling face of Chas O'Grady.

* * *

CHAS WAS GOING to be sick right here in the street. He rapidly blinked away his memories of Julia's body, broken and bloodied on the saloon floor, but the sight that greeted him was not much better.

Danna Carpenter had handled the two ruffians, both drunk, with finesse, but he still couldn't erase the memory of that knife slashing toward her. Did she know how close she'd come to dying right here on this dusty street?

He desperately wanted to rebuke her, make her understand exactly how dangerous a position she was in, but he couldn't force the words past the fear lodged firmly under his sternum.

"If you don't mind, I'd appreciate your help getting that

man"—she nodded to the drunk underneath his foot—"over to the jail."

Still unable to answer, he pulled the man to his feet and followed the marshal as she prodded the second man toward the two-story jail building on the edge of town.

Thoughts and memories colliding inside his head, he marched his prisoner along with her. Once both men were locked in adjoining cells, they continued arguing through the bars, though neither got close enough to touch the other.

Chas rounded on the marshal. "What did you think you were doing?"

"My job." Her words were said stiffly. Something was wrong. Was she hurt? He looked her up and down but couldn't detect blood on her clothing.

"You all right?" He asked the question without thinking, and stepped closer as she rolled up one shirtsleeve. A large red mark shaped like a palm bloomed on her skin and made him tremble more. He wanted to pull both men out of their cells and give them a thrashing like his older brother had given him once.

"I'm fine. Probably a bruise is all." She lifted her shoulder and didn't look at him as she ran her fingers over the skin on her forearm.

It would turn into a nasty bruise, if the red mark was any indication.

"What did you think you were doing?" she asked, eyes flashing when she finally looked at him.

"What?"

"I had everything under control."

He shook his head. In his mind's eye, all he could see was that knife coming toward her.

She slapped her hat down on the desk, stirring a stack of papers sitting on one corner. "I would have been fine." She clapped one hand on her hip. "But you had to step in, and now all those men probably think I can't take care of things myself."

"That's not what it looked like. One of your assailants had a knife." He blinked. Again. Still, the image persisted behind his eyes. She'd almost died.

"I know." She knew?

"He almost stabbed you."

"He didn't—"

"Because I stepped in!" Didn't she understand? She'd needed him!

She needed him. The realization sent him reeling. He sat in the hard-backed chair against the wall, silent. Danna still spoke, but Chas couldn't hear her words for the rushing in his ears.

How had this happened? He'd been drawn in by another female, when he'd vowed to stay away from all persons of that gender. He couldn't do this.

He couldn't be her deputy. Could he?

A knock sounded and the door opened. The well-dressed man Chas had seen in the café two days past sauntered in.

"Shut up!" Danna ordered the two prisoners, still arguing. When they didn't listen, Chas rattled the doors of the nearest cell. The men subsided, each sitting on a bunk.

"Mr. Parrott." Danna greeted him with a deferential nod. Her shoulders were suddenly straighter.

So, Chas's guess in the café had been correct. This man was a wealthy rancher, one of the two who owned the largest spreads around. No wonder Danna adopted such a respectful manner.

Chas scrutinized the other man as he took off his white hat and tucked one hand in the top of his vest. He was tanned, probably mid-forties.

"Marshal, I heard you took care of a little dustup down by

the saloon." Parrott spared a quick glance for Chas. "Everyone all right?"

"Yes, fine," Danna said quickly. "How's the missus? Anything I can do for you today?"

"The wife's doing well. She asked me to make sure you're planning on attending the dance we're hosting this Friday."

Danna glanced at Chas, but as far as he was concerned, they still had talking to do; he crossed his arms and stretched his legs out in front of him.

Her smile, when she turned it on Parrott, was forced. "I've been thinking on it. I'm not sure I'll be able to get away."

"You work too hard, Marshal. A night of relaxation will be good for you."

The marshal's frown showed she didn't agree with him, but her voice remained level and calm. "I don't know that I should leave the town unattended."

Her statement almost sounded like a question. Why was she showing Mr. Parrott such deference, when Chas had seen her talk down to other men? Chas had learned there were four men on the Calvin town council. They appointed the marshal. Mr. Parrott must be one of them for Danna to speak so respectfully to him.

"Ah. Still no luck with the deputies? I'm sorry to hear it. Well, be that as it may, you can't work every hour of every day. Besides, the wife has a few eligible men she wants to make sure you meet. You are considering remarrying, aren't you?"

Chas's breath stuck in his chest. The marshal was a widow? What else didn't he know about her?

She cleared her throat, her feet shifting and her down-turned face indicating her discomfort. She gestured toward Chas, who hadn't joined the conversation. "Mr. O'Grady and I were in the middle of something, Mr. Parrott. I'll try to come to the party if I'm able. If there isn't anything else, I'm afraid we'll have to speak later."

She hadn't given the older man a straight answer about remarrying, but the rancher accepted it with grace as Danna ushered him out the door.

After he left, she leaned against the portal, her head clunking against the wood.

"Your boss?" Chas asked.

"One of them." She huffed and blew a strand of dark, curly hair off her face, then turned her head to look at Chas. "What are you still doing here?"

"Marshal, you can consider us even," Chas said.

"What do you mean?"

"You saved my life. I saved yours."

Her lips twisted. Not a smile. They pinched together. If she didn't like that, she probably wouldn't like Chas's next statement either.

He glanced at the two men in adjacent cells. They hadn't spoken since Parrott's arrival. One looked to be nodding off, the other staring at the wall.

"I think you should hire me on as one of your deputies." Had those words really come out of his mouth?

Her jaw dropped, then her eyes narrowed. She pushed off the door. "You want me to deputize you? Why?"

He lowered his voice, so the prisoners couldn't hear. "I need a job, a reason to stay in town. Plus, it will give me some leeway to investigate without any potential cattle thieves being the wiser. And you need help."

She looked as if she would protest, so he quickly went on.

"I've been talking to people around town and found out a couple of families are missing cattle. Problem is, I don't know the lay of the land."

She half-smiled at that, probably remembering his unfortunate tumble down the ravine.

"You can relax a little, go to that party—"

"I don't need a deputy so I can attend social functions. If

you want to pin a tin star on your chest, you'll have to realize that I'm the marshal."

"I do realize that." Chas's temper burned in his middle, and he rose out of his seat and stood face to face with the marshal.

"That means I'm the boss. I make the schedule. I'm in charge. If you can't handle that—"

"I can." He hoped. "I have to put my investigation first, but as long as you stay out of my way..."

Danna shook her head and stepped back. "This isn't going to work."

He blinked and again saw that knife coming straight for Danna's heart. "We'll have to make it work. I'll be in town until I find my rustlers. You'll be my boss"—he almost choked on the word— "until then."

She started to say something else, but the door opened again, and a very pregnant woman bustled in, followed by a toddler, a blond-haired girl in a stained dress.

"Fine," Danna said, resigned. "Be here first thing tomorrow."

CHAPTER 5

*D*anna tucked her chin into the upturned collar of her coat, the chill in the early morning wind stealing her breath. She made this journey to the small cemetery just outside of town almost every morning. It never got easier, standing in front of Fred's grave.

This morning she was especially discomfited, thanks to her new deputy, Chas O'Grady, private detective.

She shook off her distracting thoughts. She shouldn't be thinking about another man, even one she planned to work with, while visiting her husband's grave.

"I'm sorry I haven't found your killer yet," she whispered, the wind snatching her words away. Three months, and she hadn't turned over one clue that would lead her in any helpful direction. As his deputy, Fred had believed she could solve any crime. So why couldn't she solve his murder?

She could still see his body lying prone in the field of dry summer grass. Shot in the back. And no one in town or out was talking.

Her only hope was to find the horse that matched the funny-shaped hoofprints she'd found near the scene of Fred's murder. The horse was shod, but not well. Something was wrong with one of its shoes. Its tracks made a crescent shape instead of the traditional horseshoe. She'd made a sketch in the leather book Fred had insisted all his deputies carry to take notes on pertinent information.

Since she'd never learned to read or write, Fred had taught her to sketch the important things about crimes she investigated.

But she hadn't been able to track down that horse anywhere.

With a sigh, Danna turned to town. She had one more stop to make before she faced O'Grady this morning.

With the sun barely up, the streets were still quiet. Not many folks stirred this early. Danna wouldn't usually, but she hadn't been able to rest this morning. Too many thoughts crowding in her head, keeping her awake.

She banged on the wind-faded door of a shanty on the edge of town. When her friend Corrine opened the door, Danna lifted the dead rabbit she'd snared with her slingshot. Why waste a bullet if you didn't have to? "Brought you a present."

"You've been out to the cemetery again." Corrine didn't sound surprised. She didn't sound much of anything, her voice emerging a monotone. She edged inside, motioning for Danna to follow.

"Lots of game out there, with the tall grasses." Danna didn't have to make an excuse to her only friend. Corrine knew about loss, too.

The smell of fresh bread wafted through the small shack. Three places were set at the table against one wall, under the only window in the house. Two of the plates were untouched and had what appeared to be last night's supper still on them.

Corrine faced Danna, unshed tears reddening her eyes. She twisted a towel between her hands, then one hand moved to cover her large-with-child belly.

"What's this? Did you eat last night?" Danna asked.

Corrine shook her head, visibly upset. "I-I made a plate for Brent, just in case he came home. But then I got so upset thinking about him that I couldn't eat."

Danna nudged her friend into a chair and sat down herself. Another failure on her part. Corrine's husband had been missing since the same night Fred hadn't come home. Unlike Fred's body, Brent had never been found. Danna, and most of the town, couldn't help thinking the two events were connected.

Patting her friend's hand, Danna did her best to comfort the distraught woman. "You need to eat. You've got to think about the baby."

Corrine nodded but put her face in her hands and snuffled. "I don't know how much longer I can keep going. Wh-why doesn't he come home?"

Danna hugged her friend's shoulders, a little afraid to touch the swell of the other woman's stomach. "I don't know. Shh." She knew better than to offer promises she couldn't keep, so she kept silent while she rocked the slight woman.

Movement from the bed in the corner caught Danna's eye. Ellie, Corrine's daughter, was asleep, but maybe not for much longer. She had to get Corrine calmed down or risk upsetting the three-year old.

"I don't know what happened to Brent," Danna said softly, still rubbing Corrine's back. "But I'll do everything I can to find him." Dead or alive. She didn't say the words, but Corrine shuddered against her shoulder.

"Do you...?" Corrine had to sniffle and swallow before she could continue. She spoke in a voice so low it wasn't even a whisper. "Do you think he killed Marshal Fred, and that's why he left?"

Most of the town did. But not Danna. "Brent might be a laggard and a bum, but that doesn't mean he killed Fred. Even if he does have a habit of running off. He's always come back before." Corrine's husband out of work so often that his wife had to take jobs in order to feed the family. But just because someone was lazy or absent didn't mean they had it in them to commit murder.

And Corrine always took him back. Even after weeks apart. Danna couldn't believe her friend would stay in a marriage like that, but what could Danna do, other than help her friend out occasionally? Corrine wouldn't accept help from anyone else.

"You're right. I know you're right." Corrine pushed away and went to the washbasin. "Not the part about Brent being a bum." Her voice came muffled from the scrap of towel she scrubbed her face dry with. "But that he always returns."

Danna hated that her friend's lousy husband had done this enough times that she could say that. "Is there anything you need?"

Corrine busied herself wrapping one of the two loaves of bread warming on the stovetop. She shook her head quickly. "No. No, we're fine. Thank you for the rabbit, though. I'll make a nice stew with it."

"Auntie, auntie!" A joyful shout erupted from the bed.

Danna barely had time to scoot her chair away from the table and catch her nightshirt-clad *niece*, Ellie, as the girl vaulted from the bed in the far corner of the room and launched herself at Danna. Holding the three-year-old's small, sleep-warm body in her arms fueled a rush of emotion that brought tears to her eyes.

She wanted a family of her own. It was her biggest dream and her deepest regret from before Fred had passed. She'd always wanted to give him a son.

Danna shoved away the familiar longing, stowed it in a deep corner of her heart, and made a funny face. "Good morning, Elf. You're late for breakfast."

Ellie giggled, as she did every time Danna used her pet

name. Danna set her down, and Ellie hefted herself up into her own chair at the table and settled her worn rag doll in her lap. "Ma, can I have jam?"

Corrine smiled at her daughter, but when she turned away to slice a piece of fresh bread, Danna could see fresh tears in her eyes. The bulge of her stomach became more defined when she reached with one hand to rub the small of her back. She didn't have long before the baby came. Would Brent return before then?

A sense of urgency sent Danna to her feet. She reached for the cloth-wrapped loaf of bread Corrine had placed on the table before her.

"I heard about your new deputy. You rushing off to him?"

She froze.

"Ya got a new dep'ty, Auntie?" Ellie's question echoed her mother's, but her blue eyes held an innocence that Corrine's did not.

Danna sagged against the table. "Don't tease, Corrine. I can't imagine this working out."

Not with Chas O'Grady, only concerned about one thing, his case. Maybe his presence would allow her to make inroads with the other men. She hoped.

"You'll be fine," Corrine said, reversing roles and patting Danna's shoulder comfortingly. "It can't be different than working with the other deputies back when Fred...was still here."

"But when Fred was marshal, I wasn't in charge. And this isn't the same at all."

More of a trial period. Chas O'Grady would leave once he'd found his outlaws. Danna only hoped she would get the respect she deserved from the people of Calvin, and maybe the help of a couple more deputies.

Corrine narrowed her eyes. "Why? Because he's a handsome fellow?'

"What? No!" A hot flush stole its way up Danna's neck and into her face, mocking her denial. "Even if he is handsome, I have no intention of noticing. He's a city dude. Likely, he won't make it long in our small town."

Corrine shrugged. "I don't know why you're getting all bothered. It almost sounds as if you want him to leave."

Danna waved her hat in front of her still-warm face. "I don't know what I want. Just to find Fred's killer and find some peace."

She was tired. Tired of working alone. Of facing the censure that nearly all the town showed for her. The town council had thought she could do the job of marshal. Why didn't anyone else? Carrying a gun, enforcing the laws, those were the things she was good at. The only things.

"Maybe that's not all that God wants for you," Corrine said softly.

Danna couldn't help it. Her eyes dropped to her friend's pregnant belly. She'd always wanted a family...until she'd made herself stop thinking about that impossible dream.

"I have to go," Danna said when she could find words again. She reached down to hug Ellie, who'd watched the exchange with huge blue eyes.

"Bye, Auntie!"

Corrine pushed the forgotten loaf of bread into Danna's hands. "You're plenty smart. You'll figure out what to do."

* * *

AN HOUR after she'd left Corrine, Danna strode out of the saloon, disgusted. She'd stopped in to find out what the owner would charge Ellery and Hamilton for damages to his properties. She'd thought a morning visit would be a mite more respectable. And she'd been the epitome of profession-alism, but the proprietor had insisted on leering at her the entire time and offered her a job as one of *his girls* on her way out.

She was steaming mad, fighting to hold on to her temper.

And that's when she saw Chas O'Grady leaning casually against the wall outside the jail in what looked to be a cheerful conversation with two of Calvin's eligible young ladies, Penny Castlerock and Merritt Harding.

Still fired up, Danna stomped toward the little group.

Penny Castlerock, the wealthy banker's daughter, stood in her frilly gown with her hair cascading in copper ringlets from her bonnet. A parasol bobbed over her shoulder. She was the picture of femininity.

Even Merritt, the schoolmarm who was a little too old to be on the marriage market, was pretty in a slightly faded gingham dress, her blond tresses bound up in a bun like Danna could never achieve.

She would never be like those women. She didn't want to be like those women. Did she?

The question stopped her in place. She turned toward the general store, pretending to admire the two gowns in its front window.

When she'd become Fred's wife at age sixteen, she hadn't known how to do any feminine things. Keep house, sew a quilt, cook...all those things had been beyond her capabilities.

And Fred had never made her learn. He'd seen her skill with a rifle and how she could track a coon in a snowstorm, and he'd made her his deputy instead. They'd shared the chores. He'd cooked most of the time, because he was better at it. She was no good at wifely skills. She'd never fit in with the other women in town, and he hadn't asked her to.

She didn't really want to be like all the others, did she?

In the reflection of the glass she could see Penny leaning flirtatiously close to O'Grady. She couldn't help straining her ears to overhear their discussion.

"Perhaps we need a man's opinion. Mr. O'Grady?" Penny's query was accompanied by a flutter of her eyelashes so big Danna could see it from here.

"Yes?" He sounded politely interested.

"I'm trying to decide between these two hats." Penny pointed to the window of the milliner's shop, right next to the jail. "Pink or yellow?"

O'Grady considered the store window for a few moments, then said, "I'm afraid I don't know much about ladies' fashion. They both look fine to me."

Danna felt a little gratified he didn't seem to be falling for the girl's overeager manner.

Penny giggled, a shrill sound that had Danna clenching her teeth.

The young woman leaned toward Chas to murmur, "You must not know much about ladies either. You never tell a woman she looks 'fine.' She may look 'lovely,' or 'pleasing,' or even 'handsome,' but never simply 'fine.'" Then she oh-so-casually placed her gloved hand on O'Grady's forearm.

The flirt. Danna stifled the snort that wanted to emerge, but she must've made some noise, for Penny and Merritt turned toward her, and Chas's head came up.

"Well, hello, Marshal." Penny said. "Are you shopping for a new gown?"

Danna narrowed her eyes. The girl's question seemed innocent, but everyone in town knew Danna never wore dresses.

"I'm not." Danna nodded to the group and considered whether she should walk past them to the jail. Since they'd engaged her in conversation, it seemed rude to go on. She stepped forward, but not close enough to be considered part of their group.

"Do you know Mr. O'Grady?" Penny asked. "Oh, of course you do. Merritt and I were just commenting how terribly brave he was yesterday to stop that horrid fight in front of the saloon."

The fight Danna had stopped?

Merritt shook her head, and Danna wondered if she was embarrassed for her friend's flirtatious behavior.

Color crept into Chas O'Grady's cheeks. "Marshal Carpenter—"

"You're coming to the dance next week, aren't you, Marshal?" Penny asked. "Papa said I could have a new bonnet and dress. Which do you like better, the pink or the yellow?"

Danna took a cursory glance into the shop window. Honestly, they both looked the same to her. Fussy frills and ribbons. "The yellow is nice."

"Hmm." Penny appeared to be lost in thought for a moment, leaning her head on one gloved hand while she gazed into the window. "Perhaps I'll wait to buy the bonnet." Penny said, giving her parasol a twirl.

Merritt, who hadn't said a word to Danna yet, grasped her friend's elbow and leaned close to murmur something in Penny's ear.

"Miss Harding reminds me that we're committed to tea with my mother this morning," Penny said. "Mr. O'Grady, it was a pleasure to meet you. I hope we'll meet again." She nodded to Danna. "Marshal."

The two women walked off arm in arm, Penny shooting a final saucy wink over her shoulder toward O'Grady.

Danna shook her head as she moved past her new deputy and opened the jail door.

"I knocked earlier but there was no answer. I wasn't sure if I should go in and wait for you. I wasn't trying to engage those young ladies in conversation."

"You don't have to make excuses to me." She stepped behind her desk.

"I wasn't. I don't... I'm not interested in female companionship"

Danna shot a look at him and noted his face had flushed so darkly that his freckles were entirely obscured. "What you do when you're off-duty is none of my concern."

"I'm not interested." His words emerged stiffly now. "I have a job to do, and that's all I care about."

"Fine." She shrugged and pulled open the top desk drawer. The items inside it clinked together, and she drew out one of the tin stars. She flipped it onto the desk. "Yours."

He picked it up, looking down at the silvery badge for a long moment. "Why did you become marshal, anyway?"

"Because I was asked." She didn't mean to be short with him, but the events of the morning had worn her nerves thin.

O'Grady exhaled loudly. "I think we've gotten off on the wrong foot this morning. Shall we start over? Morning, Miss Marshal."

She glanced up at him quickly, at his teasing reference to her title, but he didn't seem disrespectful. He extended one hand for her to shake.

She took it, and warmth ran all the way up her arm. She couldn't keep her gaze from meeting Chas's, and his blue eyes reflected the same awareness that was in hers.

She dropped his hand and hurried to fill the coffeepot Fred had always kept going on the stove. The familiar motions soothed her, and when she finally sat behind the desk, she looked composed. She hoped. Chas took the chair near the door, clearing his throat.

She shuffled the stack of Wanted posters on the corner of the desk. The silence now stretching between them was awkward, but she didn't know how to bridge it.

"Where'd the two yahoos from yesterday go?" Chas asked, jerking his thumb toward the two empty cells.

"I had to let them go once they sobered up."

He nodded, drummed his fingers on his knee. "It seems like a hard job for a woman."

She answered him in a softer tone than she'd used earlier. "My husband used to be the marshal. I was one of his deputies."

"How did he die?"

"He was murdered."

Chas didn't ask if she'd caught Fred's killer, for which she was thankful. She didn't want to talk about Fred.

"And you were asked to be marshal? What about the other deputies?"

What about the male deputies? That's what he meant.

"I'm sure the town council considered all options, but when they came to me and offered me the job, I couldn't refuse."

"Did none of the other men want to work with you?"

She gave him a look. If they had, she wouldn't need him, would she?

"Did you do something to them? Alienate them somehow?"

She threw her hands up. "Other than being born a woman? I worked mostly with my husband, but I have worked with the other men on occasion. Either they think I'm not competent to be marshal without Fred's support, or they've been paid off." She said the last part in jest. No one in Calvin would do that. Why would they?

She turned the tables on him. "Tell me about yourself, Chas O'Grady. I should know something about my new employee, shouldn't I?"

He shrugged, but his gaze dropped to the leg he crossed over his knee. "I'm from Boston. I've been a detective the past five and a half years. My mother and father still live in the East."

"No siblings?"

"One living. A younger sister. May we get down to business now? What would you have me do today?"

His choice of words was telling. He'd had another sibling

who had died. And who he clearly didn't want to talk about. She didn't push it, though. She had enough subjects she'd rather were left unexplored.

"I thought we could ride out to some of the smaller homesteads today and ask about missing cattle. If there really is rustling going on, I have a responsibility to find out."

And it still irked her that the ranchers hadn't reported any missing cattle to her. She was the marshal. She was supposed to take care of those kinds of things. Plus, by making the rounds of the ranches in the area, she would have a chance to watch for those funny-shaped tracks she'd seen at the site of Fred's murder.

"Fine." He stood and pinned the tin star to his chest. "I'll need a horse."

She'd already thought of that. "My husband's horse is stabled at the livery. You can borrow her until you leave town."

It was best to remind herself that he'd be leaving soon. That way maybe she could keep her heart from getting too attached to her attractive new deputy.

CHAPTER 6

Chas maneuvered his horse to walk beside Danna's. "Perhaps this time we should try something different. That last man, Gill, knew something. I'm almost sure of it." Chas tried to affect a tentative tone as he offered the suggestion, but he was afraid his irritation had leaked out.

At the last two small farms they'd visited, Danna had insisted on accompanying him out to the barn to talk with the men. Men who hadn't wanted to give any information in her presence. They'd been polite but hadn't offered one piece of information helpful to Chas or his case.

"What do you mean?" Danna's terse question echoed his own frustration.

"This is just a suggestion, but what if you remained inside and visited with the woman of the house?'

Danna's looked at him askance. "You want me to pay a social call?"

He lifted his shoulders. "Not exactly. Just talk for a bit. She might even offer some news."

"You don't really think that. You just think he won't talk to me."

He lifted one shoulder. "It might be easier to get somebody to without a woman present."

"*I'm* the marshal."

"I know that. And I'm on your side. But we can't change everyone's mind at once. And the women probably do know as much as the men—maybe more."

She paused, her mouth set in a frown. "But I've never gone visiting in my life!" she burst out.

"Never?"

How was that possible? Wasn't that what women did? His sister loved to gossip with her friends. She never missed a chance to pay social calls.

Watching Danna's trim figure out of the side of his vision, he still couldn't believe he'd first mistaken her for a man. Even in the men's trousers and shirt, there was no disguising her womanly form. She was too shapely. She moved with the horse, her natural grace evident.

She flushed under his scrutiny. "I'm not like other women."

"Of that, there's no doubt in my mind."

She sucked in a breath, face creasing, and he realized how she might have taken his statement.

"Wait. I didn't mean…" Chas stifled the urge to curse. "Let's not have another misunderstanding like the first night we met."

She glared at him.

"Let me explain."

Finally, she nodded.

"Obviously, I've never met a woman who dressed"—he waved a hand to encompass her from head to toe—"like that. Or can break up a fight between two drunken men. And I'd be willing to wager you can outshoot me, as well."

She gazed at him, a question in her eyes.

"You are an original, Miss Marshal. I like that." He liked her, even though he didn't want to.

"Have you ever…?" He hesitated to ask, but he found he had

to know. "Have you ever wanted to dress like the other women?"

She stared ahead for a long time. Eventually, he realized she had no intention of answering his question.

She nodded ahead, and Chas saw a couple of buildings grow larger as they approached.

"Here's the Early place."

Had he touched a sore spot? He hadn't meant to. It seemed he couldn't keep from saying the wrong thing around Danna Carpenter.

* * *

DANNA STOOD behind one of the four kitchen chairs surrounding the small table in the Early kitchen, gripping its back with white-knuckled fingers.

"Thank you...um, for inviting us in. It was very kind."

Mrs. Anna Early glanced at her with creased brows as she bustled to brew a fresh pot of coffee. "Is there sumpin' wrong?"

"No, no." Danna placed one hand flat against her stomach. "I'm just nervous. I'm not—I don't make very many social calls."

The woman turned and smacked one hand onto her ample waist. "I meant is there sumpin' wrong that you want to talk to my husband about. He ain't a thief or nuthin'."

"Oh. Oh, of course not, Mrs. Early."

"Anna. We don't stand too much on formality round here."

"All right, Anna. No, I don't think your husband has done anything wrong. Mr. O'Grady and I are investigating a possible case of cattle rustling in the area." Danna released her death grip on the chair back. "Is there—Can I help with anything?"

"Don't know nuthin' about any missing cattle. Here." Anna plopped a loaf of bread and a knife on the table. Grateful for something to do with her hands, Danna did her best to carve slices of the bread without smashing it too badly. Judging from the slightly pinched look on Anna's face, she didn't succeed.

The other woman offered Danna a cup of coffee and sat at the table. With a soft sigh, Danna sat, as well. "Neighbors have been in a ruckus lately, but I don't know no details. Mrs. Bailey and me don't get along so well."

"Mam! Mam!" A small girl raced into the kitchen through the back door, followed closely by a boy only a little bigger. "There's a dep'ty talking to da!"

Anna turned in her chair and shushed the children. "Shh, you two. Cain't you see we've got comp'ny?"

The two children faced Danna with wide eyes and dirt-smudged faces.

"Hello." Danna held out her hand.

Faces solemn, they slowly rounded the table and, one by one, shook her hand with their grubby ones.

"Are you goin' to arrest my da?" asked the little boy, who seemed unable to look away from the badge pinned to Danna's vest. His voice lowered even more. "He didn't shoot that no-account, thievin' Timmy Bailey, ya know. Even though he tried t'other night."

"Joey!" Anna stood and clamped a hand on her son's shoulder. "He didn't mean—"

"It's okay." Danna did her best to hide her smile. "I'm not here to arrest anyone," she reassured the boy. "Just to visit. Do you want to eat with us?"

For once, she'd said the right thing. Anna's shoulders released their tension, and she allowed the children to sit at the table and have a slice of bread and a glass of milk.

"Mmm..." Danna hummed as she bit into her slice. "This is delicious. I wish I could bake bread like this."

"Thank you." Anna accepted the compliment with a flush. "My own mam taught me." She sipped her coffee.

"I'm learning, too!" chimed in the little daughter.

"That's wonderful," Danna said.

"Did your ma teach you?" the girl asked.

"No," Danna said slowly. "My ma died when I was littler than you. I never learned how to cook or sew or anything."

Anna looked a little more sympathetic after that. It gave Danna the courage to ask, "So, you're having problems with your neighbors?"

* * *

FRUSTRATED that Mr. Early had been uncooperative, Chas waited near the horses for Danna to end her visit.

When she finally stepped out of the Early's small farmhouse, she squinted in the bright afternoon sunlight. Chas was graced with a view of her glorious dark head before she smashed her worn hat on.

He offered her a leg up to her horse. She accepted the boost into her saddle with a twinge of her fine black brows and a flash of curiosity in her coffee-colored eyes. She wore a small smile as they guided their horses down the rutted lane toward the edge of the Early property.

"Did it go better than you thought?" he asked.

"You were right." Her body fairly vibrated with energy. Her smile grew until he saw a flash of white teeth. The first real smile he'd earned during their brief acquaintance.

He liked it more than he should.

"The neighbors?"

She tugged on her hat brim, and the smile faded. "The husband told you?"

"Not in so many words. He was remarkably close-lipped. What did you find out?"

"It seems the Baileys have been riding across the Early property, which wouldn't normally be a problem..."

"Do go on."

"Apparently, they've been driving cattle in the middle of the night. Some got loose and knocked down a lean-to. The Earlys lost some chickens."

"Seems a little suspicious. Why would they do it at night?"

Her eyes shone at him. "That's what I thought, too. The husband didn't say anything at all?"

Chas approached a fork in the road and drew in his horse to stop. "Said he'd heard some rumors of missing cattle, but nothing important enough to remember. Said he wasn't missing any himself. But said he thought someone in the area had been moving animals."

"The Baileys."

Chas knew his admiration showed in his eyes. The marshal was perceptive and intelligent, two things he could appreciate. He nodded to the dilapidated house not far up the lane. "Let's go."

As they approached the house, he noticed there were no animals in the corral. One of the barn doors was open and waving slightly in the breeze.

He and Danna shared a glance before they split up. She would check the house and he would check the barn. Minutes later, they met back at their horses.

"Barn's empty."

"House, too. They must've left in a hurry, because the furniture and some of the clothes are still in there."

Disappointment sliced through Chas. He'd been convinced they were on the right path to finding the missing cattle and the rustlers, but there wasn't a man or beast on this place.

* * *

DANNA'S FRUSTRATION rose as she and Chas mounted up again.

"We should ride down their back pasture toward the Early property and see what we can see," she said quietly, trying to rein in the emotions that wouldn't help her solve this mystery any faster.

The afternoon sunlight would last another couple of hours. The breeze tickling the curls that escaped her braid was chilly, but not unpleasant. Sky was clear. They should have plenty of time to scout the Bailey property and get back to town before sundown.

As they neared the creek that the Earlys claimed as their property line, the grass changed from dry and brown to just tufts and then dirt, pockmarked by many hooves.

"This looks familiar," Chas commented, riding up beside her.

"Umm-hmm. Like in the canyon? Not quite so bad. Fewer cattle, I think. See how the tracks don't spread very wide?"

"I see it."

"In the canyon, the hoofmarks were spread across the whole canyon floor."

"Is it possible it was the same number of animals, just driven in a narrow bunch?"

She considered it for a few seconds. "Doesn't seem likely. You'd need more cowboys than a small outfit like the Baileys could afford."

But what were they doing moving cattle this time of year? And where had the family gone?

Chas followed Danna across the creek, but she reined in her mount before she reached the bank.

"Look." She pointed to the impression visible in the mud just above the water's edge. "It's a crescent." She hopped down from her horse, boots splashing in the shallow water as she crossed, and squatted next to the single track, peering closely to be sure. She started to shake.

It was the same. She knew it was.

"What is it?" Chas rode up the bank before he stopped his

horse and dismounted. Probably didn't want to get his boots wet.

Danna waded through the creek to her horse and dug in one of the saddlebags, finally locating the small leather-bound book. She flipped pages to the middle, to the sketch she'd made. She turned the book so Chas could see the drawing. "This was found near—" She choked on the words, had to swallow hard before she could say it. "Near my husband's body."

His gaze went from the book to her face, and she drew a deep breath, struggling to maintain control of her emotions. She wanted him to know she could do her job, didn't get distracted by feminine emotions.

When she thought she could speak again, Danna worked to make her voice even. "I'm going to track them. You can go back to town if you like."

"I won't let you go alone."

No, she hadn't really thought he would.

* * *

IT WAS after nightfall when Chas and Danna rode up to the livery and dismounted. Chas watched Danna's slow movements, her disappointment evident in the droop of her shoulders.

The tracks she'd wanted to follow had vanished not long after they'd picked up the trail. She had not been happy.

They'd ridden home in silence, Chas allowing her the time to get her emotions under control. He was impressed that she had held back her tears earlier. And he knew what it was to be disappointed a lead hadn't panned out.

Now she reached for his reins. "The stableboy will have gone home for his dinner. I'll rub these two down and make a patrol of the saloons. Come by the jail in the morning."

Chas flipped the reins into her hand, but didn't let go. He

tugged against her hold until she looked up at him, her eyes dark and unreadable. "You take care of the horses, and I'll make a round of the saloons."

"I'm the boss."

"I haven't forgotten."

There was something in the air between them, though the only physical connection was the reins they both held. "Let me help you."

"Why?" she whispered.

To keep her out of danger. That was one reason, but another he couldn't voice. He couldn't tell her that he liked the look she was giving him—a look that said he was offering her a kindness no one else ever had.

She nodded gravely, and he left before she could ensnare him even more.

* * *

EXCEPT for the piano music and raucous laughter coming from the four saloons, the town was quiet. Chas stuck his head into each of the first three to make sure things were relatively calm. They were, and he was looking forward to an early night as he headed to the fourth saloon.

It was there that things changed. Chas stepped inside and stood with his back to the wall next to the door, perusing the main room. He was about to turn and leave when he caught sight of the man with the long hair and the blond mustache sitting at the bar.

The suspicious man from the café. Chas glanced around, but didn't see Big Tim or Earl. Pale Eyes seemed to be talking to a man with a scruffy goatee and dark hair. Chas waited to get a good look at the second man's face, and when he did, everything seemed to stop around him.

A long, jagged scar down the right side of the man's face left no doubt that this was the same person he'd come to hate in Tucson.

The man who had killed Joseph and Julia.

Hank Lewis.

Rage roared through Chas, filled his head, pounded in his ears. His hand went to the gun at his belt. Then he realized two of the men at the table closest to him had turned to stare at him. What was he doing?

Even though he'd been made deputy, he couldn't shoot a man in cold blood. He'd hang for murder, even if the scoundrel did deserve to die. He would wait until Hank Lewis went outside, and then he'd do it. It wouldn't make it legal, but he wouldn't get caught.

He nodded to the men at the table and settled in a corner, waving away the bartender when the pot-bellied man approached.

Nearly an hour later, both Hank Lewis and the blond man stood. Chas waited until they'd left before he rose from the small table. The crowd had grown by then, and he had to side-step a couple of fellows on his way out. By the time he pushed through the swinging doors, neither man was in sight.

Rushing around the side of the building, Chas scoured the shadows, pistol in hand. Nothing.

Back into the street. Empty.

Hank Lewis was gone.

A man in her rooms.

Danna craned her neck, trying to get a look at the speaker over the heads of the partygoers at the Parrott's dance.

This was the third comment she'd overheard about a man being seen in her rooms. *Hers*!

Which was ludicrous, because she wasn't aware of any man in Calvin—or Converse County for that matter—who thought of her as anything other than The Marshal. Certainly not as a woman, not with her job and the way she dressed.

Who had started these horrible rumors?

"Ah, just the woman I wanted to see."

Danna turned at the booming voice of Joe Parrott as he approached through the crush of people. He had two of the other three town council members in tow.

"Mr. Parrott, lovely party. Mr. Hyer. Mr. Castlerock." She nodded to the owners of the local general store and the Calvin Bank and Trust respectively. Neither man smiled at her.

"It's, ah..." Hyer started, "come to our attention there are some rumors going around about you." He looked uncomfortable with the topic.

She stifled the groan that wanted to escape and swallowed the anger that made her want to lash out. It wasn't their fault someone had started malicious gossip about her.

"I haven't had anyone up to my rooms, male or female," she said, working hard to keep her voice level. But she must've spoken louder than she intended, because a woman nearby turned to look. Danna glared until she turned around.

"We mustn't have even a hint of scandal amongst the leaders of our town." Castlerock managed to look condescending, though he didn't meet Danna's eyes. She knew he'd been the only one of the four council members to vote against her appointment.

Parrott patted her shoulder, giving her a smile. "My dear, we know you're trying your best."

Castlerock snorted softly.

Danna eyed him but kept her mouth closed while she tried to think. What would Fred have done in this situation?

"If she can't maintain a good reputation, perhaps she shouldn't be marshal," said Hyer to Castlerock, as if she weren't standing right there.

Castlerock nodded agreement.

This was getting out of hand.

Danna kept her voice even when she spoke, but it was not without effort. "Gentlemen, I haven't done anything inappropriate. As I'm sure this will not be the last time malicious gossip is spread about a woman in a position of authority, I would advise you to ignore it."

Hands shaking, she turned on her heel and escaped into the crowd.

* * *

CHAS REINED in his borrowed horse, slowing to move through the wagons and horses gathered outside the impressive ranch house. He hadn't known where the dance was to be held, but he'd managed to find a few stragglers leaving town late and followed them.

He wasn't supposed to be here. Danna had tasked him with watching over the town while she attended the dance, but he'd had a little situation and needed her.

Plus, he wanted to mingle in the crowd and see if he could spot Hank Lewis again. He'd patrolled the entire town of Calvin in the last week, become overly familiar with its three main roads and smaller, grassy lanes. He'd memorized most of the nooks and crannies behind each store. He'd found no sign of Hank Lewis.

Each day, Chas's rage and desire for revenge had grown. He'd barely had patience to deal with the marshal, and he could sense she'd been frustrated with him, as well. There'd been no further leads about the cattle rustlers. He could no longer bring himself to care about his case. All he wanted was to get revenge on the man who had murdered Julia.

Chas took a moment to adjust his horse's saddle, eyes taking in the yard filled with buggies and horses. The dance appeared to be in full swing, the sweet sounds of a fiddle and banjo floating over the din of many voices.

The six-shooter at Chas's waist seemed heavier than usual. He kept touching it, reassuring himself he was ready to do this.

Even as his urge for revenge built, he'd been struggling with his conscience. He wanted to do right, but he couldn't forget the promise he'd made to himself when he'd awoken on the doctor's table after Julia's death. He'd promised himself if he ever came upon the man who killed her, he'd return the favor.

Chas was out for revenge, plain and simple. Lewis deserved to die. An eye for an eye. That was biblical, wasn't it?

Chas shrugged off the distracting thoughts and approached the house.

The porch spanned the width of the building, and Chas was

halfway up the steps when a shadow moved near the far corner. Suspicion had Chas jumping into one of the dark patches between the rectangles of light shining from the windows. Could it be Lewis? No one with good intentions would be hiding outside.

Crouching close to the outside wall of the house, Chas crept toward where he'd seen the movement. Subdued voices reached his ear, but he couldn't make out what they were saying. He moved closer, careful not to make noise.

"...boys are getting ready to move the cattle after they take care of this other matter. They'll have to take 'em to Rock Springs instead of Cheyenne, or someone might notice the brands, but it shouldn't be a problem."

Now, that sounded promising for his rustling investigation. Chas settled one knee on the wood planks of the porch, giving his other leg a reprieve from the uncomfortable crouch.

"And what about the marshal?" This was a different voice, another male.

"She don't have any idea what's goin' on," the first man replied.

Chas didn't think either of the voices was Lewis.

"Besides, the marshal's got other things to worry about. She's goin' to be tied up with the robbery. This gossip about her is an extra bonus."

What robbery? What gossip? Were these men involved in the cattle rustling?

He had no idea if they were armed, but they could be dangerous. Chas leaned his head against the wall behind him, unsure what to do. Two against one wasn't the best odds, and what if Lewis was here and he missed his chance to kill him?

Maybe if he could get a look at the men... He shifted closer until he could see a boot and a dark pair of trousers. The man seemed to be leaning on the adjoining wall, around the corner, so Chas couldn't see his face, but he held an expensive-looking black bowler hat against his leg. In the dim light, Chas thought he could make out a mark of some kind—a tattoo?—on the man's wrist, but he couldn't be sure. The second man wasn't in sight at all.

Just then, two horses rode up into the yard, hooves thundering. If they approached the house, they would see Chas. He had no choice but to scramble across the wooden planks and go inside.

Once in the front door, he slipped into the crowd. There were plenty of people around. No one seemed to notice him. He skirted the room, torn between returning outside to try to find out the identities of the two men and staying inside to find the marshal and look for Lewis.

He was concentrating so hard on his dilemma, he nearly missed the familiar dark braid on the woman with a badge on her chest.

* * *

DANNA HAD SENSED O'Grady the moment he walked into Parrott's front parlor, even though the room was filled with people. So many people, she was having trouble making her way toward the door.

What was the man doing here? Couldn't he follow instructions? She wanted him available for any emergencies back in town.

He'd been moody and distracted since they'd ridden out to visit the Earlys and Baileys last week, but coming to the dance tonight was outright defiance.

She wasn't sure if she was more irritated by that or by the distance he'd been building between them. If only her awareness of him would fade, but it had only grown stronger in the past few days.

She'd spent much too long finding her hostess to thank the

woman for inviting her, and now all she wanted to do was return to her rooms. She had no desire to confront her deputy right now; she could talk to him in the morning.

Other than the three town council members, hardly anyone had spoken to her all evening. She'd thought she had learned to be tough while being Fred's deputy, but she found herself close to tears at the rejection of the people who had been, if not friends, then acquaintances for the last seven years.

And now O'Grady was blocking her exit. She didn't want to see his admiration for Penny Castlerock or the other ladies in lovely gowns who would undoubtedly flock to him.

Unfortunately, he saw her heading toward the door.

"What are you doing here?" she asked.

Light from the gas lamps highlighted the red in his auburn hair. Sandy stubble covered his chin, making him look disreputable and a bit dangerous. Because of the press of bodies in the crowd, she stood close enough to smell him. Leather and soap and man. She didn't want to feel the tingle of awareness that trembled deep in her belly. She focused on glaring at him for not following her instructions.

"We've got a situation in town." His gaze slid right over the top of her head, as if he was looking for someone else. Her insides pinched to think it was the banker's daughter he searched for. His indifference shouldn't matter to Danna, but it did.

"You couldn't handle it on your own?" If her words were on the caustic side, she hoped it couldn't be heard above the voices surrounding them.

Chas looked down at her, his eyes glinting in the lamplight. "Not this one. What say we switch places? I'll stay here and you head back to town?"

She'd been prepared to leave the party, but his request ignited her ire and made her question him. "What kind of situation are we talking about?"

"I've detained someone." Again, his blue eyes swept the room above her head. Was the person he looked for so important he couldn't have a conversation with her?

Irritation surged, and she tried to push past him. "I'm sure Miss Castlerock is around somewhere so you can admire her new gown."

He grasped her elbow. "That's not why I came—"

"I shouldn't have said that." She tried to shake his hand away, but he held fast to her arm.

"Dance with me, Miss Marshal." His demanding tone sparked something inside her, like iron on a tinderbox, and she opened her mouth, but her refusal was muted when she noted the set of his jaw.

"Please," he murmured.

Without waiting for an answer, he swept her into the crowd of dancers. Reacting quickly, in order not to be stepped on by the swirling couples, she clutched his shoulders to keep her balance. The fiddle seemed muted now, or was that the blood rushing in her ears? Though he was only a couple inches taller than she, his very presence seemed larger. Almost protective. Like she could lean on his broad shoulders and be safe.

Belatedly, his hand met her waist, and she jumped. No one had touched her since Fred. And how did this touch, in the middle of a crowded room, feel so intimate?

"What's the matter?" she asked, struggling to focus on her words instead of the unsteady feeling he evoked in her.

"Do you know that man? There, in the corner. With the long blond hair?" He twirled her, and she caught a glimpse of a man with stringy blond hair and a long mustache standing near the food tables in the second parlor. Her quick glance revealed he was dressed as many of the cowboys were, in their nicest denims and starched white shirts.

She shook her head. "Who is he?"

"I've seen him in town a couple of times. Last time with...a suspicious character."

Danna could feel the tension in his grip. There was something he wasn't telling her. But what?

* * *

CHAS KNEW he'd made a mistake the moment he took Danna in his arms. Holding her felt natural, right, the same way it had on horseback when she'd rescued him. And it scared him.

But when he'd seen Hank Lewis's crony across the room, he'd faced an irrational urge to keep her near. If Hank Lewis was here, anyone in the room could be in danger, including the marshal.

If he blinked, he could imagine Danna sprawled across the floor in a pool of blood—just like Julia had been at the hand of Hank Lewis. He couldn't let that happen.

He hadn't counted on what the feel of her in his arms would do to him. The simple smell of soap and woman rose above the other scents.

For a brief moment, he forgot about Hank Lewis. He couldn't stop himself from gazing upon Danna. He let his eyes roam her face from forehead to chin. She was flushed with the exertion of swinging and stomping around the dance floor, Wisps of her dark hair had come loose from her braid and curled at her temples and over her forehead. She wasn't looking at his face, more like his shoulders, and her dark lashes contrasted with the golden skin of her cheeks. She hadn't dressed up like the other ladies here tonight. She still wore her trousers.

She was vibrant.

And he wanted her as far away from Henry Lewis as he could get her.

The music ended, and they stepped away from each other.

"We probably should head back to town," she murmured, not looking at him now. "And see about this situation of yours."

He cleared his throat. "Yes."

When he regained his senses and looked up again, the blond man was gone.

* * *

THE SITUATION WAS...A girl locked in one of the cells. Danna stopped in the middle of the floor, shock holding her immobile. Dark, stringy, unwashed hair obscured Danna's view of the girl's face, but the slight person huddling on the cot behind bars was certainly female, even if she were disguised by the tattered man's shirt and trousers.

Was this what Danna looked like in her marshal's clothes?

"Let me out of here!" the girl shouted when Danna and Chas walked inside. She stood, and Danna got a good look at her dirt-smudge face. Not familiar.

The girl shook the cell door, rattling the metal. "You can't keep me here!"

"You were caught stealing, so yes, we can keep you here." Chas spoke calmly, ignoring the girl's ire. Again, almost distracted.

Danna turned to him with raised brows. "Which store?"

"Hereford's Grocery. I caught her myself when she ran out with a half a ham in her hands."

Danna walked up to the bars, and the girl backed away. As if she were afraid.

"I don't know you." Danna said quietly, hoping to calm the girl. "Do your parents live in town? What's your name?"

The girl crossed her arms over her middle.

"If you don't talk to me, I can't get you back home."

"Store owner didn't recognize her either," Chas said. "She can't be more than fifteen. I would've turned her over to her parents, but there was no one else around, and I couldn't get anything out of her." Chas sat in his now customary chair and propped his feet on the desk. Danna frowned at him. She'd told him twice not to put his boots there. He ignored her glare and went on. "I wasn't sure you'd want to leave her locked up all night."

The girl's face blanched at his casually spoken words.

Danna considered it for a moment. "I don't know that we've got a choice. She's a minor. I can't just turn her out on her own. Maybe a night in that cell will make her want to tell us who she belongs to."

Now the girl's shoulders slumped.

Danna felt sorry for her. She approached the cell and touched the bars. "If you're afraid your parents are going to be angry, I could talk to them. They're probably worried about you right now."

The girl curled up on the cot, giving Danna her profile. She swiped at her face with one hand, and Danna thought she saw a bit of moisture before it was whisked away. But what choice did she have if the girl refused to cooperate?

Moving to the pot-bellied stove in the corner, Danna stirred the coals and fed in two sturdy logs. The autumn nights were getting cooler, and the girl didn't have a coat. Danna didn't want her to get chilled overnight.

Chas's booted feet hit the floor with a thump.

"You heading out?" Danna asked, intent on her task. His attention had been diverted all evening. She didn't want him to know it mattered.

"Mmm-hmm. See you in the morning." And he was gone.

Danna turned to give the girl one more chance. "I want to help you. Won't you tell me who you are?"

Still no answer. The girl only sunk her chin into her folded arms, a ball of misery.

* * *

CLIMBING the stairs to her room, Danna considered what she could do. The mystery girl couldn't stay in the jail indefinitely, especially if any men were arrested. But who was she? Why weren't her parents looking for her? Was she an orphan?

The questions had no answers, at least not tonight. Danna toed off her boots and changed into her nightshirt, but her thoughts stayed with the girl below. If she was an orphan, was she lonely?

Like Danna was? Maybe that was the key to getting the girl to open up. Just spending time with her. Showing her that Danna could be trusted.

Danna pulled on a pair of pants, tucked her nightgown into them, and threw her coat on over that. She pulled the extra quilt off the end of the bed and added Fred's pillow on top.

She ducked back outside and made her way down the steps without really looking, even though the moon was mostly hidden by clouds. She was pushing open the door to the jail when a hulking figure loomed over her.

Resisting the urge to shriek, she reached for her pistol and realized she'd left it upstairs when she'd started getting ready for bed. Could she run back to get it?

The moon came out from behind a cloud and threw the face of Chas O'Grady into relief. Danna's shoulders dropped, and she let out a silent breath. It was just her deputy. But...

"What are you doing here?"

* * *

CHAS GRINNED at the marshal's discomfited expression. "Scare ya?"

She shook her head, but he didn't believe her. Seeing her vulnerable put a hitch in his stomach, just like he'd felt when he'd seen the mercantile owner grab the teen girl Chas'd taken into custody.

Women. They brought out the best in him—his desire to protect, take care of them. And also the worst—he seemed unable to stay away, even when he knew he should.

He spotted the bundle in Danna's arms and couldn't help his smile. Something warm unfurled in his chest. Danna had the same idea about making friends with the mystery girl.

"You felt sorry for her, too," he whispered. "Figured she'd have to be pretty desperate to steal from the grocery. So I brought some things from the hotel." He held up the burlap sack.

She nodded. "Perhaps, if we show her that we care, she'll open up."

His thoughts exactly. He could put aside his quest for vengeance for a few hours. On his walk down from the hotel, the town had been almost deserted. Most folks were probably still at the Parrott's party. Finding Hank Lewis could wait until morning.

Chas pushed the door open and allowed Danna to brush past him. In the warmth and light inside, he held up the burlap sack he'd filled with the goods begged from the hotel manager.

"So you brought some leftovers from the hotel?" Danna asked, probably for the girl's benefit, since they'd just discussed this in whispers outside.

"Unfortunately, the hotel's kitchen was closed. I had to bribe the manager for some eggs and bacon from tomorrow morning's breakfast."

He waved the cast-iron frying pan in the air, moved across the room to the pot-bellied stove. "I borrowed this, as well."

The girl did her best to appear disinterested, but Chas saw the way her eyes tracked both his and Danna's movements across the room. Danna moved to the desk, putting the bundle of cloth and pillow she carried on its top.

The girl's head came up off her folded arms.

Danna reached for the coffeepot on the shelf near the stove. "You want me to make some?"

How could he cushion his answer? He didn't have to.

Danna's eyes narrowed at his hesitation. "You don't like my coffee." It wasn't a question.

"Your coffee is a little...ah..." He started to say *strong*.

She shook her head, cutting him off. "Don't say it. I'll fetch some water. You can make the coffee."

When she brought the pot back in, he had to push back the skillet to make room. The stove was made for heat, not cooking, but it would work for their purposes. The food should be edible, at least.

"Are you sure you know what you're doing?" Danna asked as Chas cracked several eggs into the skillet, where they sizzled.

"I've been a bachelor long enough to know how to fry a couple of eggs." He added some bacon to the far side of the pan, and the scent of cooking meat wafted through the air. When he looked up at her, Danna's mouth was pinched and white.

"My husband used to say that."

"He cooked?'

"One of us had to," she said, a bit of humor in her soft smile.

Chas jerked his focus back to the frying pan and away from her mouth.

A glance from the side of his eyes revealed the girl had sat forward on her cot and was watching them. If they kept the conversation going, would she eventually say something?

"I thought most mamas taught their daughters how to cook."

"My ma died when I was little. And my pa."

She said the words so matter-of-factly that the fork scraped across the bottom of the frying pan with a screech. "Sorry."

Was he apologizing for the noise or for her mother's death?

She always tangled his emotions until he didn't know which way was up.

"Who raised you?" He hadn't meant for the words to come out of his mouth, hadn't meant for the conversation to turn serious, but he couldn't take them back now.

"My brother. Until I was sixteen and he sent me away."

"Let me guess. He sent you to a finishing school, but it didn't take?" he said it with a hint of a smile.

She shook her head stiffly and sat on the edge of the desk. "He sent me away to get married."

The sound of bacon grease popping was the only noise in the room.

Finally, not knowing what to say, Chas scraped the bacon and turned it over. "Almost done."

Danna popped up from the desk and scurried to the door. "I'm going to run upstairs and get a plate for our...guest." She nodded toward the girl now sitting on the edge of the cot.

"Bring a couple," he said, not looking away from what he was doing.

"Hmm?"

"I got a glimpse of that fancy spread at the party, but I didn't get to partake." He pointed the fork he was using to turn the bacon at the girl in the cell. "I can hear her stomach growling from here. I think you're the only one who ate supper tonight."

"I didn't eat either."

"Why not?" When she didn't answer, he looked up from the popping grease in the pan to see her turn for the door with a faint trace of a flush on her face.

"I'll get the plates." She closed the door behind her with a snap. A few moments later, Chas heard movement above his head.

Chas tried to make sense out of Danna's comment. From the way she'd said it, it seemed her brother had pushed her into marriage. But why? And was it inappropriate for Chas to ask more questions of his boss?

The door banged open again and Danna reappeared holding tin plates and cutlery in her hands. "Are you burning that bacon?"

She was going to ignore his question if he let her. So he didn't. "Why didn't you eat supper at the dance?"

She shrugged, but she wouldn't meet his eye as he waved her over. He scooped eggs and bacon onto the plates.

"Goodness, there is a lot of food here. I was too busy avoiding rumors to stop and eat," Danna said, all in a rush. "Someone believes they saw a man in my rooms, and it has scandalized everyone in town. Even the council members cautioned me about my behavior."

The thought of someone calling on Danna put a hot rock in the center of his chest, but he instantly knew she wouldn't allow any inappropriate behavior. She was too straight-laced for that.

He tried to make a joke out of it. "I'm sure once the idea of you accepting callers gets around, things will settle down."

If he'd hoped to calm her ire, he'd failed. She sputtered, "I haven't had any callers. And I don't want another husband."

The pressure on his chest eased a bit. Chas took the girl's plate before Danna could dump it on him and carried it to the cell. The teen still sat on the cot, her eyes fastened on the food in his hands, hope shining from their depths.

"For you."

She was slow to get up, hesitated before she accepted the plate from his hands, but then shoveled the eggs into her mouth with her fingers, not even using the fork.

Chas turned away to give her privacy, leaned against the wall. He was too tense to sit down, even to eat.

Danna sat behind the desk, eating slowly, staring at a point across the room. Had he offended her by his teasing comment?

He could easily see her getting remarried. She was uncommonly beautiful with her dark hair and eyes. The men's clothes couldn't hide it. The attitude she carried couldn't hide it. And her sense of duty was strong. Her dedication to the people of this town proved it; as a wife, she would never betray her husband.

Scooping the last of his eggs into his mouth, Chas let his gaze linger on Danna. As he watched, she slid open the top drawer and fingered something just inside.

He'd snooped one afternoon when she'd been out visiting a sick friend and knew that the only thing in that drawer was a worn leather journal. Her husband's journal. He'd glanced through the first few pages then decided it was too personal to keep reading.

This wasn't the first time Chas had seen Danna touch the object. Did she miss her husband? Did she keep the journal near as a reminder of him?

It was another reminder of how deep her loyalty ran. Even after the man's death, she sought to uphold his honor by defending this town.

"I suppose your sister is a good cook? Pays lots of social calls?'

Danna's quiet question surprised him. He didn't want to talk about his family, about home, but he could feel the teen's eyes on him.

"Erin? Yes, I suppose my mother has been instructing her on how to best run a household." Although his wealthy Boston parents would have a very different opinion on what that entailed from anyone in this small town. "She was only fourteen when I left home. Still having lessons with her tutors."

And it made him ache to think about home. He couldn't speak of it any more.

"It's late," he said, pushing off the wall. "Wouldn't want any more rumors to get started about you, Marshal." He winked at Danna.

Chas collected the frying pan and fork he'd borrowed from the hotel kitchen and moved toward the door.

Danna gathered the plates and utensils on the desk and took the bundle from her desk to the cell.

"I brought you a blanket," Danna said, offering the girl a folded quilt. "I know the cots in those cells aren't the most comfortable, but this will have to do if you won't tell us your name or where you come from"

The girl slid her hands through the cell bars and accepted the quilt and pillow.

She went to the cot and began spreading out the quilt.

"My name's Katy."

* * *

THE NEXT MORNING at the office, Danna finished a quick sketch of the man Chas had pointed out to her at the dance, She wanted to put his likeness on paper while it was still clear in her mind. If Chas thought the man was a suspicious character, perhaps she had a Wanted poster on him.

Her next task was to flip through the stack of hand-drawn faces and see if she could match her sketch to any of them.

It was a little hard to concentrate with Katy humming a bawdy tune that she only could've learned in a saloon.

Seated with her elbows propped on the desk, Danna flicked her eyes up to watch the teen.

Katy seemed much more relaxed today than she had last night. The shadows behind her eyes had lifted somewhat, and her humming showed her mood had lightened. Now all Danna needed to do was find out where she belonged and get the girl out of her jail.

"I brought breakfast." The cheerful, masculine voice

preceded Chas into the jail as he backed through the door, two piping plates in his hands. How kind of him to bring breakfast to share with Katy.

She looked down at the Wanted poster, but she couldn't make her eyes focus on the face it depicted. Chas's casual statements last night about his sister's tutor and running a household had thrown another obstacle in the way of her silly emotions. He obviously came from money. Somehow, he'd ended up here in the West, but his roots mattered, even if he didn't talk about home much.

If she was right and his family was well-off, she would never fit in with them. She was no lady. That was if her silly, female emotions ever came to anything.

Who was she kidding? Those silly emotions would never amount to anything.

A gilt-edged china plate, much nicer than the tin ones she owned, plonked onto the table, and her head came up.

Chas quirked a half smile, just a corner of his lips turned upward. "I grabbed breakfast at the hotel. Didn't figure you had."

His kindness flustered her. She could feel a flush creeping into her cheeks. He didn't seem to notice as he crossed the room to glance out the window.

* * *

CHAS KEPT one eye on Katy, who was again shoveling the food into her mouth, ignoring the fork he'd put on her plate. Was she still that hungry? Or had she never learned basic manners?

In the reflection of the window's glass, he caught a glimpse of Danna with her head bent over the papers on her desk. Before he'd turned away, he'd seen her blush.

She was sweet on him. The thought was terrifying—and crazy. Surely, he was mistaken. She couldn't be.

"I think I've found your man with the blond mustache."

He turned to find Danna waving a piece of paper in his direction. "You're kidding."

Surprised, he took it from her outstretched hand and looked into the face of the blond man he'd seen first in the café and then in the saloon with Hank Lewis.

"Well, what does it say?" Danna demanded.

"Jed Hester." Chas read aloud. "Wanted in Kansas, the Indian Territory, and Colorado. For robbery. There's a reward."

"Robbery? Not rustling? Are you certain it is the same man you've seen around town?"

"I'm sure," he replied grimly.

"But what is he doing around this area?"

And what was his involvement with Hank Lewis? Hank had been a cardsharp in Arizona before he'd killed Julia and Joseph.

"How many times have you seen this man?"

"Three."

"Then he isn't just passing through."

"It would appear not." What did it all mean? "Do you mind if I borrow this?" Chas wiggled the Wanted poster. "I might check around and see if he is staying at the hotel or boardinghouse."

"Do you think that's likely?" From her skeptical frown, it was obvious Danna didn't think so. Someone with a wanted poster wouldn't stay out in the open, would they?

"It wouldn't hurt to ask."

* * *

"MARSHAL?" The quiet voice from the girl huddled in a blanket next to Danna's bed brought Danna from the brink of sleep instantly. It was the first time Katy had spoken since telling Danna and Chas her name the night before.

"Hmm?" Danna levered herself up on the bed with an elbow in order to see the girl. In the dim light, she could only make

85

out an outline. Katy appeared to be curled in on herself, even though the room was warm.

A barroom brawl earlier in the evening had filled the two cells, and Danna's conscience wouldn't let her leave the girl in the jail with the men. Danna'd brought Katy into her room, telling her sternly that she was still under Danna's custody.

"Did your brother love you?"

The question was utterly unexpected. Stunned, half-asleep, she spoke before thinking. "I suppose he must've."

"Then why did he send you away?"

Danna had asked herself the same question for years after she'd married Fred. She'd never come up with a satisfactory answer. She barely spoke to her brother.

"My brother had lived on the ranch his whole life. Didn't even go to school. I don't think he knew what to do with a sister. A girl."

Katy was quiet for so long that Danna almost drifted off to sleep again. When the girl finally spoke, her voice was almost a whisper.

"What would have happened to you if...if there wasn't a husband to take you in? If you had nowhere to go?"

Danna took a breath and reminder herself to tread carefully, hoping she could get more information on the girl's identity.

"Well, Katy, I guess if I hadn't married Fred, I probably would've found a family that I liked and that liked me, and I would've stayed with them and helped work their farm. I was used to outdoor work from being on my brother's ranch."

"What if you didn't know how to work?"

Danna followed her instinct and reached down to rest her hand on the girl's shoulder. Katy flinched, but she didn't pull away. A moment passed, and she seemed to relax.

"Honey, if you're worried about what's going to happen to you, you don't need to."

Danna felt more than heard the girl take a shuddering breath.

"Do you have any family?"

"N-no," came the whisper. "My p-pa died."

"What about schooling?"

"I can't read, but I can cipher some."

"Well, come tomorrow, we'll see if we can find you a place to stay and some work to do. You promise not to steal anymore?"

The girl grunted, and Danna decided to take it for a yes. She should probably feel good that she finally had a plan on what to do with Katy, but something about it sat like a stone in her stomach.

Was it because the girl reminded her so vividly of herself at that age? Alone, uncertain, unloved? Because despite her automatic answer to Katy, despite all the times she'd told herself that of course her brother loved her, Danna could never quite convince herself.

It was a long-time before she drifted off to sleep.

CHAPTER 8

he next night, Danna moved wearily up the stairs to her room above the jail, looking forward to her bed and some rest after breaking up a barroom fight after one gambler had declared the man playing against him was cheating.

She'd nearly taken a broken bottle to the ribs. Chas would've been upset if he'd seen her in danger, but this was his evening off. Finally, in the wee hours, the saloons had closed, and she was free to get some sleep.

She pushed open the door, careful not to wake Katy, whom she'd settled earlier in the evening. A sliver of moonlight from the open door fell on the blanket Katy had used the past two nights.

The girl was gone.

A horrible feeling clenched Danna's insides. She struck a match and lit the oil lamp she kept on the small round table in one corner of the room and found the entire space was empty.

The blanket was folded neatly and sat with the extra pillow in the middle of Danna's bed. No signs that the girl had ever inhabited the room.

It had been dark when Danna had brought her up here for the night. If she'd left, she probably wouldn't have gotten far. But why would she leave? And where would she go?

Questions swirled in Danna's mind as she raced back outside and clomped down the steps, her boots echoing loudly in the darkness.

She slipped in the small space between the stairway that led up to her rooms and the outside wall of the milliner's building, pausing before she reached the boardwalk.

Something felt wrong. Call it instinct, call it something else, but her skin crawled. Something was going on. Something she hadn't felt two minutes ago when she'd gone upstairs.

Taking her time, just like Fred had taught her, Danna peeked around the corner of the building, but the street was empty, the buildings dark.

Danna crept down the street, taking care to stay in the shadows under the buildings awnings, keeping her bootsteps muted against the boardwalk.

As she crossed Third Street, she thought she glimpsed a flash of light from inside the Calvin Bank and Trust. She froze, eyes glued to the front window. Was someone inside? Straining her ears, Danna heard a soft whicker. A horse?

Everything was still. Then—*there*. The flash of light came again.

From this distance, she couldn't make out any details through the bank windows. She needed to get closer.

A prickle of unease skittered up the back of her neck.

She needed to be sure, needed to see into the bank.

She crouched down and crept along the boardwalk, keeping close to the front of the grocery. She jumped when something warm bumped into her leg. She barely stifled her scream.

"Wrong Tree." She hissed the dog's name, and he sat in front of her. He was supposed to be at the livery with Will. "Go home."

His tongue lolled and his tail swept the dirt-packed lane.

"Go. Home."

He whined and turned away from the jail house toward the saloon across the street.

"I don't have time to deal with you right now." She tried grasping the piece of rope around his neck to usher him toward the jail, but he turned back toward the saloon, and this time he barked.

"Hush." Danna released him and let him gallop away. She couldn't worry about him. She had work to do.

The bank had two entry points. The main customer entrance at the front and the employee entrance at the rear. Both of those doors were to the east side of the building, so it was possible someone could be watching both exits at once from the alley between the bank and the doctor's office next door. That would make it harder for her to get near the building. And the bank's entire front wall was composed of large windows. If they had a sentry inside, there would be no sneaking up on the building from Main Street. The closest she could hope to get without being seen was the doctor's office. And it had no windows that looked toward the bank.

But the doc's office was only a single story tall. If she could get on the roof, she could use her field glasses to see into the bank. And she'd have her rifle in case she needed it.

It wasn't much of a plan, but she had to try. She didn't have time to track down Chas at the hotel if the bank was being robbed.

* * *

CHAS HAD HAD a bad feeling all evening that Hank Lewis was still in town. This was his third patrol through Calvin's streets tonight, and he was exhausted, his eyes heavy from scouring the shadows for trouble. He'd been having a hard time sleeping, knowing Hank Lewis was nearby, he'd been taking extra patrols on his own.

Everything was quiet, the streets deserted, the saloons finally closed down for the night.

Then he saw movement on top of one of the buildings a few blocks down.

Heart pounding, Chas pulled his pistol from his gun belt and ran across Main Street, then jumped up onto the boardwalk.

At the corner of the bank, he paused with his back against the bricks beside the windows that stretched all the way across the front of the building to the door.

Noise from inside surprised him into stillness. Scuffling...and voices.

From here, Chas couldn't get a look at the roof of the building next door. To do that, he'd have to cross in front of the large windows overlooking the boardwalk. Was there a lookout up there? Was this a bank robbery?

Chas peeked around the corner and through the window closest to him. He thought he could make out some movement, but the inside was too dark for him to be sure.

The soft neigh of a horse brought his head up. Ready for escape?

He didn't have time to rouse the marshal from sleep.

Ducking low, he half-crawled, half-shuffled across the boardwalk toward the front door of the bank, pistol in hand. He needed a glimpse inside, to see the layout of the bank, see if there was a sentry standing just inside the windows.

Halfway across the front of the bank and from his crouched position, he could see the roof of the building next door. He caught a flash of movement. Was that a hat? A glint of moonlight on metal told him there was weapon up there. Then the figure shifted, and he caught a glimpse of a dark braid.

Danna? No. He blinked, straining his eyes for another look,

but he couldn't see anything. Had it really been her, or just an illusion prompted by his imagination?

Before he could raise his head above the windowsill to see inside, a shot rang out, then the sound of breaking glass.

He froze.

Julia fell to the ground at his feet, blood seeping from underneath her crumpled body. He followed her to the ground, moaning her name.

But she didn't hear him. She was already gone.

* * *

DANNA DUCKED when she saw the muzzle-flash from the darkened back door of the bank.

Okay. It definitely wasn't the bank manager inside. Not if someone'd taken a shot at her.

If they'd seen her, she'd lost the element of surprise and the chance to go get help.

She couldn't let them get away.

She quickly rose on her knees and fired a shot at the person-size shadow in the bank's side window. Glass shattered. Had she hit him?

A man on horseback below held the reins for three other horses. She could hear the animals stomping and whinnying their agitation. The man probably had a gun. Could she trust that he was adequately distracted by the horses?

She stuck her head over the roof's edge for a look. A blur of snarling dark fur launched across the alleyway.

Wrong Tree! All four horses whinnied and then thundered off, hoofbeats fading. The lookout shouted but couldn't get control before they disappeared into the night. *Thank you, Wrong Tree!*

She left her rifle on the doc's rooftop and dangled her feet off the edge, then dropped. Landing in a crouch, she fumbled for her pistol, moving toward the broken window. With a little hop, she vaulted the window's lip and inside the building. She slammed into a moving body.

* * *

CHAS FOUGHT the mental and physical paralysis that held him pinned in a ball on the boardwalk. All he could see was Julia's form crumpled before him, see his bloodstained hands.

"We got comp'ny!"

The muffled shout shook Chas from the dark place.

A woman's shriek brought him to his feet, though it almost cost him his last meal. He shook with the adrenaline and revulsion coursing through him.

He clutched his pistol against his shoulder, breathing hard. A glance at the rooftop showed it was empty. Shards of glass were scattered across the boardwalk. Someone had broken the far window.

Had Danna gone inside?

He had to go in there. He couldn't save Julia, but he could rescue her.

He used his elbow to break the glass in the nearest window and then rolled over the sill.

It was even darker inside the building than out. Something —someone?—scrabbled over to his right and he steped in that direction when he was tackled from behind.

* * *

DANNA GRAPPLED with the man trying to take her arm off, using both her shoulder and elbow to get some leverage. The man grunted, but instead of releasing her, he shoved her into the wall, and she cried out.

Her gun had been knocked from her hand when she'd

barreled into this human ox, and she could really use it right about now.

Over the sounds of their struggle, she heard glass breaking and a muffled shout. "Danna!"

Chas?

The large man's rancid breath hit her full in the face, and she knocked her head into his. He let go of her arm, cursing.

She dropped to the floor and scrambled for her weapon. The ox-man walked into her, knocking her flat. Where was her gun? It couldn't have gotten far.

"Let's go!" A third voice rang out from behind the wall separating the bank's teller area from the vault room.

The man Danna had been struggling with turned, but she swept her leg out and caught his ankles. He stumbled, but didn't go down. She tackled his knees, and he fell.

* * *

CHAS and his assailant were evenly matched. He couldn't get the guy to go down and stay there.

"Shoot her!" someone shouted.

"No!" The cry ripped from his throat. The exchange was enough of a distraction for him to lose track of the fight. He registered a sharp pain in his temple and knew no more.

* * *

DANNA HEARD the sound of a body hitting the floor, but she was too busy struggling with the human ox to do more than hope someone on the street would hear the ruckus and come to her aid.

Something metal clanged against wood. Oh, no! Had the big man somehow gotten hold of her gun?

He shoved her away, and she rolled to one side. Light from

a torch glinted off the barrel of a pistol, which the man held in his beefy hand. Pointed right at her.

She leapt to her left. The crack of the bullet whizzed by, but it didn't hit her. She ducked behind the teller counter.

A deep thud and soft moan turned her head. The light illuminated two bodies lying on the floor. Was one of them her deputy?

"Get out, get out!" shouted the voice from the back.

From her vulnerable position crouched on the floor, Danna saw the huge shadow of the man she'd been grappling with move away. The robbers were leaving? Two pairs of boots thumped against the wooden floors, one with a noticeable drag to one of his footsteps.

Silence fell.

Danna knelt behind the desk, trembling. She'd nearly been shot. In all the years she'd worked at Fred's side, she'd never been so close to dying before. Correction, never except two weeks ago, when she'd nearly been run over by a stampede.

Her heart drummed in her ears about as loud as the gunshot had been. She was alive. That's what mattered.

Another moan from nearby drew her gaze up from her shaking hands. The body closest to her was moving, his head rolling from side to side.

"Mama," he whispered.

She crawled toward him, frowning when her palms met with something warm and sticky on the floor. Blood? She hadn't been shot, but apparently this man had.

The body she reached wasn't her deputy's, but she saw Chas's tousled head a few feet away and sucked in a quick breath. What had happened? How had he known something was wrong and come in here? Had he been shot?

A shaft of moonlight filtered through the shattered window and illuminated her deputy's face, slack and unconscious. No blood marked his body, thankfully.

The unknown man groaned again, and she crouched next to him, kicking away the weapon lying nearby. Even a wounded man could shoot.

A quick examination told her he was in serious danger. Blood seeped from a wound in his abdomen.

Danna bit back a cry and reached into her pocket for her bandanna. She pressed it against the man's stomach, trying to stanch the flow of blood. Wounds in the torso were almost impossible to treat. If she didn't get help, he might not make it.

"Marshal?" came a wavering voice from the vault room. Danna wished she'd found her pistol, but there wasn't time to locate it now. She held pressure on the man's wound.

A light appeared behind her, and its beam bounced and shook on the walls until she could see the face of Zachariah Silverton, the bank manager. Danna swallowed a groan. Zachariah was not known for his calm.

"Silverton, I need you to bring the light closer, then run for the doc. This man's in a bad way." She used her marshal's voice, the one Fred had taught her to cultivate on a laughter-filled afternoon so many years ago.

"Th-th-they made me open the vault. They held a g-g-gun on me. Said they'd sh-shoot me."

Splendid. He was so shaken he didn't seem to have heard her.

"Zachariah. Zachariah!" He started and looked up at her. The lantern he held wobbled so much, she was afraid he might drop it.

"Bring the light here. Put it on the desk." His eyes grew large when he saw the bloody body under Danna's hands. The lantern banged against the corner of the desk, and he nearly dropped it before he settled it on the edge. He backed away, overturning a wooden chair and almost falling.

"Zachariah." She waited until he focused on her face before she went on. "I need you to go find Doc."

He nodded, his head bobbing awkwardly. He edged toward the door.

"Hurry! This man needs help."

He turned and bolted, shoulder banging into the doorframe before he passed out of sight. The sound of his boot steps faded, and Danna could hear Chas's deep breathing and the wavering breaths of the man underneath her hands.

Her handkerchief soaked through, she looked around for something else to help stop the flowing blood.

She needed the doc now. This man was dying.

* * *

CHAS HEARD noises as if from far away. Shouts, voices, then moaning. A ringing filled his ears, his head ached.

He remembered. Following Danna into the bank right into the middle of a scuffle—a robbery. Was she alive?

It took some effort, but he cracked one eye open. Light sent shafts of pain pulsing through his head, but he refused to close his eye now that he had it open. He rolled his head to one side and saw the broken window he'd busted.

Where was the kid now? He turned his head in the other direction and forced both eyes open. There was a body, lying on the floor And Danna leaning over him.

He closed his eyes against the intensity of his relief. She was all right.

But the kid didn't appear to be. What had happened? Had Danna shot him?

Confusion and pain beat at the inside of his head, muddling everything.

He tried to push himself up with one hand, but throbbing pain made it impossible, and he slumped to the floor.

"Stay still for now." Her voice sounded curt, angry. "Are you hurt?"

Was he? All he could feel was the pounding in his brain. "Took a wallop on the head."

"It's a good thing, too, or you might've ended up shot."

"Like him? Did you shoot him?"

Her lips flattened. "No."

Chas's throat closed. More bloodshed. He hadn't been able to prevent it. Gingerly, he sat up, head spinning.

"O'Grady, stay where you are."

Hurried steps pounded on the boardwalk, and Chas turned in time to see two tall forms pass the broken window. They clattered inside.

"M-marshal, I got the doc." The nervous man hung back while an older man with a bushy white mustache and full head of silver hair came to Danna's side.

"Can't get a good look. Need more light," mumbled the man that must be the doc.

"Silverton," Danna barked. "Bring the light down here."

Silverton didn't move. His face was a pasty white, and Chas wondered if he was about to faint. Chas stood, fighting for equilibrium.

"O'Grady," Danna barked his name, but the rushing in his ears made it hard to tell if she said anything else.

He used one hand to hold onto the desk, to make sure he didn't embarrass himself and fall. With the other, he picked up the lamp and handed it to the doc.

"You don't look real good either, son."

That's when Chas blacked out for the second time.

* * *

"—ROBBED—"

"Four or five men..."

"—headed out of town—"

An irate voice yelled over all the other chatter.

"Where's the marshal?"

The other voices receded into more of a whispered murmur. Chas forced his eyes open, noting that the pain in his head wasn't as bad as it had been before.

The bank was lit up now, several more lamps joining the first. A short, balding man stormed through the front door, past Chas where he lay half-behind one of the desks, to where Danna stood conversing with a man Chas didn't recognize and the man named Silverton near the rear of the building.

"Marshal—"

She ignored the balding man, continuing her conversation with the two other men in low tones.

Chas pushed himself up to a sitting position.

The man Danna had ignored obviously wasn't used to being treated that way, because his face turned a deep shade of purple, and he began to splutter.

Danna nodded at something the doc said and turned. "Yes, Mr. Castlerock?"

Ah. The owner. "Marshal, why aren't you out catching the men who did this to my bank?"

"I've been tending to a man with a bullet wound in his gut. My deputy is injured. I'm doing the best I can."

She walked past him toward Chas. "I'll let you know when I have something to report."

The man sputtered, but Danna's gaze was fastened on Chas as she crouched next to him.

He couldn't look away from her face. Unscathed. She was perfectly unharmed. He had to swallow back the emotions that wanted to burst from him.

He realized her hands were covered in blood.

It unnerved him. Look at what had almost happened to her. He'd frozen up, let her down. Couldn't protect her. She hadn't been killed, but she could've been.

He needed distance. Forcing himself to stand, he closed his eyes to counteract his roiling stomach.

"All right?" Danna's soft-spoken question came from too close.

"I will be. You?" He opened his eyes but didn't look at her. The dizziness began to fade.

Out of the corner of his eye, he saw her shrug. "Maybe a little bruised. No worse than breaking up a saloon fight."

It made him itch that she spoke of throwing herself into danger so casually. What could he say? She was the marshal.

He followed her out the front door, boots crunching on glass from the window he'd broken.

Danna knelt in front of one of the watering troughs. She spoke as she scrubbed her hands. "I'm going to take a swing around town, make sure they haven't holed up anywhere. I doubt they would, but best to make sure. I'll gather a posse and ride out at first light."

She hadn't looked at him the whole time she'd been speaking, but now she glanced up. He could see weariness etched in the lines bracketing her mouth. "You should have Doc check out that bump on your head. Maybe rest a while. I want you to sit in the doc's office until the wounded robber comes around. Assuming he survives."

CHAPTER 9

The door to the jail half-open, Chas picked his aching head up off his arms when he heard a distinct set of bootsteps approaching.

Danna was back.

Then a second set of footsteps, this one much heavier than Danna's, thudded on the boardwalk, coming from another direction.

"Marshal, did you catch the men who robbed my bank yet?"

The bank owner. Castlerock.

"Not yet, sir." Weariness was evident in Danna's voice.

"I want my money recovered and the men apprehended."

"They will be, sir."

"Soon, or I'm going to call for your job."

Now her voice lost what was left of its politeness. "I'll be in touch when I have more information to share."

Through the open doorway, Chas saw her push past the larger man. She stepped through the door, her huff of annoyance audible as she closed it with a snap.

"Problem, Miss Marshal?"

She was apparently so tired she didn't even react to his

teasing use of her title. She moved to her desk quickly and started opening drawers, making a pile of items on top of the desk. He recognized the leather journal from the top drawer, a pair of field glasses, a length of rope.

Chas glanced out the window. The sky was lightening. Dawn would be here soon.

"When's the posse get here?"

"There won't be one." Her actions contradicted her flatly spoken statement. She seemed to be preparing to leave for a length of time.

"You found them, then?"

She laid her hands flat on the table, closed her eyes, and tucked her head so her chin rested on her vest. "No one will ride with me. But I'm going anyway."

"Alone?"

She must have heard the sharpness in his tone, because she looked up with a glare. He didn't care if he'd offended her. The thought of her chasing down Hank Lewis alone made his stomach roil.

"Is it such a surprise? You didn't want to work with me either. You're only here because you need my help getting around the countryside."

She went back to her packing as if he hadn't lodged a protest. "The tracks close to town were obscured, but I picked up four sets of hooves outside of town, heading toward the mountains."

"You'll be outnumbered."

She muttered under her breath as she loaded a pair of saddlebags.

Something whined outside the door, and Danna stomped across the room to open it. The ugly mutt he'd met on his first day sauntered in.

"Wrong Tree. Where've you been, boy?"

She patted the top of the dog's head, ruffled his ears. "You helped me last night, didn't you? Chased off that lookout. But how did you get loose from Will Chittim?"

The dog only lay at her feet and offered his belly to be scratched.

"He likes you," Chas said, the only words he could force past the lump of fear lodged in his throat.

"He never has before." After a cursory pet of the dog's belly, she returned to the desk. "He was Fred's dog before we married. He's been staying at the livery."

The dog lolled its head toward Chas, as if inviting him to take Danna's place. Chas knelt to oblige, and the dog grunted its appreciation.

Chas stood when Danna finished packing her saddlebags and turned for the door. "I'm going with you."

"Your head still hurt?"

Her eyes were too perceptive not to catch him if he lied. She could probably see the pulse pounding on his temple.

"I can ride."

She shook her head. "There's a storm threatening, and I've got to move fast. If you get dizzy and fall off your horse... You're too much of a liability."

"I'm not letting you go alone. We should really have more men, too."

"You're welcome to try. Go talk to the same men I've just been to see. Maybe they'll listen to an outsider instead of a woman."

The bitterness in her voice scared him; she was normally even-tempered, even in the face of the others in town doubting her. If she was giving chase to Hank Lewis and a gang of violent men with her emotions leading her, she was liable to get killed.

The thought Chas. He grasped the marshal's arm just above her elbow. "Would your husband have faced multiple armed men alone?"

It was the wrong thing to say. He knew it as she clenched her fist against the wooden door. She looked over her shoulder, her face set and fierce.

"Fred would've done whatever he needed to do to apprehend these men."

"And you need my help," he said it softly, as close to pleading as he'd ever come. "I'll ride with you. I won't take no for an answer."

* * *

DANNA RODE a few paces in front of her deputy, eyes on the terrain in front of her horse. She might be watching for tracks in the brushy foothills, but she remained extremely aware of the man behind her.

He'd been vehement about not letting her do this alone, and he was probably right. But she worried about that bump on his head. Head injuries could be tricky. What if he hurt himself worse on the hunt?

So far, he'd not fallen, but his face was gray with the strain. Of course, that could be from the chill. The temperatures had been falling all day.

They needed to round up the bank robbers and fast or risk getting caught in the snowstorm banked in gray clouds that were getting closer with every hoofbeat. A stinging cold wind, strong enough to cut through her leather slicker, had descended about the time they'd ridden out of town.

She hated riding into the mountains. When she'd still lived with her brother, she'd ridden after a lost cow and calf and had gotten injured and lost. Ever since then, the mountains had spooked her. After following tracks all day and into the early afternoon, they were already well into the foothills, and she was starting to get jumpy.

And even though it irked her to admit it, her deputy had

been right when he'd said Fred would never have walked into a situation like this alone.

It still hurt that the men from town denied her request for help. The same men her husband had counted on. Hadn't she proved herself enough yet? Would she ever?

Chas made a low sound, and Danna looked back to find he was hunched in the saddle with the collar of his jacket turned up.

She drew up on the reins. Chas followed suit.

"You okay?"

He nodded, but it didn't reassure her, not with the strain on his face. She knew he most likely wouldn't be able to find his way back to town on his own, and she didn't want to leave him when he had a head injury. If he lost consciousness and fell without anyone to assist him, he could die out in the elements.

But if they stopped now, they'd lose the trail. There were no good options.

He rested the reins against his thigh and raised his hands to his mouth, blowing on them. "Just cold," he said, voice muffled by his hands. "Do you really know where we're going?"

"I'm tracking them," she said.

His expression remained skeptical.

She dismounted, her joints protesting after being in one position for too long, and motioned Chas to do the same. "It won't hurt to get down and get some blood flowing, warm up a bit."

When her deputy hit the ground, she beckoned him to her side, a few feet in front of the horses. She squatted and pointed to the leaf knocked from its branch about a foot off the ground.

"See how it's broken off? This jagged edge here? Something stronger than the wind had to do that." She walked forward a few paces before bending over a patch of soft dirt that showed a partial print from a horse's hoof. "This track didn't come from a wolf or a bear."

Chas knelt beside her and traced the imprint with his forefinger. She tried not to be aware of his close proximity. She failed.

"How did you even see it?" He looked up at her, his hat shading his eyes so she couldn't read them.

"The more time I spend in the woods, the easier it is to spot things like broken leaves or footprints."

"Where did you learn all this? Following your husband around?'

She shook her head. "My granddad taught me and my brother a lot before he died. The rest is a matter of staying in practice."

She pointed to another pair of hoofprints a few feet further along. "These are shaped a little differently. See here? It's a different horse, but the tracks are just as fresh. I've seen four different prints, best I can tell."

"Amazing," O'Grady muttered. His tone reminded Danna of his voice when he'd called her a doll on the first night they'd met. But surely his sentiments weren't tender toward her, not after seeing her do a man's job.

Her emotions toward her deputy certainly didn't need to get any more tangled. She knew he was leaving when he completed his assignment. He was a city boy. She was happy in Calvin. At least, she had been before Fred's death.

They would never suit. But her heart didn't seem to want to listen. "We need to keep going if we've got any hope of catching up with the robbers." Danna swung her foot into the stirrup and boosted herself into the saddle, not looking back.

* * *

THE SKY KEPT GETTING darker and darker, and Chas watched Danna get jumpier and jumpier the farther they rode into the foothills.

She hadn't spoken to him since they'd taken off for the second time. He couldn't get a good look at her face, couldn't tell if she was getting antsy because of her tracking or for some other reason.

Her constant reactions to little things, like the snap of a branch in the wind, put him on edge. Plus, he was bone-aching cold, and the wind seemed to keep getting worse the longer they were in the saddle.

"Can we stop for a rest?" he called out when he couldn't take her silence or the cold any longer.

She wheeled her mount around but showed no signs of getting off.

Her jaw was set tight, almost like she was holding back a scream. "I hate to stop now. Once it starts snowing, we'll start losing the trail."

"Do you think we're close?"

"I don't know." Her fatigue and frustration were evident as she shifted in the saddle and wiped her face with a gloved hand. "I've lost two of the sets of hoofprints. I don't know if they've split up or if I'm so tired I'm not seeing straight anymore."

Part of him wanted to comfort her, to make everything all right again. Another part wanted to find Hank Lewis at all costs, to enact his revenge.

"Danna," he said quietly, and she raised her eyes to meet his. "Why don't we rest for a few minutes, and you can catch your breath?"

She tapped her thigh with a fist. "I'd rather keep moving."

Something cold stung his cheek, and he raised his face to the sky. Snowflakes whipped downward in a crazy dance toward the ground. He looked to Danna to see her face fall. "I think we're out of time."

"Not if we hurry!" She jerked on her mount's reins and kicked him hard, spurring him into a gallop.

Chas followed, but his heart wasn't in the chase any longer. He still felt an urgency to find Lewis, and he would find him, but his concern for Danna was more pressing.

He concentrated on keeping pace with her, not an easy feat, since her horse's legs were so much longer. Her braid flew out behind her, the tails of her long coat flapped in the wind. Snow and sleet stung his face as they raced through the trees and hills.

He was forced to fall back, his mare lathered and getting winded. He managed to keep Danna in sight but fell farther behind.

He'd topped a ridge when he saw her lying on the ground, a dark shape against the gathering snowdrifts.

CHAPTER 10

*C*has kicked his horse, riding past Danna's horse, which limped on three feet, several yards away from where her body lay. He threw himself to the ground before he could stop the beast.

"Danna." He dropped to his knees, took her shoulders, and turned her over as gently as possible. Other than a scrape on one cheek, her face was unmarred. Her dark eyes blinked open and focused on his face.

Her hat had fallen off, and her hair fell loose in the wind, dark strands tickling his fingers as he clutched her shoulders. She gasped for breath.

"Danna."

She struggled against him, and for once he was thankful for her stubborn independence. "I'm all right. Just winded."

She pushed his arms away, tried to sit up, finally catching her breath.

The sense of relief he felt nearly crippled him. She was all right. Again. Did the woman have to constantly put herself in danger?

"Let me..." His throat threatened to close. He ran his hands through the hair that had come loose, checking for bumps on her head. Large, fluffy snowflakes landed in her hair, stark white against the dark locks.

"I'm all right, Chas."

Her quiet words stopped his erratic movements but not the frantic beat of his heart. Before he could think, he leaned in and took her mouth in a kiss.

He felt her surprise in her utter stillness, was conscious of her hands trembling against his chest. When he pulled back, hands on her shoulders, she stared at him with large, dark eyes.

"What...was that?"

"Relief," he said quickly. "Probably shouldn't have done that. We work together—"

She stood, cutting off the rest of his words. Good thing, since he had no idea what he would have said next.

She moved toward her horse.

* * *

DANNA COULDN'T STOP SHAKING. Not from adrenaline or fear from when her horse had thrown her.

From Chas's kiss. The kiss that he thought was a mistake.

She went to Thunder. Something was wrong. A quick examination revealed it had thrown its shoe. She patted its neck, intensely relieved that nothing worse had happened.

"He won't be able to carry a rider, not with a thrown shoe."

Chas had moved to his horse, too. He wouldn't look at her. She closed her eyes, realizing he must regret kissing her.

"So, what do we do?" Chas asked.

"We can both ride on your mount, but the snow's getting worse."

It was coming down in clumps, the cold wind buffeting it in all directions.

She hated that it had come to this. "I think we're better off buckling down here for a while. We wait until the worst of the storm is past."

She wouldn't be able to track the bank robbers in this weather. It galled her to have lost them, but even a Fred and a team of deputies wouldn't have been able to stop the snow.

Shelter was scarce this high in the mountains, but Danna scouted for their best option. She showed Chas where to look for dry kindling in the wet weather, then picketed the horses in the driest spot she could find.

Nearby, she found a hollow between a hill and a large fallen tree. It would give her and Chas the most protection possible. Hopefully, they wouldn't be stuck for long. Especially with the awkward tension between them.

He'd pulled away so quickly. Had he been able to tell how it had affected her? Her heart had beaten like a big bass drum she'd heard once at a parade in Cheyenne. She hadn't been able to breathe correctly.

It was nothing she'd ever felt before. Not even with Fred.

She couldn't be falling for her deputy.

She got a fire going with Chas's twigs and motioned him to sit close to the flames after they'd hauled their gear over, including the saddle blankets that they would use to keep warm.

* * *

CHAS WATCHED the marshal settle in to their campsite. She was agitated, but tried to hide it. He couldn't miss the dip of her frown, the set of her shoulders turned slightly away from him.

All because of that kiss.

He wished he hadn't done it.

He would never forget it. How she'd felt in his arms, her scent... His head pounded, but not with pain.

He shook those traitorous thoughts away as she sat, near enough to touch.

She tipped her head back and glanced at the sky. He watched, entranced, as snowflakes fell on her face and into her dark hair. She didn't seem to realize the long tresses had come loose from her braid.

"Snow's coming down faster." Her voice was hushed, awed. "It's a good thing we didn't try to go back. If we couldn't find our way, we might freeze to death. Your head all right?"

"Fine." He didn't know what to say. He was completely off-balance.

She tucked her knees up toward her chest, wrapped her arms around them, and loosely clasped her hands toward the fire. "It's my fault." The words were so soft, Chas barely heard them over the popping of the fire. "We should've turned back earlier. I wanted to race the snowstorm."

"Do you think the bank robbers holed up somewhere? Why would they come up into the mountains like this?"

"I don't know. There are lots of caves in these mountains, even some old trappers' shacks where they could've taken shelter."

She was silent a long time. Chas watched the fire until he finally felt compelled to say, "It's not your fault we got stuck here. The weather..."

She shook her head. "Fred would never have gotten in a pickle like this."

"You compare yourself to him too much."

Her eyes flashed up to his, and he saw the surprise in their depths. "I do?"

"All the time. You make coffee like Fred used to make it. Patrol the town at the hours he used to patrol. What's wrong with making the job your own?"

A flush ran up her jaw and into her cheeks. He hoped he hadn't offended her.

"I don't know." She unclasped her hands and held them toward the fire. The air was biting cold on his exposed skin, mostly his face, and he shifted closer to the fire's warmth.

"Fred was a good marshal. He'd been doing it for years. And he was a good teacher."

The affection in her tone when she spoke of her husband wasn't surprising, but his reaction was. Jealousy. "You're not the same person he was. No reason you have to be marshal the exact same way he did. The town council appointed you for a reason."

"Why did they?" Her abrupt question seemed to surprise her as much as it did him. She went on a rush. "You asked me that, and once I started thinking about it, I realized it really didn't make sense. Why me instead of any of the other deputies? Why not hire someone from another town?"

"Maybe none of them wanted to be marshal."

Her brows wrinkled in skepticism. "I can think of at least two men who would've taken the job."

"Perhaps the council considered all the candidates and decided you were the best."

Something changed in her eyes, some softer emotion that he didn't recognize. Didn't want to recognize. "I doubt that. And anyway, I'm still sorry you're caught in this snowstorm with me."

He shrugged. "I guess there could be worse things than being stuck in the wilderness with a beautiful woman."

She turned her face away, but not before he saw the flare of hurt in her expression. "I'll thank you not to mock me, even though we shared…even though you stole that kiss earlier."

What? She thought he was jesting? The cold, and his still-roiling emotions, made him scoot across the damp ground, reach out for her, and pull her flush against his chest. He braced for an elbow or a fist he was sure would come his way.

"I wasn't mocking you," he said quietly.

"What are you—?"

"It'll be warmer this way." He settled his arms loosely around her and rested his cheek against her brow. The softness of the hair at her temple made him close his eyes. He forced them open, forced away thoughts better left alone. "Who'd have thought this city boy would be camping with a pretty marshal in a snowstorm?"

She was silent for so long he thought she wasn't going to respond.

"I'm not...pretty." Her whisper was nearly inaudible. He looked down at her. Was she blushing? Yes. Warm color lit the side of her cheek. How could she doubt herself?

"You are. Why, at least half the men wanted to dance with you the other night at that rancher's shindig."

She didn't speak, but somehow, he knew she didn't believe him.

"Didn't your husband ever tell you how pretty you are?"

He nearly bit his tongue as the words escaped. He didn't want to talk about her dead husband.

"Fred told me that I was a good shot. That I could outride him most days, and that I had a good memory for details. He told me the truth."

"Well, he didn't tell you everything. Your eyes and your smile are...incredibly lovely." His voice stuck on the word, so caught up was he in making her believe him. He went on, voice lower. "And your hair is like silk."

He didn't dare touch her hair, not the way he wanted to, although a few strands tickled his chin and neck.

One of the horses blew, and Danna turned her head, her temple grazing Chas's jaw. They both remained quiet for a long while, Chas simply enjoying the marvel of the falling snow, enjoying the heat of the fire, enjoying the opportunity to be close to her.

The woods were silent until she burst out, "If they wanted to dance with me, why didn't they ask?"

* * *

DANNA FELT Chas's breath catch in his chest, and she thought he was going to laugh at her.

"Maybe they're a little afraid of you," he suggested. "Or it could have something to do with that weapon you carry and the badge you wear."

"Or because I don't dress like the other women?" she asked, knowing her curiosity betrayed that she cared more than she let on.

She ached to belong. To walk into one of the stores and be welcomed like the other wives and daughters, not with the grim, condescending smiles she always received.

"Maybe. Although I can't really picture you jumping into a brawl at the saloon in a skirt."

She tilted her head to see his face. Was he mocking her now? He wasn't smiling. He was staring out into the night. Why was it that being close to her deputy made her want to open up to him? He wasn't even holding her tightly; his arms loosely covered hers. His head rested against hers in an almost brotherly way.

But the thrills coursing through her veins didn't feel sisterly at all.

He blew out a breath. "If you want to blame anyone, it's really my fault we're stuck out here."

Her brows scrunched as she followed his change of topic. "How so?"

"Outside the bank. I was there sooner, but...I froze."

"I wondered how you came to be there."

"I was patrolling. I've been...anxious since that blond man has been around town."

Something about the way he finished his sentence was off. She sensed that he'd started to say something else.

"I saw a light in the window. And I thought I saw you...on the roof?"

She nodded. "I was there. I was out looking for Katy. Katy..." How could she have forgotten the girl? Yes, Danna had been extremely busy with the robbery and its aftermath, but—

"What about her?" Chas asked.

"She'd disappeared. That's how I stumbled on the bank robbery. I was looking for her. I'd tucked her in and left, and when I came back she was gone. I haven't even thought about her." Guilt pressed heavy. Danna should have remembered the girl, should have told someone before she'd left town.

"She'll be all right. She survived until we found her."

"I hope so." It was true, but it didn't make her feel any better. "I interrupted. You were telling me why you thought the robbery was your fault?"

He shrugged, eyes on the fire. "I heard your shot, heard scuffling, but before I could make myself go inside, I just...couldn't move."

Again, she sensed he hadn't said what he'd wanted to say. She waited for a moment to see if he would.

When he didn't speak, she said, "Even if you'd come into the building right away, we were outnumbered. And since I didn't know you were there, I might've shot you."

"How do you do it? Walk into dangerous situations like that alone? You could've been killed."

"I wasn't alone. God was with me."

He snorted, and she drew away. He let her go easily.

"It's true," she said. "He is with me every day, every moment. You don't have to believe for it to be true. It just is."

He didn't reply.

"When He calls me home, I'll go. But I'm not going to stop living life—that includes doing my job—until then."

He flipped a twig into the fire. It sizzled until it was engulfed in flames. "I used to be religious."

She stifled the urge to tell him that her relationship with God was more than "religion," but something held her silent.

"Then someone I loved, someone I was close to, died."

A wife? She couldn't bear the thought. "God didn't make her die."

He was silent for a long time. "No. No, he didn't."

Had he realized she'd assumed it was a woman. But his words were confirmation and made her insides twist.

He didn't say more, and with the closeness between them broken, she shifted to reach the saddle and opened one of the saddlebags. There was hardtack and jerky inside a wrapped pouch. Fred had always insisted on traveling with a little food in case of emergency. It wouldn't be much, and if she needed to hunt up a rabbit for supper, she could. At least it gave her a distraction right now. She handed a portion of the dried meat to Chas, who took it and ate silently.

Where was the canteen? She reached back into the saddle-bag, but this time her fingers brushed against soft leather, and she pulled out Fred's journal. She'd forgotten sliding it into her bag this morning.

She flipped open the journal and ran her fingers over the writing. How many nights had Fred sat at his small desk in their room above the jail, writing in this book?

She blinked away her memories and returned the journal to her saddlebag, where it would be safe from the snow.

"You ever read that, or do you just like touching it?"

Danna looked up to find Chas's eyes on her.

"I've seen you handle that book several times, but never read it."

It was already a night for sharing confidences. What would it hurt to reveal this, too?

"I can't read," she answered, ashamed by the admission.

"It's one of the many things I don't know how to do. Cooking, sewing, keeping house. It was good my husband was a bachelor for years before we married, or we'd likely have starved."

* * *

CHAS FELT the tension crackling in the air between them. It mattered to Danna how he reacted. He could feel it.

He noted the distance she'd put between them when he'd scoffed at her mention of God, saw how she stared into the fire with her arms crossed protectively over her middle, a shiver coursing through her.

She thought he would think less of her because she couldn't read? Or cook?

"Not knowing those things hasn't stopped you being marshal, hasn't stopped you doing a good job of it, either."

"You really think so?"

"Yes." He was surprised to find it was true. He did think she did a good job. Her loyalty to the people of Calvin couldn't be questioned. She'd ridden into a blizzard to chase down those thieves.

Now that he took the time to think about it, he should have recognized the clues right in front of him. The way she'd squinted at his letter of introduction from the detective agency, the way she'd pushed the Wanted poster for Jed Hester to him to read.

"Come back over here. It's cold," he said when a second shiver shook her shoulders.

She shifted into place at his side, and he couldn't ignore the brush of their shoulders. She spread one of the horse blankets over both their legs. Chas knew it was just to keep them warm, but the intimacy of the action had him scrambling for a distraction.

He choked out the words, "Now that I know you a little, I can't imagine you doing anything else."

Sitting so close, he had only a profile view of her face, but still he saw the wry smile. "Can't picture me as a seamstress or cook?"

"Perhaps a ranch foreman...or running your own spread."

Her lips quirked but didn't quite form a smile this time. When she spoke, her words held a wistful quality. "When I was a child, I often dreamed of having my own homestead. Raising cattle."

"What changed?"

She was quiet for a longtime. "I got married."

She'd told him her brother had sent her away, not to finishing school but to get married, and he desperately wanted to ask what had caused the rift between them. She seemed to sense his question.

"When I was fifteen," she started, "I took a horse from my brother's barn to chase down a heifer that was due to calf any day. I ended up in the mountains alone, and my horse threw me. I broke my leg."

"Is that why the mountains bother you?"

She looked at him, eyebrows lifted.

"You've been jumpy all afternoon. Reacting to little noises, shadows."

A flush crept up her cheeks, and she rested her head lightly on his shoulder. So he couldn't read her expression?

"Maybe I am a bit anxious. Anyway, because of my leg, I couldn't get home. It took my brother nearly a day and a half to find me." She inhaled deeply, her shoulder moving against his chest. "I'd never seen him so angry before."

"And that's why he sent you away? Because he was angry?"

"I think...I think he didn't know what to do with a sister. If I'd been born a boy—or maybe if he'd had more time with my parents—he might have known how to handle me."

She yawned. He knew how she felt. Neither of them had slept the night before, and as the sky was darkening, he struggled to keep his eyes open.

"Should we rest a while?" he asked. "The blizzard doesn't seem to have slowed."

Her head came off his shoulder. "One of us should probably keep watch. We don't know if the bank robbers are nearby. Once night falls, our fire will be a beacon in the darkness."

She sounded bone-tired.

"I can stay awake," Chas said, shifting his arm to support her shoulders a bit more.

"You're sure?"

"Yes."

Her head lolled against his shoulder, and her breathing evened out. That quickly, she'd fallen asleep. It told him just how much she trusted him. It was a sobering thought.

Mind whirling, he watched the flames flicker, watched shadows dance against the trees.

He was getting too entangled with the marshal. The things she'd shared tonight had served to open his heart toward her. Before, he'd thought her crude, out of place as she fought to be marshal, but that impression had been completely wrong.

He couldn't imagine her brother sending her away. She was so strong, unbelievably beautiful, independent. She'd taken the circumstances life had given her, like the loss of her parents, and gone on. Not just existing, but living. She'd made a place for herself, provided for herself.

She was amazing. How could someone who claimed to love her abandon her?

His thoughts went to his sister Erin back in Boston. Hadn't he done the same thing? He'd left her to the devices of their overbearing father and matchmaking mother? What if she needed him?

Not for the first time, he thought of sending for her. He

could make a home for his sister in St. Louis or another western town. The question was, did she hate him the way his parents surely did?

He thrust thoughts of Boston, of home, away, and focused instead on his growing feelings for the marshal.

He genuinely liked her. But he still hadn't told her about Hank Lewis or his thirst for revenge. Danna was a straight-shooter. She'd never approve, but Chas couldn't give up on his mission. Lewis had taken everything from him.

Including a chance at winning the marshal's heart.

CHAPTER 11

*D*awn arrived with a lightening of the steel-gray sky and the absence of snow falling.

Chas woke to a hand on his shoulder to find himself wrapped in one of the horse blankets and the fire already extinguished.

"You all right?" Danna asked, crouching near. "Is your head paining you? You were mumbling in your sleep."

The nightmare. Just before Danna'd woken him, he'd watched Julia fall away from him, lifeless.

Chas scrubbed a hand over his face. "I'll be all right in a minute." It was a lie. He'd never be all right again, not after what he'd let happen to Julia.

He squinted up at the sky, then back at Danna, who'd moved to the horses, one of which was already saddled up. She was ready to move.

He remembered waking her several hours into the night, when he could no longer keep his eyes open. She'd gone after more firewood, and he'd wrapped himself in the blanket to wait for her. That was the last thing he remembered. Had he slept through? And only had the nightmare there at the very end?

It seemed impossible. The dream usually recurred multiple times, waking him often.

With the return of his nightmare came the return of his hatred for Hank Lewis.

"Any chance of finding fresh tracks in this snow?" Chas gestured to the several inches of powder on the ground. A smaller layer dusted his blanket.

She considered him. "Depends. If they were nearby, it's possible we could pick up their tracks. We should get back to town soon, but we could spare a little time scouting."

Too soon Danna declared they had to return to Calvin. The disappointment was sharp in his chest, but he had no choice but to follow orders. Plus, they only had the one uninjured horse between them. Danna's original horse followed behind, its reins held loosely in her gloved hand.

By midday, they had descended the mountain and were only a few miles out from Calvin.

Riding double in the silent, snowy landscape was much different than when they'd ridden into town coming out of the canyon.

He was different. The dynamics of their relationship had changed last night. They were no longer simply marshal and deputy. Two people couldn't share the things they had and remain in a cordial working relationship.

But were they friends? He cared about what happened to Danna and wanted her to be safe in her job, but there couldn't be more than that between them.

He couldn't allow it.

Because the only other woman he'd loved had died, and it was his fault.

Safely back in town, Chas and Danna parted ways at the

livery. He desperately wanted his bed, but a grumble of his stomach had him stopping in at the café first.

He still didn't know what to do. He needed to find and kill Hank Lewis. He needed to protect himself, protect his heart. And that meant distancing himself from Danna Carpenter.

Inside the café, he was greeted by the smell of frying meat and the familiar waitress.

"Afternoon, hon." She set a mug of coffee down and motioned him to sit at one of the few empty tables. "Meatloaf or stew?'

He grunted what must've been a satisfactory answer, because she smiled and left.

How could he find Lewis? At this point, he didn't even care about the job he'd been assigned. The WSGA could send someone else to find the rustlers.

"Marshal come and claim that boy yet?" a male voice asked from a table nearby.

"He's still in the doc's office. Heard he's in bad shape," another voice answered.

A plate appeared in front of him, and Chas tucked in to the fare, trying not to listen to the talk swirling around him.

Someone slurped their coffee. "...said she gut-shot him. Poor soul didn't have a chance."

Chas choked back words in Danna's defense. She'd been alone for most of that robbery. It was a miracle she hadn't been killed.

"I've seen her shoot. Wouldn't want to be on the other end of her gun, that's for sure."

"Nor her temper. I heard she let it fly at Harold's wife once for no reason a'tall!"

The young waitress from before rushed through the door and joined her mother a few tables over. "Mama! You'll never guess who I saw riding into town this morning, proud as could be. The marshal!"

Chas's head came up. The mother was carrying two plates to a table at the far side of the room while her daughter followed at her elbow.

"Put your apron on. We've got a full crowd," the waitress said, not appearing to pay attention to her daughter's words. She stopped for a moment at Chas's table to refill his coffee.

"But, Ma! She was out all night with her deputy. Everyone saw her leave town." The girl looked at him and must've just realized who she was gossiping about. She turned red.

The men sitting nearby who'd been talking about the marshal now sat silent, staring at Chas.

Danna would be furious.

* * *

DANNA DARTED toward the jail and the safety it represented. How could those awful rumors have spread through town so fast?

Her visit to the doctor hadn't provided any good news. The outlaw was still in serious condition and hadn't roused except for a few lucid moments. After she'd left the doctor's office, she'd heard two people talking about her going out overnight with Chas. Disparaging her reputation.

She couldn't help the anger that clenched her fists. She neared the jail and quickened her steps, wanting nothing more than to escape to the privacy of her room upstairs.

She hadn't paid any attention to who might have seen her yesterday when she'd left town. No one else would help her. What was she supposed to do?

She'd been so relieved to have his help, she probably wouldn't have cared if the town had staged a parade to see them out of town. And she'd never expected to be caught in the snowstorm. Hadn't even considered she had a reputation to be damaged.

Nothing inappropriate had happened. But rumors were swirling through town. She'd never had to worry about rumors or inappropriate behavior when she'd worked with Fred. No one would have dared start a rumor about her then. Fred wouldn't have stood for it. But now, she was on her own. And how did she stop something like this?

CHAPTER 12

*U*p early after a restless night, Danna came down the stairs from her room, intending to run a quick patrol. She'd let the gossip scare her into hiding last night, afraid of coming face-to-face with her deputy. It would be bad enough to know he'd heard the rumors, worse if she saw an inkling of humor in his eyes. The thought of him realizing her feelings for him and feeling sorry for her made her physically ill.

But she needed to find Katy and make sure the girl was okay.

Boots hitting the boardwalk, she drew up short at the sight of two men obviously waiting for her outside the jail.

One of them cleared his throat. "Mrs. Carpenter." Mr. Castlerock.

"Marshal." Mr. Parrott.

Two members of the town council.

"We need to speak to you for a few moments."

She motioned them toward the door and unlocked it. They filed inside behind her.

Still dark due to the early hour, Danna lit the lamp on her desk and the two that hung on each side of the room.

The men stood inside the door, Parrott looking decidedly uncomfortable. Castlerock wore the familiar scowl.

She didn't know whether to sit or stand, so she did what Fred would've done and perched against the side of the desk with her hands clasped in front of her. "What can I do for you gentlemen?"

Surprisingly, it was Parrott who spoke. "We're, er...that is, the town council is..." He took a deep breath.

Danna braced for the worst. They were going to demand her resignation. They'd warned her not to be a subject of the gossip, but this hadn't been her fault.

"Well, let's just say there is a bit of concern that you haven't made much progress on the bank robbery." He glanced at Castlerock and left Danna no doubt as to who was really worried. "The people of Calvin need to feel they're safe in this town."

The people of Cavin her foot. This was about Castlerock and his desire to get his money back. "Have there been any complaints about the job I'm doing?" Danna asked.

Parrott's eyes shifted to Castlerock again, and away. "Not officially, but—"

"Perhaps the town council could show its support by recommending that able-bodied men volunteer to be deputies." She forced her voice to stay even, not betray her emotions. "More manpower would certainly help."

"Yes, well—"

"Have you contacted the sheriff?" Castlerock put in.

Even in the dim light from the lamps, she could see his face had begun to flush. He shifted on his feet.

"Of course," she replied, though it was getting harder to keep her tone calm. "I wired over to Glenrock just after the robbery. I haven't received a reply, but I assume he'll get here when he can."

She hadn't wanted to ask the sheriff for help. He had a whole county to watch over. And Fred had never relied on the sheriff for help. But she'd wired him anyway, knowing she didn't have much choice.

"You lost their tracks?" Castlerock's eyes were hard. "What are you going to do next?"

Danna stood, propelled by her anger. "I don't recall the town council ever questioning Fred about how he did his job."

He took a step closer. "Answer the questions, Mrs. Carpenter. I want my money back."

Danna registered that this was the second time he'd called her by name instead of Marshal. Had a decision already been made about her career? Or was Castlerock simply trying to intimidate?

Parrott was no help to her now as he stood stoically behind Castlerock, though his expression seemed a little apologetic.

Danna expelled a rough breath. "My deputy and I tracked the robbers as long as we could, but we lost the tracks when the snowstorm hit—"

Castlerock exploded. He turned to Parrott, nearly yelling in the other man's face. "Do you see? She shouldn't even be marshal. My money is no closer to being found."

"Hold on—" Danna started.

"I want her resignation."

Silence descended in the wake of Castlerock's demand. Danna froze, unable to believe he'd said the words aloud. Until now, she'd thought she still had time. That she would be able to find the robbers, that she'd...what? Be a town hero, like Fred had been?

What would she do now?

Parrott stepped between Danna and Castlerock and held

out a hand toward each of them. "Now, George, we'll proceed as the council already decided."

Danna wanted badly to sit on the desk behind her. In her exhaustion, and with emotions stampeding over her, her legs threatened to fold. But she refused to give either man the satisfaction of seeing her weak. She would hear the remainder of what they had to say standing.

"Marshal," Parrott said, "The town council is concerned. We'll give you a few days—"

"Three," Castlerock said.

Parrott shot a quelling look at the other man. "A few days to find the bank robbers. If you can't, I'm afraid we'll have to start looking for a replacement."

Surprise, along with a renewed sense of hope, surged through her. There was still time to solve this.

Parrott cleared his throat. Apparently, he wasn't done. "There is another matter we need to discuss."

Castlerock's eyes gleamed. "I can't wait to hear her excuse for this."

"Hang on." Parrott tried to calm the other man. "I'm sure there's an explanation. Marshal? Did you spend the night alone with a man?"

Danna couldn't believe it was coming down to this. "We had no choice." she lifted her chin. "We were caught in the snowstorm. But nothing inappropriate happened."

The two men shared a glance. "I'm afraid it doesn't matter if anything happened, Marshal," Parrott said. "We can't have even the appearance of impropriety. Where is this man now? Because I'm afraid he's going to have to marry you."

* * *

CHAS RAPPED on the door and pushed it open. "Mornin', Miss Marshal. I know it's early—"

He froze. Danna stood between two older men, one he recognized as the owner of the bank. The other looked vaguely familiar, probably from the dance several nights ago.

"O'Grady." The growl from Danna didn't sound too pleased to see him.

"Hello, hello." The taller of the two men moved toward him and extended his hand for Chas to shake. "I assume you're the groom. Joe Parrott. Nice to meet you."

"Groom?" What? He couldn't have heard right. He looked to Danna and saw the answer written on her face.

Deep lines were etched around her eyes. Had something else happened last night?

The banker moved forward, appraising Chas with a flickering glance. "I'm afraid the marshal's reputation is tarnished beyond repair, thanks to your little jaunt out into the woods. If the two of you don't marry, she'll be removed from her position."

The man's supercilious manner irritated Chas even more than Joe Parrott's false cheerfulness. Then he registered what the other man had said.

"What?"

Danna started. "Chas—"

"Perhaps we should leave the two of you to discuss what arrangements should be made," The rancher said. "Mr. Castlerock and I will notify the preacher. Shall we meet at the parsonage at, say...two o'clock?"

They must've taken Chas's silence and Danna's pale skin as agreement. The two men excused themselves, Parrott sending a shrewd glance over his shoulder.

Once they'd gone, Danna slumped in the chair behind her desk and rested her head on folded arms. "What are we going to do?"

Numb, Chas dropped into his usual straight-backed chair near the door. "We can't get married."

"Thank you very much for that," she sniped, but her words were muffled by her arms, and was she... It almost sounded like she was...

"You're not crying, are you?"

She raised her head far enough to glare at him, and he was enormously grateful to see that she wasn't crying, but the terrible emotion revealed on her expressive face didn't do much to relieve the ache in his stomach. She laid her head back down on her arms.

A racket started up outside. A dog bayed. Someone pounded on the door. Danna called a somewhat muffled "Come in," without raising her head again.

The bank manager, Silverton, pushed the door open and shoved Danna's ugly dog inside the room. The mutt stopped his baying and howling and moved to Chas's side, sitting on his boot.

"Um, Marshal, I'm real sorry to bother you, but your dog was, um, serenading me from my front porch this morning. I thought you might be looking for him."

Chas idly scratched the top of the dog's head. His brain was still spinning. Marry the marshal?

"I'm sorry about the trouble," Danna said, still not raising her head.

Silverton shared a glance with Chas, brows furled. "Marshal...um...are you...? I hope you don't mind me asking, but are you all right?"

She didn't respond. Chas had never seen her this hopeless. Even when she'd planned to ride out after the bank robbers alone, she'd been determined.

It was as if she were giving up. But he couldn't marry her. He liked her, admired her even. But he couldn't marry her.

Could he?

* * *

"MARRIED?" Silverton echoed as Chas finished an abbreviated retelling of what had just happened. Maybe it was because she'd come to his rescue during the bank robbery, but Silverton had seen her upset and refused to leave. Chas had told him everything.

Danna couldn't look at either of them. Did Silverton have to sound so appalled? Was she that undesirable?

"Yes," she said, hiccupping a little as she finally sat up. "Hitched. Wed. United. Till death do us part."

She stood, shaky, and paced across the open floor in front of her desk. Silverton wisely moved out of the way.

"They said I am no longer above reproach." She laughed bitterly. "Other towns have made marshals out of criminals, killers even, but Calvin's town council is going to remove my badge because of a scandal." No wonder no one else had wanted to partner up with her. Who'd want to get trapped with *her*?

"But they can't do that," Silverton said. "They can't force you to marry."

"They want to."

"I could leave," Chas said.

Danna froze, facing the wall, so neither man could see the hurt she knew etched her face.

"That would solve your problem," Silverton said, "but what about the marshal? If she doesn't marry you, they'll call for her job."

Why did Silverton have to sound so reasonable about it? She wanted to rage at the unfairness. She'd just been doing her job. She and Chas hadn't done anything immoral. And if she were to bow to the council's demands, then it might seem as if the gossip were true.

Oh, God. The cry came straight from her heart. Her breaking heart.

"Danna." A touch on her shoulder. She turned to face Chas,

137

doing her best to keep her emotions from showing in her expression.

He looked more serious than she'd ever seen him before. "I can't leave. I have to see this case through," Chas said, voice low. "I—"

There was something behind his hesitation, but her mind was too muddled to sort it out right now.

She rubbed a hand over her suddenly aching eyes. "But you don't want to marry me."

His silence was answer enough.

He didn't get a chance to answer because Silverton spoke. "You could have the marriage annulled later. Coercion is a valid reason for annulment in this state. I'm not a lawyer, but it could work."

And then what? Chas would leave. Go back to his life, be a detective somewhere else.

And she'd still be in Calvin, probably without a job.

Right now, what choice did they have?

* * *

DANNA TURNED IN A SLOW CIRCLE, perusing the room that had belonged to her and Fred. After tonight, it would belong to her and Chas.

They were going to go through with the wedding. And hope that the marriage could be annulled later.

Problem was, she didn't know how to keep her heart from getting involved. She was already half in love with Chas O'Grady. And now, he'd agreed to this crazy farce of a marriage in order to help her. Because he could stay in town, find the rustlers, and be on his way regardless of what happened to Danna. But instead, he'd chosen to marry her, even if it wasn't real. He'd chosen to risk his future on her, just to protect her job. Nobody had ever been that kind to her.

She closed her eyes, forced the thoughts to the back of her mind. When she opened her eyes again, she focused on her surroundings. What would Chas think of this place?

The room wasn't very homey. In fact, it was almost bare. She'd never had the inclination to weave rugs or hang curtains —the ones she'd hung in the jail downstairs had been out of necessity, to keep folks from looking in. The quilt on the bed had been a gift at her wedding to Fred.

Plain writing desk, table and two chairs, stove, small cupboard. Nothing frilly or womanly here at all.

The one decorative item was the wooden chest sitting at the end of the bed. It had been her mother's and was the only thing she'd taken from Rob when she'd left home at sixteen.

Sitting on the end of the bed, she ran her hand over the smooth wood of Mama's chest. She flipped the lid open and clutched the side of the box as memories rushed over her.

She couldn't remember her mother, except for a sense of warmth and a vague, feminine scent. But she remembered being about five years old and going through this very chest. She knew that under the wedding dress were a few letters tied with a ribbon, a family Bible, a portrait of her mother and father, a partial piece of lace. Each one was a piece of her mother.

Rob had come in as she was going through the contents all those years ago, and when he'd seen what she was doing, he'd erupted in a fit of anger. She hadn't realized at the time that he'd been hurting, too, missing their parents. She'd only known she'd done something wrong.

She hadn't touched the chest again, not until Fred had moved it into the tiny cabin they'd lived in at the time. A wedding present from Rob, after he'd shipped her off to Fred, made her Fred's problem.

Now she touched the pale blue fabric lightly, then picked up the dress. Her mother's wedding dress. She hadn't worn it when she'd married Fred. It had been too long, and at the time, she couldn't bear to have it hemmed.

But she'd grown two inches in her seventeenth year, and she'd filled out some, too. It might fit now. And a woman shouldn't be married in pants, should she?

Danna considered it for a long moment before sliding out of her shirt and trousers and slipping the dress over her head. Her hands trembled as she buttoned it up, then smoothed out the lines from where the dress had been folded.

She turned to the small looking glass Fred had used for shaving, almost afraid of what she would see.

A woman with large, dark eyes stared back at her. Glossy hair, almost black, pulled back from her face. Skin tanned by hours outside. But in the dress, she no longer looked like the marshal. She looked like a woman.

Danna slowly unbraided her hair and ran her hairbrush through the thick, long locks. She watched the mirror, the play of light on her hair as it shifted over her shoulder.

Chas seemed to like her hair down. When they'd been trapped in the snowstorm, with her hat gone and braid unraveled, he'd touched her hair more than once. She tried to imagine walking through town with her hair down past her shoulders, like this, and couldn't do it. It would have to be enough that she wore the dress. She searched in the trunk until she found a piece of ribbon. She pulled her hair into a bundle and tied it at the nape of her neck. When she looked at the mirror, a few tendrils had come loose, but most were held by the tie.

She smoothed a hand over her brow. Her hands were shaking.

Was marrying Chas really the right thing to do?

* * *

DANNA DELAYED LONG ENOUGH PAST the appointed hour that Chas wondered whether she'd come at all. A soft knock sounded, and he halted mid-pace in the center of the preacher's parlor.

The minister ushered her inside.

Danna wore a delicate blue dress. She'd pulled her hair out of the braid, and soft pieces framed her face now.

A soft gasp came from behind him from either Parrott or Castlerock, but his senses were filled with Danna. He couldn't take his eyes off her.

He'd been attracted to her when in trousers, but with a long skirt swirling around her legs and the bodice of her gown clinging in all the right ways, she took his breath away.

Danna was focused on the preacher, who was speaking quietly to her. Chas used the time to examine the two curls trailing down her cheek, following the line of her jaw and down her neck.

He swallowed hard.

"Thank you," she said, and turned to face him.

Grateful she hadn't caught him with his mouth hanging open, Chas cleared his throat and prayed his voice wouldn't crack when he spoke.

When she looked up and met his gaze, he knew she wasn't as calm as she seemed. Her eyes shone with panic, then flicked to the two council members standing behind Chas. She schooled her expression.

"You look lovely," he said, and his voice emerged steady. Nothing like the raging turmoil he felt inside. How had it come to this?

Her hands shook when the preacher directed Chas to take them. His might be shaking, too. It was hard to tell.

They faced the preacher, who held the Good Book in his hands. The vows they spoke only took a few minutes, and it was done.

"You may kiss the bride," the preacher said. Danna's eyes met his—the first time she'd looked up during the whole ceremony—and he could easily read the trepidation in their depths. She started to shake her head. "We don't—"

He stopped her protest with a gentle touch of his mouth. It was nothing like the way he'd kissed her on the mountain. That had been a kiss of relief, a way of expressing the emotions that had pounded through him. And yet...when he brushed his lips against the velvet softness of hers, raised his hand and cupped her jaw...it was the same.

The emotions bursting in his chest were enough to make him feel like he was in front of that stampede again, with his heart drumming in his ears. Sweat popped out on his brow. He stepped away, unable to take his eyes from her face, the contrast between her lashes and her cheeks.

Beautiful. His wife. For now.

"I'll need you two to sign the marriage license, and we'll be done."

The preacher had a document in front of him on the table. Chas took up the pen the other man had produced and scribbled his name on the line the man indicated. He passed the pen to Danna, and she squinted down at the paper, hesitating.

Something inside him opened, wanting to protect her from the men who stood close and who probably didn't know she couldn't read.

Chas touched a finger to the line where she needed to sign. It was a simple gesture, but she looked up at him with something other than the panic or anger that he'd seen in her eyes since the men had left her office this morning. The look she gave him was pure appreciation.

CHAPTER 13

*D*anna approached the jail, fingering the simple silver band on her finger. She'd removed it a few weeks after Fred's death. Chas had returned it to her finger today. It felt foreign. New. Strange.

Their marriage was a farce.

She slowed her steps as her feet his the boardwalk. She supposed Chas would be back soon from gathering his things at the hotel.

She'd needed some space after the wedding, and the kiss, so she'd changed clothes and gone on a patrol, keeping her eyes open for any signs of Katy. She hadn't found the girl or any sign of her.

And now she had to face her new husband. Who hadn't wanted to marry her. Who was planning to leave.

She didn't want to be married again either, she reminded herself.

Except she loved Chas.

A boy she recognized as belonging to one of Corrine's neighbors came running down the street as she neared the jail.

"M-miss Marshall," the lad stuttered, "Missus Jackson needs you. Her baby's comin'."

Corrine was indeed in labor, crying out in pain, as Danna let herself into the shanty. A neighbor stood over the kitchen table, but the instant she saw Danna, she turned for the door.

"Glad you're here. I've got my own young'uns at home. Cain't stay. I'll take that'un for the night."

With that, the other woman swept out of the shack with three-year-old Ellie in tow, leaving Danna with the wailing Corrine.

"What—"

"Danna."

"I'm here!" Rushing to her friend's side, Danna saw the face creased in pain, the sweat on Corrine's brow, the marks where she'd obviously clutched the sheets in her fists. "What can I do?'

Corrine let out a long breath, muscles easing. "Nothing yet. I think we have a bit to go, even though the pains have been coming all day."

"Should I get the doctor?"

"He's tied up at his office. The young man from the robbery took a turn for the worse. He's in surgery."

That was bad. The wounded thief was quite possibly the only lead Danna had to find out the outlaws' location.

"What about your neighbor...?" And why had she rushed out like that?

Corrine clasped Danna's hand as another pain came. Her lips pinched white. "She doesn't... She thinks...Brent killed...your husband." The words came out in spurts and gasps as Corrine panted through the contraction.

Danna found a clean cloth on the end of the bed and dabbed at her friend's forehead. "Shh. Shh. It's okay."

The contraction eased, and Corrine relaxed again. "I don't suppose there's any news...?"

Danna wished she had something positive to tell her friend, but there was nothing. "I'm sorry."

"And Mrs. Burnett"—the preacher's wife—"is visiting her sister out of town," Corrine spoke as if the question about her husband hadn't been uttered. "So I sent the neighbor boy to fetch you. Will you stay with me? Help me labor this baby?"

Tears sparkled in Corrine's eyes.

A lump formed in Danna's throat. "You don't even have to ask," she told her dearest friend.

* * *

IT WAS DARK OUTSIDE WHEN, hours later, Danna trudged toward her room above the jail.

She hadn't wanted to leave, but Corrine insisted she and her new baby boy would be all right for a few hours—long enough for Danna to get some rest.

The labor had been grueling. Danna had done her best to distract Corinne from the pain, telling her about the recent events as marshal, even about the wedding. But Danna had seen it in Corrine's eyes that her friend just wanted her missing husband.

And it hurt that Danna hadn't been able to produce him. The guilt ate away at her.

In those last few moments, the baby had come quickly. He'd been a squalling, wriggling mass of flesh and goo. He'd been the most handsome thing Danna had ever seen.

Even now, the memory had her clutching her empty hands together.

For so long, Danna had wanted a family of her own. More than just a husband. Fred had wanted sons and she'd wanted to give them to him. She'd wanted to be more than just the marshal's wife.

And, yes, a part of her thought that if she had a child she

145

would be able to relate to the other women. Not be so much of an outsider.

But she'd never so much as missed her monthly time, never suspected she was pregnant. Fred had never spoken his disappointment aloud, but she knew he must've felt it. Oh, he'd never come outright and say he regretted marrying her, but sometimes she wondered.

And then he died. And she had no one. And she'd been fine with that. Just fine. But this business with Chas O'Grady, this temporary marriage, was stirring everything up in her heart again.

She wanted children of her own. Why wouldn't God give her even one dream of her heart?

She rounded the corner past Hereford's Grocery and looked up. A light shone out the window to her room. So her new husband had made himself at home already.

And had left a light on for her.

CHAPTER 14

The next morning, Danna watched Chas charm Ellie over a bowl of porridge, a little glad for the distraction.

Last night, he'd been wrapped in a bedroll on the floor when she'd entered the room. Asleep, or at least pretending. With his back to her, she hadn't had the courage to find out. She'd quickly snuffed the light. And then lay in the bed for a long time, listening to his breathing.

This morning had been awkward. Sharing the washbasin. Stumbling over each other in the small space. The keen awareness she had of him, though he'd avoided mostly her eyes.

When he'd offered to accompany her to check on Corrine, she hadn't known how to refuse. At least Ellie and the new baby were proving a much-needed distraction from the tension between Danna and Chas.

Not from her longings for a family of her own.

Danna tried not to imagine what it would be like to hold a son of her own the way she cuddled Corrine's son next to her sternum. But the image wouldn't be shaken.

The little one stirred and fussed, which roused Corrine, so

Danna left the boy to be fed and joined Chas and Ellie at the table.

"There's some more porridge left," Chas said, glancing at her, then pushing a bowl in front of her. "You look exhausted."

Danna flushed.

"Did you not sleep well last night?"

His concern was disconcerting.

She shifted her shoulders, trying to remove some of the knots. "I'm all right."

He rose, stepped behind her, and closed his large hands over her shoulders, making her jump. Their warmth burned through her shirt. His thumbs made comforting circles, fingers relaxed her aching muscles.

His touch made her feel as if he cared. And that was dangerous to her emotions. When was the last time she'd been touched like this? Tears burned her eyes when she couldn't remember.

"All right?" Chas asked.

She couldn't answer. The intimacy of the moment was suddenly too much for her. She wanted it to be real.

And knew that it couldn't. She pulled away, returning to Corrine in the corner. Her friend watched with weary, wide eyes, but thankfully remained silent.

* * *

DANNA WATCHED, Chas at her side, as the doctor woke the outlaw who'd been shot. Doc thought the young man had made it through the worst of his injury, but Danna knew that type of wound could be tricky. She couldn't wait any longer to question him.

"He's conscious," the doctor said over his shoulder, and she and Chas stepped closer.

"Where were they going to take the money? From the bank?" Chas asked quietly.

The other man spoke, his voice so soft and raspy that Danna could barely make out his words. "Cabin... mountains."

"Where?'

"A little stream," he paused, his head rolling to the side. He groaned. "Big, gnarled oak tree."

The description was too vague. Danna knew the mountains, the terrain, but she needed more landmarks than that.

"Who was leading the gang?" she asked, leaning down a bit so the boy didn't have to strain so much to talk.

"H-hank...Lewis."

Chas inhaled loudly. A glance at his face revealed a muscle ticking in his cheek. Who was Hank Lewis? And why did Chas react to hearing his name?

The kid closed his eyes. Moaned.

"Anything else?"

"Supposed to...meet with..." That was it. He'd fallen unconscious again.

"Sorry, Marshal," the doc said, and sounded it, too. "If he comes awake again later, I'll send someone for you."

Chas turned away, his blue eyes dark as a coming storm.

Danna was disappointed, too. The kid was their only lead, and she was running out of time.

* * *

DANNA ALLOWED Chas to steer her into the café for a midday meal.

Instantly, all eyes were on her. Eugene Hamilton, who ran the freight office and was one of the drunks she'd arrested last week, raised his brows. The milliner's spoon clanked against her bowl. The nearest conversations stopped.

She wanted to go right back out the door. But Chas had

crowded in behind her, and she had no choice but to move toward an empty table in the corner. She lifted her chin high, reminding herself she'd done nothing to be ashamed of.

Chas's hand branded her lower back. She reached for a chair, only to have her hand swallowed up in his. His shoulder brushed hers.

"I'll get the chair for my wife."

She sank into the chair he'd pulled away from the table. His wife.

Marilee, the teenaged waitress, stopped short from their table. "You got married?" The girl gasped the question, then seemed to realize what she'd done. She came the rest of the way to the table, stammering. "I-I'm sorry. Didn't mean to be rude. C-congratulations."

Heads at the two nearest tables turned. Chas smiled widely. "Thank you."

The girl set two menu cards down, and Danna saw her hands were trembling. "Would you like coffee or water?"

Danna mumbled her response. She looked at the next table over and saw the two men staring. She nodded pointedly, and they had the good grace to look away.

She hated this. Hated all the eyes on her.

Chas reached across the table with his palm turned up. Danna raised her brows, and he wiggled his fingers. "Give me your hand."

"What?'

He lifted his eyebrows.

She gingerly placed her hand in his, and his fingers closed around hers. The strength and firmness of his hold reminded her that she wasn't alone in this. She met his eyes across the table, and they held.

They would take on the robbers together. Take on the rumors together. A team, like she and Fred had been. Only, this was temporary.

A shadow fell over her shoulder, and Danna looked up to see the one person she least wanted to see right now. Castlerock.

"Marshal." He nodded to her, then Chas, his lips a thin line. "Any news?"

Danna tried to reclaim her hand, but Chas clasped it too tightly, and she didn't want to draw more attention than they already had.

"Not yet." It was too much to hope the banker would leave them in peace. He tapped on the edge of the table.

"While I am *delighted* that you've resolved your personal issues, there is still the matter of my missing money."

Danna bristled, but it was Chas who answered, his voice cool. "The marshal hasn't forgotten about your money."

"Is that so? And how is her investigation going at the moment? Well enough for her to dine with her new husband, is it?" Castlerock's voice was rising, as was the blood to his face, which began to mottle red and white.

Danna stood, extracting her hand from Chas's. He stood beside her and touched her side lightly, but she moved away from him.

She was the marshal; she would handle this. "I don't remember my first husband being questioned during an investigation, and I'll thank you not to question me, either. I will apprehend the men responsible for the theft, or you and the rest of the council can fire me."

"You can be assured, I'll see to it. You're on borrowed time, Marshal." Castlerock's threatening words weren't spoken very loudly, but Danna knew every ear in the room had heard.

She sensed Chas shift next to her. They'd spent enough time talking, so she sat. Castlerock stalked off.

Their food arrived, the waitress whisking it on the table and leaving quickly.

Chas stared down at his plate while he ate, a contemplative

look on his face. After a while, he commented, "The banker seems awfully interested in muddling with your investigation."

Appetite gone, Danna played with her fork. "He's interested in looking out for himself," she murmured, not wanting others to hear the disparaging comment.

"I didn't see it before..." Chas said softly, as if to himself. He lifted his gaze. "Can you remember specifically what all those men who refused to be deputies had to say?"

What did that have to do with Castlerock? "No, not really. Why?"

"In the beginning of my own investigation, I started asking questions around town. About the rustling problem."

She knew her face showed the puzzlement she felt.

"And the responses I got were a bit...unusual."

"In what way?"

"Everyone I spoke to seemed loath to share information. I could understand if one or two didn't want to talk to me, but this was every person I talked with."

She'd gotten the same response, but attributed it to being a woman.

Chas was staring off into space again, and she cleared her throat.

"Sorry." He shook his head. "I'm trying to put together how it might be related. Perhaps we should..." He nodded toward the door.

They settled their bill and were soon on the boardwalk heading toward the jailhouse. Chas offered his arm, and she took it. Anyone who looked at them would think they were out for a stroll, but when he spoke, his urgent tone belied the casual air he put off.

"At the dance. I overheard two men talking about it."

"About the robbery?"

"Yes, before I came inside. I didn't recognize the voices, and I couldn't see faces, but they seemed to know an awful lot about what was happening with the rustling. Unfortunately, I had to go inside or risk being found out.

"And the other day, in your office, something seemed...I don't know, off about Joe Parrott. I couldn't place it at the time, and then we got distracted by the wedding, but does he have a tattoo or a mark on his left wrist?"

She nodded. "There's some sort of mark, yes."

"I think he was one of the men I overheard at the dance. What if the town council has set you up to fail? And they've bribed the former deputies not to help you?"

"Why would they do that?"

"To keep from being found out, maybe?"

She slowed her steps. "Then why would they threaten to fire me?"

"I don't know, but there's something going on in this town that's bigger than some missing cattle and a bank robbery."

$\mathcal{D}$anna perched on the edge of the bed, flustered and ill at ease. Last night, after helping Corrine birth her baby, she'd fallen into bed exhausted. Chas'd already been settled on the floor.

Tonight, she was alone with Chas. And it was completely different than when they'd been stuck in the snowstorm. They hadn't had a choice that night, and they didn't have one tonight either, but she still felt...discomfited.

A soft knock on the door announced his presence. She called, "come in," and he stepped inside, filling her small upstairs room with his broad shoulders, his very presence.

He took off his hat and ran his hand through the auburn curls plastered to his head. She'd seen him do that before. Did it mean he was as nervous as she was?

Chas looked around the rooms, and Danna refused to be ashamed of the simple furnishings. They might not be as fancy as something he'd find in Penny Castlerock's home, but they were functional.

Chas reached into his chest pocket and withdrew a small bundle, distracting her from her thoughts. "I...this is for you."

He stepped forward and handed her the cloth-wrapped item, then stuffed his empty hand in his trouser pocket. "It's not much of a wedding present, but I thought perhaps it was something you'd get some use out of."

Heart pounding, Danna unwrapped the small bundle of cloth to find a pair of spectacles with round lenses and thin wire frames. She looked up at Chas, puzzled.

"What—?"

"To help you read." The words stretched in the sudden stillness between them, the last thing she'd expected him to say. He'd been so kind, so considerate all day.

And now he'd touched on the one thing she'd never been able to accomplish, no matter how hard she'd tried. Would he be ashamed of her, like Rob had been? She averted her face, set the spectacles on the desk, and gripped the wood.

"I've seen you...the way you squint sometimes..." His voice trailed off, and she glanced at him to see his gaze focused on the wall, as if remembering something. "Just like a friend I used to know."

"There was no school here when I was a child." Danna said, her eyes trained on his shoulder. "Fred tried to teach me for months after we were married. I never took to it."

He turned to her, watched her face. He picked up the spectacles from the table to hold them out to her again. "My friend could see fine at far distances. Maybe better than I could. But up close"—he held his hand about a foot in front of his face—"everything was a blur."

She didn't take the spectacles from him; neither did he lower his outstretched hand.

"I can't do it," she said.

"Wouldn't you like to read your husband's journal?"

She glared at him. "That book is not your concern."

"Will you just try?" His hand remained extended, his eyes serious.

Exasperated, she took the spectacles from him, expecting him to gloat, but he watched her in silence.

She slipped them over her nose, tucked the curves behind her ears. She reached for the sheaf of papers in one of the desk drawers. When she looked down at the top sheet, she expected to see the same thing she always saw, blurry lines that made no sense. To her surprise, the words came into sharp focus. She could make out each individual letter clearly.

She looked up at Chas in amazement. "I can see!"

* * *

CHAS COULDN'T TAKE his eyes off her that night. Danna slept with her face to the door, one hand tucked under her cheek. She looked so young. Not old enough to have been married twice or in charge of keeping in the peace in this town.

Chas watched her for a long time, this woman he...had feelings for. He'd been fighting against himself all evening, against the greed inside that claimed her as his.

She was his, but not forever. Just for long enough that she didn't get herself killed. They would ferret out whatever secrets the town council was hiding, and she'd be free. Then they'd get an annulment, and he'd leave.

He still felt warm from the giddiness she'd shown when she'd tried on the spectacles. They'd sat at the small table, heads together, reviewing the alphabet and sounding out some small words. Each brush of her hand against his had sent his senses spiraling.

Now he looked down at the leather-bound book he'd palmed as Danna had readied for bed earlier. Part of him felt guilty for what he was about to do, but the other part wanted to know if her first husband had left them any clues.

He flipped the book open, toward the end. The writing was cramped, but legible. It seemed to be the middle of an entry.

...when will she understand that she is loved, both by her Heavenly Father and by me? She is so alone. She needs to be able to rely on someone greater than herself. But she won't open her heart—I still can't find a way inside, not after searching for the key all these years.

Neither can anyone else. I saw Mrs. Poe approach her in the general store today, but Danna ignored the older woman's overtures of kindness. It is as if she can't see her own worth. She still won't talk about Rob. The man was my best friend but didn't know anything about females—not like I knew much either, before I married Danna.

Chas slapped the book closed. It felt wrong to read the inner thoughts of the man who'd been Danna's husband. And yet a part of him wanted to know more. More about what this other man saw in Danna. Part of him seethed with jealousy that Fred had known Danna intimately, had known her secrets.

But not all of them. Chas remembered the night—was it just two nights ago?—he and Danna had spent tucked next to the small campfire she'd built. She'd told him her brother had basically thrown her away. From her first husband's words, it didn't sound like she'd ever told him.

And several things she'd said about herself made him think she didn't know her own worth, like the late husband said. She saw herself as a deputy, a friend. Not as a woman.

Chas slapped the lid closed on his wishful thinking just as he'd closed the journal a moment ago. He wasn't here to woo Danna. He was here to help her with her problem. Then he was gone. Once he enacted his revenge on Lewis, he'd need to make a quick escape. He'd likely never return to Wyoming.

That was it. No happy ending for him. He didn't deserve one.

* * *

DANNA WOKE WITH A START, instantly alert. What was that noise? She shifted her gaze to the floor and saw that Chas's head was rolling, tossing, though he appeared to be asleep. His face was creased in a frown.

What did a man like Chas dream about? He still hadn't revealed much of his past.

Had he moaned? Or had she imagined the noise? No, there it was again. She slid off the edge of the bed and quickly pulled on her overshirt and trousers. She tiptoed to where he sprawled across the floor. She didn't want to wake him if she didn't have to.

His head thrashed on the pillow, his lips moving, his brow wrinkled.

She reached out her hand to touch him, wake him, but she froze when his moan turned into a word.

Julia.

Feeling as if she'd been punched in the stomach, she backed away until her calves hit the bed.

Who was Julia? A sister? Friend? Wife?

She was shaking. She clasped her hands together in front of her to try and stop them trembling. She'd known he'd lost someone, but for him to call out another woman's name...

A noise from the street made Danna jerk her head toward the window. That had definitely been a horse's whicker. It was the middle of the night. Who was out there?

She carefully pulled the edge of the curtain back. The moon was only half-full, but it was enough to see the three men on horseback, just below her window. They wore bandanas over their faces.

With no time to categorize her emotions, to stifle the hurt that Chas's Julia had caused, she fell back on the training learned from years of working with Fred.

She darted across the floor, slapped her husband's shoulder, and held a finger to her lips when he started awake.

"There are masked men downstairs. I don't know what they

want, but I don't wish to be trapped up here with only one way out."

He rose without a word and reached for the weapon he'd left on the table.

He glanced at her over his shoulder, and she prayed he couldn't read the turmoil in her face.

"I'm going out the window," Danna said. "You'd better sneak down the stairs. Now."

Quick and silent, Danna slid the window all the way open and swung one leg over the sill.

"Wait!" Chas had found his voice. He grasped her arm above the elbow. She flinched but forced herself not to pull away. She couldn't read his face in the darkness, but the rasp of his breath was rapid, almost anguished. "Please be careful."

She nodded, not sure if he could even see her in the dark, but she couldn't make words emerge from her suddenly parched throat. He sounded as if he cared.

She pulled away from his grasp and slipped out the window.

* * *

CHAS WOKE from one nightmare to be thrust into another.

The stench of blood and death was strong in his mind, and he didn't have time to shake it off before Danna was halfway out the window.

He clung to her for too long, afraid this whole thing was going to end badly. He couldn't watch another woman he cared about die.

He opened the door with a soft snick, but he didn't even have a chance to step outside before he heard the thump of boots on the staircase. He shut the door with another near-silent click and latched it, for all the good it would do.

Now what?

He made for the window, swung one leg over to try to find the footholds Danna had used a moment ago. Where was she?

"What are you doing?" A sharp hiss from above his head answered his unasked question. She was on the roof.

"How did you get up there?" Before she could answer, a loud thump sounded on the marshal's door. Chas needed to get out of the window. He swung his other leg over the windowsill and supported his weight with his posterior and a white-knuckled grip.

"Chas—" He didn't hear the rest of Danna's words, because the sound of wood splintering obscured her whisper. He slid off the windowsill and hung by his fingertips, dangling like a monkey at the circus.

He didn't think it would hurt too much if he fell to the ground. He couldn't be more than eight or ten feet up. He was more afraid of the noise he'd make when he hit the boardwalk.

Angry voices from inside the room preceded the sound of boots stomping, moving toward the window. Chas had run out of time.

He let go.

* * *

WHAT A DISASTER.

She could make out two voices from inside the room. The two men weren't making any effort to be quiet. Their rapid, pounding steps told Danna their exact location inside. They swore when they realized the room was empty.

Where was Chas? He hadn't followed her onto the roof. Clouds blew in and covered the moon, limiting her visibility to the ground. But the men didn't sound like they'd found him inside. Where was the third guy?

She couldn't call out again.

How she wished Fred were here. She could trust Fred to

cover her flank. But her instincts and Chas's seemed to always be at odds.

She closed her eyes. No more time.

Careful to stay light on her feet, she darted across the roof and hopped down to the platform at the top of the stairs. She slammed the door of her apartment closed. A muffled curse came from inside.

The door rattled under her hands as someone tried to wrest it open. It wouldn't hold them for long.

She ran down the stairs and paused behind the corner of the building. She strained to hear over the pounding of her heart.

Hearing nothing, she skirted the building, keeping to the shadows close to the wall. She unholstered her pistol and held it at her side.

Where was Chas?

Three horses stood saddled in the alleyway between the jail and the saloon behind it. One of the shadows behind the horses moved, and she was able to make out a head and shoulders of someone standing on the other side. She edged closer.

"Hold up a minute." The harsh, deep voice, undeniably male, came from behind the horses.

There was a thud from upstairs, and in the silence that followed, Danna heard the unmistakable sound of a pistol hammer being cocked. She froze a few paces from the horses, crouching close to the ground.

"Where's the marshal?"

"Don't know." That was Chas's voice.

"You was jest in her room. Saw you twist yer ankle comin' out the window."

Oh no. It sounded like Chas was hurt *and* caught.

Danna tucked even closer to the ground, moving toward the horses.

"I'm gonna ask ya one more time. Where's the marshal? I aim to get my colleague outta jail. Tonight."

He'd come for the injured outlaw? He must not know how badly the kid had been injured or that he was being kept at the doctor's office. Not if they were trying to break into the jail looking for him.

Wood splintered loudly. The door. Loud footsteps sounded on the stairs.

She crept beneath the hooves of the first horse, moving as slowly as possible. She prayed nothing would spook the horses. If they startled, they'd crush her.

She could also see her husband's booted feet near the corner of the boardwalk by the clothing store.

Danna sprang up between the horses, vaulted over the nearest one, and used her foot on its saddle as a springboard to launch herself across the back of the second one. All the way over. Her momentum took the outlaw to the ground, and she pinned his gun arm with her weight and both hands.

The horses shied at the unexpected movement and trotted out into the middle of the street.

Chas kicked away the outlaw's gun and rushed to kneel next to her. He stuffed the other man's hat against the lower part of his face as a gag.

"That was crazy," he said, voice low. "You could've been killed."

At this close proximity, she could see the anger in his drawn brows and clenched jaw.

"So could you!" she returned. She took one of the rawhide strips she had tucked into her pocket and tied the man's wrists together.

The man continued to struggle as booted footsteps drew closer.

"What's going on?" A voice and flickering light came from the saloon.

Shouts from farther down the street alerted Danna that the other two robbers had seen the horses in the open. She yelled, "Watch out!" to Mr. McCabe as she ducked behind the corner of the building, pulling her deputy with her.

Multiple shots rang out, and fire ripped through the inside of her upper left arm. Stifling a cry, she turned to check on Chas. "You okay?"

"Fine. What do we do now?"

"I doubt they've figured out that the kid's at Doc's office, so we're good there." The pain in her arm throbbed, but she ignored it. "But if they keep shooting, innocents are liable to get hurt."

"What should we do?"

"Let's herd them toward the railroad tracks. Hopefully, one of us can cut them off in front. If they manage to escape, I can track them down, as long as the weather holds."

CHAPTER 16

"*C*an we please stop now?"

Chas pushed his hat off his forehead to get a glimpse of Danna. Icy rain snuck down the back of his neck and he winced.

He may not know much about tracking, but surely the driving rain had erased any tracks that might have been left from the two men who'd disappeared last night. It was well into the morning now, dreary and wet.

Danna wheeled her mount toward town without speaking. She'd been silent since they'd mounted up outside the livery.

At least they had one outlaw in custody. This one uninjured. He was one of the men Chas had spoken to in the café on his first day in town. If they could just get him to talk.

Chas was the first to admit he didn't know much about women, but he was smart enough to know her silence meant she was upset. But what was she upset about? Losing track of the two other outlaws?

Still wrapped in his thoughts, he barely noticed when they arrived in town and dropped their horses off with the boy in the livery. He did notice when Danna stomped off down the boardwalk without him.

"She's sure got a bee in her bonnet this mornin', huh?" the livery hand said as he took the bridles of both horses. "I'm guessin' y'all didn't catch up to them robbers." He seemed disappointed. Was he one of her admirers?

Chas frowned. Danna hated people in town talking about her. "That's the marshal's business."

"I reckon everyone's going to be in the marshal's business if she came back to town without them."

That's what he was afraid of. He hurried off after her.

"Danna. Danna!" He shouted her name the last time, his frustration making his temper spike.

She spat her next words over her shoulder, her eyes inscrutable under the brim of her hat. "Please refrain from spreading my business all over town."

He caught up to her in front of the jail and grabbed her arm to force her to face him. Something flared in her eyes, and she jerked her arm away. "Don't—"

"Why are you angry with me?"

"Who is Julia?"

He blinked, stepped back, and looked down, unable to contain the surprise and pain he knew would show in his face.

Before he could answer, he noticed a stain on her white shirt inside the flap of her jacket. "Are you—?" He swallowed a lump of fear. He could barely force the words out, so sudden was the sensation of the breath being squeezed from his lungs. "Are you hurt?"

She shrugged off his hand, and it was only then he realized he was still clutching her shoulder. He forced himself to focus, deny the roaring in his head. Danna was injured and needed his help.

"Let's get you to the doctor." He tried to steer her toward the doc's office, but she jerked away from his hand.

"It's just a scratch. I'll take care of it myself."

He didn't believe her, but had no choice but to follow her up to her room.

Was she angry enough to deny him entrance? Apparently not, because she left the door ajar.

Danna turned her back and took off her long coat, revealing a bloodstain along her left side.

Chas bit off a curse and strode toward her. He gripped her shoulders and spun her so she faced him. He wanted to see her eyes, needed to gauge how bad it really was.

The sight of her blood did things to his insides he hadn't felt since Julia. But having tender emotions for Danna was impossible, wasn't it? He'd promised himself he was never going to fall in love again.

Danna half turned away from him and shook loose of his grasp. "I'll undress and take care of this, if you don't mind." She twirled her finger, and he turned his back to her.

Staring at the wall, Chas began methodically taking off his coat, boots, vest. He left the rest of his clothes on, even though his pants were soaked through, his shirt nearly so.

"How did it happen? Where is it?" he asked, not sure he wanted the answer. It seemed everything had gone wrong last night. How much of it was his fault?

"Upper part of my arm. On the inside."

A drawer opened and closed behind him, and then cloth rustled, and a soft tinkling noise came. What was she doing?

Her voice sounded muffled. "When that first volley of shots came"—now clearer—"the bullet grazed me. It's not that bad." But her voice was tight, and he wasn't sure he believed her.

"Not that bad," he repeated. Not that bad. Only shot a little. A scratch. He felt as if the top of his head floated away from the rest of him as his temper ignited.

She was so quick to put herself in danger...

What if he asked Danna to give up her quest to apprehend

the robbers? Bad idea. But what if he put her on a train to Boston? He hadn't talked to his parents in years, but they wouldn't turn away his wife.

Too bad Danna would never agree to go. He did know her well enough to know that.

He wanted to hunt down Lewis's gang himself, to show them as much pain as they'd showed him—and now Danna. He'd longed for revenge before. Now he hungered for it in a way he'd never known. Lewis needed to pay.

"I can't quite..." Danna's voice interrupted the roaring tempest of his thoughts.

"Do you need help?" He waited for her answer before he turned.

Danna sighed, a little huff of air to let him know she wasn't happy about it. "I can't reach the wound."

He faced her and had to swallow hard. She wore an undershirt and had the quilt from the bed wrapped around her, so only her shoulder and injured arm emerged. It was her hair that unmanned him, the dark locks falling in waves down her back. She must've loosed them from the braid so they could dry.

His knees threatened to knock together as he approached. She flushed under his gaze and averted her face, pointing to the array of doctoring supplies she'd laid out across the bed.

"You'll need to clean it out first," she said. "The wound isn't bad, but if infection sets in..."

"Yes, I know." And he did know how bad infection could get. He'd met plenty of men missing limbs or on the brink of dying because of infection from injuries. "I can't believe you went all morning with a bullet wound and didn't tell me."

He located an antiseptic and some clean cloths and moved in front of Danna so her crown was at his chin. He wiped the blood off the inside of her arm. He was too conscious of how soft her skin felt against his palm, and how she smelled sweet, even though the rain must've washed away any scent of soap or perfume.

"There wasn't anything you could have done, even if I had told you."

"You would've told your first husband."

"Fred—" She bit out the one word. That was it.

He kept his gaze on what he was doing, but he could see her jaw flex from the corner of his eye.

He leaned away so he could look her in the face. He didn't release his hold on her upper arm. "Fred what?"

Her gaze didn't waver from his. "Fred would've known without me telling him."

Well. Chas looked down to apply the antiseptic to a rag, pretending her words hadn't stung. He dabbed the rag against the bloody furrow in her skin and heard her soft intake of breath. She was lucky the bullet hadn't entered her flesh.

He hated that she was injured. Hated that they hadn't been able to capture the outlaws. Hated that he had no control over any of this.

He shifted behind her to get a better look at the other side of her wound.

"This was my fault," he muttered. Maybe he never should have come to Calvin in the first place.

"It's not." Danna's soft but firm words startled him. He didn't realize he'd spoken aloud. Their eyes met in the small looking glass hanging above her desk.

"What?"

"It's not your fault I got shot," she said, and the look in her dark eyes confirmed her words. "It just happened." She took a deep breath and said, "What about Julia? Who is she?"

Chas closed his eyes. He should have known Danna wouldn't forget. But what should he tell her?

The truth. The simple words reverberated in his head. "She was a childhood friend." The words stuck in his throat like molasses, gummy. He had to push each one out. "Our parents traveled in the same social circles. When we got older, we became sweethearts."

Danna had been sitting still before. Now she was motionless. Chas tried to control the bitterness seeping into his voice. She'd asked, after all.

"And then...and then our parents arranged a marriage."

She nodded.

But he wasn't finished. "For Julia and my brother." Now her spine went rigid beneath the hand he'd placed there as he doctored her arm.

"She was my brother's wife."

"But you loved her."

He had. It had been his downfall. "Yes, and I killed her, too."

* * *

CHAS'S WORDS, so casually spoken, turned Danna's world topsy-turvy.

She spun and pushed away from him, creating distance between them while he watched her with stormy eyes.

He set his rag on the table and turned his shoulders so she couldn't see his face.

"Julia and Joseph hadn't been married for six months before he came up with some hare-brained idea to head west and make his own fortune, even though he was in line to take over our father's empire." He looked up for a moment. "In Boston."

Danna sat on the bed.

"He sent Julia a couple of letters, and then all correspondence stopped. She was sure my brother had been caught up in something immoral or illegal, or both." He paused. Ran a hand through his damp hair. "She asked me to find him for her."

"And you said yes?"

"Of course. At the time, I thought it would be a better

choice. It was too hard to be near her in Boston, knowing I couldn't be with her." He stared at the wall. Lost in the past?

She couldn't imagine him hurting a woman. Not one that he claimed to love. Not any woman, actually.

"So you came west looking for your brother. Did you find him?"

He turned back to her. His eyes had gone from stormy turquoise to darkened sapphire.

"I made the mistake of telling Julia what train I was taking out of Boston. She showed up, sat down right next to me a few minutes after the train left the station."

"She traveled with you?"

He nodded, a small smile quirking the corners of his lips. "I didn't know she had that much gumption. She'd always done what her parents wanted."

Even marry Chas's brother, came the unspoken emphasis.

"I tried to put her off at the next station, but she would have none of it. She insisted she could handle the travel, the long hours. She said she'd stay in the hotels and let me find Joseph. She said she just wanted to be there when we found him."

"And you gave in."

"I was stupid," Chas spat, his brows slashing downward. "I should've known she was fibbing."

"Most women have certain...wiles they can use to get men to do what they want."

Chas looked up at her as if surprised she was defending him. She was a little surprised herself. She motioned for him to go on, but he continued to stare at her. She prompted him, "So when you found Joseph..."

He shook his head, eyes again going to the floor, to the past. "I found him in a saloon, in the middle of a poker game, surrounded by—"

He cut himself off and flushed a little. As if she didn't know what sort his brother would have been surrounded by in a saloon. She nodded for him to go on.

"He didn't even look like Joseph. The Joseph I knew was fussy about his clothing, always neat and groomed. This Joseph had a scraggly beard and unkempt clothes. His shirt was torn in two places, and he smelled like he hadn't bathed in weeks. I barely recognized him."

Danna knew that feeling, knew how it burned inside. Like when the person you thought would always take care of you suddenly didn't want you anymore. You couldn't help loving them, but oh, it hurt.

"Before I spoke to him, the man sitting across the table accused Joseph of cheating. He probably was." Chas went silent again. Danna saw the muscles move as he swallowed hard.

"And Julia came into the saloon behind you." She could guess the rest. Maybe he needed to tell it.

He nodded, his throat still working. Finally, he continued. "The men had their guns drawn before I even knew she was there. Several men started shooting. It was wild. Julia was shot twice. There was blood everywhere." He rasped the words now, rushing, as if he couldn't stop. "I got hit, too, but I didn't even feel the bullets. I tried to save her, but I couldn't."

Again his throat worked. Danna expected to see tears on his face, but though his eyes were luminous, no moisture fell.

What would it feel like if Chas loved her the way he'd loved his Julia? Would she feel treasured, the way she never had with Fred?

Finally, she had to ask. "And your brother?"

"Dead before he hit the ground." Chas rubbed both hands down his face, and Danna worried there was more to the story. He spoke evenly now, the words seeming to come easier. "I haven't been home since it happened. I promised myself I'd find the man responsible and kill him. And now I'm so close."

Close. He'd been searching for cattle rustlers when he got

here, but it was the way he'd reacted to the name spoken by the injured outlaw that had her speculating. "Hank Lewis?"

He nodded. No wonder he'd been so fixated on the man, enough that he could draw an accurate portrait.

"You should've told me he was a killer."

Chas simply shook his head.

"You know I can't let you kill him," she murmured.

He shook his head, not quite meeting her eyes. "Then you'd better hope you find him before I do."

The air crackled between them. Danna stood, breaking the awful tension between them. "Will you wrap my arm? I want to talk to the man we locked up last night. Maybe see if our boy over at Doc's is awake."

He returned to her side, and the heat of his hand on her bare skin made her wish things were different.

"Would you really arrest your husband?" He didn't look up, but his words held a tinge of amusement.

She shrugged. "I'd prefer not to have to make the choice."

"I know. I know. Your first husband was perfect." He said the words as if he were joking, but it sounded as if they were tinged with a hint of jealousy. Chas was jealous of Fred?

She tried not to examine the warmth spreading through her.

"I never said that. Fred never would have told me what you just shared with me."

"Really?"

She shrugged. "We didn't talk about our feelings, or...things that were difficult for us." Like Rob.

"I haven't told anyone else."

"Not even your parents?" she asked.

"I told you I haven't been home since it happened."

"How long ago?"

"Four years."

"You haven't even sent a letter or a telegraph to let them know you're all right?"

"I can't."

"Why not?"

"I just can't. Leave it be."

She wanted to press further, but the answer was so obvious, she didn't bother. Obviously, he blamed himself for Joseph's and Julia's deaths. His guilt was keeping him from his family, and it didn't sound as if he'd found any healing.

"Do you think your husband wanted to talk about those other kind of things?" he asked.

Chas's words brought her out of her thoughts. What a funny thing to say.

"Fred wasn't the type of man to keep things inside. If he wanted to say something, he usually did."

"Maybe he wanted to, but he wasn't sure how you'd react."

Chas tied off the white cloth he'd used to wrap her arm. His hand remained on her shoulder, thumb brushing the edge of the cloth. His touch sent shivers down her spine.

"Thanks." Was that really her voice, that breathy whisper?

Their eyes met and held, and Danna wished for a repeat of the kiss they'd shared in the preacher's parlor.

Chas must've seen her wish reflected in her eyes, because he leaned in until his chin brushed hers and his breath warmed her lips.

But at the last second, as her eyes were closing, he jerked away and moved to the opposite side of the room.

"We shouldn't."

"Oh—" Her voice emerged broken, so she cleared her throat before speaking again. "Will you go down and check on the prisoner? I'll finish getting dressed and join you in a minute. We should check on the wounded outlaw, too."

He nodded, already half-turned toward the door.

She dressed quickly and then stood inside the door with her hands pressed to her stomach, trying to breathe.

She felt as if she would fly apart with one wrong breath, one wrong move. Her husband was in love with a dead woman. A woman that Danna would never be able to compete with. It sounded like this Julia had been cultured, refined...and manipulative.

Danna shook the jealous thought away. She needed clarity. She had no hold over Chas. They'd agreed to annul their marriage after they'd found the robbers and the cattle thieves.

She couldn't go back on their agreement, not now. No matter what she'd started to hope in the last two days.

She needed focus, needed it desperately. What she really needed was to catch the remaining two or three outlaws, keep Chas from killing Lewis, sleep for two days straight, and then work through her feelings about Chas.

She needed divine help. Danna turned and fell to her knees at her bedside. She poured out her heart, begged for God to help her with the tasks she found to be insurmountable. What she couldn't ask for in words, for Him to love her, she secretly hoped He heard anyway.

When she got up to face the town and her job again, she found her cheeks were wet, but a weight had been lifted from her shoulders.

Until she got to the bottom of her staircase, and it dropped right back in place. A crowd of people jostled between the jailhouse door and where she stood, murmurs rippling through it.

"Gone."

"Marshal's done."

"...resignation."

She found Chas in the center of the crowd, pushing his way toward her. In tow was the man she both did and did not want to see.

Sheriff Halverson.

CHAPTER 17

*T*he crowd parted for Danna's passage. She met Sheriff Halverson in the middle. Over his shoulder, she could see Chas's grim expression.

"I'm afraid we've got a bit of a problem," the sheriff murmured.

The crowd went silent around them, but the last thing Danna wanted was to discuss any business in front of the town busybodies.

She nodded toward the jail. "Let's go inside."

She followed the sheriff through the group of residents, using a strategic elbow more than once. The townspeople knew better than to ask her for details, but several men shouted questions at the sheriff.

Thankfully, he didn't respond.

Once she stepped up on the boardwalk, she noticed Chas had halted outside the doorway. She motioned him toward the door. "I'd appreciate it if you'd—"

Come in. Support me.

The words stuck in her throat, but Chas must've known

what she meant, because he stepped right behind her and placed a hand at her hip as she entered the jail.

The sheriff stood at the cell. The door stood open. No outlaw in sight.

"Oh, no." The words fell from Danna's lips as a near silent whisper, but Chas was close enough to hear. He squeezed her waist before he let go.

The outlaw was gone. Halverson was bent over, examining the lock mechanism, and Danna stepped up beside him.

"I rode up about twenty minutes ago and came in here to find you." The brim of the sheriff's hat shaded his eyes, and she couldn't make out his expression. "I've been on a case and only got your telegraph yesterday."

She nodded, words still failing her as panic gripped her throat. The town would call for her badge now for certain.

The sheriff continued. "Some scratches here, like someone tried to pick it. See here..." Halverson pointed to the outside of the locking mechanism, where there were indeed several deep gouges in the metal.

"They're impossible to break into," she returned, finally finding her voice. "Fred had a friend who could get through any kind of lock or safe, and he couldn't break through these."

She looked over to Chas, who stood behind the desk. He bent and reached for something behind the desk. What was he doing?

"Was there a spare key, then?" the sheriff asked, diverting her attention from Chas for the moment.

"Yes, it was—"

"In the third desk drawer, in a hidden compartment," Chas finished.

She'd never told Chas that. "How did you—?"

Words failed her again as he held up the desk drawer, revealing the broken compartment.

"But who could've done it?' Danna wondered aloud. She

crossed to where Chas stood behind the desk and groaned when she observed the mess of Wanted posters, papers, and other paraphernalia strewn across the floor. Apparently, whoever had released the outlaw had felt it necessary to dump the contents of all the desk drawers.

Their best chance of tracking down the bank's money had waltzed right out the door.

"Perhaps you should've left a guard," Halverson said, and his tone had Danna looking up to examine his face. Instead of the concern he'd shown up until a few moments ago, his expression and voice were hard as steel.

She knew it was over. "I didn't have anyone to leave behind."

* * *

TWO HOURS LATER, it was done. Danna had surrendered her badge and her responsibilities at the request of the town council. The Sheriff Halverson was taking over the bank robbery investigation. She'd shared her suspicions about the town council, but Halverson had laughed it off.

Maybe he was right. Maybe she wasn't the investigator she'd thought she was.

She and Chas had three days to vacate the room above the jail.

Chas stood silently by her side, aching to do something. Knowing that at least part of this mess was his fault. His only consolation was that Danna hadn't gotten herself killed.

They'd returned to her room without speaking. Once inside, she'd wilted onto the bed, not looking at him. He stared out the dingy window, trying to figure out a way to comfort her that didn't involve touching her. He'd nearly kissed her earlier, and that would've been a grave mistake. He had to leave soon, and pulling her—or himself—deeper into this would only cause more heartache.

179

What he needed to do was figure out a way to track down Hank Lewis, exact his revenge, and move on to the next job. Alone.

Problem was, he was tired of being alone. Spending time with Danna had shown him how lonely his life had become. He wasn't sure he could return to the way things had been before. Without Danna in it, his life seemed empty. His life *was* empty.

But he'd made a deal with himself. Ensure Danna's safety, then leave so he didn't endanger her again. He had never reneged on a promise, and he wouldn't now, not even if fulfilling it felt like a bullet to the gut.

He just needed to figure out a way to extricate himself from the situation gently.

"...for me?"

He started, realizing he'd missed Danna's words. He had to clear his throat before he could speak. "Sorry. What?" He faced her and leaned against the windowsill.

"I said, why didn't you speak up for me?"

The pain on her face hammered him. He'd never seen her so vulnerable, and somehow he knew he was the only person she'd shown it to. It made what he had to say so much harder.

"I thought...I thought their decision was best."

Her lips opened in a silent gasp. "Why?" Tears glittered on her eyelashes. It cut him to the bone. She'd stood silent and proud while her job, her entire life, had been stripped away. But now he had reduced her to tears.

He was a cad. The worst sort.

* * *

DANNA HAD the strangest urge to shake some sense into Chas, But her muscles had atrophied in the short time since she'd slumped onto the bed, and she found she couldn't move.

In light of everything that had happened in the past few

days and weeks, she should've been too numb to feel any more hurt.

On the mountain, during the snowstorm, he'd said he thought she made a good marshal.

"If you didn't think I should be marshal, why did you marry me?" Her voice betrayed her emotions. "It was only to save my job."

He was silent for a moment. "I needed you to help me find Hank Lewis. I have to... He killed Julia. I can't forget it."

"Julia," she whispered. She should have known.

It had all been for her. He'd loved Julia—still loved her—so much that it colored all of his decisions. Danna would never be able to compete with a memory.

"If you want, I could write a letter to my parents in Boston. I have a little money left, and I can send you to them. I know they won't turn you away."

She knew it cost him to make his offer, considering he hadn't made contact with his parents since his brother died. Still, it was a worthless offer.

"What would I do in Boston?" she asked with a little teary laugh. She stood and turned away, wiping at her cheeks. She didn't want him to see how much this was hurting her. Not now.

"You could see the sights." He lowered his voice. "Remarry."

She laughed again, and this time it was bitterness coloring her voice instead of tears. "If no one in the Wild West will have me, I doubt I could find a husband in a city like Boston."

"Danna." He spoke her name like it hurt him to say it, but she couldn't bear to face him.

"Thank you for the offer, but I can't accept." She turned to face him, and looking into his craggy face hurt as much as she thought it would. She forced a small smile to her lips. "I think I'll stay with Corrine for the time being, if she'll have me."

He swallowed once, his eyes never leaving her face. "And if her husband returns?"

Finding Brent would give her something to work on. "Then I'll find something else."

"What about your brother?"

The thought of going to Rob and admitting her failures tasted a lot like dirt. She shrugged anyway. "It's a possibility."

He looked like he wanted to say something else, but she couldn't handle much more of this.

"You don't have to worry about me, O'Grady." She teared up at the distance she was putting between them. "I'll be fine."

A sharp twinge in her shoulder and arm had her clutching it.

Chas's brow wrinkled. "You should have the doctor look at your wound." She couldn't help but notice he didn't offer to look at it again himself.

Maybe it meant he'd felt something when he'd doctored her before.

"What will you do? Hire a tracker to go after your outlaw?' The words were out before she could catch them.

"Maybe." He opened the door, turned, met her eyes. "Good-bye, Danna."

CHAPTER 18

*D*anna waited in a chair in Doc Crittendon's outer room, ignoring the room's two other occupants. She didn't want to talk to anyone in Calvin right at this moment. Not while the shame still made her cheeks color at each knowing look people gave her. She'd been too upset to visit Corrine. She didn't want to disturb her friend's fragile happiness with the new baby. So she'd come here instead.

And waited. Finally the doctor emerged from one of the two examination rooms and motioned her inside. She showed him her injury and told him what Chas had already done for it.

The doctor hummed low under his breath as he re-cleaned the wound and wrapped it again.

"Not any worse than you've had before," he said when he was done, moving to the counter to pump fresh water to wash his hands. It was true.

"No sign of infection," he continued. "Just keep it clean."

She nodded. "How's the outlaw who got shot up?"

The doctor frowned. "Somewhat better. The sheriff fetched him, even though I recommended keeping him here for observation for a while longer."

"What?" Shock held Danna immobile. "Halverson took him?"

"Hours ago. Said he was taking him to the jailhouse."

Suspicion tickled Danna's overwrought brain. She hadn't heard any movement or voices in the jailhouse when she and Chas had been talking or after he'd left. Had she been so wrapped up in her own misery that she'd somehow missed activity beneath their feet?

Surely he hadn't meant to take the outlaw to the county lockup in Glenrock, not in his injured condition. An awful idea had begun to dawn on her. What if Halverson was in on it? She'd suspected the council, but could this conspiracy have reached him?

The doctor wrinkled his forehead. "I'm sorry you didn't get to question him again. He did say some things in his delirium last night...something about a hideout in a big cave. He mentioned Glenrock. I told the sheriff when he was here."

Her heart thrummed. She knew that cave. It was near where she'd hurt herself, a few miles from her brother's ranch. If it was true, there was a chance she could still recover the bank's money. She probably wouldn't get her job back, but it galled her to leave the job undone. Especially because of how Castlerock had treated her. If he hadn't thought she'd be able to handle the job, why had he appointed her?

The doc must've seen the change of attitude in her expression, because his hand tightened on her arm. "You aren't going to do something foolish, are you?"

She smiled a wan smile. "More foolish than anything I've done in the last few days?" *Like marrying a man I barely knew? Or worse, falling in love with him?* She knew her voice held a tinge of desperation, and she worked to remove it as she reassured the doc. "No, sir."

The thud of her boots sounded heavy and final on the

boardwalk as she made her way to the livery. She would find that money or die trying.

* * *

CHAS HAD GATHERED up all his belongings and now stood in the doorway to Danna's room, looking over the small, bare area.

It didn't even look like a female lived there. No frilly embellishments or fine china to be seen. Knowing Danna the way he did now, he wasn't surprised at the lack of femininity. She was much too practical to waste time on frippery, and she would see it as showing weakness, which she couldn't afford to do.

But underneath her strong exterior existed a sensitive, beautiful woman.

Why else would she have donned a dress for their wedding day?

Was he making a mistake, going to Cheyenne to hire a tracker?

He didn't know. Every choice felt wrong. In his attempt to protect Danna, he'd ended up betraying her. He didn't know anything anymore.

Except that it had scared him—absolutely terrified him—to see the blood on her blouse earlier. She put herself in harm's way too often. As marshal, she would do so every day.

His heart couldn't take the strain, the worry, knowing how vulnerable she was. How close to danger she lived. He couldn't stay here and watch her risk her life. Couldn't leave knowing she still would. But now that she'd given up her badge, she should be safe. She'd never forgive him for not sticking up for her. And now she knew she couldn't count on him, not really. It was better this way. The distance between them would grow when the annulment was filed. Better to cut ties now.

Only it didn't feel better. It felt wrong.

The sound of approaching boots on the stairs alerted him to her presence. Perhaps that's what he'd really been waiting for— one more chance to see her again.

She was focused, her mind busy with whatever was putting the determined frown on her face. She didn't see him until she'd stepped into the room and kicked the door partway closed.

When she realized he was there, she froze, surprise and something else flashing over her features. Hurt, maybe?

"You're still here?" Her voice held no emotion.

He raised the saddlebags in a salute. "I'll be back from Cheyenne in a couple days. With the annulment."

"Fine. Goodbye." She didn't look at him.

He winced at the curt dismissal. Stopped in the doorway for one last look.

She crossed to the bed and tossed her hat onto the coverlet, followed by her coat. She pulled a sweater from one of the drawers in the stand next to the bed and yanked it on over her shirt, causing several tendrils of her dark hair to escape the braid hanging past her shoulders.

He remembered the way her hair had looked as it cascaded down her back in those thick, rich curls. He'd never forget it.

He watched her yank off first one boot, then the other, and add a second pair of thick wool socks before jamming the boots on again.

Where was she going? Worry slithered down his spine.

Not his business. Not anymore.

He turned to go, whispering, "Goodbye, Miss Marshal."

* * *

Danna's entire body shook as she scooted down the stairs and untied her mare from the hitching post out front.

She gulped air, working to calm herself because the horse

would be able to read her agitation, and she had no desire to fight it. Judging by the clouds darkening the sky, she had a few hours to find the outlaws before the storm hit. She'd need the animal's cooperation to make it into the mountains on time.

Danna didn't speak to anyone on her way out of town. Contrary to what she'd told herself all this time, their acceptance *did* matter. Once she captured the bank robbers, she would move somewhere else. Maybe try her hand at ranching. Fred had left her a little savings, and she hadn't spent much in her short tenure as marshal. She could buy herself a little homestead and a few cattle.

But she didn't know if she could do it. After all, it had been years since she'd worked with Rob on his ranch. After the way the town had treated her, maybe a solitary life was for her.

A shout came from down the street. She looked up to see a man on a horse trotting down the end of Main Street toward the open prairie.

"He stole my horse!" came a second shout from a man running down the boardwalk.

Danna kicked her mare and took off after the thief. The rider looked over his shoulder once, then spurred the stolen horse to a gallop.

She heard another yell as she raced past a group of people on the boardwalk, their faces a blur. It sounded an awful lot like, "You get him, Marshal!" but that couldn't be right, because her badge had been rescinded.

As she passed the edge of town, she urged her mare for more speed, and they gained on the stolen horse and its rider. A cold wind ate through Danna's long coat and the sweater she'd added beneath it.

Drawing abreast of the rider, she was astonished to see Sam Castlerock at the reins. What was the banker's son doing? Why would the boy steal a horse when his father was rich enough to buy him as many as he wanted?

Sam caught sight of her. His face paled.

"Stop!" she shouted, but the boy hunched forward in the saddle and used the end of the reins to whip the horse to move faster.

She considered launching herself onto the other horse, but at their speed, one or both of them might break something when they hit the ground. And she still had to catch Lewis's gang, so that wasn't an option for her.

Instead, she slipped a length of rope from atop her saddle horn and fashioned a lasso, Sam saw what she was doing and tried to steer his horse away, but she watched the movements of his torso and guessed his next move. She drew closer to horse and rider and, with a quick flick of her wrist, tossed the lariat over the other horse's head. She slowed, and so did the horse, even though the young Castlerock continued to kick its flanks. The horse's lather and tossing head told enough of the story. It wasn't used to running like this, nor did it appreciate the boy's treatment.

"Your little jaunt is over," she shouted. "Stop!"

When it became apparent his horse was no longer obeying his commands, Sam threw himself out of the saddle and raced away on foot.

Danna growled low in her throat. The boy was causing her an unneeded delay. She left the stolen animal behind and took off after the boy. She fashioned a second lariat from another length of rope out of her saddlebag and within minutes had looped it around the boy's shoulders. In no time, she had him trussed like a turkey and slumped over the saddle in front of her. They returned to the stolen horse at a slower pace, and she tried to talk some sense into the young man.

"I don't think you're going to get away with this, Sam. Horse thievin' is a hanging offense." And with the number of witnesses on Main Street, there was little chance of his father buying his way out of this. "Why'd you do it?"

"You wouldn't understand, Marshal." He spat the title in a mocking voice and didn't say another word. In the distance, she could see riders heading toward them.

She made the boy dismount from her horse and waited as several men from town rode up.

"I thought he'd get away for sure," said Dodie Bennett. "You sure didn't waste any time, Miz Marshal. Thank you." She ignored him when she should have corrected him. She wasn't marshal any longer.

"You'll want to take him to the jail," she told the blacksmith. She left it up to him whether he'd make Sam walk or allow him to ride.

"Too bad the town council wasn't here to see this." Undertaker Burr McCoy almost sounded impressed. But that couldn't be right.

"Yep, maybe they'da changed their minds about firin' ya." That from Ellery Pyle.

Danna frowned, "I didn't run him down for recognition." She removed the lariat from around the horse's neck.

"Why'd she do it then?" another voice asked as she wheeled her horse to the open plain.

Someone answered, barely audible as she rode away. "She did it because it was the right thing to do, ya goose. Hey, where's she goin'? Town's the other way—"

Soon enough, the prairie gave way to small conifers, and she was crossing the foothills. Before the disastrous ride up here with her deputy, she hadn't been closer than viewing distance to the mountains in over a year. She hadn't had any desire to return to the place where she'd broken her brother's trust, where her life as a little sister on his ranch had ended. She wasn't superstitious, not really, but ever since that night, she'd felt like her life was one long mountain journey, her feet just inches from a cliff she couldn't see.

She guided her mare around an outcropping of rock,

thankful for the horse's surefootedness on the changing terrain.

Her mind whirled. How was she going to sneak up on the outlaw camp by herself?

What was she doing?

Was Chas right? He'd agreed with the town council that she shouldn't wear the badge. Since she'd met him, she *had* taken unnecessary risks. Charging into the bank building alone. Tracking outlaws in a snowstorm.

She glanced up at the menacing slate-colored sky. And winced.

Tracking outlaws in a snowstorm. *Twice.*

Fred wouldn't have taken risks like she had. But Fred had had support from both his deputies and the town council.

It had been her choice to stay on as marshal with no deputies. Had her pride gotten in the way of this investigation? Because she'd had something to prove. To the town council. To herself.

Why hadn't she asked the men who'd ridden out after Sam for help? She'd assumed they wouldn't ride along with her.

Chas had conjectured that someone was paying off the former deputies and any other men in town who might be obliged to help her. If he was right, she should've ridden to Bear Creek or even Ash Grove to round up some help.

Instead, she'd galloped out of town to take on a gang of outlaws. Alone.

Without a plan.

She *was* going to get herself killed.

No. Not today.

She reined in her horse to turn back.

At the sharp crack of a pistol's hammer being cocked, the mare faltered and whinnied.

"Hands up," a thin, menacing voice snapped. A familiar voice.

Heart hammering, Danna turned in her saddle to find herself staring down the barrel of a mean-looking Colt .45, not a handful of yards away. Even a bad shot wasn't likely to miss from such a short distance. Her gaze followed the pistol's barrel back to a craggy face. Halverson.

"Do it, or I'll shoot." His voice brooked no argument, but she considered reaching for her own pistol anyway, until she saw the second man a few paces behind Halverson. Pale and trembling, it was the injured outlaw. He, too, had a gun trained on her, a rifle that lay across his horse's shoulders, balanced against the saddle horn. She had no choice but to release the reins and push her hands above her head. There would be no chance to ride for help now.

CHAPTER 19

Standing on the boardwalk as he waited for the stagecoach, Chas let his gaze roam over the town. That was no good. Every place he looked reminded him of Danna. Trying to keep his mind off her, he dug through his saddlebags, looking for the letter with the name of his contact at the WSGA in Cheyenne.

Instead, his hand closed over a smooth leather item, and he drew it out so he could see it. Fred Carpenter's journal. How had it ended up in Chas's things?

In all the chaos of the previous night and this morning, the journal must have been tucked into his saddlebag by mistake.

He snorted. Mistake, or subconscious desire to be close to Danna in any way he could?

Well, it wouldn't work. He could return the diary when he brought the annulment papers, after all the trouble with Lewis died down.

Idly, he flipped open the book to a spot near the middle. Anything to help pass the time.

Danna and I spent the day picnicking and then several hours of target practice. It was a nice break from our normal routine. We watched the sunset down by Pa's Crik, and she started to open up to me.

It's been years since she's revealed her inner thoughts, and that she felt comfortable to do so today meant the world to me.

Chas closed the book with a snap. He didn't want to read about Danna and Fred Carpenter's relationship after all. The man had obviously never meant for this to fall into the hands of Danna's second husband.

Morbid curiosity had him flipping the book open again, searching for that same entry. He had to know what happened next. Spying a familiar name on a different page stopped him cold.

Halverson in town again. I wish I had firm proof he was behind the rustling, or just proof of his involvement, but in the six months since Stevenson saw him settling a sale of cattle at the Cheyenne train station, he's proved more wily than I thought.

Perhaps he has help?

Reaching the end of the entry, Chas stared down at the page and let the words blur out of focus.

Chas knew lawmen weren't above reproach—he'd taken down a marshal near Houston, Texas, who'd murdered several men in a gambling den and had almost gotten away with it.

Fred Carpenter suspected Halverson?

In the distance, thundering hoofbeats and the rattle of the stagecoach signaled its approach. Chas was running out of time.

He flipped through the book rapidly, looking for more entries that mentioned the sheriff or suspicious activity. Several mentioned suspicions of a gang of rustlers, most likely the very same ones Chas was hunting. Carpenter didn't know identities but had found the prairie cabin. On the last page, Chas came upon an underlined entry.

Halverson's involvement confirmed. Meeting tomorrow at 3:00

*p.m. Will follow Halverson to cattle holding location then return for
backup. Will tell Danna when I'm sure. No need to put her in danger
before then.*

There were no further entries. Fred Carpenter must have
been spotted as he'd tried to take down the gang. Danna said
he'd been murdered in cold blood, but nothing about his suspicions. Because he hadn't told her, Chas realized. And she
couldn't read his journal for herself.

He couldn't go to Cheyenne. Not with Halverson out there
gunning for Danna.

He needed a horse. He needed help, but he wasn't likely to
find it in Calvin. Not when everyone here had turned their
backs on Danna.

Outside the livery, a small group of men were giving a
teenaged boy a talking to. He paid them little attention until,

"—can't believe she rode out toward the mountains," a
voice said.

Chas drew up short. There was only one woman he knew
who would dare ride out alone.

And then he remembered her donning a heavy sweater and
socks. Like she was getting ready to ride out.

He was an idiot.

He grabbed the man who'd spoken by the arm, not caring
that it was rude. "The marshal?" he demanded.

The man shook of Chas's hold, frowning.

"The marshal," Chas pressed. "Is that who you're talking
about? Who rode out alone?"

"Yeah, bud."

She'd gone after the gang alone.

All the blood rushed from his head in a dizzying rush.

"And none of you went with her?" Of course they hadn't.

One of the nearest men bristled. "Whatever she was doing,
it ain't our business."

Chas shook his head, anger rising. "I know some of you

rode with Danna when her first husband was still alive. You know her abilities."

The first man who'd spoken—the blacksmith?—shifted his feet.

"You should be ashamed of yourselves. Danna has worked herself to the bone, lost sleep, and now put herself in danger. All for this town that doesn't even appreciate her."

"A woman shouldn't be marshal," someone from the back of the crowd called out.

"She cain't handle the job!"

Not exactly the response Chas wanted.

The teenaged boy who ran the livery sidled up to Chas. He hadn't even noticed the boy. Had he been listening from inside the livery? "The marshal can do just as good a job as any man," the boy said. "Last week she broke up two fights at the saloon before things could get out of hand. She's the best tracker around, and y'all all know it."

They were wasting time. Danna was out there, tracking the outlaws. Alone.

"I'm riding out after her," Chas said. "And I need help. Anybody willing to ride with me?"

The men grumbled. No one raised a hand. Most of them wouldn't even look him in the eye.

"Is there some other reason you won't ride with Danna?" he asked, desperate now. "Is someone paying you off?"

Heads lowered, no one said a word.

He growled under his breath. Turned to the stablehand. "Will you loan me a horse?"

The boy nodded, face grave. "I'll ride with you."

Was he serious? Chas supposed one teenager was better than no one. "What's your name?"

"Will Chittim."

"I'd be obliged if you'd ride with me."

The kid nodded and ducked into the livery.

As the crowd of men started to disperse, a group of eight rough-looking men on horseback thundered into town. They reined in nearby, horses blowing.

The man out front pushed his stained Stetson off his brow, allowing Chas a good look at his face. Dark stubble covered his cheeks and chin while a full mustache hid the man's mouth. His coffee-brown eyes were familiar, but he couldn't place the man.

"I'm looking for the marshal," he called out to

Chas bristled. He didn't like the looks of these ruffians. "Who's asking?" he demanded loudly.

The man wheeled his horse in the street, his dark gaze honed in on Chas. Dangerous.

Someone else spoke from the boardwalk, breaking the tension. "Ain't got no marshal no more."

The man on horseback looked at the speaker, face going white beneath his tan. "What?"

"She resigned."

"She was forced to resign," Chas muttered.

Will appeared in the stable doorway holding two horses by the reins.

Chas nodded to him. "Let's go find my wife."

He swung up on his mount and turned the horse toward the mountains, visible over the roofs of the town buildings. He didn't make it far before the sound of hoofbeats joined those from his own. The stranger with dark hair came abreast of him.

"We'll ride with you," the stranger said, and made it sound like a command, not a request.

"Thank you, but I don't know you."

"I'm her brother." The man's terse words were offset by the

jumping muscle in his jaw. "Rob Darcy. Sounds like we're family now."

A kernel of hope bloomed in Chas's chest.

Darcy motioned to the six men following. "These are a few of my hands. One of my men heard about Danna's troubles while passing through. I came when I could, but it sounds like it wasn't soon enough. So Danna's taken off to chase a group of outlaws on her own?" Darcy didn't sound surprised.

"It's worse than that," Chas told him, itching to move faster, to get out of town, but knowing it would be impossible to talk once they let the horses go. "I think the sheriff is involved. Danna doesn't know."

With a glance to the rapidly darkening sky and the snowflakes swirling around them, the set of the cowboy's mouth turned even grimmer. "We don't have much time. I don't suppose you know where she was headed?"

"I can take you there," a female voice called out.

Katy. She shied from Darcy when his horse sidestepped toward her. Approached Chas instead.

"I can take ya right to the hideout. It's in a cave in the mountains."

"How do you know it? Who are you?" Rob demanded.

"We can trust her," Chas put in. She might've run away, but he knew she liked Danna.

When Katy spoke, it was to Chas. "My pa used to run with that awful Jed Hester. Then a few months ago, that lyin', no good snake shot him in the back. Tried to come after me, too, but Pa had taught me how to disappear in the woods."

So, she'd been on her own for months, probably near to starving when Chas had caught her outside the grocery. No wonder she'd eaten as if his eggs and bacon had been her last meal.

"Anyways, I want that no-account varmint dead, and I guess

hangin's the next best thing to shootin' 'im when you lot catch up to them."

Even though he was used to Danna and her trousers, the violence spewing from this girl surprised him. He supposed she was only expressing the same thing he felt about Hank Lewis.

Right now, he'd kill Hank Lewis with his bare hands.

* * *

DANNA'S MIND whirled as the three horses neared the crude campsite spilling out of the mouth of the yawning black hole of the cave. With her hands bound in front of her, it had been all she could do to cling to the saddle horn and not topple as her horse followed Halverson's mount, traversing the difficult terrain in the foothills. Never mind reaching for a weapon to help her escape or to overpower Halverson.

She looked over her shoulder again. The kid who'd been shot wasn't doing well. His complexion matched the color of the snow swirling around them. If his injury was getting worse, maybe she could convince Halverson to let her help him. And if she could get close to him, maybe she could get his weapon loose.

It was a risky plan, relying on an awful lot of maybes. But it was all she had.

Halverson reined in outside of the camp and dismounted. He hauled her off her horse, none too gently. Her ankle jarred when she landed on the ground, but he didn't give her time to even catch her breath before he shoved her in the direction of the cave.

She stumbled forward. "Halverson—"

"No talking," he ordered. "I've got a job for you. Now move it." He unholstered his gun in an obvious silent threat.

She didn't argue. She ducked through the mouth of the cave, carefully stepping over a man laid out on the ground, snoring, and had to start breathing through her mouth at the overpowering stench of unwashed flesh. Halverson kicked the sleeping man, who roused with a disoriented huff.

"You're supposed to be on watch, Wilson. If I catch you sleeping again, I'll put a bullet in you."

The man didn't respond, but Danna read anger in the set of his mouth before he spit a stream of tobacco juice against the cave wall. He stood and stomped outside the cave.

Halverson motioned her farther inside with his pistol. She walked around the small fire in the center, noting how little warmth it exuded, and moved toward a man with a distinctive handlebar mustache squatting next to a bundle of rags. Jed Hester.

"He any worse?" Halverson asked, and the man looked up, his face grave.

"No change." That's when she realized the bundle of rags was a man. One who was seriously injured. Between the flickering firelight and shadows, his pant leg appeared nearly black with slick blood. It seemed to have come from a wound in his upper thigh.

That answered her question of why Halverson hadn't killed her outright.

The sheriff glared at her. "Fix him up. No funny business or you're dead."

"I can't—I'm no doctor" she stalled. The injured man already appeared close to death. He was so pale, she didn't know if there was anything she could do for him.

"I know you ain't a doctor, girl. But you saved yer Freddie-poo when he got shot up a coupla years ago, an I 'spect you to do the same for my boy here."

She knelt next to the injured man, wobbling, since her tied hands put her off balance. She pushed aside the ripped shirt used to bind the wound, and blood poured from the leg. Hastily, she re-covered the wound as best she could.

"You're going to have to untie me. There's a few medical supplies in my saddlebag. And we'll need some clean cloths. How long has he been like this?"

"Stu, get the woman's saddlebags." Halverson nodded to the other outlaw. "Take off his gun belt. Then untie her."

He didn't answer her question, but she could guess. He must've been shot last night during the melee in town.

Once her hands were freed, she shook them, and pinpricks like needles of ice ushered the return of feeling to her fingers. Holding her emotions in check, she rummaged in the saddlebag that was thrust in her face. It was hard to think with the gun barrel mere feet away, focused directly on her. Was there anything in her bag she could use to escape?

Even if there was, could she leave the man to die?

"Hurry up," a voice from behind her warned.

She had to find a way out of here.

"What's your name?" she asked softly as she removed the blood-soaked cloth from the wound.

He didn't respond, instead focusing his pain-glazed eyes above her head.

"His name's Hank," grunted the man who now squatted near the fire, gun in hand. Danna glanced around the small cavern, but Halverson was nowhere to be seen.

Danna's muscles tensed as she returned her gaze to the man beneath her hands. So, this was the man who'd killed Chas's sister-in-law, the woman he loved. The outlaw's breathing was irregular, his face pasty. He was obviously in a lot of pain, and if Danna couldn't remove the bullet, there was a strong possibility he would bleed out.

It wouldn't take much to let nature take his course. To let him die.

Chas thought he deserved to die. She was inclined to agree.

If she let him die, would God forgive her? If she let him live, would Chas forgive her?

Whatever she chose, Halverson would kill her once she was no use to him anymore.

ight had fallen and bitter wind cut through Chas's coat and all the layers he wore. After hours of hard riding, the mountainous terrain became difficult and Darcy had insisted the search party stop until the blizzard waned or morning light, whichever came first.

Chas chafed at the delay.

Most of the cowboys were asleep, but he remaining sitting near the large campfire Darcy had built, staring into the flames.

His soul felt frozen. Danna was out there somewhere. In danger. Because of him.

The tracks she might have left were quickly obscured by the blowing snow. Katy assured them she knew were the outlaw hideout was. Were they already too late?

Sitting so near the fire reminded him of sharing another fire with Danna. He remembered how she'd trusted him with her past, with feelings she hadn't even shared with her first husband. And he'd thrown that trust in her face when she needed him most.

He loved her. And he'd failed her.

"So, you're married to my sister."

The quiet statement shook Chas from his musings. He hadn't realized the other man was still awake, but with a shift of his head, he saw Rob Darcy's eyes shining in the light from the campfire, though the man didn't look at him directly.

Chas didn't know what information the man was fishing for. He went with the simple answer. "For a few days."

"She's a special woman."

No argument there. "She is."

"And a lot to handle."

Chas couldn't contain a rueful quirk of his lips. "I don't think there is any such thing as handling your sister. She makes her own way."

"You're probably right." Darcy shifted under his horse blanket. "Is that why she went off after this gang alone?"

Chas's guilt made him unable to look at the other man. "I'm not good with women. I thought she'd stay in town. If I'd known she'd go after Hank Lewis's men alone, I never would've planned to go to Cheyenne."

"I ain't real good with women myself. She tell you I was the reason she left home?"

"She told me."

"I didn't know what to do with a kid sister. It wasn't that I didn't want her around. She was a pretty good kid. Hard-headed, but then, so am I. I didn't know nothin' about raising a girl."

Darcy's voice grew softer. "She scared the life out of me when she went off into the mountains by herself. I knew what could happen to a grown man alone, and she was just a girl. And then she got hurt. It terrified me. But I never would have sent her away."

Chas had guessed as much after reading Fred Carpenter's journal entries. Darcy went on talking.

"Fred loved her so much. Even then. I remember him telling me he wanted to marry her. I lost my temper when she got lost in the woods, and I told him he could have her and good luck. She was a handful at sixteen. I couldn't imagine what she'd do at eighteen.

"Then, the next morning, she just marched out of her room —well, hobbled with that broken leg—and announced she was ready to marry Fred. Right then." He shook his head, a sad smile on his lips. "I had a time convincing her to wait a couple of weeks while her leg healed. She was determined. Never did know what the rush was."

"She overheard you and Fred talking the night you rescued her. She thought you didn't want her around anymore."

"She told you that?" Chas nodded, and the other man was silent for a long time. "Things weren't the same after she married Fred. Didn't see her much at all, and then they moved away. I stayed away because she didn't seem to want me around. It makes sense now, if she thought I wanted to get rid of her.

"Fred wrote once a month, kept me up to date on how she was doing. But he never said she asked about me."

It was obvious the man cared about Danna, even if he didn't know how to show it.

"One thing I know about your sister," Chas said, "is that she hides the most important things close to her heart. She misses you. I'm sure of it."

Rob Darcy stared into the fire. "I hope you're right. I feel like I've lost too much time with her already."

"Well, let's find her, and you can tell her."

Darcy grunted in response, but Chas was only half-joking. The waiting was killing him. His feeling that Danna was in danger intensified by the minute. But the snow continued falling, and he knew he wouldn't convince the others to leave until it let up.

His inner turmoil was compounded by Darcy's presence. On one hand, he was grateful the man was here to help him find Danna. On the other hand, Rob's presence meant that Danna had someone to take her in once all this craziness was over. If the town wouldn't return her badge, it sure sounded like her brother wanted her to come back to the ranch with him. Which would be great for her, once Chas got the annulment and they'd gone their separate ways.

So why did the thought leave him empty inside?

* * *

DANNA SHIFTED on the frozen ground and brought her knees up to conserve her body heat in any way possible. Her hands had been tied again, this time behind her back. Around a tree. Tightly.

She was going to freeze to death if she couldn't get loose.

Hank Lewis's wound had been deep, and with her every move being scrutinized by the outlaw Halverson had left behind, it had been nearly impossible to snitch anything that might help her escape.

Nearly impossible. But she'd done it. She had a small knife up her sleeve, and Halverson hadn't found it when he'd brought her out here, well away from the cave, and tied her up.

She couldn't imagine why he hadn't shot her outright. Maybe he wanted her to clean Hester's wound again in the morning? Or maybe he was afraid someone would hear the report of the gunshot. When Halverson had returned to the cave, he'd been acting cagey. Like maybe he'd seen signs that someone was on their trail.

She could only hope.

Hope was all she had left.

She was alive, for now. She had to escape.

* * *

206

HOURS LATER, Danna hadn't managed to free the knife from her shirtsleeve, no matter what she tried.

She was settled in a small dip at the base of the tree, and snow had been piling up against her left side, providing insulation against the colder night air. It wasn't enough.

She was getting sleepy, but she couldn't give in to it. She knew better. How many times had Fred told her that, once a person dozed off, hypothermia would set in, and then they'd be goners? Probably dozens.

She was going to fail. She was going to die.

If only she hadn't rushed out of town alone. If only she hadn't been so careless that she'd allowed herself to get captured.

She hoped Chas would remember her with less pain than he remembered Julia. She didn't want him carrying around another load of guilt for something that wasn't his fault.

She wished she could see him one more time. If she saw him, she'd tell him she loved him. She'd never told Fred, and even though her first love had felt more like a comfortable friendship, she regretted that Fred hadn't known before he died.

She also regretted that no one had ever told her the same. All these years, she'd thought she didn't need the softer things in life, didn't need love. But she'd been wrong.

She wanted it. And if by some miracle she got out of this mess, she was going to find it. Even if she had to make herself into the most ladylike woman in the West. Wear dresses. Learn to read.

She might not have all her toes by then, but she'd make do. Danna kicked both feet against the ground to keep the blood flowing, keep them from going numb. It wasn't working.

She would try one more time. She bent her wrist to a nearly impossible angle, biting back the cry of pain that wanted to slip past her lips. There. Somehow, she'd managed to wedge the knife into her palm. Now if she could just angle it around...

The tip of the knife slipped off the frozen rope, and she almost dropped it. Her numb fingers weren't working right. The ties were so tight that her circulation was nearly cut off. She couldn't operate the knife like she needed to.

She wouldn't give up! She had to stay awake. So she began to sing. Loudly. All the hymns she could remember. The effort it took to sing sent blood pumping through her veins and made her feel more awake.

And she remembered the last time she'd been trapped on a mountain. Back then, she'd believed the words to the hymns. Believed God was faithful. Believed He would take care of her. Maybe it had been naive. Had she been blind in her faith?

Was Chas right that God didn't really care about individuals?

Just like she couldn't give up, she couldn't believe that, either.

Hadn't He kept her from freezing in this mountains once before? He'd brought Rob to her in time, and her leg had healed from the fracture. She hadn't suffered any lasting effects from her near-disaster—getting tossed from her horse. And marrying Fred had been a blessing in her life, even if she hadn't seen it as such in the beginning. Fred had taught her about being a lawman, about being a wife, even though she hadn't been a conventional one.

But what about all of the bad things that had happened lately? Fred's death, getting fired from her job?

All of a sudden, a sharp whine broke through the silent blackness and shook her from her thoughts. Danna sang louder, determined not to get eaten by a wolf, either.

The sound of a branch breaking nearby had her craning her neck to try and see where the intruder was coming from. A shape took form, a shadow darker than all the others. It grew bigger as it neared, and she prepared to kick it with her feet.

It came even nearer, and the whine turned into a yelping bark. One she recognized.

"Wrong Tree?" Her dog came nearer, right up next to Danna, and snuggled to her side, offering its furry warmth and comfort.

"Good boy," she cooed, and for the first time since Fred had brought the mutt home, she meant it. "How did you find me?"

The dog whined again, a pitiful sound.

If he'd come all the way from Calvin, was it possible someone else was out there?

"Hello?" she called out.

Nothing.

And the hope that had sprouted when she'd recognized the dog waned as precious minutes ticked by.

"Okay," she said, when it was obvious no one else was coming to her rescue. "I guess you're better than nothing."

The dog barked. He moved away, taking his warmth with him, then turned back a few feet away, as if beckoning her to follow.

"I can't, boy, I'm stuck here." She pulled against her bonds, then shook her head. Why was she reasoning with a dog?

Wrong Tree tipped his head, looking at her with a quizzical, lopsided doggy grin.

"Come here, boy," she urged, shivering as another gust of wind sliced through her clothing and made her insides quake.

For once, the animal listened to her, scooting so close she got a noseful of wet, smelly dog.

"What a good boy," she cooed. "You'll keep me alive."

Thank you, Father. Maybe with Wrong Tree, she could survive the night.

She nuzzled her face into the ruff of fur on his neck. *God, please don't let him leave again.*

With renewed hope and the bit of warmth she took from Wrong Tree, Danna tried the knife again. Her frozen fingers ached with each draw of the knife against the cords.

She might've drifted off.

The dog shifted, and cold blasted through the layers of Danna's clothing, jarring her into wakefulness.

The dog grunted and moved away, leaving only freezing air to take its place.

Had she fallen asleep? She'd been sawing against the frozen ropes binding her hands for what seemed like forever—hours, at least.

The first fingers of light showed slate-gray against the horizon. She'd survived the night. And it had stopped snowing.

A limb snapped behind her, cracking like a gunshot in the early morning stillness. Wrong Tree turned, hackles rising.

"Danna?"

CHAPTER 21

*A*t first, Danna thought she must be imagining Chas's voice. But the shock of heat when his hands touched hers was real. He untied her ropes, and her hands fell to the cold ground, free. She stretched them, rubbed at her sore shoulders, and watched as the man she loved rounded the tree and crouched in front of her.

Time seemed to suspend itself as she stared into his impossibly blue eyes, and all she could think was, *he came for me.*

"How did you find me?" she asked in a hushed voice, afraid to disturb the silence that surrounded them. Afraid he was an apparition she'd conjured with the strength of her wish to see him again.

Chas nodded to the side, toward a figure as he moved into her line of vision.

* * *

"Rob?" Chas watched Danna's brother rush to her and gently wrap her in a hug, and still he couldn't make his feet move.

Danna was alive.

She and Rob didn't speak. She jerked her thumb over her shoulder. Over the hill? Was that were the outlaws were? He could only assume she'd been captured by Lewis and left to die of exposure.

Brother and sister moved toward Chas. Rob held her tightly to his side, supporting her weight, and Chas feared that maybe she'd been hurt. He jogged to the horses, just over the crest of the hill.

He pulled down his bedroll to wrap around Danna. He was still facing his horse, trying to school his rioting emotions into submission, when he sensed her approach.

"I can't believe you came." The soft-spoken words threatened his composure. He spun to face her, needing to see for himself she was all right.

Tears sparkled in her brown eyes, and he the blanket around her shoulders and pulled her to his chest. One hand clung to her waist while the other cupped the back of her head, his fingers threading through her hair, "I never left." In his arms, she felt fragile, but he knew it was an illusion. She was strong and capable. She'd almost cut through the ropes. Another quarter inch and she'd have been able to pull free.

"We should get going and meet up with the others," Rob said quietly from where he'd already mounted up.

"Others?" Danna wiped her face with the corner of the blanket and stepped away from Chas. He didn't like being so close to the outlaws without the rest of their backup and carefully slid into the saddle.

Rob answered. "There were ten of us crazy enough to come out here after you. We got halfway up the mountain last night and had to stop because of the snow. Your husband refused to wait until morning, though. He dragged me away from a warm fire and my bedroll to get to you sooner."

Danna's upturned face revealed her surprise. When Chas reached for her, she used his boot in the stirrup to boost herself into the saddle in front of him. Chas wrapped his arms around her, unable to keep from noticing how perfectly she fit there. He didn't ever want to let her go. Careful not to bump her, he guided his horse to follow Darcy's down the same way they'd come. Danna's dog followed a little off to the side, silent, its tongue lolling out of its mouth.

"Men from town?" Danna murmured over her shoulder, giving Chas a good look at her profile. She didn't have a single bruise on her face.

"I'm afraid not. Your brother brought several hands from his ranch. And your stablehand friend brought a little gal who happened to know where this cave was located."

He read her disappointment in the tightening of her lips before she nodded and turned her face forward again.

"The girl was Katy."

Her face lit up. "You found her?"

"She found us. Just before we left town. Said her pa used to run with Lewis's gang until Hester killed him. She ran away. I think she's been afraid all this time that they'd track her down and kill her, too." His thoughts jumped from the outlaw gang killing Katy to what he'd feared the most since yesterday afternoon—them killing Danna. He hated riding away. He'd never been closer to enacting his revenge on Hank Lewis than right now.

"How'd you know where I'd gone, though?" Danna's asked.

"Bunch of men from town saw you ride out. And I ... found a passage in Fred's journal that implicated Sheriff Halverson as part of the rustling ring."

"You read the journal?"

He couldn't tell if that made her angry. He had invaded her privacy.

"I would've come anyway, once I learned you'd gone off alone."

She wiped her face with the blanket. Laughed a little. "I'm a mess."

He squeezed her waist. She had a right to cry after being out in the elements all night, after surviving Halverson.

"I was coming back to town," she admitted. "To get help."

* * *

THEY RODE into camp to find Darcy's cowboys saddling up. The scent of coffee had her stomach gurgling before Chas let her down from the horse.

A little embarrassed by her teary breakdown, Danna wiped her face with the blanket again and averted her eyes. But Chas wouldn't let her hide. He tipped her chin up, kissed her cheek gently before he propelled her to the blazing fire and urged her to sit on a log. Wrong Tree settled a few feet away.

The fire was almost painful in its warmth. Her limbs and extremities were still bone cold.

"Let's get some coffee into her," he called out, and men jumped to do his bidding.

He pulled off her gloves. Her hands were chapped but not discolored like they'd be if she had frostbite. Chas chafed her hands between his, and the warm that infused her came from more than just from the fire and his hands.

It felt like he cared.

Wrong Tree butted his head under Chas's arm, looking for attention from the man he'd liked from the beginning. Chas gave the mutt a playful push out of the way and settled close to Danna's side.

"All right. So what's the plan?" Rob squatted next to Danna's other side. He handed her a tin cup, steam rising from its rim.

The rest of the cowpokes stood near enough to listen without intruding on their conversation.

"The plan?" she echoed.

"You mean to tell me you weren't working on a way to round up those outlaws while you were tied up?" Rob's voice held both a teasing quality and a note of seriousness.

"I'm sorry." She shook her head, feeling as if it were stuffed with cotton. "I'm not thinking real clearly yet." She drank a big gulp of the coffee, hoping it would help.

"You didn't think we came all the way up here just to save your hide, did you? We're going to help you bring in those outlaws."

She risked a glance at Chas, who was staring hard into the fire, his jaw tight. Had that been his intention? She couldn't tell. But she had a job to do, even if she didn't have the official title, and if these cowboys were willing to help, she'd be foolish not to take them up on it.

"I saw four men in the cave last night, plus Halverson. Two are injured. The way they were talking, there might be another man, but I never saw him."

"Who are the two injured?"

She couldn't look at Chas when she told them. "Hank Lewis and the man who was shot during the robbery."

Chas stiffened. "How bad is Lewis?"

She shrugged. "He'd lost a lot of blood. The gunshot was in his upper thigh. He was alive when I got done patching him up, but I don't know if he made it through the night."

"You patched him up?" Chas vaulted to his feet. His face and neck had gone red, making his freckles disappear. "After what he's done? He murdered my—" He cut himself off, but she could still hear the words, as if he'd said them aloud. *He murdered my love.* The reminder burned a hole in her gut.

"He killed my brother and his wife," Chas said in a slightly more controlled voice. She could still hear the undercurrents of anger in his tone. "He doesn't deserve to live."

She'd known his temper would blow when he found out she'd helped Lewis.

"I'm not a judge," she replied. "I can't make the decision whether he should live or die. Plus, they had a gun on me. If I refused to treat him, Halverson would have shot me."

Chas's face paled, all the red seeping out of his cheeks, but he still stared at her as if she was a stranger to him. Slowly, he shook his head, then ran a hand from forehead to chin. The action wiped all the expression from his face, leaving only a hard-set jaw and empty eyes behind. "So, what do we do now?"

Rob shifted in his crouch, clearly uncomfortable to have witnessed their conversation. "We can assume they've figured out Danna's disappeared. We need to move fast."

After a moment of tense silence, Chas said what was on all their minds. "If Halverson knows his cover is blown, he's going to want us dead."

Rob's hands all murmured their agreement. They all looked to her, and their gazes were like a weight on her chest. She'd wanted this responsibility?

Chas turned to her, one hand massaging his neck. He hadn't looked her in the eye since he'd blown up about Lewis. "Tell us what to do, boss lady. You wanted deputies. Now you've got 'em."

* * *

DANNA TOOK command of the situation, like Chas had known she could. She sent four of Rob's men to scout for anyone who might have left the camp after the snow had stopped. She instructed them to fire a sequence of shots if they caught the men or needed help. She ordered Will Katy to stay put and to keep her ornery dog tied up with them. That left five of them to figure out a way to approach the outlaw's campsite without getting shot.

Anger simmered in his gut. Hank Lewis was close. This was his chance to enact his revenge.

He still couldn't fathom that Danna had doctored the man. If it would have been him, he'd have let Lewis bleed out. It was an easier death than the man deserved.

"We came in from the south last night, and there wasn't much cover at all." Danna seemed to have regained her equilibrium. She paced a tight ring around the fire, alternately clasping her hands in front of her and waving them around when she spoke. She was adorable.

"Is there another way into the cave?" Rob asked as he checked his weapon.

Danna shook her head. "The inside walls are solid rock. I couldn't see any other way in or out, and believe me, I looked."

"From what I could tell, we'd have the most cover approaching from the east," one of the cowboys said.

"Or we could hang a rope, and someone could shimmy down to get to the cave," a second cowboy countered.

It was risky. Chas hadn't gotten much of a glimpse of the cave through the trees this morning, as Danna had been tied pretty far from the entrance, but he'd seen enough to know it was a sheer drop of thirty feet.

"Danna could do it," Chas said. "She likes to climb things. Like roofs." He couldn't find the humor in it today.

He glanced at Danna and tension arced between them.

"I guess you never grow out of some things," said Rob, shattering the moment.

Danna averted her face, but then she turned to Chas. "Do you have Fred's journal with you? And a pencil?"

He'd thought she would be angry that he'd violated her husband's memory, but did what she always seemed to do when faced with a situation that needed to be handled—she put aside her emotions to work.

He retrieved the book and a stub of a pencil from his saddlebag and brought them to Danna. She flipped to a blank page near the end of the book and completed a quick sketch of the area around the cave, including trees, rocks, larger impressions in the hills. Her memory was impressive.

She tapped a corner of the page. "If your two hands come from this direction, and I slip down from above the cave, you"—she nodded to Rob—"and Chas can approach from here." She indicated a thick stand of trees. She shook her head. "I think this is the best we can do. Y'all ready?"

She didn't wait for an answer as she strode to her horse and swung up into the saddle, confident they'd follow. Chas hopped up behind Danna. It didn't take long to retrace their route to where they'd found Danna in the woods. The storm clouds had dissipated after sunrise, and now the sunlight sparkled off every surface, almost blinding in its intensity.

Shortly before they reached the place where Danna had been tied, Rob and Chas broke away from the other two men to circle around the other side of the little valley.

Letting Danna down from his horse and watching her slip away into the snowy mountain was difficult for him. Especially when she'd come so close to death the night before. Chas clamped his teeth together to keep from calling her back.

He had to remember how capable she was. And she was armed this time, with one of Rob's pistols.

Chas and Rob moved quietly into place, hobbling the horses a fair piece away, in case gunfire erupted. They snuck through the winter-white landscape together.

Not as comfortable as Rob was at sneaking, Chas followed the other man and tried to stay behind barren trees or outcroppings of rocks. Once, he even crawled in the snow, so as not to be seen.

When the mouth of the cave was in sight, Rob slowed his pace. He found a spot he liked and pointed out a covering of brush not far away, mouthing instructions for Chas to go over there and wait for Danna's signal.

Lying there with his belly wet and cold wasn't Chas's idea of a good time, but he did as he was told. He wouldn't endanger Danna as he had the other night. Sighting his rifle, he drew a bead on the cave, black against the white landscape.

In minutes, a length of rope unfurled down the ledge above the cave. He saw Danna's dark head at the top of the cliff, and then her backside as she began to lower herself hand over hand, right down the wall of rock.

Chas's heart drummed in his temples at her being so exposed. If any of the outlaws were in the woods, they'd have an easy shot. He sent up a desperate prayer that no one with nefarious intentions would be near enough to do her harm.

For a moment, his breath cut off, and he thought he was going to get caught up in a memory of those few moments before Julia and Joseph died, but instead of the images he expected, all he could see was Danna hanging off that dangling rope, her life in the balance.

After she was out in the open so long he was beginning to feel sick to his stomach, she braced her legs against the rock wall and raised one hand in a prearranged signal.

"Halverson!" Rob roared, and Chas jumped, even though he'd been expecting it. "We've got you surrounded. Toss your weapons outside the cave and walk out with your hands up!"

No sound emerged from the cave. The woods were eerily quiet without the normal sounds of birds and small animals moving about, as if even they knew something was happening. The snow muffled everything, but Chas knew the layer of pure white could be hiding death and danger.

Danna fisted her hand and pumped it once in the air—the signal they were waiting for—and a voice from across the clearing called out this time. "We know you're in there, and we'll wait you out."

Still no answer, no movement. Had the men discovered Danna was missing and left?

Chas watched breathlessly as Danna found footholds on the

rocky cliff face and leaned until she was nearly horizontal. Her braid hung down like a pendulum as she peered into the cave. A shot rang out, and she scrambled a few feet up the rope.

His heart pounded erratically.

There was at least one man in the cave. Chas squinted, cursing the bright sun glinting off every surface, as he tried to determine if she'd been hit. He couldn't see any blood on her face or neck. That was a good sign, right?

"Stop worrying so much," came Rob's voice, this time so quiet, Chas knew it was meant for his ears alone. "She knows what she's doing."

That might be true, but he didn't know if he could accept the risk. Chas knew how quickly a life could be snuffed out, and Danna was putting herself in danger. And she did it every single day.

"You have to let it go." Rob said. "Her life is in the Lord's hands. If He wants to take her home today, He will, and nothing we can do will stop it."

But I need her, Chas wanted to cry out, and he would've, if he could've wrenched his mouth open.

If only Danna had a safer job. Of course, just living out here in the West was more dangerous than his parents' home in Boston. But he couldn't picture her living in his parents' world, with their society parties and boring lives. If she sat down to tea with his mother, Danna would likely send the older woman into a swoon.

He loved her the way she was.

He loved the marshal. He just didn't know if he could handle her dangerous job. He was so afraid of watching her die, like he had Julia. And although Julia's death had devastated him, Danna's would rip him to shreds. Because he loved her. Not the love of a childhood friend, but the deep, abiding love of the woman he wanted to spend his life with.

As they watched, a lone man walked out of the cave, arms raised to the sky.

"It could be a trap," Chas said to Rob. "A distraction to get us out in the open so they can shoot us."

He nodded. "My men'll be careful."

Chas watched as the other two cowhands came into sight on the far side of the clearing. He kept his rifle aimed at the cave, waiting. His finger tapped the trigger, nervous anticipation mounting.

Nothing.

Rob's men reached the outlaw and yanked his arms behind his back.

"How many more are there?" one of the cowboys demanded.

"Just the two hurt ones."

One of those was Hank Lewis.

Chas dared to go out in the open. He approached the cave. He had to know if Lewis was alive. Danna's boots scraped against rock as he passed beneath her.

He slipped in to the cool darkness, keeping close to the wall, and let his eyes adjust. The kid sat against the farthest wall, unconscious, though a gun lay near his thigh.

Lewis was there, too. Unarmed, from the looks of it, lying prone on the ground.

Which meant there was nothing to stop Chas from killing him. Chas stood over the man who'd taken so much from him, and pointed his pistol at Lewis's heart.

* * *

DANNA DROPPED to the ground as Chas ran into the cave.

Foolish man. They didn't even know if the outlaw was telling the truth. Halverson could be lying in wait inside.

She rushed in after him, foolish herself. She had to stop Chas before he did something he'd regret.

Her eyes adjusted, and she saw Chas standing over the prostrate Lewis, his pistol aimed. His hand shook, but the tension in his shoulders told her everything she needed to know.

He was ready to shoot the man that had killed two people he loved.

Heart in her throat, she started toward him.

"You deserve to die," Chas said.

"Chas."

He didn't acknowledge her.

She prayed he wouldn't shoot. She'd have to arrest him if he did.

Lewis didn't respond. She was nearly there, but from this distance, she couldn't tell if he was even conscious.

As she drew near, she saw that Chas's whole body was trembling.

"Chas."

This time he turned his head, and even from the side, she could tell he was struggling with himself.

Please, God, don't let him do this. Slowly, feeling as if she were swimming through molasses, she touched Chas's arm.

And he let her push it down until his weapon pointed at the floor.

CHAPTER 22

*T*hey rode into town to a hero's welcome, the three surviving outlaws strapped to the saddles of three horses.

Rob's men had made the difference. They were experienced operators and had tracked and captured Halverson and Big Tim. If Danna'd had men like them to help her, she wouldn't have lost her job in the first place.

And the best part was, Rob's cowhands had agreed to go with her to track down the last outlaw, the one the kid had admitted was probably guarding the rustled cattle. Before they could go after the cattle, they had to get the outlaws they'd already captured locked up in the jail.

Big Tim wouldn't shut up and had revealed that it'd been a chance sighting Danna riding in the ravines that had made them attempt to get rid of her. They'd caused the stampede that had nearly killed Chas and Danna.

Earlier in the day, Danna had realized that Halverson's horse created a crescent-shaped hoofmark. She'd been riding behind the animal when she'd noticed it. Her husband had been killed by a man who'd sworn to uphold the law. She would do her best to prove it to the judge when he came to town, and to see Halverson receive what he was due—the noose. To her surprise, people lined the streets and clapped as they walked their mounts through town to the jail. Several people called out to her, and one child even cheered and called her "the marshal."

It sounded like they respected her, or at least respected the job she'd done, bringing down the bank robbers.

But too late.

Castlerock waited with Albert Hyer, one of the other town council members, on the steps of the jailhouse.

"Where's my money?' he demanded before she'd reined in.

She wanted to tell him off so badly that she had to grit her teeth to keep the words inside.

"The marshal's brother has custody of it," Chas said, pulling his mount to a halt next to her and jerking his head to indicate Rob. "Kindly thank the marshal, and you can take your cash right over to your bank." His voice brooked no argument.

Why did he keep calling her that? She hadn't gone after the robbers to reclaim her job, and it wasn't likely the council would agree to give it back to her. She hadn't been able to do the job alone, after all.

Castlerock looked a mite green, but he uttered the words, though it was obvious by his demeanor he didn't want to. "Thank you, Miz Carpenter."

"That's Mrs. O'Grady or Miss Marshal to you," Chas said.

What? She shook her head even as Castlerock stalked off. The banker's words were a reminder that her marriage was almost over. But what was Chas's statement about? He'd been the one ready to go to Cheyenne for an annulment.

She looked away from him and waved to Katy, who rode in the back of the pack of riders, and pointed to her room above the jail. Danna had offered to let the girl stay with her as long as she needed to. She remembered the girl's questions from before. Danna also remembered how Fred had taken care of a similar teen who was lost and alone...and she determined that she would make Katy her family, like a little sister.

Rob tied off his mount at the hitching post across from the jail. She needed to talk to him, as well, to find out why he'd come for her. Maybe she'd get her brother back, too.

But she wanted a husband...a particular husband.

Will joined their group in front of the jail, but he ignored the group of businessmen. She warmed at his loyalty. "I'll take your mounts over to the livery, Marshal."

She dismounted and handed the reins over to him, but she didn't let him leave without an impulsive hug. Without his help, Chas and Rob might not have reached her in time.

Hyer cleared his throat and stepped forward to the edge of the boardwalk. "Mrs. O'Grady, we'd like to reinstate you as marshal. We made a mistake in firing you."

Her heart thudded in her ears. It seemed too good to be true.

"Where's Parrott? And Shipley? Did they agree to this, too?"

Hyer shook his head. Castlerock looked away. It was Hyer who spoke.

"After yer husband made such a passionate plea for deputies, several people came forward and admitted they'd been threatened not to help ya do your job. Parrott and Shipley ran outta town pretty quick. A coupla fellas went after 'em. We didn't have no part of their plan, and we want ya back as marshal."

She looked to Castlerock, who nodded. He still looked green, but his mouth was set and he didn't argue.

"You've got some loyal friends," said Hyer. "They made quite a case for you yesterday evening,"

She shot a look to Chas and mouthed *they?* But he shrugged.

"We've got three men who've agreed to work as your deputies." He listed three men who'd worked for Fred "And a possible fourth, as well. We've agreed to pay them a salary—not much, mind you—and they'll answer to you."

That would change everything. Make her life a whole lot easier. She wouldn't have to be in charge of the whole town, all day and all night. She'd have some help, men she knew she could trust.

Chas stepped to her side. "You should take the job back," he said quietly. "You deserve it. You'll do a good job."

She looked up at him, her hat brim shading her eyes and hopefully hiding them from the watchful gazes of her bosses. She could read the truth on his face, that he wanted her to take the job, and that he couldn't stay.

Not with a wife who had such a dangerous job. They needed to have a serious conversation, but this wasn't the place or the time. She looked at the councilmen and nodded. "Calvin is my home, and I'm proud to protect it."

She shook their hands, and they left. Rob's men were already untying the outlaws. She went to the jail to get their cells ready, leaving her temporary husband behind.

* * *

CHAS MEANDERED DOWN THE BOARDWALK, vaguely heading toward the hotel, his saddlebags over one shoulder.

Danna disappeared into the jail to lock up the three healthy outlaws and Hank Lewis. She wasn't willing to take the chance of putting Lewis at the doc's office, not after what had happened with Halverson springing the kid. He'd followed, but she didn't need his help, not with all these men available.

She'd looked exhausted. He hadn't wanted to add to her strain by trying to have a serious discussion after the night and the day she'd had.

So he'd slipped out, figuring she wouldn't even notice he was missing.

What was he supposed to do now?

When he'd become a deputy, the arrangement had been beneficial to both of them. He'd needed her help conquering the Wyoming terrain. She'd needed his support.

Now that she had all these other men to help her out, and now that his case was wrapping up, he was free to go.

But he didn't want to. The realization was powerful.

He loved his wife, and he didn't want to leave Calvin.

But how could he convince Danna not to go through with the annulment?

* * *

EVENING WAS FALLING as Danna and Rob settled in to her room above the jail. Katy had pled exhaustion and was already asleep in Danna's bed.

"You did a good job today, Miss Marshal," Rob said, borrowing Chas's nickname. He sipped from his coffee mug.

Danna waved off his compliment.

"I'm serious. I was proud to ride with you."

"I wish you could stay longer," Danna said. Rob was leaving at first light, headed back to his ranch.

Rob leaned back in Fred's old chair, his lean form stretched out, legs turned toward the center of the room. "That's saying something, coming from someone who didn't want to see me for years."

A flush stole up her cheeks. "I wanted to see you. I just...I thought..."

"That I'd gotten so mad I stopped loving my own sister?"

She looked down at her hands clasped on the table. "I heard you and Fred that night. I think you must've thought I was out from the pain or exposure, I don't know. You said..."

"I said that Fred could have you and good luck. I didn't mean it."

"No?"

"No. And the only reason I let you marry him was because I knew how crazy he was about you."

Her face hot once again, Danna scratched at a scar in the tabletop. "I miss him, but..."

"But you've fallen in love with your deputy."

She nodded miserably. "The marriage was only to appease the town council. We'd planned to have it annulled on the grounds that we were coerced into it. He's... still in love with someone else."

"You sure about that? The man was sure fired up to come to your rescue."

She closed her eyes briefly so he wouldn't see the hope that unfurled in her heart. "There's something else I wanted to ask you. Chas said Fred had made notes about Halverson's involvement in his journal. Would you read it to me? I want to know if there are any more clues as to why Parrott and Shipley would pay off the men in town."

* * *

LATE INTO THE NIGHT, Rob closed the journal and placed it on the table. Danna wiped tears from her eyes, knowing Fred had given his life for this little town she loved so much. Knowing how much he'd loved her.

Rob stood to go and surprised her with an embrace.

"We won't go so long without seeing each other again," he said. "You and that one." He nodded to Katy, asleep in Danna's bed and softly snoring. "Come for Christmas. You've got enough help now to take a few days off." He paused for a moment, his eyes scrutinizing her face. "And bring your husband, too."

CHAPTER 23

he timid knock came soon after Danna had descended from her room to the jail, leaving a sleeping Katy upstairs. Braced to face her husband, Danna was surprised when the door swung open to admit several women.

"Good morning, Mrs. Kendrick. Mrs. Stoll, how are you? And Anna! What are you doing in town so early?"

"It's Martha, dear."

"Marianne." Several more women crowded into the jail behind the others, although all of them stayed a careful distance away from the cells and the rough-looking outlaws within.

"What—what are you all doing here?"

"We brought you some breakfast." One of the women held up a cloth-covered basket.

"And jam." Someone else pressed two jars of ruby-red preserves into Danna's hands.

Their smiles surrounded her, warming her. But... "Why?"

Martha Stoll stepped forward. "Young lady, I know I've complained about your dog, but you've done a fine job as marshal, and you should know it."

"We want to thank you, Marshal," came a voice from the back. "For sticking with the job, even when our men weren't a bit of help to you."

Danna didn't know what to say. She'd thought the women had never liked her, but this outpouring of goodwill said just the opposite.

A second soft knock came and the door opened to reveal Corrine, who froze in the open portal, a bundle of baby in her arms. The women closest to her turned their heads away; one even went so far as to sniff and put her nose in the air.

"Oh," Corrine said quietly, her eyes widening and a flush creeping into her cheeks. "I'll go—"

"Corrine!" Danna moved through the throng of women and grasped her friend's forearm, pulling her to the side of the room. "I was going to come see you this morning. I found out that Brent was working with Fred on the rustler case. Actually, Rob found out. It was all in the journal."

A whisper rustled among the women. Maybe it was best they'd all heard. She couldn't bear for her friend to be slighted when her husband had actually done something good for a change.

Corrine's eyes filled with tears. "Was?"

Putting an arm around her friend's shoulders, Danna led her to the desk chair. "I'm so sorry, Corrine. One of the outlaws told us he'd been killed. Helping Fred. Two of my new deputies went out to recover his body early this morning."

Corrine began to sniffle, but these weren't the sobs Danna had expected. A hand pushed a lacy handkerchief at Corrine, and she accepted it without looking up.

"Honey." A buttercup-yellow skirt swished around Danna's desk, and Mrs. Burnett, the preacher's wife, put a comforting arm around Corrine's shoulder. "That man tried his best for you. He really did." Danna wasn't so sure about that, but the other woman was still talking. "You should be proud he died helping Marshal Fred."

Corrine nodded, still pressing the handkerchief to her eyes with one hand while cradling the baby with the other. Suddenly she looked up with her teary eyes. "I forgot I came in here to tell you that I saw your deputy...er...your husband at the stagecoach office, buying a ticket."

Danna's face flamed. "We're not really married. It was all a show for the town council. We're getting an annulment."

"But you love him, don't you?" Marianne asked.

"Yes," she said, because she couldn't deny it anymore.

"Then you should fight for him." Corrine gripped Danna's arm. "Do whatever you have to do to make him want to stay."

Danna looked around at the expectant faces around her. She took a deep breath. "I'm going to need your help."

"All of us?"

"All of you."

* * *

SHAKING WITH NERVES, the skirts of her mama's blue dress swirling around her feet, Danna made her way down the boardwalk.

She felt foolish with this dress on and her hair put up as if she were attending a fancy ball. Was it too late to run back to her room?

"Miss Marshal, Miss Marshal!" Young Cody Billings ran up to her on the boardwalk, waving both arms. "Them deputies brought back those dirty council members. They're comin' to th' jail now."

She altered her direction to meet the deputies, grateful for any reprieve from facing Chas. She wanted to convince him to stay in Calvin, and trying to be feminine had seemed like a good idea until she'd seen the stranger in the looking glass. But with a roomful of expectant women behind her, she couldn't back out of the plan.

She was getting lots of stares on the street.

The lead deputy reined in his horse, eyes wide as if he didn't recognize her. He tipped his hat to her, then seemed to change his mind and took it off. "M-Miss Marshal. We got 'em." He waved to Shipley and Parrott, riding with bound hands between two other deputies.

"Good job. I've taken to carrying the jail keys with me, but I'll turn them over to you for a bit." She took a deep breath. "I have to go over to the train station and settle some business."

She'd stepped around his horse and was headed across the street when Shipley dropped to the ground. His hands wrapped around her neck and choked off her air.

She tried to break free, but he was strong and determined. She swung her elbow back and caught Shipley in the midsection. She heard the distinct sound of fabric ripping.

* * *

CHAS'S HEART raced as he left the stagecoach office and headed toward the jail and a much-needed talk with his wife.

He stopped a moment to breathe deeply of the crisp Wyoming air. He did love it here.

Loved the weathered buildings. The bustling activity on the streets. Even the crooked boardwalk that took him to the jailhouse.

Except, there was something different about Calvin since he'd headed into the mountains yesterday. There was a peace in the air, a sense that the town was safe, wholesome.

He was halfway to the jail when he saw the scuffle, a man choking a woman in a pretty blue gown. He was already moving toward them when he recognized Danna.

Two deputies moved to help her, reaching for Shipley.

He saw it unfolding before his eyes but was helpless to run faster. From horseback, Parrott pulled something from his boot.

A derringer. The man had a gun and was using his rope-bound hands to point it straight at Danna.

Chas drew and fired his pistol before he even blinked.

Parrott screamed in anger as Chas's bullet struck his wrist. His weapon dropped to the ground. Chas approached on shaking legs to find Danna with one pretty knee in Shipley's back.

"Why?" she asked, still panting from exertion. "Why did you do all this? Have Fred killed? Why did you hate us so much?"

The man beneath her remained silent.

"You've ruined it all," Parrott spat, as one of the other deputies took him roughly off his horse. "Your husband was eliminated because he started asking too many nosy questions. You were only appointed because you weren't supposed to figure any of it out."

Danna stood and let her deputy haul Shipley to his feet. The man looked beaten, defeated.

Chas approached, met her eyes, tried to offer a tiny smile.

Danna turned to Shipley. "I don't understand."

"We had a plan," Shipley said, voice nearly a monotone.

"Shipley..." Parrott warned. "Don't say another word."

"Parrott thought he could run the smaller ranchers out of the area if they lost enough cattle. He brought in a gang and had a few unsavory cowhands of his own."

"Shipley." Parrott lunged for his fellow town council member, but the deputy who had hold of his arm yanked him back.

"C'mon," the deputy said. "We'll Doc to patch up your hands, and then you're going to jail with the rest of 'em."

Shipley continued as if Parrott hadn't spoken at all. "It was unfortunate that Marshal Fred and Brent Jackson had to die, but they started asking questions of the wrong people. They got too close.

"With Halverson on our side, we planned to start extorting money from the businesses in town. We've heard of other...businessmen making good money that way."

"The only problem was Castlerock. He may be a selfish lout, but he's arrow straight."

"So you set up the robbery," Danna whispered, "thinking his bank would fold if the money was never recovered."

"It would've been best if Castlerock had left town, yes."

Chas couldn't believe the man spoke so calmly of the criminal enterprise they had masterminded.

"And the payoffs?" Chas asked. "So the men wouldn't help Danna?"

"At first no one wanted to work with a woman. They were glad to take the money. After that, we threatened to reveal they'd been bribed. They feared they'd ruin their standing in town, and that's how we kept them quiet."

"Marshal, I'm going to take him in now." The deputy stepped forward.

"Have him write out his confession first," she murmured. "For the judge when he gets to town."

With the mess sorted, Chas took Danna's arm and swung her up onto the boardwalk and out of the dusty street.

She looked up at him, her dark eyes questioning. She was something else, with her dark curls falling out of the coif, dirt smudged across her chin, one sleeve missing and a tear in the hem of her gown. He'd never seen anything so beautiful.

He wanted to sweep her into his arms, but he wasn't sure that gesture would be welcome.

"Hello," he said instead. "I was coming to talk to you."

Danna looked down at herself, and when she looked up again, he could see the distress on her face.

"You all right?" he asked, wondering if she was shaken up. "He didn't hurt you, did he?"

"No, that's not it," she said, shaking her head. With a tiny sigh, she tried to smooth away the wrinkles and dirt from her skirt. Then she seemed to realize her sleeve was torn, and her shoulders slumped. "I guess I'm not meant to be a lady."

Her words confused him, as did the sudden tears that sprang to her eyes.

She looked down again, fingered her dusty skirt. "I had this grand plan," she whispered, "to show you I could be a lady as fine as your friends back in Boston. I put on this dress, let them put perfume on me—"

"You do smell nice."

"I let Marianne Kendrick do my hair." She fingered the hair that had fallen down around her ears. "And Merritt Harding promised she'd teach me to read. I thought I could impress you."

"You did all that for me?"

"Yes." She swallowed hard, and for a moment he was afraid she might cry. "Only..."

"Only, you had to do your job," he said, busting with pride.

Tired of looking at the crown of her head, he chucked her on the chin, waited until her luminous eyes met his gaze. "I won't complain if you want to wear a dress, but I like you fine in your trousers and vest."

Murmurs from nearby interrupted everything else he wanted to say. He looked around to find several townspeople on the streets, watching his interaction with Danna and not bothering to hide their curiosity.

"Can we talk someplace private?"

She nodded. "Katy went home with Corrine for the day, to help her take care of Ellie, so the room should be empty for now."

He tucked her hand into the crook of his arm so he could escort her home. Home. He liked the sound of that.

And he was dying to kiss her, but he didn't want to do it in front of the whole town.

She was unusually quiet, until they reached the staircase leading to her room. She hopped up on the first step and whirled to face him, pressing both palms against his chest. "Are you leaving town or not?"

They were out of sight of the main thoroughfare, so he did what he'd wanted to do since he'd caught sight of her on the street.

The extra height of that first stair put her face a few inches above his, but it was easy enough to grab her waist and draw her in for a kiss. A sweet, deep kiss, to tell her everything he wanted to say.

And from the way she kissed him back, it sure seemed like she returned his sentiments.

With a last, lingering touch of his lips, he joined her on that first step and pressed her close, her cheek against his shoulder. "I'm not leaving," he said, voice husky.

"Hmm," she hummed, seemingly content to stay resting against him. He couldn't get enough of having her close like this.

Then, abruptly, she pushed away from him, eyes a little wild.

She took a step backward, moving up another step. Putting distance between them. His hands felt empty, so he braced them on both sides of the stair railing. "But you were at the stagecoach office. Corrine saw you at the ticket window."

He groaned. "Are there really no secrets in this town?"

Danna crossed her arms. She looked so vulnerable with her mussed hair and dress, her eyes shining like they were filled with tears.

"Darlin'." He purposely lengthened out the endearment, his voice a soft drawl. "I'm here to stay."

She blinked, looking a bit like a sleepy owl. "To stay," she repeated. "But..."

"I was inquiring as to the cost of a *pair* of tickets," Chas said slowly, "So I could take my wife to Boston. I thought we might go on a honeymoon trip."

She blinked. "You're going home?"

He nodded. "If you'll go with me."

"To make peace with your parents?"

"It's past time, wouldn't you say?"

Then she frowned. "But the annulment. We agreed."

He couldn't help the grin that quirked his lips. "Maybe you misunderstood my kiss. I thought it was pretty clear I'd changed my mind, but perhaps it wasn't." He kissed her again. And again, trying to show her everything he'd felt since he'd realized she'd gone after the outlaws alone, everything he wanted to share with her now. When they parted, he spoke into that crown of beautiful hair. "Just so there's no misunderstanding, I love you. I want you to be my wife forever."

"I love you, too," she whispered. "I'm glad I got the chance to tell you."

She squeezed his middle, burrowed her face into his chest. "I almost hate to ask, but...will you mind terribly if I'm still the marshal?"

"I won't mind. I'm going to talk to the town council—what's left of it—and see if they'll let you keep me on as deputy, I think we work pretty well together."

"You won't mind me having a dangerous job? Getting into trouble sometimes?"

"Not as long as I'm there to help get you out of it." He paused, but this seemed like the right moment. "And in the future, if we want to buy a homestead, you can teach me to ranch."

EPILOGUE

CHRISTMAS EVE

*C*has woke in the gray of early morning to the sound of someone getting violently sick.

He touched the space in the bed beside him only to find it empty. "Danna?"

She hummed from across the room—the chamber pot?—and retched again.

He vaulted out of bed, the wooden floor freezing against his bare feet, misjudged the distance, and banged his shin against Katy's cot. He bit off a cry and sensed the teen sit up in the semi-darkness.

"Wha's goin' on?" Katy mumbled.

"Sorry, kid." This apartment had never been meant for three people. He couldn't even imagine how Danna and her first husband had managed in the small space.

He heard rustling sounds, like Danna was moving. "I'm fine. It's nothing."

He wasn't sure he believed her. Those noises hadn't sounded like *nothing*.

"I promised I'd stop by the saloon early to assess the damage from last night's brawl," she said. "I'll catch up with you in a while."

Before he could get one word of protest out, the door opened, sending a shaft of morning light into the room. It closed just as quickly, plunging the room back into shadows.

Why would Danna rush out like that, right after she'd been sick?

Suspicions swirled. He sat on the edge of the bed, trying to make sense of it and still groggy from the split-second waking.

"She sick again?" Katy asked.

"Again?"

There was a beat of silence from the girl. "Uh—"

Chas threw open the curtains over the bed—the same window he and Danna had escaped from those months ago. The first rays of sunlight illuminated Katy's tousled head and guilt-filled expression.

He raised one eyebrow and waited her out.

She groaned and put her head in her hands. "I guess you were having breakfast with the town council that morning."

The monthly meeting had been one of the first things Danna had delegated to him. Meeting with the three-man council kept the marshal and her deputies apprised of their priorities, and things had run fairly smoothly of late. The banker Castlerock had even come to appreciate Danna and her deputies.

"She asked me not to tell you, said it was probably some kind of bug."

Obviously not, if she was sick again today.

Katy peeked through her fingers. "I don't mean to intrude in y'alls business," she said softly. "It's just..."

"The room is too small for all of us," he finished.

It wasn't a new problem. Both she and Danna were secretive and embarrassed when it came to their womanly time. He'd been hard-pressed to think of a hiding place for Christmas gifts for both females and had called in a favor from the mercantile owner to hold their gifts at the store until later today. The three of them couldn't cook a meal or relax properly in the evenings without bumping elbows or stepping on each other's toes.

In the autumn, he'd pressed Danna about finding a homestead, like she'd mentioned in those crazy first days they'd been married. She'd claimed she wasn't ready.

But he'd wondered—quite a few times—if she meant *he* wasn't ready. His horseback riding skills had improved markedly, but he didn't know anything about farming, raising crops or animals, carving a living out of the land.

Things had been good, if crowded, in their little family. Oh, they'd had bumps along the way. He and Danna occasionally knocked heads, and the independent Katy had a teenage temper tantrum every once in awhile.

Was it possible Danna wasn't as content as she seemed?

Katy pulled a shawl over her nightdress, making no move to get up. School had let out for a week for Christmas, and he supposed she was in no rush to get around.

"If she doesn't want you to know she's in the family way, you should probably pretend you didn't hear anything this morning," Katy suggested.

Suddenly, his ears were full of rushing wind.

"In the family way?" he asked weakly.

Katy's eyes grew big. "I mean—she didn't tell me she was expecting. It's just a guess."

A conclusion he hadn't jumped to.

But the girl could be right.

And if she was, why hadn't Danna told him?

Did she even know?

She'd been raised by her grandfather and a much-older brother. Had the topic of conception ever been broached? Then again, didn't being raised on a ranch mean one saw animals in all stages of childbearing?

"I'm sorry," Katy mumbled. Her expression revealed genuine distress.

"Nothing to be sorry for," he said. "This apartment is just too small."

And now he had one great big reason to find them a new place to live.

* * *

DANNA TAPPED the pencil she held against the school desk. Her eyes watered from the smoky fire Merritt was lighting in the classroom stove.

Or maybe it was more of the overflow of emotions she'd been experiencing over the past week and a half.

For so long, she'd thought something was wrong with her. That she couldn't have children.

Apparently, she'd been wrong. And after a visit with doc earlier in the week had confirmed her suspicions, she'd been constantly near tears with joy. And a little bit of fear.

Would she be a good mother? What would Chas think? Would he expect her to resign her position as marshal?

All the riot of emotions had kept her from telling Chas. She needed to do things right. And dissolving into a blubbering mess wasn't the way she wanted to handle it.

But this morning had proved that she needed to tell him. She hated getting sick, hated even more having others witness it.

"Is everything all right?"

At Merritt's question, Danna glanced up from the primer on the school desk. Her spectacles slipped, and she nudged them up the bridge of her nose with one knuckle. She was wedged into one of the students' desks, the same way she had been every morning this autumn.

The schoolmarm had generously given of her time for an hour each morning before classes started, often setting up the classroom for the day and of late, lighting the stove while Danna worked on reading.

She'd made more progress than she'd thought she would and had already progressed to the third-level book. Merritt was a good teacher.

But right at this moment, she stared at Danna with unabashed curiosity. "You've been distracted all morning."

Danna flushed, sure all the emotional turmoil she was feeling showed in her expression. "It's not—"

The door opened on a gust of wind, and Penny Castlerock blew in. Penny had made a habit of coming to visit the last ten or fifteen minutes of Danna's time. She gave lessons, too, in styling Danna's hair.

"You look terrible," the young woman said upon glancing at Danna. "Are you sick?"

Danna dropped her pencil and put both hands over her cheeks to hide the hot blush that rose. "No." Not really.

Penny's sharp eyes didn't miss a thing. They narrowed on Danna. "Are you—?"

"I can't say." Danna stood from the desk so quickly that she bumped it, sending the pencil flying to the floor. "I have to go."

Penny was grinning as Danna passed her on the way to the door. It blew open in the brisk wind, but she caught it before it banged against the wall.

"What?" asked Merritt.

"She's expecting," Penny murmured as the door snapped closed behind Danna.

She needed to find Chas. And tell him before anyone else figured out her secret.

Her stomach started roiling again as she checked in at the jailhouse. Deputy Cal Newton sat behind the desk. No Chas.

"What do you mean he went to the livery?" Before he could answer, she said, "Never mind." She left the wide-eyed deputy behind and went to the stable to find Will.

He was just as clueless as the deputy had been, but he saddled Danna's horse, and she rode out.

She reined in her horse at the edge of town.

It was pointless, she knew. Chas could've headed in any direction. She didn't even know what his errand was. If a crime had been committed, wouldn't her other deputy know about it? And why hadn't he come to find her? He knew she'd be at the schoolhouse. And it was Christmas Eve. What possible errand could he have, today?

The secrecy bothered her.

Which was ironic, considering she was keeping a secret from him, too.

She tucked her chin into the lapel of her slicker, vacillating between returning to the apartment or finding further distraction in town.

And then she saw Chas, riding in from the east. She turned her mount to meet him.

"What're you doing out in the cold?" he called out before she'd even come near.

What a funny thing to say. She narrowed her eyes, but his expression didn't reveal any clues.

He'd become a much more accomplished horseman and now reined his mount before quickly sliding down. He reached up and helped her from her horse. "Is there something you'd like to come clean about?"

Heat rushed into her face. "You know? About the baby?" This wasn't the way she'd wanted to tell him. She tipped her face up but couldn't read his expression at all. Was he angry she hadn't told him directly?

"I didn't suspect until Katy said something."

"Are you angry?"

His eyes glittered. "Are you?"

She shook her head. "Of course not. I was... surprised when Doc told me. After being married to Fred for so long..." She blushed again, because she didn't know if Chas really liked hearing about her first husband, though he'd always listened when she'd spoken of Fred.

He reached out for her hand. His clasp was cool and dry.

"Surprised, and... happy?" he asked. His eyes searched her face.

Emotion boiled up and tears filled her eyes. "Yes," she whispered. "Happy."

A smile spread across his face. "I wonder if she'll look like her ma." He reached to cup her cheek. "I hope so."

She gave a wet giggle.

"Where've you been, anyway?"

That glitter in his eyes got lighter. "When we talked about it before, you put me off. But with a little one on the way, I don't think we can put it off any longer. I staked out a homestead for us."

Her surprise must've shown in her expression. "You what?"

He gave her a dry smile. "I didn't pick it out all on my own. Last time Rob was in town, we rode out and visited a few places. He gave me some good advice."

"So you've been thinking about this for a while, hmm?"

He smiled down at her. "I've been thinking I might like to have my morning coffee at a real kitchen table. And sleep in a real bed, a big one. And that I'd like to have room for a cradle and rocking chair for that babe when she gets here. A room for Katy to have all to herself, so she stops feeling like she gets in our way all the time."

She'd thought she was the only one who noticed how careful Katy was not to cause too much trouble. After being on her own for months, the girl seemed incredibly worried about being thrown out. Which Danna would never let happen. Katy was part of their family now. She just had to believe it.

"We'll want to make sure she knows the baby won't be edging her out of our affections," Danna said softly.

"Yes," Chas agreed. "And what about the town's affections? I'd hate for you to get 'a little bit shot' wearing that badge."

She pursed her lips. "Perhaps we can discuss me being behind the desk more until the baby gets here."

"I appreciate that." He looked beyond her toward the wide prairie. "If you're sure you aren't too cold, we could ride out and see the new land. I've got a two-bedroom cabin plotted out."

A home of her own. A teenage daughter and a baby on the way. And a husband to love forever.

"That sounds perfect. Happy Christmas."

* * *

ACKNOWLEDGMENTS

To the God who gave me everything needed to make this book a reality—all praise.

To those who have pushed me: my beloved Luke, Denice Stewart, Margaret Daley, Vickie McDonough. Thanks for not giving up on me.

To those who have encouraged me: Mon and Dad, Haley, Sean & Megan (and all my family), Janet Barton, Linda Goodnight, Darlene Franklin & the rest of OCFW and WIN—thanks for believing in me.

To those who have made this book better through critique, brainstorming and more: Megan Yager, Mary Brookman, Haley Yager, Denice Stewart, Mischelle Creager—thank you for pushing me to make this a better story.

ALSO BY LACY WILLIAMS

WILD WYOMING HEART SERIES (HISTORICAL ROMANCE)

Marrying Miss Marshal

Counterfeit Cowboy

Cowboy Pride

Courted by a Cowboy

TRIPLE H BRIDES SERIES (CONTEMPORARY ROMANCE)

Kissing Kelsey

Courting Carrie

Stealing Sarah

Keeping Kayla

COWBOY FAIRYTALES SERIES (CONTEMPORARY ROMANCE)

Once Upon a Cowboy

Cowboy Charming

The Toad Prince

The Beastly Princess

The Lost Princess

HEART OF OKLAHOMA SERIES (CONTEMPORARY ROMANCE)

Kissed by a Cowboy

Love Letters from Cowboy

Mistletoe Cowboy

Cowgirl for Keeps

Jingle Bell Cowgirl

Heart of a Cowgirl

3 Days with a Cowboy

Prodigal Cowgirl

WYOMING LEGACY SERIES (HISTORICAL ROMANCE)

The Homesteader's Sweetheart

Courted by a Cowboy

Roping the Wrangler

Return of the Cowboy Doctor

The Wrangler's Inconvenient Wife

A Cowboy for Christmas

Her Convenient Cowboy

Her Cowboy Deputy

NOT IN A SERIES

Love's Glimmer

How to Lose a Guy in 10 Dates

Santa Next Door

The Butterfly Bride

Secondhand Cowboy

Wagon Train Sweetheart (historical romance)

Made in the USA
Monee, IL
11 July 2021

73382238R00152

All inquiries should be addressed to:
Barron's Educational Series, Inc.
250 Wireless Boulevard
Hauppauge, NY 11788

Library of Congress Catalog Card Number 96-37522

International Standard Book No. 0-7641-0061-0

Library of Congress Cataloging-in Publication Data

Renckly, Richard G.
      Human Resources / Richard G. Renckly.
        p.   cm. -— (Barron's business library)
      ISBN 0-7641-0061-0
      1. Personnel management. I. Title. II. Series.
      HF5549.R4594   1997
      658.3—dc21   96-37522
                                      CIP

PRINTED IN ITALY
9 8 7 6

BARRON'S BUSINESS LIBRARY

Human Resources

Richard G. Renckly
Senior Professional, SPHR

Contents

Preface

New personnel managers, human resources managers, or directors or vice presidents of human resources will find no scarcity of books, magazine articles, videotapes, conferences, and seminars on the subject of how to be successful in human resources. They will discover that there is much in the literature regarding the organization and maintenance of a personnel/human resources operation within a corporate structure. A great deal of that information will include statistical and technical charts, graphs, matrices, and other helpful data explaining the details of operations, staffing, budgeting, compensation, employment, personnel relations, and practically any other management function. And I definitely urge new HR managers to take full advantage of every opportunity to read and study the data most closely related to and applicable to their corporate situation.

Although you will want to keep up with new state-of-the-art developments and ideas in our chosen field, you will probably not have the time or inclination to read and check into anything but a fraction of the material written about business management in general and personnel management in particular.

So, if you begin to feel overwhelmed in terms of complex or conflicting expert recommendations, and theories of human resources management, in particular, keep in mind some of the basic thoughts and ideas offered in this book as they relate to employees, AKA people:

1) People always have been, are, and always will be the most important and valuable asset any corporation could ever hope to have.

2) Despite everything you may read and hear in our modern era of rights rather than responsibilities, the vast majority of people (employees, customers, vendors, suppliers, and outside agencies) will respond and react favorably to any company management that genuinely treats them with dignity and respect.

3) When employees are regularly informed by management about the status of the business relating to profits, losses, problems, new expansions, hard times—or any other matter concerning their company, they consider themselves part of the team, and communication then flows rapidly up as well as down. Also, in such companies, employee loyalty is just about assured, even in difficult economic times when reductions in the work force are unavoidable, since employees will be confident their management has done its best to keep layoffs to an absolute minimum.

4) Employees usually expect equity and fairness from their employer in all aspects of business including wages, promotion, and discipline, as well as in work rules and working conditions. Companies can always gain the trust of employees when they sincerely try to earn it.

5) The personnel or human resources manager can and must become one of the most valuable members of the management team by doing everything possible to ensure that the above recommendations and philosophies become a basic part of company culture. If these commitments are made and kept, a company is almost always guaranteed to be successful, since its most important asset and the company now have a common cause and can merge into one unbeatable team.

The era of the employee, the customer—the "person"—is <u>now</u>, and promises to continue as such for many years into the future. You are privileged to deal with the challenge of people. You have a serious responsibility to make sure to the best of your ability that your top management is fully aware that *the company that handles this asset properly is the company that prospers and survives.*

With this reference to the true, real-life human resources person, I would like to open this book with a quotation from Theodore Roosevelt in 1910:

> It is not the critic who counts, not the man who points out how the strong man stumbles, or where the doer of deeds could have done them better. The credit belongs to the man who is actually in the arena, whose face is marred by dust and sweat and blood; who strives valiantly; who errs, and comes short again and again (but)...who knows the great enthusiasms, the great devotions, who spends himself in a worthy cause; who at the best knows in the end the triumph of high achievement, and who at the worst if he fails, at least fails while daring greatly, so that his place shall never be with those cold and timid souls who know neither victory or defeat.

Acknowledgments

No man is an island. Similarly, authors may not claim complete isolation and total credit for what they think, organize, write, edit, and correct. Even when the first creative idea reveals itself to the author, selecting the ground, planting the seed, nurturing, feeding, and maintaining the embryonic idea is often (to one degree or another) the result of the efforts of others who may have an instinctive belief in the value and worth of the author's original concept.

In the case of this book, the author, having had quite a few years of experience in the personnel/human resources field, and has seen a myriad of positive changes and new developments in the profession. There are probably any number of others who can claim the same length of experience, but I am convinced that not many could have had the same amount of encouragement, guidance, cooperation, and enthusiasm shown to me in the course of making this book a reality.

In all truth and fairness, I first must mention my dear wife Mary Elizabeth, whose patience and understanding in enduring many lonely hours enabled me to spend those hours in planning, researching, and writing my work. Her encouragement, praise (when merited), and candid critiquing of the book were all absolutely invaluable in bringing it to life.

My mentor, Alan Weinstein, a friend and business associate, was extremely instrumental and encouraging on so many occasions in recommending to me which path to take and how to stay with it once the choice was made. Alan, himself an accomplished author and editor, was my sounding board for many important aspects of the book and especially in helping to make it acceptable for publication. I have no idea of how any comments of mine may have influenced his own new book (if at all), but I cannot measure the importance of his advice and encouragement to me regarding my own.

Others who must be mentioned include my ever-supportive family, especially my son Michael as well as my son-in-law Dave Cameron, both of whom, together with another son Tom, constituted my inexhaustible pool of knowledge and information relating to electronic communication, particularly the personal computer, the Internet, and the World Wide Web. Their skills and patient cooperation would be impossible to overstress. The advice and counsel of friend and attorney Brad Gardner were especially meaningful and deeply appreciated. Friends and business associates Rich Lee, Neil Dempster, and Erv Spille graciously provided necessary support and buoyancy.

A former employer, U-Haul International, must also be recognized for its most cooperative attitude in allowing me to draw on some of its HR forms and policies for inclusion in this work. Retired U-Haul Senior Executive Vice President John M. Dodds gave unceasing encouragement and support to me as the book was being written, as well as later. U-Haul Executive Vice President Harry B. DeShong was, as always, most helpful in arranging for me to utilize some company facilities and equipment when necessary. My former business associates, Marti Patton and Bob Platek, gave unselfishly of many hours of their own time in helping to prepare the manuscript and advising on information systems. Liz Jolly, Debbie Tooker, and Connie Bartlett were also of great assistance in gathering and providing information to me. These folks are all members of the U-Haul International Human Resources department, the most capable and enthusiastic group of HR professionals it has ever been my pleasure to be associated with.

As with any book or work of this scope, I have probably omitted some people I should have acknowledged. If so, it is purely unintentional and my thanks for their help is extended to them with the same sincerity as for those mentioned.

Finally, although no names are mentioned in this book, I find no fault with and mean no disrespect to any former subordinate, peer, or superior whose ideas, philosophy, or management style may be referred to in the text. I learned **much** from each of these associations and would be the last to criticize them for "...always following a sensible strategy for getting along in the kind of world they think they live in."

RGR
1997

The Structure of Human Resources

INTRODUCTION AND MAIN POINTS

This chapter examines the structure of the human resources function. To demonstrate how widely the structure can vary, three examples of organizational charts from variously sized organizations are included. The rest of the chapter describes the flow of human resources operations to illustrate HR's key areas of responsibility. The description may be considered a cross-section of the principal, typical functional elements found in the modern, proactive human resources department.

After you have studied the materials in this chapter:

■ You will be aware of the different areas of responsibility that comprise the structure of a typical human resources department.

■ You will know that there can be great variety in the structure of the human resources function.

■ You will understand the internal relationships of different functions within a human resources department.

STRUCTURE IS BASED ON FUNCTION

In this chapter, we will examine the structure of a typical human resources department. We know that not every company will be large enough to have either a separate human resources department or one containing all of the personnel functions or areas of responsibility that are mentioned here and described in greater detail in following chapters. Even some of the largest corporations are not necessarily structured in the same manner as we have described below. Nevertheless, similarities exist among organizations and thus it is possible to show the essential functions in which every human resources department should be involved. For an overview of three different structures of the human resources function, see Tables 1-1, 1-2, and 1-3.

TABLE 1-1

Human Resources Organizational Chart
(Example for organization with 10,000+ employees)

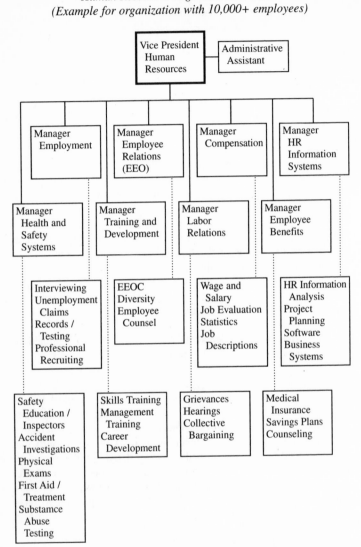

TABLE 1-2
Human Resources Organizational Chart
(Example for organization with 500–1,000 employees)

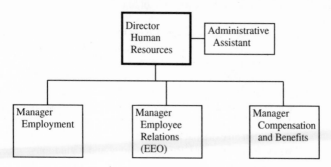

TABLE 1-3
Human Resources Organizational Chart
(Example for organization with 25–100 employees)

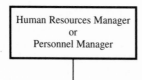

Human Resources Manager
or
Personnel Manager

Job may include a wide variety of other duties in addition to HR, including the supervision of the bookkeeping, payroll, hiring, sales, and clerical functions, and the personnel who perform them.

Office Manager
or
Administrative Assisstant

In smaller companies, the office manager may direct other office employees in the performance of HR as well as other functions mentioned above. The owner of the company may also reserve these responsiblities for himself or herself. The advantages of such flexibility often disappear, however, as companies grow in size and revenue.

HUMAN RESOURCES' TYPICAL AREAS OF RESPONSIBILITY

A brief description of the flow of human resources operations through the department might help to illustrate HR's key responsibilities and how they interact with the rest of the organization.

> **NOTE:** It must be emphasized here that the HR functions and responsibilities set out below, although intended to describe duties performed in companies having the luxury of their own HR departments, are nonetheless applicable and important in any size company. Whether the HR responsibility rests with the company owner, the office manager, administrative assistant, accounting clerk, or others (as is usually the case in small HR environments), the HR responsibility is often an extra hat that people need to wear, but they must still be aware of current HR methodology and regulations.

Employment

The human resources employment staff begins its work by designing and developing policies, procedures, and programs to recruit the most able and qualified applicants available for the job openings the company is attempting to fill. It then begins the actual recruiting process by employing a wide variety of sources including media advertising, private employment agencies, state employment services, schools, churches, local civic organizations, and chambers of commerce, and by using whatever sources are available in order to find and attract the most qualified individuals for the company.

Once sufficient applicants are found, employment then begins the task of screening, interviewing, and testing candidates (including coordination of preemployment drug testing programs, where applicable), and referring the best of these to appropriate line or staff managers for further interviewing prior to the final hiring decision being made.

In some organizations, the human resources department also makes the hiring decision and sends the applicant to work in the department where the job opening exists. This is especially true when production or assembly line job openings are being filled. In most cases, however, managers and supervisors usually prefer to personally select the employees who will be working in their departments. Whatever procedure applies to or works best for your company should be the preferred method.

Having found the most capable people available to fill your job openings, you must now be in a position to offer them a salary or wage commensurate with the duties and responsibilities of the position, and one that is generally competitive with comparable job openings at other companies in the local area. If the successful applicant accepts the job at the salary offered, he or she now joins the company as a bona fide employee (system member, associate, or whatever the company's nomenclature might be).

Compensation

Next, it becomes the responsibility of the human resources compensation staff to establish the proper wage and salary guidelines, pay scales, and other compensation programs, including well-designed employee benefit packages and strategies, to ensure the company's ability to retain the capable employees that have presumably been hired with great care and effort, not to mention expense.

Training

The human resources training section now begins its function of providing whatever training and orientation the new employees might need in order to make certain that they are well equipped to perform their new duties, and that they have some idea of the history and policies as well as the culture of the company.

The training group also performs the functions of designing and implementing management training programs in which new recruits, it is hoped, might some day be involved.

Employee Relations

As some of the new system members eventually find their way into management positions, the human resources employee relations staff will undoubtedly be of assistance in providing guidance and counsel to them on discrimination matters as well as on other human relations opportunities or challenges. These concerns are ever present in today's sensitive business environment, and they promise to become even more evident in the future.

Benefits Staff

The human resources benefits staff is charged with the responsibility of administering, recommending, and monitoring all phases of the company's employee benefits program. Group insurance plans, paid time off (vacations, holidays), retirement programs, service awards, and a host of other benefit features are all within the scope of the HR benefits function.

One of the more challenging areas of this group's duties is to ensure that existing retirement programs are properly designed, developed, managed, and communicated to participants, and that they fit in with the overall objectives, strategies, and philosophy of the company.

They are also responsible for presenting and recommending tax-favored retirement programs such as 401(k)s, Individual Retirement

Accounts (IRAs), and other tax-deferred and government-backed savings plans, as well as perhaps a well-designed and implemented Employee Stock Ownership Plan (ESOP). Such savings programs are designed to assist these new hires as well as all of the current, eligible employees, to be able to enjoy a comfortable retirement at the end of their career and service with the organization.

The human resources benefits group should also be committed to rendering every assistance possible by answering employee questions and providing and explaining benefit policies. This same courtesy, of course, should also be shown retired employees as well. By so doing, the company not only conveys its wishes for their happy and successful retirement, but also lets them know that they are still considered members of the organization family.

CHAPTER PERSPECTIVE

This chapter examined the internal structure of a typical human resources department by tracking the flow of its operations, from advertising a job and hiring a new employee to the employee's promotion, retirement, and beyond.

Three examples of organizational charts from differently structured organizations were included.

The Human Resources Function

INTRODUCTION AND MAIN POINTS

This chapter defines and then illustrates through numerous examples the function of the personnel or human resources department within an organization. When and how the HR department should become involved in employee problems or complaints is delineated.

Here we describe the tools and techniques of the HR profession in resolving employee problems or complaints, and how they are best used in specific cases. In all cases, however, an attentive and helpful manner and good listening skills on the part of the HR staff are stressed.

The conditions that give rise to a union drive are described. The rights of organized labor, as guaranteed by the National Labor Relations Act, are explained. Possible outcomes of a representation election are discussed.

This chapter stresses that the human resources focus remains a genuine concern for employee welfare and application of the People Principle, whether or not the employees are represented by a union.

After studying the material in this chapter:

▬ You will learn what the function of the Human Resources department is.

▬ You will gain an overview of the proper procedures for investigating and resolving an employee problem or complaint.

▬ You will become aware of the underlying causes for a union drive.

▬ You will understand the importance of human resources' role in reassuring employees that management is genuinely concerned with their welfare.

▬ You will learn about the application of the People Principle in all situations.

THE HUMAN RESOURCES FUNCTION DEFINED

The primary function of the human resources (HR) department is:

▬ to essentially establish, develop, maintain, and communicate personnel policies to the entire company and

■ to represent, help, advise, and consult with the employees of the organization.

At the same time, the human resources staff members must never forget that they are to represent first, last, and always, the best interests of their employer—the top management of the corporation.

While on the surface it may seem to be a conflict to claim it represents both the employee and employer equally well and at the same time, the HR staff must, nonetheless, acquire this highly complex and technical skill. It is the hallmark of the well-run and more qualified human resources department.

EMPLOYEE RELATIONS

From Personnel to Human Resources

Most companies, large or small, normally include in their table of organization a department known as "personnel." In more recent years, this department's name has evolved into "human resources." Many experienced people in this field resisted the term human resources, because they felt that human beings should not be categorized as mere resources, especially if they are a company's most important asset. Eventually, however, the term became generally accepted in the industry without really changing the primary objective of all such departments, namely, serving their most important and special clients—the employees of the organization.

Industrial Relations Department Defined

The personnel principles stated in this work generally apply equally well in a unionized as well as nonunionized corporate setting, however, in some unionized companies, the industrial relations department may be a component part of the human resources operation. For the purposes of this book, we will assume that industrial relations staffs that deal directly with union contract matters are separate and distinct from the human resources function, in which case the industrial relations department is the sole and exclusive representative of management, and not of those employees who may be union members.

THE HUMAN RESOURCES DEPARTMENT AS NEUTRAL GROUND

The employees of the company, in turn, should regard the human resources department as neutral and impartial ground where they can
■ take their problems or complaints;
■ expect help, information, and advice; and
■ certainly anticipate a fair and impartial hearing, and assume an environment of trust and confidentiality.

Successful personnel or human resources managers, through their staff, create the atmosphere in which this will happen.

THE CHAIN OF COMMAND

It is also most important to know and to remember that the primary responsibility for resolving employee complaints and grievances lies with the immediate supervisor. No human resources department has the time or inclination to hear, investigate, and resolve every problem that arises in day-to-day operations, nor should it! The immediate boss—manager, supervisor, or working leader—is by far the best first line of defense in resolving personnel problems, and thereby protecting the company's best interests.

In the event, however, that the problem situation is not resolved at the immediate supervisor stage, it should then be referred to the next level of supervision, and ultimately up the chain of command to the top of the organization, if necessary. Again, depending on how company personnel policy is structured, the human resources department must be brought into the picture by management. Often, the employees involved will not wait for upper management intervention but, assuming the human resources staff has created the proper climate or environment of listening and concern, employees will ask human resources to work with them.

Assuming that the human resources department is involved, we will examine some of the tactics and strategies the HR professional should and should not use in attempting to resolve problems successfully.

DEALING WITH PROBLEMS EFFECTIVELY

Avoid the Quick Draw

If you are currently in human resources or have had experience in the HR field, you may have known staff members who could be overly influenced by an employee complaining about his or her supervisor. In their righteous indignation, and without bothering to thoroughly check out the employee's complaint or quarrel with the manager or supervisor involved, they may make snap judgments based solely on the employee's input. Thus, the supervisor is judged guilty without benefit of hearing or trial. The old expression, "There are two sides to every story" certainly applies here.

Get Both Sides of the Story

About 99 percent—or perhaps even more—of employee complaints or problem situations are never totally one-sided. In most cases, the truth lies somewhere between the contentions of both parties in the nebulous "gray" area. For example, an employee may be upset because the manager allegedly reneged on a promised wage increase. The manager may, perhaps, claim the employee did not accomplish his or her goals, such as meeting expected performance standards as previously agreed upon, and is therefore not deserving of an increase.

The skilled professional always looks for and considers facts on both sides of the story. The most important responsibility you as a personnel professional have when employee problem situations are referred to your attention, is to make sure you have absolutely *all* of the facts you can possibly get your hands on before you make any decision or recommendation to the personnel or human resources manager, or to the operating manager.

The Personnel File

Most companies, even the smallest ones, maintain what is known as a personnel file. Such a file may consist of

▬ an elaborate, titled folder of documents and data; or

▬ a manual, even handwritten, employee work history card; or

▬ an on-line computer listing of the person's work history and employment record with the company.

No matter what your format may be, you will find that the number one, most helpful, and just about the most essential tool you can have for any and all aspects of your personnel job is the personnel files of the employees. It matters not how well you *think* you know your employees, including the department where they work, their rate of pay, date of last increase, and so forth; you must have the personnel record in front of you before you even begin your research. And, if available, the same applies to personnel files and records of employees who may no longer be employed with the company but who may in some way be involved in the case or problem at hand.

First you must satisfy yourself that you know

▬ *who* the person or persons are,

▬ *what* their jobs are,

▬ *where* they work, and

▬ *when* they were hired, transferred, promoted, rehired, and so on.

All this information is indicated in personnel files and records. Then the next questions are:

▬ *Why* are we having a problem?

▬ *How* can we resolve it?

It is hoped that the solution will be to everyone's satisfaction—or nearly so.

Given the importance of the personnel file, never let anyone talk you into letting the personnel files and records be stored, warehoused, or kept in any way outside of your HR department. You may be advised that, since they are just another type of record, they should more properly be kept in the corporate records area or department together with other company statements, accounts, contracts, or payroll logs. Not so! From the standpoint of confidentiality, convenience, and quick and after-hours accessibility, the personnel files are *not* run-of-the-mill documents or data and they belong in the human resources department! Even if you input and maintain these files in your computer database, or keep them on microfiche or microfilm, you will still find value in having hard copies available within your department, or at least stored under your immediate access and control.

Talking with People

Before you make any judgments or decisions, of course, it might be a good idea to talk with several people, such as the complaining party or parties, and all supervisors involved, as well as any witnesses, coworkers, or other persons who might possibly have some knowledge of the situation, the person(s) in question, and the events leading up to the present impasse.

The Investigation

Once you've assembled and studied all the facts, you're now finally in a position to begin the investigation. As described at the beginning of this chapter, you, as a human resources manager or specialist, represent your company or corporation first and foremost, but you must also fill the role of employee representative to assure equity to the individual. By maintaining this balance, you are truly performing your job, benefiting your company's reputation, and undoubtedly adding to its bottom line.

Resolution of the Problem

When the investigation reveals that an understandable disagreement or impasse exists, it may mean that an honest mistake was made between supervisor and employee; therefore, some kind of compromise or settlement is probably in order. In the case of legal actions involving charges of discrimination or wrongful termination, for example, the experienced human resources staff member knows that sometimes a modest financial settlement makes sense. This is especially appropriate if the company's position has some weaknesses and the administrative or legal costs of defending it in the future are anticipated to be far greater than any settlement amount that may be involved.

It is most important to know when to settle or to comply with the employee's request and when it is wiser to fight for and to defend the company's position to the limit. In the latter event, you must really feel that the company has a strong case and that the manager or supervisor involved acted in good faith. When the company's position is valid, refusing to concede or to settle an issue for money most always sends the right signal to other potential claimants that here is a company that will *not* give in under pressure if it feels it's on solid ground.

Listening Skills

Regardless of the circumstances, good listening skills are most important and should never be underrated. For instance, when employees or their spouses persist in calling every company official from the chairman of the board on down in order to right a perceived grievance, the best response may be to simply listen to what they have to say. Sometimes these complaints have merit, but other times people just want someone to listen to them and they may be satisfied to have a willing ear. Often, the payment of as little as one week's additional (severance) pay or even a neutral reference to employment inquiries from outside companies will remedy what initially sounded like a serious complaint against the company. Similarly, if complaints from customers are listened to with the same sense of helpful attention and respect, customers will often express satisfaction that a representative of the company took the time to listen to them and at least tried to help them with their problem or complaint. While employees are the company's most valuable asset, customers pay their salaries and, therefore, merit the utmost consideration and attention.

In some cases, had the employees with complaints been handled by their immediate or first-line supervision with the attention and dignity due to a company's most important asset, no further time-consuming phone calls up the chain of command or to human resources might have been necessary.

THE UNION CONNECTION

We will later discuss (in Chapter 3 and elsewhere) the value and importance of an employee to a company. Therefore, it must be stressed that it becomes one of the primary functions of the human resources department to play a major role in reassuring employees of management's concern for equity and fairness in all employee relations matters—assuming such concern does in fact really exist!

Failure to Reassure Employees of Equity

If human resources fails in this effort, it is highly likely in the nonunion company that employees will at some point turn to a union with the frequently mistaken hope that this third party will represent their best interests to their employer. More often than not, if the general attitude of a company toward its people is one of mere tolerance, or if employees are viewed by top management as simply necessary overhead, most any union has a better-than-average chance of winning a representation election by convincing a majority of people in the bargaining unit just how much improved their wages, benefits, and job security will become when they are represented by the union.

In addition, depending on how much or how little regard was paid to the employees by management before the union arrived, union allies within employee ranks will make every effort to convince their co-workers how improved their lives will be when they are represented by Local 754 of the Amalgamated Ironworkers of America, the Machinists Union, or the Food and Commercial Workers of America.

Intimidating Managers, Supervisors, or Leaders

Allowing for the inevitable exceptions to the rule, experienced HR and labor relations managers would probably agree that the root cause of a union drive is not necessarily issues over wages or benefits. Many nonunion companies have found that the reason they have a letter or phone call from a union claiming to have sufficient authorization cards signed by company employees to represent them is in no way related to increased compensation or benefits. It is, in fact, a result of the unfeeling, intimidating management style of a particular manager, supervisor, or even working leader.

This lack of considerate and decent treatment of people is assumed to be condoned by top management or ownership of the company, inasmuch as nothing ever changes and no one up the line seems to care.

Such union drives are often instigated by one employee or a small group of employees who have found working for such an individual simply intolerable. When people find themselves working for a tyrant with no hope whatever of relief or redress, including going to higher company authority, they will inevitably go to an outside third party (such as a union), to help them. At this point, the company's battle is totally uphill, and what could have been a relatively small and inexpensive ounce of prevention relating to employee respect and consideration, now becomes a tidal wave of resistance by employees to all of management's efforts to convince them that "we're a team, and we want you to believe we really do care about you."

It is also very interesting to predict as well as to observe how a company's "take-'em-for-granted" attitude, philosophy, or culture suddenly takes on a new dimension and reverses its field at the first hint of union presence or activity. Management professes to be aghast as well as deeply shocked and hurt to think that its work force did not first bring their complaints or problems to their supervisor or to their boss's boss, or, as a last resort, to the office of the chairman of the board whose door has been perpetually open. To make matters worse, the human resources staff, as well as any labor lawyers or consultants on the scene, will now dutifully remind the chairman that all activities must be in accordance with provisions of the National Labor Relations Act.

The National Labor Relations Act

Under the provisions of this act, the company's management
— can make no **T**hreats of retaliation against employees for union interest;
— cannot **I**nterrogate employees about their union views;
— cannot **P**romise increased wages, benefits, or better working conditions; and
— cannot undertake **S**urveillance of union activities, including watching who goes in and out of the union hall or spying on union/employee meetings.

The use of any of these unlawful practices, which comprise the familiar **TIPS** acronym, could result in the National Labor Relations Board charging the company with an unfair labor practice. In flagrant cases, such a charge might even mean automatic certification of the union by the board as representative of the employees without the formality of a secret-ballot election. Thus, the chairman's hands are effectively tied so that it may even now be too late to try to convince people that the corporation—and particularly the chair—has always listened to their problems, and has certainly always tried to provide them with competitive wages, generous benefits, and good working conditions.

The Representation Election

The Captive Audience Doctrine. Under the so-called Captive Audience Doctrine, employers may speak to their employees in a mass meeting on company time about the union campaign, and may require employees to attend the meeting. A union may not do the same on company time, and must limit its campaigning to employees' homes and to distributing literature and answering employee questions and inquiries.

The 24-Hour Rule. The general exception to the captive audience doctrine is known as the *24-hour rule*. The NLRB will set aside a representation election if an employer gives a speech to a mass employee audience on company time within the 24-hour period just prior to the election. The employer may *start* a meeting prior to the period but must *complete* his or her speech *before* the 24-hour period begins. Even if it runs a few minutes into the 24-hour period, the board will set aside the election and, due to precedent, will make no exceptions.

This speech which many company CEOs will try to give as close to the restricted deadline as possible (but not beyond it), has come to be known as the 24-hour speech, and in most instances would probably sound something like the following.

My Fellow Workers:

You will very soon have the opportunity to vote on whether or not you want union representation.

Our management doesn't want a union, and we believe that a majority of you feel the same—but it's your vote that will decide this. Both you and our management will be bound by the choice you and your fellow workers make tomorrow.

In its campaign, the union has "pulled out all the stops," since it has nothing to lose and everything to gain. The union has made wild promises; the union has used false figures and untrue rumors to mislead you and to tear down our management; and the union has threatened and pressured our workers to try and prevent those who don't want this union from having their say. In short, the union has done anything to get your vote.

Our management has not made a single promise or uttered a single threat. What we have done is try to give you straightforward answers and honest facts. We believe that the facts can lead to only one decision—no union here!

The decision you make tomorrow is your decision. This is the way it must be because you are the ones who will be most affected.

The union can only gain, through your dues, if you vote it in. If the union loses, it will simply try to organize at some other company.

Our management will operate, union or no union. We are not concerned with any strike threat. We are not worried about union pressure forcing an increase in our costs. We would deal with this union, as the representative of our family members, in the same way we deal with any outsider: on a cold, hard impersonal basis. There would not be and could not be consideration for the individual. We would be buying labor through a labor broker, a union, and we would pay only competitive prices for it.

But where do you stand? You would be bound by any contract the union negotiated, whether it was for your best interest or not. You would be pressured to join the union and pay dues. You would be subject to possible strike action, and the trouble and violence that goes with strikes, not to mention your personal loss of wages and other problems. You would face the day-to-day bickering and backbiting that goes with the union and its supporters. You would have to deal with two bosses—the union and its stewards and your supervisor.

It's your job. It's your working conditions, it's your decision.

Albert B. Collins
Chairman of the Board and CEO
ABC Company

A very stirring and emotional appeal indeed, but in most cases, probably just a bit overdue, and a perfect illustration of too little, too late! In many cases, it is probably years too late.

If by some serendipitous turn of events the company does succeed in obtaining even a simple majority of votes in its favor, the union attempt is thwarted for at least another year, in accordance with the National Labor Relations Act. The chairman and company management breathe a long sigh of relief and, though some tangible improvements in employee/employer relations will usually occur for the moment, chances are good that before too long *business as usual* will prevail, memories will become faded and dim, and employees will find themselves in the same environment that created the union interest in the first place.

Now let's also consider the scenario where employees, despite all of management's pleas, veiled promises, and rosy portraits of the future, still feel they want the Amalgamated Clerks, Ironworkers, or some other labor organization to represent them and they vote them in accordingly. We now have a new ballgame, especially in the case of a previously all nonunion company. The employees have mandated the union to help change and improve real or perceived miserable working conditions, low wages, or benefits. In point of fact, however, the benefit they probably want most is to have their management pay some attention to them and to show them the care and respect they could and should have long before the day a union came on the scene. But now the opportunity is lost, and a union from here on in becomes a part of everyday corporate life. Thus, another company is unionized, and the oft-heard statement that the company that gets a union deserves one again proves to be true.

A GENUINE CONCERN FOR EMPLOYEES' WELFARE

The principle of showing respect toward employees and allowing them dignity also applies whether a company has just acquired a union, has had one for 20 years, or perhaps has no union at all. In human resources, you are still dealing with people either directly or through a third party, and they are still the company's most important asset. Even if a union is well entrenched, with apparently little or no chance of decertification, employees will still respond favorably to a management that demonstrates a genuine concern for their welfare.

Apply the People Principle

If the people principle is really properly understood and applied, even in a unionized situation you will find there are fewer (if any) strikes, jurisdictional disputes, boycotts, work stoppages, and similar work actions. This is because the majority of employees truly believe and want to believe that "...this is a pretty good place to work...," and that their company considers them something more than a necessary evil or overhead item. Keep in mind that this principle operates the same, regardless of whether you do or do not operate in a union environment!

CHAPTER PERSPECTIVE

This chapter focused on the functions of the personnel or human resources department: The department must maintain fairness to individual employees while simultaneously representing the interests of the company's management. Also, on a day-to-day basis, the department is responsible for establishing, maintaining, and communicating personnel policies to the entire company.

We also discussed how employee problems or complaints are properly routed though an organization, how an investigation of a problem is fairly conducted, and how problems and complaints can be resolved.

The origins and development of a union drive were described in relation to the HR function in reassuring management's concern for equity and fairness in all employee relations.

Finally, the chapter stressed the importance of the people principle, treating employees with respect and allowing them dignity in union or nonunion situations.

An Organization's Most Important Asset

INTRODUCTION AND MAIN POINTS

This chapter demonstrates that an organization's most important asset is its employees.

Through positive and negative examples from the American business community, the effects of respect and loyalty in human relations are explored.

The employee relations of a large, nonunionized, Fortune 1000 corporation are profiled as a model of success.

The idea of individuals within companies and of companies within society, both "making their own personnel records" through their performance is developed.

The chapter closes with the practical need for establishing the personnel or human resources function to represent the interests of all employees, including management.

After studying the material in this chapter:

■ You will know why the success of a company is dependent upon its people.

■ You will be able to recognize the values of top management that produce positive results for companies, as well as the opposite.

■ You will understand the need for a personnel or human resources function in any size organization as a means of maintaining a company's most important asset.

THE VALUE OF PEOPLE

In newspapers, magazines, and business journals, on television, at seminars, in boardrooms, and around office water coolers, the word is out: Employee loyalty to companies is no more, and the trade-off of loyalty for job security has gone the way of the slide rule, typewriter, and adding machine. Even though downsizing, restructuring, reengineering, and job elimination dominate the current corporate business scene, industry profits are the highest in ten years. So how important can loyalty to an employer really be with results like that to reinforce the opinions of so many business analysts and experts? One certainly would have an uphill battle refuting the effectiveness of these practices, especially in the short run.

The really savvy companies, large and small, recognize that people have never been more important to business success than they are today. Every business depends upon its employees for tomorrow as surely as it does for today. Getting and keeping the best will be a priority for every employer who expects to have any chance of competitive survival, and this book tells the decision makers just how to do it.

Most large companies today were once small organizations with some very good personnel. When these businesses were small, they genuinely believed in and practiced the principle of primary reliance on their employees for the success of the corporation. But as they grew larger, they published bigger and better recruiting brochures, annual reports, and operating statements, and began to forget that their people brought them to where they were and would take them to where they're going. Many of those growing businesses who forgot to practice the principle of primary reliance on their employees ultimately failed.

Lincoln Electric Company

One major and outstanding example of a company that has always considered employees its most valuable and important asset is the Lincoln Electric Company of Cleveland, Ohio. This large Fortune 1000 corporation is a nonunion manufacturing plant founded almost 100 years ago. It is a world leader in the manufacture of arc welding and thermal cutting equipment and AC electric motors. Good piecework rates, annual multi-million dollar bonus programs, and a guaranteed employment policy are a few of the reasons Lincoln can boast of superb quality products, and a long waiting list of applicants for as far back as anyone can remember. However, the genuine attention and concern of top management for its employees has to be the primary reason for Lincoln's success, such as its reputation for recognizing its most important asset.

Managers and executives from all over the country come to visit Lincoln Electric to learn its techniques and secrets of success. The traffic is so great that the company conducts guided tours of the plant each month. After tours are completed, these greatly impressed and highly respected executives return to their respective companies on Monday morning to tell their colleagues of this very moving management experience. Unfortunately, implementation is another story in that, in most cases, changes rarely occur in the management style of these companies that parallel or even vaguely mirror Lincoln Electric's employee policies. However, Lincoln Electric's long-standing success and its openness as a role model in the HR field, have triggered great interest in performance-based bonus programs that have recently been featured in *The Wall Street Journal.*

Other Cases

Malden Mills, a 2,400-employee company in Lawrence, Massachusetts, was largely destroyed by fire in 1995. The company owner, Aaron Feuerstein, kept the entire workforce on the payroll during the rebuilding of the plant, at a payroll cost of $1.5 million per week.

Today, the company reaps the benefits of this action of employee concern; current fabric production is up to 200,000 yards per week, compared with the 130,000 yards produced before the fire.

Mr. Feuerstein comments:

They [employees] have paid me back nearly tenfold. We must show workers the kind of loyalty they extend to us. I'm prepared to say that, not in the short term but in the long term, when companies act in an ethical way, it's good for business and good for the shareholder.

(*The Arizona Republic,* January 23, 1997)

The following case illustrates a norm in the American business community today. A board chairman of a large corporation tells employees that there is no way he can ever pay them what they are worth. This is scientifically and empirically a true statement indeed! Presumably acting on this premise, he discouraged any overt attempts at compensation equity via formal merit reviews, performance appraisals, and job evaluation systems as advocated by those "bureaucrats" in the personnel department. His objection to formal performance reviews stemmed from the fact, he said, that he informally reviewed his own subordinates every day, and therefore no six-month, annual, or other periodic formal written appraisal was necessary. He alone determined wages and salaries on the basis of what he perceived to be a living wage, and he insisted that there be a relatively small differential between the wages of supervisors and managers and those employees they directed.

The personnel department was partially able to convince the chairman of the value and practicality of performance appraisals, but he insisted that the performance and merit reviews be separate and distinct events. He believed the practice of combining them tended to cloud the performance issue: The employee's concentration would presumably be fixed on getting through the appraisal process as soon as possible to see how much of a wage or salary increase he or she might anticipate if the appraisal was favorable. Therefore, company policy prohibited the mention of wages when discussing performance appraisals or reviews with employees. Since the company did not allow for any general or automatic wage increases, the personnel department would review wage surveys and studies and usually propose new wage and salary merit range guidelines based on U.S. Department of Labor cost-of-living and other indices for the preceding year. However, the chairman's views kept the personnel department's wage range reviews and guideline increases down to once every three or four years on the average rather than annually, as good compensation policy and practice dictate.

The personnel department of this large corporation had, almost secretly, installed a formal job evaluation program that included written job descriptions for all jobs in the company. Again, some individuals viewed these actions as just another example of the personnel staff attempting to make the world safe for bureaucracy, while alleging these programs were initiated more in the spirit of artistic joy rather than for commercial advantage. Nevertheless, these programs did survive top management filibustering, sometimes ridicule, and often direct attack, primarily because presidents and managers of the company's large field operation who had to hire, fire, compensate, attract, and retain good employees demanded that the personnel department provide them with the systematic and effective wage guidelines and people-oriented programs they needed. Of course, the personnel department was not only obligated but happy to comply.

In many respects, this company was no exception to the pattern of the typical American business organization that just cannot under-stand the direct-line relationship between employees and that lifeblood of business known as *profit*. Employees are *not* a means to an end, similar to any other necessary commodity; rather they are an end in themselves since they are the most important asset a company possesses. This is definitely not intended to imply that employers should give the store away to their employees. The Lincoln Electric Company mentioned earlier certainly does not, as the following examples of its policies will attest.

■ Employees on the shop floor, called *direct production workers*, receive no base salary. Their compensation is based strictly on output known as *piecework*.

■ The company observes holidays, but it grants its employees *unpaid* time off.

■ The company encourages continuing education, but it has no tuition reimbursement program.

■ Lincoln Electric wants their employees to enjoy needed time off from their jobs, but it doesn't pay for personal time off, sick days, or other missed time; generous vacation pay is given, based on years of service.

■ And what company today does not pay at least in part for health care benefits? You guessed it—Lincoln Electric. At the end of each year, health care benefit costs are deducted from the employee's bonus, based on the individual employee's use of the medical program during that year.

Yet, despite all of these apparently negative benefits, the long waiting list of applicants still exists. And with the average length of service at about 17 years, Lincoln Electric must be doing something right! Of course, their employees appreciate the following:

■ a generous annual profit-sharing bonus, which averaged 98 percent of each employee's earnings over a 50-year period, such as, from 1934 through the early 1980s; an annual bonus that for the years from 1984 to 1996, hovered between 52 and 75 percent of an employee's earnings;

■ guaranteed employment for anyone with at least three years of service;

■ an employee stock ownership plan (ESOP) and 401(k) match;

■ promotion from within; and

■ open lines of communication through an elected advisory board to the president and chief executive officer.

These features are highlighted to call attention to what one company has accomplished in the field of human relations and to the not-so-coincident phenomenal success it has enjoyed for the past century. Undoubtedly, other companies both large and small offer some of these same advantages to their employees to one degree or another, but the difference lies in the almost total attention and focus of Lincoln Electric on its people. From the early beginnings of the company, brothers John C. and James F. Lincoln recognized the inherent advantage of treating employees as valued business partners, and the concept has flourished ever since.

When any company structures its employer-employee relations philosophy on the principle of genuine concern for its people, you can be sure that company has the respect of its employees, its customers, and the community it serves.

We should not and do not assume that this loyalty and attention on the part of the company to its employees is only a one-way street from company to employee. It is quite the contrary. Similar to one of the basic laws of physics, employees must demonstrate their goodwill and loyalty by their own equal and opposite reaction to the actions of their employer. Loyalty to one's company may not be too popular an idea in our modern business world, but today's employees can and always will respond in the same positive manner as their parents and grandparents did to their employers, if they perceive that respect and loyalty come from their companies in return.

23

The Lincoln Electric and Malden Mills companies cited previously are real-life, present-day examples of the rewards of employer/employee interactive loyalty.

YOU MAKE YOUR OWN RECORD

From time to time, we all come across quotes or sayings in some publication that appeal to us because of their wisdom or clever expression. The following statement (author anonymous) is worthy of preserving and framing, namely:

You make your own personnel record, we just keep it!

If we think about it a bit, in the long run we're all employees and, in general, most of us do have the ability to advance in whatever field we choose. Sometimes, the opportunity may not be there; other times, sickness or injury intervenes. Occasionally, fate takes a hand. However, by and large, employees in our country, in particular, can and do control their own destiny. Sometimes they succeed only after a number of unsuccessful starts, but sooner or later hardworking, conscientious, and honest effort wins out over mediocre performance or the lackluster, unplanned approach to the work ethic. So the somewhat corny axiom, "the harder I work, the luckier I get," will probably always have application in business, as well as in life in general.

Hard-working, conscientious people with reasonable intelligence and competency usually succeed in any business field and with practically any employer they choose. However, the Lincoln Electric-type company attracts more than its fair share of this kind of employee. Its people-oriented personnel policies and its sincere concern for employee welfare practically assure a continuing supply of highly-motivated and competent personnel who consider this company to be *the* place to work. In other words, it assures its own continuing success, almost without regard to the product it sells or the service it provides. Here again, we could almost say that, *Each company makes its own personnel record; its customers just keep it.*

Now that we have demonstrated, through the above examples, that in any business organization people are the most important asset, how shall we guard, protect, and nurture this asset so that it continues to flourish, and may eventually be taken for granted as *the* most essential element of our U.S. corporate culture?

We have advanced the hypothesis that without question this precious resource grows and thrives in direct proportion to the genuine concern of top management and the amount of attention it pays to its employees. As we progress through this book, we will discuss the ways and means corporate managers have at their disposal to convince their employees that they are indeed appreciated, and that they are the most valuable line item on any profit and loss statement or on any company balance sheet.

One very practical means of emphasizing and maintaining this valued resource would be to establish, as most companies have, a department or function known as the personnel or human resources department to represent the best interests of their employees and thereby of management as well.

The truly effective, proactive, and functional human resources (HR) department can be the key that unlocks the doors of apathy, unconcern, or, in some cases, outright hostility toward employees that some chief executives and boards of directors seem to feel toward the people who work for them. The personnel staff must first understand and believe in its own mission and role of emphasizing the value of people. Then it must aggressively act as a catalyst in making the necessary changes in corporate attitude toward people. Pursuing this theme, we will explore what makes a good human resources department work and how it can be structured to operate with maximum effectiveness through people recognition in the following chapter.

CHAPTER PERSPECTIVE

This chapter demonstrated how important positive human relations are to any business organization. It provided a clear profile of a long-standing, successful corporation as a model for good human relations. The value of mutual respect and loyalty within a business organization was observed. In addition, the chapter offered some negative examples of top-management philosophies that were unproductive and subsequently changed. Parallels were drawn concerning how individuals and companies create their own personnel records. The importance of establishing a human resources function as a means to maintain a company's most-valued asset was stressed.

The Human Resources Executive and the HR Managers

INTRODUCTION AND MAIN POINTS

This chapter focuses on the human resouces executive position, the selection of HR managers, and the relationship between HR executives and their managerial staff. The executive position is described, as well as the best temperament needed to match the requirements of the job. The qualities most necessary for the HR managerial staff are clearly delineated, with people-orientation at the top of the list for the "people" department. Lastly, guidelines for the relationship between HR executives and their staff of managers are given.

After reading the material in this chapter:

■ You will understand the role of the HR manager and which personality traits best suit the job.

■ You will know which functional areas the HR management staff has responsibility for.

■ You will understand how important people-orientation is in the people department and others.

■ You will know what other personal qualities are needed to succeed in HR management.

■ You will understand the parameters of a good working relationship between the HR executive and the HR managerial staff.

THE HEAD HUMAN

The position of human resources manager, director, or vice president, also known in some circles as the *head human*, is a multifaceted job, a fact that cannot be emphasized too much. The job consists of many complex and technical aspects, as does that of lawyers, engineers, doctors, CPAs, and others, but the human resources executive must deal exclusively with the most complex of all organisms—the human being. With that in mind, it is probably true that the variety of potential problems and challenges to which the human resources manager is subject exists in almost no other profession. It is true that practicing physicians also deal exclusively with humans, but they are primarily concerned with the physical or mental state of a person. While physical and mental states can also present complex problems, the personnel director must be concerned with an employee's physical and emotional well-being, as well as with other components such as competency, morale, attitude, personality, and conscientiousness.

A Challenging Profession

Those in the HR profession find the job challenging because they handle so many diverse subjects at one time and rarely meet the same problem twice. In addition, human resources executives are patience personified. Their phone voice never discloses the frustration or anger they have just experienced from the preceding call when they may have learned that a new program, procedure, or special event that could not go wrong, did. If they remember to maintain their equilibrium, to use righteous indignation at the proper time and place, and especially to learn what to delegate and what to do themselves, their job should proceed well.

Quality of Persuasiveness

Human resources executives must be able to sell their programs to the top executives and managers in the organization. Sometimes the interface of long-standing relationships within a company can be helpful in obtaining approval and enthusiastic acceptance of a proposed new program. HR managers may first have to win the support of those who are in a stronger position than they are, in order that the program be accepted by key persons. At times the political process becomes just as important an ingredient in the human resources profession as it is in public life.

STAFFING THE HUMAN RESOURCES DEPARTMENT

Similar to the captain of a ship, the first thing the head humans will want to do is to pick their own crew. Of course, this may be impossible under certain circumstances, for example, when HR managers are put in charge of an existing department. In such a situation, they must, at least for the moment, go with the current staff, but sooner or later, they will probably need to designate their own managers or supervisors. If, however, the task at hand is setting up a personnel/human resources operation from the ground up, the HR manager will want to staff each job in the department with the persons he or she wants and thinks will do the best job.

Human resouces executives should not worry about mistakes they make in the selection of people. The most experienced and respected human resources vice presidents or employment managers in the world can never guarantee that they will always hire the right person for a job opening—such an employment executive does not exist. So, by having the self-confidence and courage to move people laterally, down, or even out when they finally decide they are not right for the job, HR managers can be of great value to a company.

If called upon to do so, HR managers can effectively set up a new human resources function or reengineer an existing department in many different ways. No one table of organization can possibly fit every situation; nevertheless, similarities exist among organizations, and thus it is possible to show the essential functions in which every human resources department should be involved. Most of these functions are often the direct responsibility of the HR department, and HR staff members should have at least a working knowledge of each of the areas listed, even if it is not their direct concern.

HR Jobs and Titles

The organization of HR duties and responsibilities into formal jobs and titles is usually determined by company size and availability of resources. If a company is relatively large and the HR department has sufficient personnel, staff members may have the luxury of specialization. On the other hand, if the personnel/human resources department consists of only one person, the personnel/human resources manager can expect to wear many different hats.

In either event, the suggested job titles listed below represent all of the aspects of personnel management with which the modern-day personnel/human resources operation should be concerned. The job titles listed are not necessarily in the order of importance, nor are they meant to be literal: When a job title of "Manager" is used, that function could also be named "Supervisor" or even "Leader." For example, especially in larger companies, it is common to have a "Manager, Benefits," a "Supervisor, Benefits," and one or more "Leader, Benefits" positions. The structure above a "Manager, Benefits" might well include a "Director, Benefits," and at the top in the largest organizations, a "Vice President, Benefits." Some companies may also combine different personnel functions while others keep them separate. For example, the "Manager, Benefits" and the "Manager, Compensation" positions in one company may be combined into a single "Manager, Compensation and Benefits" in another. In addition, practice varies regarding the use of the functional designation before the individual title on all the titles listed, such as, "Employment Manager" and "Compensation Manager."

The following job title listing stresses function rather than format:

- Manager, Employment
- Manager, Compensation

- Manager, Benefits
- EEO, Coordinator (or Manager, Personnel Relations)
- Manager, Information Systems (This title is appropriate in those organizations where all programming and management information systems—MIS—personnel are assigned to their respective user groups, such as in Human Resources.)
- Manager, Wage and Salary Analysis
- Manager, Training and Development
- Manager, Payroll
- Manager, Unemployment Compensation
- Manager, Executive Compensation
- Manager, Retirement Planning
- Manager, Employee Assistance Program
- Manager, Outplacement Services
- Manager, Union/Labor Relations
- Manager, Community Relations
- Manager, Quality Circles/Suggestion System
- Manager, Health, Safety, and Wellness Programs
- Manager, Workers' Compensation Administration
- Manager, Organization Development
- Manager, Medical Services Administration

In effect, at least some 15 managerial titles are possible in a human resources operation, in addition to all the other levels of supervisor and/or leader that might be associated with each functional area. However, rarely would the HR department actually include all or even most of these managerial job titles in its organizational chart. They are spelled out here to demonstrate the extent of human resources responsibilities. Small companies, of course, might have one individual covering all 15 bases. As the company begins to increase in size and scope, the need to divide some of the major functions becomes apparent, and the head of the department then has the duty and the challenge to convince top management to adjust the human resources budget to allow for the new position(s) within the department.

Choose Leaders on the Basis of People-Orientation

HR executives should choose team captains and leaders carefully and on the basis of people-orientation. Filling these key managerial slots with individuals who are first and foremost people-oriented men and women is extremely important. Technical competence, education, and job knowledge are important, of course, to the success of any job; however, individuals who relate to people easily and who are normally patient and understanding with customers are the proper choice in any business situation and especially in a retail sales operation. In addition, the person hired will inevitably hire into his or her group employees who share the manager's values and approach to handling customers and others, thus perpetuating good customer service and satisfaction, as well as success and profits. The corollary to this is that HR executives should have no hesitancy whatsoever in replacing those managers who, for whatever reason, forget their people/customer-orientation.

The ability to relate to people is extremely important in every leadership or supervisory role; in fact, it is important in any job, supervisory or not. From the standpoint of the human resources function, the credo is clear and simple:

> It is absolutely vital that each personnel staff member be an unabashed, all-out, proud-of-it *people* person whose primary goal is to help and to serve the people of the organization with enthusiasm, competency, and cooperation. There must be a willingness to go the extra mile, to do whatever is necessary to investigate and resolve problems, answer questions, and do everything within his or her power to assist others in the effective performance of their jobs.

This is the human resources/personnel mandate, and it has universal application whether the HR manager *directs* a department of 100 people or *is* the department.

Other Important Qualities for Success in HR

In addition to the all-important quality of relating to people, success in human resources also requires a sense of fairness and tough-mindedness with the ability to make objective decisions based on the analysis of facts rather than on appearance, assumption, or emotion.

The HR managers and staff must also have the courage of their convictions to tell management as well as employees when they believe them to be wrong. While human resources first and foremost represents the management of the company, it also must represent the employees, the company's most important asset—this is good business. Regardless of how the organizational chart is designed, these are the kind of people an HR manager will need to fill the positions.

HR EXECUTIVE AND MANAGERIAL STAFF RELATIONSHIPS

Human resources managers' actions, attitudes, and motivations will essentially determine whether HR executives succeed or fail. These people are a head human's first line of defense. Although they report to the executive and the executive is their boss, things will go much more smoothly and successfully if HR executives can subtly convince the boss that they primarily work *with* him or her rather than *for* him or her.

The staff must respect HR executives as their leader, and the best way for HR executives to gain that respect is to earn it. In dealing with people —whether they are employees, customers, or the public in general—it is often the so-called little things that cause the biggest problems. As with most procedures that work, many are the result of trial and error, successes and failures, until the right solution is found. While the following guidelines do not apply to every company's individual circumstances they may nevertheless apply to a future situation. They concern the relationship between HR executives and the HR management staff:

1) No employee, whether manager or operative, always makes the right decision, and there is no such thing as an employee who never makes a mistake. Regardless of these truths, however, one of the first principles to be observed between HR executives and the management staff is that HR executives must back them up and support their decisions to anyone outside the department. This does not imply that they can never be wrong, nor that HR executives openly support them when they *are* wrong, but it does require that HR executives not condemn their action or concede that they were wrong until they have had the opportunity to discuss the matter with them first. If their decision was wrong or even questionable, the matter can then be corrected without embarrassment, and the human resources management staff will admire and respect the stand of the HR director and will undoubtedly make every effort to prevent a repeat situation.

2) In any human resources operation, regardless of the size of the company, a great variety of events, problems, situations, and opportunities will occur, primarily because the function of human resources is to deal with people. The challenges are literally endless; therefore, HR executives will want to keep in daily contact with their managers. To have detailed knowledge, HR executives should hold weekly or biweekly staff meetings with them, as well as require written, but brief, weekly status reports from them covering their current and anticipated projects. Many chief executives and some managers dislike meetings of any kind and characterize meetings as events where minutes are kept and hours wasted. Nevertheless, a well-conducted, stick-to-the subject session will prove a highly effective communication tool for all participants, and especially for HR executives. Staff meetings do not have to be dull or boring; the more interesting and lively they are, the more the management staff will look forward to them and will participate and contribute productively. A bit of genial and genuine humor from time to time can further enhance staff meetings.

3) Before HR executives make any kind of substantive business decision, they should ask the management staff what they think about the matter. While executives still reserve the right to make the final decisions, the input of the managers might provide that additional bit of light to guide their thinking. The staff may even be flattered that they have been asked for their opinion. By asking for the advice of the management staff, executives give the staff recognition, and earn their respect.

4) HR executives should be careful when dealing with their staff, either privately or in a meeting environment, not to put down or harshly criticize the company for some decision or action taken by the CEO or board of directors. All employees at some time or other gripe about their company, even considering it their prerogative to do so, and directors and managers are no exception However, as the head of the human resources department, the executive must demonstrate dedication and loyalty to the organization and its top management in his or her speech and actions. It is also advisable to not let HR management staff members be overly critical or outspoken about company management policies, programs, or procedures. These people also represent the HR department and their opinions do influence other company employees and supervisors. The expression, "we ride for the brand" implies that we either support top management fully or seek employment at another ranch.

5) HR directors must at any cost maintain the harmony of the group; they must never let petty differences between staff personnel go unnoticed or unattended. They must all understand that, although the HR director may have the highest regard for each of them individually, they will not permit constant internal arguments and disagreements, which might easily lead to a polarization of their group and be damaging to the department, the company, and the HR director. If necessary, the HR director should hold a meeting with the managers who are not seeing eye to eye, and make it unmistakably clear to them that, regardless of how valuable they are to the department and the company, their behavior will not be tolerated. Unless they agree to work together in harmony and to cooperate with each other, they can no longer continue as members of the human resources department. By being straightforward, HR directors can usually manage to bring the dissident members together in peaceful coexistence.

6) The management staff needs to understand that each of them has his or her primary specialty within the department, and that all

questions should be referred to the appropriate individual. By adhering to this practice, HR executives can eliminate or reduce the possibility of misinformation regarding HR programs, company policies, and so forth. It must be noted, however, that staff personnel should be able to handle general inquiries that overlap into other areas. In fact, managers should have at least a working knowledge of each other's areas of responsibility because human resources functions interlock with each other. For example, the employment group relies on the compensation staff to create accurate job descriptions and establish competitive wage ranges for hiring purposes. The equal employment coordinator depends on employment interviewers and recruiters to ensure that company hiring practices are nondiscriminatory. All human resources managers trust that the HR management information systems or computer people are providing them with reliable recommendations as to which software and hardware systems will enable them to economically and effectively carry out their job responsibilities.

7) Another important procedure that the HR director should require is the dating of all letters, memos, notes, reports, or other documents generated in the human resources department for either external or internal communication. Nothing is more frustrating than to find an important note in a personnel file, for example, which is dated August 6th, without indicating the year. It is best to avoid the confusion and time wasted to reconstruct the year of the writing. A corollary to this policy is for HR executives to require authorship of various notes and memos to be made clearly, directing, for example: "Please sign your name to everything you write or, at least, initial it."

8) Finally, a brief word on some "housekeeping" matters is appropriate:

    (a) The HR executives should socialize with managers as little as possible, except in the environment of company-sponsored or related events. Socializing under other circumstances can create erroneous impressions and make disciplinary situations more complex and difficult and invariably sends the wrong signals to other members of the HR staff.

    (b) When dealing with managers in a staff meeting, individually, or any other time, it is important for HR executives to display a sense of humor. When used properly and discreetly, a genuine sense of humor can often ease tensions, while letting the management staff know that the HR director personally enjoys association with them in a business context.

(c) Say "Good Morning" to them when you arrive at work and "Good-bye," "Have a good evening," or similar greeting or good-bye when you leave at night—you might be surprised at the goodwill this small but thoughtful action generates.

CHAPTER PERSPECTIVE

This chapter concentrated upon the key positions in the human resouces department: the executive and the management staff. What types of personal characteristics are necessary for success in these positions was discussed. The importance of people-orientation for the "people" department was emphasized. The important relationship between HR executives and their managerial staff was explored using specific guidelines.

Compensation: Surveys, Wage and Salary Guidelines, and Job Descriptions

INTRODUCTION AND MAIN POINTS

This chapter focuses on the following areas of responsibility: analyzing wage and salary data and statistics, conducting surveys, analyzing and evaluating job duties and requirements, and writing and maintaining job descriptions for all jobs within the organization—all part of the compensation function of human resources:

The tools that the compensation professional uses to accomplish the above objectives are defined, and the proper sequence and use of the tools are discussed.

The chapter describes how to conduct a survey for information regarding wages of specific job descriptions. Included are useful hints and examples on how to motivate competitor companies to participate, how to maintain anonymity and how to ask the right questions to get specific information.

An overview of how wage and salary guidelines are constructed is given.

The chapter also gives practical and detailed instructions on how to analyze jobs and how to write good job descriptions.

After studying the material in this chapter:

— You will know what is involved in making job data analysis and surveys, wage and salary guidelines, and job descriptions.

— You will be familiar with the tools that compensation professionals use to accomplish their objectives.

— You will be acquainted with the general concepts of constructing wage and salary guidelines.

— You will know how to go about analyzing jobs and how to write good job descriptions.

THE COMPENSATION FUNCTION

Compensation's primary responsibility is to study and analyze wage and salary data, surveys, and statistics. This is to insure internal pay equity and to maintain the company's competitive edge in recruiting, hiring, and retaining qualified people.

If the company has a formal wage program, this group will also have the following responsibilities:

■ Analyze and evaluate job duties, requirements, and responsibilities
■ Write and maintain job descriptions for all jobs within the organization.

Listing the compensation function first among human resources responsibilities is not necessarily intended to indicate priority ranking, however, compensation always ranks high—and in most cases *Number One*—in importance on the wish list of the average wage earner. This despite the much-publicized scientific conjectures about compensation being an issue far down the list of wants and needs of employees.

Compensation Staff
The compensation group is often comprised of the following types of employees:

■ Wage and salary analysts
■ Statisticians
■ Administrative and clerical support

The Tools
The compensation group accomplishes the above objectives just as all professionals do—by employing to the fullest extent the tools of their trade. Some of these tools are

1) a wage and salary program.
2) a point-scoring plan based on job duties.
3) computers and specialized software.
4) trade publications.

A formal wage and salary program and a point-scoring plan based solely on job duties and responsibilities are of primary importance. Probably the two most popular wage plans used by companies with a formal compensation program include those of the American Association of Industrial Management (AAIM) and the Hay organization. Before choosing a plan, the compensation manager and staff should thoroughly research and analyze different plans for their applicability to the company's particular needs. There is no one best plan for all companies; the best plan is the one that will work for you.

Other tools available to compensation professionals today are personal computers and a wide variety of software programs, which are not only convenient but absolutely essential in the gathering, calculation, maintenance, and retrieval of wage and salary data. From a practical standpoint, the processing and storage of data such as wage surveys, cost-of-living, and competitive salary information cannot be done without the management information and data processing hardware and software that exist today (and that will be even more helpful tomorrow). The constantly changing and improving state of the art of these tools insures greater speed, accuracy, storage, and retrieval capabilities of information so vital to compensation as well as to most other company functions.

The human resources professionals today have available to them any number of valuable HR software programs and systems. Listed below are some of the better-known HR software vendors, their products, and contact information:

GENESYS CORPORATION

Features human resources; benefits software designed to handle large as well as small volumes of data including employment EEO, life and history, wage and salary; defines contribution, benefits, and retirement plans.

For information: Genesys Software
5 Branch Street
Methuen, MA 01844

ABRA HUMAN RESOURCES MANAGEMENT SOFTWARE

Software covers EEOC, affirmative action, OSHA, worker's compensation, COBRA, immigration laws (I-9 forms), compliance with complex governmental regulations and standards.

Company also offers other related software, including:

ABRA Payroll.
ABRA Attendance.
ABRA Recruiting Solution.

ABRA Products Group is a division of Best Programs, Inc., St. Petersburg, Florida.

For information: ABRA Software
888 Executive Center Drive W
St. Petersburg, FL 33702-2402

D & B SOFTWARE

Offers multitiered approach to human resource management solutions, including:

host-based human resource management systems.
PC/LAN-based THR.
client/server-based HR stream.

These approaches facilitate integrated solutions for manpower management and compensation-support problems.

For information: Dun & Bradstreet Software, Inc.
66 Perimeter Center East
Atlanta, GA 30346

SPECTRUM'S HR VANTAGE SYSTEMS

This software features:
benefits administration.
compensation analysis.
government compliance.
(Optimized for Microsoft SQL server and Windows NT server.)
For information: Spectrum Human Resources Systems Corporation
1625 Broadway, Suite 2600
Denver, CO 80202

CYBORG SYSTEMS

Client/Server Human Resource Management Systems (HRMS) Options.

Software features:
human resource management.
payroll administration.
time and attendance applications.
ISO 9000 quality standards registration.
For information: Cyborg Systems
2 North Riverside Plaza
Chicago, IL 60606-0899

COMPUTER ASSOCIATES

Has developed new CA-HRISMA Software, a completely integrated system covering:
payroll.
personnel.
benefits.
The system uses client/server GUI-based software that supports both distributed and centralized processing.
For information: Computer Associates International, Inc.
Islandia, NY 11788-7000

In addition, a number of trade publications can assist compensation managers and their wage and salary analysts in keeping aware of what goes on in this most vital and key world of compensation. These publications are sources of wage and salary survey data by occupation within different geographic areas, federal and state wage law information, and a myriad of other data relating to compensation practices, policies, and procedures. They are published by organizations such as the Bureau of National Affairs (BNA), a Washington DC-based management information service; and Commerce Clearing House (CCH), a management business/legal service headquartered in Chicago, Illinois.

Now let's turn to the practical usage and application of all these tools and data available to the human resource professional.

USING THE TOOLS

First, let's assume that you have just been appointed manager or director of compensation in a company that possibly has always had its own informal wage program, but it has perhaps never used (or even heard of) standardized or formal wage ranges, rate positions, job descriptions, job analyses, relation-to-range techniques, or similar useful items. From a practical, economic, and efficiency standpoint, you may justifiably ask, "Just where do I start?" Good question. Several possible answers will be considered below.

In order to have competitive, equitable, and reasonable wage ranges, you must first determine what these ranges should be in the environments or areas in which the company operates or is located. Since local companies all bid for employee services for their available job openings, you naturally will want to know—and indeed *have* to know—what the competition is paying for the services of its work force. If your company is a national or international one with many outlets or facilities, your scope broadens, because you must know just what it takes to attract and keep good employees at each and every company location, domestic and foreign.

SURVEYING

How do you find and develop such highly confidential and competitive information? There is only one proven and effective method: You *ask* for it, meaning you dig, you write, you call, you listen, you discuss, you do everything in your power to find out from other companies, from chambers of commerce, from local personnel associations, from any source you can, just what hourly and salary rates other employers in the area pay for generally the same kind of work or jobs you may have in your company.

The general term for this type of inquiry is *surveying*, which ranges from telephone surveys and the other informal methods mentioned above, to the more formal written survey or questionnaire forms sent out to other companies, especially those in the same community in which your company operates. Incidentally, you might be surprised at how many of these companies will accede to your survey request, even knowing that you will probably be in competition with them for employees as well as for customers. Don't be discouraged or skeptical about how much success you'll have in getting this data from other companies. It is unlikely you'll get a 100 percent return rate, but you normally can anticipate a sufficient number of responses to provide some insight into what these jobs generally pay. Some motivators are as follows:

1) If you commit to give all participants a copy of the survey results, you may have offered enough enticement to insure a reasonable response.

2) Your assurance of strict confidentiality regarding the identities of participants should also help to increase your rate of return.

If you do not use company names, no participant will be able to identify any other company. Usually, each company in the survey is assigned a symbol or letter, such as A, B, C, D, and the only company that can be identified by participants is, therefore, their own.

In the cover letter or survey form, you should

▬ ask for their cooperation and assistance in providing this information, including a request that they complete and return the survey by a specified date;

▬ briefly describe the duties and responsibilities of the job categories in which you are interested, for example, accountants, engineers, mechanics, programmers, or janitors; and

▬ ask for compensation data on these jobs, such as low, midpoint, and high *actual* salaries, as well as salary *ranges*.

You would normally request return of the survey forms within four to six weeks. Once they are returned, they, together with other research you've done on your own, should put you in a position to begin constructing a compensation range for each of your jobs. See the sample survey cover letter and questionnaire form below.

FIGURE 5-1
Sample Survey Cover Letter

July 1, 1996

DEF Manufacturing Company
132 East Main Street
Hartford, CT 06163
Attention: Director of Human Resources (or Compensation Manager):

Dear Sir or Madam:

ABC Company is asking you and a selected group of private and public employers in our community to participate in a wage and salary survey designed to provide wage and benefit information on the positions listed on the enclosed survey form.

FIGURE 5-1 (continued)

Your responses to this survey will be kept in strictest confidence, and all survey participants will be assigned an identification letter (A, B, C, etc.), in order to identify their own organization when survey results are published to all participating companies.

If you are interested in participating in the survey (and we sincerely hope you are), we ask that you complete and return it (mail or fax) to us at the address given below on or before July 25. If you have any questions concerning the data requested in the survey form, please do not hesitate to contact me for clarification.

We very much appreciate the investment of your valuable time in answering the survey, and we would be more than happy to reciprocate by providing whatever wage or salary information you may need from us in the future.

Very sincerely yours,

Jennifer Rankin
Manager, Compensation
ABC Company, Inc.
2818 Asylum Avenue
Hartford, CT 06161

Voice - (203) 422-6871
Fax - (203) 422-6775

Enclosure: Survey Reply Form

FIGURE 5-2
Survey Questionnaire Form

Date: _____   Your assigned survey letter: (A)

Company Name: DEF Manufacturing Co.
Location: (City/State)   Hartford, CT
Company Size: (# employees at this location): F/T____ P/T____

JOB TITLE(S)	PRIMARY DUTIES	SALARY RANGE		
		MIN	MID	MAX
_____	_____	$____	$____	$____
_____	_____	____	____	____
_____	_____	____	____	____

FIGURE 5-2 (continued)

_____   _____   ___ ___ ___

_____   _____   ___ ___ ___

BENEFITS PROVIDED	COMPANY PAID	EMPLOYEE PAID
Medical	_____	_____
Dental	_____	_____
401(k)	_____	_____
Profit Sharing	_____	_____
Other Benefits (list) (such as apt. furnished, vacation pay):	_____	_____
	_____	_____

Pay increases based on Merit _____   Other _____

GENERAL COMMENTS:

At this point, you are now beginning to get a fairly good idea of the going rate needed to attract and keep good job candidates. Incidentally, no matter how thorough you are, your survey efforts will probably not cover each and every job title or position the company will have. However, it will normally give you enough information to build wage ranges for your key jobs and to slot in the nonsurveyed jobs, based on their individual scoring analysis, which will be described later in this chapter.

WAGE AND SALARY GUIDELINES

At this point, a matrix or series of numerical grade levels can be constructed and a wage or salary range guideline can be assigned to each grade level. You can set up a table or chart of perhaps ten grade levels for nonexempt jobs and an equal number for the exempt job categories. There is no specific recommended number of grade levels but ten is a reasonable number to work with. A grade level table for executive jobs should also be created later, after the exempt/nonexempt wage tables have been constructed and placed in effect. Any number of grade levels may be selected for the wage and salary program, depending upon what you, as compensation manager, determine is right for the company and its wage and salary program. The following is a sample illustration of what these wage and salary guideline tables might look like.

TABLE 5-1
Nonexempt Wage Schedule Guidelines
Hourly Rates (with Monthly Equivalents)

Grade Level	Rate Step 80	Rate Step 90	Rate Step J	Rate Step S	Rate Step T
1	5.15 (892.)	5.80 (1005.)	6.45 (1117.)	7.10 (1230.)	7.75 (1343.)
2	5.65 (979.)	6.35 (1100.)	7.05 (1221.)	7.75 (1343.)	8.50 (1473.)
3	6.15 (1065.)	6.90 (1195.)	7.65 (1325.)	8.45 (1464.)	9.25 (1603.)
4	6.65 (1152.)	7.45 (1291.)	8.25 (1429.)	9.10 (1577.)	10.00 (1733.)
5	7.15 (1239.)	8.00 (1386.)	8.90 (1542.)	9.80 (1698.)	10.75 (1863.)
6	7.65 (1325.)	8.55 (1481.)	9.50 (1646.)	10.50 (1819.)	11.50 (1993.)
7	8.15 (1412.)	9.10 (1577.)	10.10 (1750.)	11.15 (1932.)	12.25 (2123.)
8	8.65 (1499.)	9.65 (1672.)	10.75 (1863.)	11.85 (2053.)	13.00 (2253.)
9	9.15 (1585.)	10.20 (1767.)	11.35 (1967.)	12.55 (2175.)	13.75 (2383.)
10	9.65 (1672.)	10.75 (1863.)	11.95 (2071.)	13.20 (2287.)	14.50 (2513.)

In Table 5-1, each grade level hourly range is constructed using flat 50 cent increases from grade levels 1 through 10 at the 80 step; and a 50 percent dollar spread from rate steps 80 through T, at each grade level. Each rate step is then rounded to the next higher 5 cent increment.

The various rate steps may be identified with any type of symbol, number, letter, etc. Here we have chosen to identify the steps as 80 (as in

80 percent of job standard); 90 (90 percent of job standard), J (normally referred to as job standard, the point at which the employee on a particular grade level is performing all phases of that job in a satisfactory manner); S (used to identify superior performance); and T (meaning top performance,) is the maximum point on the wage scale, and implies that the individual employee who achieves this rating is doing the job in an excellent or top-notch manner, or as well as it can possibly be done by anyone!

Current (September 1, 1997) Federal minimum wage—$5.15 per hour.

The wage schedule is constructed to increase the dollar potential for an employee who is promoted to a higher grade level. For example, employees on a grade level 3 job who have attained the J, S, or T step of that particular grade, and who are promoted to a grade level 5 job, increase their maximum potential from 9.25 per hour (grade 3 T), to 10.75 per hour (grade 5 T). This method of increasing money potential is also true in the Exempt Salary Schedule shown in Table 5-2.

TABLE 5-2
Exempt Salary Schedule Guidelines
Monthly Salaries (with Annual Equivalents)

Grade Level	Rate Step 80	Rate Step 90	Rate Step J	Rate Step S	Rate Step T
21	1300. (15,600.)	1460. (17,520.)	1620. (19,440.)	1785. (21,420.)	1950. (23,400.)
22	1430. (17,160.)	1605. (19,260.)	1785. (21,420.	1965. (23,580.)	2145. (25,740.)
23	1575. (18,900.)	1770. (21,240.)	1965. (23,580.)	2165. (25,980.)	2365. (28,380.)
24	1735. (20,820.)	1950. (23,400.)	2165. (25,980.)	2385. (28,620.)	2605. (31,260.)
25	1910. (22,920.)	2145. (25,740.)	2385. (28,620.)	2625. (31,500.)	2865. (34,380.)
26	2100. (25,200.)	2360. (28,320.)	2620. (31,440.)	2885. (34,620.)	3150. (37,800.)

TABLE 5-2 (continued)

27	2310.	2595.	2885	3175.	3465.
	(27,720.)	(31,140.)	(34,620.)	(38,100.)	(41,580.)
28	2545.	2860.	3180.	3500.	3820.
	(30,540.)	(34,320.)	(38,160.)	(42,000.)	(45,840.)
29	2800.	3150.	3500.	3850.	4200.
	(33,600.)	(37,800.)	(42,000.)	(46,200.)	(50,400.)
30	3080.	3465.	3850.	4235.	4620.
	(36,960.)	(41,580.)	(46,200.)	(50,820.)	(55,440.)

In Table 5-2, each grade level salary range is constructed using 10 percent increases from grade levels 21 through 30 at the 80 step; and a 50 percent dollar spread for each salary range, as from steps 80 through T at each grade level. Each rate step is then rounded to the next higher $5.00 increment.

The various rate steps may be identified with any type of symbol, number, letter, etc. Here as with the nonexempt wage schedule (Table 5-1) we have chosen to identify the steps as 80 (as in 80 percent of the job standard); 90 (90 percent of the job standard); J (normally referred to as the job standard, the point at which the employee on a particular grade level is performing all phases of that job in a satisfactory manner); S (used to identify Superior performance); and T (meaning Top performance), the maximum point on the salary scale, and implies that the individual employee who achieves this rating is doing the job in an excellent or top-notch manner, or as well as it can possibly be done by anyone!

The exempt salary schedule, similar to the hourly nonexempt schedule in Table 5-1, is also constructed to increase the dollar potential for an employee who is promoted to a higher grade level. For example, employees on a grade level 25 job who have attained the J, S, or T step on that particular grade, and who are promoted to a grade level 27 job, increase their maximum potential from $2,865 per month (Grade 25 T), to $3,465 per month (Grade 27 T).

Any type or combination of symbols, letters, and numbers may be utilized in constructing the wage and salary tables, but there must be some system of tables, charts, and wage cards in order for employees and managers to be aware of the guidelines for all jobs in the company. Once completed, the wage and salary guidelines should be distributed to all supervisors and managers for their use in compensating their employees. All company supervisors will appreciate the wage and salary tables printed on wallet-size cards and preferably laminated, for their convenience in usage.

Having constructed the tables based on the most accurate, current, and competitive information available, you should be sure to review them at least yearly and make adjustments based on inflation, cost of living, and wage increase data from the past 12-month period. The success of your entire wage and salary program is in many respects dependent on how up to date the charts and tables of the wage and salary guidelines are kept.

OTHER IMPORTANT TOOLS

The next and probably most complex part of the human resources compensation function involves the determination of just what jobs are needed in the program and how they are to be evaluated and described. In order to accomplish this, you will need some additional tools to help the compensation staff properly perform their analytical and evaluation duties. These tools include the following:

- Organization charts
- Questionnaire forms
- Personal interviews
- Job descriptions

Organization Charts

An organization chart is a graphic representation of all jobs in which the reporting relationships are delineated by boxes, circles, lines, captions, and so forth, to demonstrate how the unit is functionally organized. Normally prepared and approved by the manager of the department whose jobs are being evaluated, the organization chart provides the wage and salary analyst in the compensation group with an overview of the unit's organizational or reporting structure.

To assist the wage and salary analyst in gauging the weight or importance of lead, supervisory, or managerial jobs in the unit, the chart should also include the total number of employees classified in each job in order to determine the scope of any supervisory responsibility. See Table 5-3 for a sample organization chart.

In addition, the organization chart should have the signature approval of the respective department or line manager involved, which gives the compensation group the authority to begin the analysis and evaluation of the job or jobs in question. There is probably no greater source of frustration or waste of time and money than the discovery, after having completed or even partially completed a difficult job evaluation project, that top department supervision had *not* given final approval of the chart. The evaluation project might then be shelved either temporarily or permanently.

Table 5-3 is an example of an accounting department organization chart:

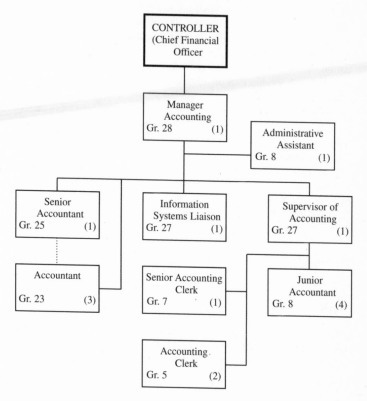

TABLE 5-3

Accounting Department Organizational Chart
(Example for organization with 500–1,000 employees)
Total Department Personnel: 15

Questionnaire Forms

The questionnaire is a useful document that simply asks the incumbent of the job certain standard and basic questions regarding the job, such as

- the day-to-day duties and responsibilities of the job;
- the type and nature of the work;
- how often certain activities are performed;
- the frequency, nature, and level of contacts involved;
- the most difficult aspects of the work;

■ the type of decisions that must be made; and

■ the consequences of probable errors.

Designed by the compensation group, the questionnaire form requests current incumbent job holders of jobs being analyzed to fill out and return the form to compensation prior to the start of the job evaluation project.

The questionnaire gives the wage and salary analyst a preliminary yet basic overview of job functions and duties. It is intended only to supplement, rather than to replace, the recommended one-on-one personal interviews by the analyst with job incumbents and managers. While the questionnaire is not an absolute requirement for every evaluation, it is especially useful in analyzing highly technical jobs, and for multi-job evaluations involving new or completely reorganized departments or groups.

When company departments or job groups are being organized, reorganized, or reevaluated, and there are no incumbents in the jobs in question, the manager or director of the job or jobs in question completes the questionnaire. The manager answers the questions therein based on how he or she intends the job or jobs to operate, once incumbents are hired, promoted, or transferred into these positions. The evaluation process then proceeds on the basis of the input from the department head involved. See the sample questionnaire form in Figure 5-3.

FIGURE 5-3

Position Description Questionnaire (to be Completed by Manager)

CO/DEPT.:_____   DATE:_____

NAME:_____

INSTRUCTIONS: The purpose of this form is to describe the position below in terms of its PRIMARY AND FUNDAMENTAL duties, responsibilities, and other requirements. Please fill out the questionnaire completely.

CURRENT JOB TITLE:_____

THIS POSITION REPORTS TO:_____

PRIMARY/FUNDAMENTAL DUTIES (MOST ESSENTIAL REQUIREMENTS) OF THIS POSITION: Indicate the percent of time spent performing these duties daily. USE COMPLETE SENTENCES, INDICATING THE DUTIES PERFORMED, WHY THEY ARE PERFORMED OR HOW.

FIGURE 5-3 (continued)

OTHER DUTIES PERFORMED: (Marginal duties). Duties and responsibilities that are performed either very infrequently or that could be performed by others without altering the underlying reason the job exists. NOTE: A marginal function may be essential, however, due to the limited number of employees available to perform the particular duty(ies). Use back of this page to continue. *(Indicate the percent of time spent performing these duties daily.)*

SUPERVISION: LIST TITLES OF ANY SUBORDINATES REPORT-ING TO THIS POSITION, IF APPLICABLE.

1. WHAT IS THE MOST DIFFICULT OR COMPLEX PART OF THIS JOB?

2. WHO ASSIGNS DAILY OR REGULAR WORK? (IF NOT SUPER-VISOR, GIVE TITLE.)

3. HOW MUCH INSTRUCTION IS RECEIVED FROM THE SUPERVISOR IN DOING THIS WORK, AND WHAT PARTS ARE CHECKED BY THE SUPERVISOR?

4. WHAT KINDS OF DECISIONS OR JUDGMENTS DOES THE EMPLOYEE EXERCISE ON HIS OR HER OWN? (GIVE SPECIFIC OR CONCRETE EXAMPLES OF EACH.)

FIGURE 5-3 (continued)

5. WHAT CONTACTS DOES THE EMPLOYEE MAKE WITH PEOPLE IN THE PERFORMANCE OF THE JOB? (LIST DEPARTMENTS NOT NAMES.) TELL FREQUENCY, PURPOSE, AND TYPE OF CONTACT (WRITTEN, IN PERSON, BY PHONE).

6. WHAT PROGRAMS/PROJECTS IS THE EMPLOYEE DIRECTLY RESPONSIBLE FOR, IF ANY? (EXPLAIN THE PURPOSE OF EACH.)

7. PHYSICAL SKILLS: CHECK BELOW THE OFFICE MACHINES OR OTHER EQUIPMENT REQUIRED TO PERFORM THE PRIMARY/FUNDAMENTAL FUNCTIONS OF THIS JOB. INDICATE THE AVERAGE PERCENT OF TIME REQUIRED FOR EACH.

MACHINE	PERCENT OF TIME USED	DAILY	WKLY	MTHLY
a. Telephone				
b. Calculator				
c. PC/computer terminal				
d. Dictaphone/ Transcriber				
e. Forklift				

f. OTHER (list), for example, hand tools (hammers, screwdrivers); power tools, cameras/video recorders, etc.

8. INDICATE BELOW (X) THOSE PHYSICAL ACTIVITIES (ABSOLUTELY ESSENTIAL) TO THE PERFORMANCE OF THIS JOB. DESIGNATE THE PHYSICAL ACTIVITIES REQUIRING THE MOST EFFORT AND THAT ARE ABSOLUTELY NECESSARY TO PERFORM THE PRIMARY/FUNDAMENTAL DUTIES REQUIRED OF THIS POSITION.

FIGURE 5-3 (continued)

PHYSICAL ACTIVITIES

____Walking	____Jumping	____Running	____Balancing
____Climbing	____Crawling	____Standing	____Turning
____Stooping	____Crouching	____Kneeling	____Sitting
____Reaching	____Lifting	____Carrying	____Throwing
____Pushing	____Handling	____Fingering	____Feeling
____Talking	____Hearing	____Seeing	____Color Vision

____Depth Perception   ____Working Speed (as in assembler)

____Pulling   ____Grasping

If lifting or carrying is a requirement, what are the MINIMUM number of pounds required to be lifted or carried? _____

Is driving a motor vehicle a requirement of this job?_____

9. PHYSICAL REQUIREMENTS(DEMANDS): CHECK BELOW (X) WHICH ADEQUATELY DESCRIBES THE PHYSICAL EFFORT REQUIRED TO PERFORM THE JOB DUTIES):

a. Light tasks requiring a minimum of tiring physical effort. Performance of work provides intermittent sitting, standing, and walking._____

b. Light physical effort required in working with lightweight materials and office supplies. Occasional operation of office machines or equipment resulting in some fatigue._____

c. Almost constant or repetitive work of a mechanical or machine nature. Almost continuous sitting at computer terminal. Walking. Occasionally difficult working position. Small amount of lifting and carrying._____

d. SUSTAINED physical effort required in working with average or lightweight materials and/or office supplies with continuity of effort. CONTINUOUS SITTING OR WALKING. CONTINUOUS OPERATION OF OFFICE MACHINES OR EQUIPMENT RESULTING IN CONSIDERABLE FATIGUE._____

e. CONTINUOUS STANDING OR WORKING IN DIFFICULT POSITIONS. WORKING WITH AVERAGE OR HEAVYWEIGHT MATERIALS AND/OR OFFICE SUPPLIES._____

FIGURE 5-3 (continued)

10. WORKING CONDITIONS: CHECK BELOW (X) ANY WORKING CONDITIONS THAT APPLY TO THE PRESENT WORK LOCATION FOR THIS POSITION:

_____Work primarily inside   _____Work primarily outside

____Hot   ____Cold   ____Sudden Temperature Changes   ____Humid

____Dry   ____Wet   ____Dusty   ____Odors   ____Noisy

____Adequate lighting   ____Adequate ventilation   ____Vibration

____Mechanical hazards   ____Moving objects   ____Cramped spaces

____High places   ____Exposure to burns   ____Electrical hazards

____Explosives   ____Radiant energy   ____Toxic conditions

____Working with others   ____Working around others   ____Work alone

11. TRAINING: List any degree or on-the-job training essential to this job (licenses, certificates, degrees). (Give minimum requirements.)

12. EXPERIENCE: What are the minimum years of job-related experience necessary to perform all of the normal duties required in this position._____

13. CONFIDENTAL DATA: Does employee have access to confidential data? YES____ NO____ If YES, what is the general nature of the confidential data?

14. TRAVEL: Is the employee required to travel for business purposes? YES____ NO____ If YES, approximately how many days per year? _____

OTHER COMMENTS:

FIGURE 5-3 (continued)

_____

MANAGER'S SIGNATURE

DATE COMPLETED:_____
CO./DEPT.: _____

NOTE: THIS QUESTIONNAIRE MUST BE RETURNED TO HUMAN
RESOURCES ALONG WITH A CURRENT ORGANIZATION
CHART APPROVED BY THE MANAGER'S VICE PRESIDENT,
GENERAL MANAGER, OR DIRECTOR.

Thank you,

HUMAN RESOURCES DEPARTMENT.

Personal Interviews

A critical responsibility of every good wage and salary analyst is to talk
with as many people as possible who occupy and perform the duties
of the jobs being evaluated. It cannot be performed at the analyst's
desk, but must be experienced out on the shop floor, in the engineering lab, at the office, or wherever else the job in question is being done.
Once again, if there are no job incumbents, then the respective manager
or department head must be interviewed by the analyst in order to determine how the job will interact and what its duties and responsibilities
are expected to be.

Although the personal interview may not be considered a tangible
tool of the job evaluation trade, the interviewing of those who are already
performing the job or jobs being evaluated becomes a formidable,
essential aid in producing a good, well-written job description.

JOB DESCRIPTIONS

The written products of the wage and salary analyst's job evaluation,
job descriptions should clearly and concisely describe the duties and
responsibilities of each of the jobs in question.

In the preparation of the job description, the experienced wage and
salary analyst uses the organization chart (see Table 5-3) to help determine the proper weight and credit for job-scoring purposes. Although
opponents of organization charts may deride them as being hanging
trees, bureaucratic red tape, artistic nonsense, and the like, they are
nonetheless valuable aids in writing realistic job descriptions.

Whether the job is an hourly wage, salaried, blue-collar, or white-
collar job does not change the process of analyzing the job. The only

practical and objective way a wage and salary analyst can prepare a clear, accurate, and comprehensive job description is to know the duties of the job *thoroughly*, and to skillfully and carefully describe those duties and responsibilities as they actually exist, not what one might suppose or assume them to be.

To fully understand and be familiar with the duties of the job under study, the analyst would be well advised to consider the following formula for success. As the human resources director, the wage and salary analyst, or whoever is evaluating the job, take the following steps.

1. Get up off your chair.
2. Take your portfolio or notebook in hand.
3. Leave your office.
4. Observe the incumbents (if any) on the job performing their work.
5. Make notes or an outline of your findings.
6. Ask for information or data from them as to *how*, *what*, *where*, *when*, and *why*, they do what they do.

Writing the Job Description

Assuming you now have an approved organization chart, have received your completed questionnaires from the department in question, and have conducted your personal interviews with job incumbents and/or the department manager, all that now remains is to begin your task of preparing a clear, accurate, and comprehensive job description.

You should also give credence and weight to anticipated future duties and responsibilities, even those that might not necessarily be a part of the job at the time it is first written.

A clear, concise, and well-written job description normally enables the reader to understand exactly what the job duties and responsibilities are. Ideally, it is written to describe what the duties of the job should be, as determined by the supervisor or manager of the job in question. A good rule is to write the job as generically as possible, as though there were no incumbent on it, and to build the description on the specific duties management expects future occupants of the job to perform.

This does not mean that you ignore the work that the incumbents are currently performing and what they tell us they do—far from it! However, you must always keep in mind the purpose and reason for having such a job at all, and where it fits into the overall department structure. This again is where preliminary job knowledge gathered from the chart and questionnaire can be of tremendous help in getting the feel for job duties and responsibilities before the actual analysis begins.

The format, or technical construction of the job description also deserves your attention. You will find that the most effective techniques in writing a job description are

1. to summarize the duties and responsibilities of the job as clearly and completely as you can in the first paragraph, sometimes referred to as the topical or summary paragraph, and

2. to elaborate on these duties in the subsequent paragraphs.

The description should be concise, just long enough to adequately acquaint the reader with the essential duties and responsibilities of the job without unnecessary details. Contrary to some popular beliefs among wage and salary analysts, a sign of a good job description is not how long it is, such as, how many paragraphs or how many pages. Similar to Abraham Lincoln's famous comment that a person's legs should be just long enough to reach the ground, so should a well-written job description be just long enough to acquaint the reader with all of the principal job duties and responsibilities of the position. It rarely needs to exceed one page, with one-half to two-thirds of a page normally adequate to get your main points across.

The language should be simple, clear, and straightforward. It should not be sprinkled with oblique, flowery, or 64-dollar words. When you read a job description that does have such words, it's a fairly sure bet that the analyst who wrote it did not have a full grasp of the job and is probably just trying to meet an assigned quota of jobs written. Of course, it may also be an attempt by the analyst to get signoff approval of the description draft from his or her supervisor or checker by dazzling that person with big words and impressive language. The experienced analyst knows that tactic seldom works. Again, when too many big and important-sounding words are used in a job description, chances are pretty good that the analyst really didn't understand the duties of the job or what it was all about.

If you follow the above guidelines for researching and writing job descriptions, you will find it is the guaranteed, fail-safe way to success in the job description writing business.

Sample Job Descriptions

Figures 5-4 through 5-9 are sample job descriptions illustrating the above-recommended methods of preparation.

FIGURE 5-4
Job Description

Job Title: MECHANIC A   GRADE LEVEL: 7

Job Code: 2030   Exemption Status: NONEXEMPT

Company Name: ABC CORPORATION, INC.

Department Name: REPAIR SHOPS   Department No.: VARIOUS

PRIMARY FUNCTION: Under the direction of the shop manager, or shop foreman, provide technical direction and instruction to less-experienced mechanics. Check progress of work being performed to ensure meeting quality standards and delivery schedules. May perform all levels of complex repair and preventative maintenance on vehicles and equipment including removal and installation of engines and transmission overhaul and repair. Initiate repair statements, work orders, parts requisitions, inventory forms, condition reports, etc.

Responsible for the repair of all mechanical defects and complete campaign modifications of vehicles and equipment. Road test trucks after repairs are completed. May be required to assist in the repair of vehicles disabled while in road service.

Must be familiar with motor vehicle repair manuals and company repair policies and procedures. Recommend new or revised operations to improve equipment repair, performance and quality. May recommend campaigns to retrofit specific types of vehicles for reasons of safety or better performance. Maintain good housekeeping and safety practices in the work area. May perform other related duties as required or assigned, especially those that involve serving the customer.

PHYSICAL/MENTAL REQUIREMENTS: Walking, balancing, standing, turning, climbing, stooping, crouching, kneeling, sitting, reaching, lifting (at least 50 pounds minimum daily), carrying, pushing, handling, digital dexterity, feeling, talking, hearing, seeing, depth perception, working speed. Must concentrate mental and visual attention closely on work, matching manual dexterity with mental and visual attention for sustained periods.

Must have valid driver's license and be able to drive vehicles with manual transmissions. Must comply with local and state license requirements for test drive purposes.

Wage and Salary Analyst:_____

Approvals: _____

          (Name)   (Title)

          _____

          (Name)   (Title)

FIGURE 5-5
Job Description

Job Title: OFFICE MANAGER　　　　Grade Level: 7

Job Code: 1650　　　Exemption Status: NONEXEMPT

Company Name: ABC CORPORATION, INC.

Department Name: VARIOUS　　Department No. VARIOUS
(This job may be used in any department authorized to have a position of Office Manager on its staff.)

PRIMARY FUNCTION: Under the direction of the department manager, responsible for supervising office clerical personnel.

Supervise clerical personnel on the basis of economy and effectiveness. Maintain office and personnel records, and ensure that supplies and clerical support are available for staff. Gather data and prepare periodic reports. Assist with budget preparation and control. Select, train, and motivate personnel, initiate wage increases, promotions, and transfers, as well as disciplinary action including termination when warranted.

Conduct new-employee orientation and explain benefit programs. Must be familiar with ABC Company policies and procedures. Supervise the ordering of supplies and recommend the purchase of new office equipment or furniture.

Input special hours (sick time, vacation, and personal time off into payroll system, and finalize payroll.

Perform other related duties as required or assigned.

PHYSICAL/MENTAL REQUIREMENTS: Flow of work and character of duties involve the coordination of manual dexterity and normal mental and visual attention. Activities: Fingering (55 percent of time spent on keyboard), seeing, sitting, talking, walking.

Wage and Salary Analyst:_____

Approvals: _____
　　　　　　　　(Name)　　　　　　　　　(Title)
　　　　　　　_____
　　　　　　　　(Name)　　　　　　　　　(Title)

FIGURE 5-6
Job Description

Job Title: PARTS COORDINATOR A   Grade Level: 8

Job Code: 2688   Exemption Status: NONEXEMPT

Company Name: ABC CORPORATION, INC.

Department Name: REPAIR SHOPS   Department No.: VARIOUS

PRIMARY FUNCTION: Under the direction of the shop manager or shop foreman in a repair shop, order and stock all parts, materials, tools, and supplies used in the facility. Maintain adequate inventory levels to assure continued availability of same to avoid work stoppages. Keep informed of vendor lead and delivery times. Establish and maintain minimum stocking levels of all parts, based on usage history. Order and maintain adequate inventories of specialty tools, lubricants, tires, batteries, and all other most-used parts and items. Take accurate inventories as scheduled in accordance with company policy and procedures.
May deliver parts directly to user or using area. Originate and process all internal and external purchase orders. Approve invoices for payment. Maintain a clean, safe, and well-organized parts operation. Perform duties with a minimum of supervision.

May be requested to operate a forklift.

Perform other related duties as required or assigned, and particularly with regard to serving the customer.

PHYSICAL/MENTAL REQUIREMENTS: Walking, balancing, climbing, standing, turning, stooping, crouching, kneeling, sitting, reaching, lifting (minimum 50 pounds), carrying, pushing, handling, feeling, talking, hearing, seeing (with color vision) depth perception. Use of telephone 30 percent daily, fax machine and computer terminals. Duties involve the coordination of manual dexterity with normal mental and visual attention, or of part-time normal and part-time concentration and coordination.

Wage and Salary Analyst:_____

Approvals: _____
                    (Name)   (Title)

              _____
                    (Name)   (Title)

FIGURE 5-7
Job Description

Job Title: RECEPTIONIST/CLERK   Grade Level: 4

Job Code: 1675   Exemption Status: NONEXEMPT

Company Name: ABC CORPORATION, INC.

Department Name: WAREHOUSE   Department No. 950

PRIMARY FUNCTION: Under the direction of the warehouse manager, or office manager, responsible for performing a variety of clerical duties, including one or more of the following:

Type reports, charts, graphs, correspondence, and memos. May take or transcribe dictation using dictating equipment. Enter data into computer terminal. Greet visitors or customers and direct them to appropriate individuals. Answer telephones. Take messages, answer questions, and direct callers to appropriate parties. Open and distribute incoming mail and prepare outgoing mail. Maintain office files, order office supplies, and operate a variety of office machines such as an adding machine, transcription machine, computer terminal, personal computer (PC), fax machine, and photocopier. Maintain good housekeeping in work area.

Perform other duties as required or assigned.

PHYSICAL/MENTAL REQUIREMENTS: Flow of work and character of duties involve the coordination of manual dexterity, and normal mental and visual attention, or part-time normal, and part-time concentration and coordination. Activities: Walking, stooping, reaching, talking, handling, hearing, standing, carrying, fingering (50 percent of time spent on keyboard), seeing, working speed, sitting.

Wage and Salary Analyst:_____

Approvals: _____

          (Name)   (Title)

          _____

          (Name)   (Title)

FIGURE 5-8
Job Description

Job Title: SENIOR CLERK   Grade Level: 6

Job Code: 1681   Exemption Status: NONEXEMPT

Company Name: ABC CORPORATION, INC.

Department Name: WAREHOUSE   Department No.: 988

PRIMARY FUNCTION: Under the direction of the warehouse manager or office manager, responsible for performing a variety of clerical duties, including one or more of the following:

Keep accurate, current records of all warehouse transactions. Send copies of invoices to appropriate persons. Process bills for payment, and maintain accurate records of all bills paid and invoices received. May order stationery and supplies as needed. May fill supply orders as requested by authorized company personnel. Enter data into computer terminals, maintain shipping logs, and distribute all incoming and outgoing correspondence to appropriate departments. Maintain and update an accurate filing system. Assist with picking orders and inventory counts in the warehouse as necessary.

Audit, input, and transmit personnel/payroll information into computer network for warehouse personnel. Maintain vacation schedules and sick leave accumulations. Work with division or headquarters human resources personnel to answer employees' questions regarding pay, benefits, and related matters. May type correspondence, memos, take dictation, or transcribe from dictating machine. May gather data for preparation of periodic reports, act as receptionist, or perform other clerical duties in support of office staff. Must be able to operate a variety of office machines including a fax machine, computer terminal, personal computer, transcribing unit, photocopier, etc. Maintain good housekeeping in work area.

Perform other related duties as required or assigned.

PHYSICAL/MENTAL REQUIREMENTS: Flow of work and character of duties involve the coordination of manual dexterity and normal mental and visual attention; or part-time normal and part-time concentration and coordination. Activities: Handling, seeing, hearing, sitting, talking, fingering (70 percent of time spent on keyboard.)

Wage and Salary Analyst:_____

Approvals: _____
          (Name)   (Title)

          _____
          (Name)   (Title)

FIGURE 5-9
Job Description

Job Title: SHOP FOREMAN   Grade Level: 23

Job Code: 4427   Exemption Status: EXEMPT

Company Name: ABC CORPORATION, INC.

Department Name: REPAIR SHOPS   Department No.: VARIOUS

PRIMARY FUNCTION: Under the direction of the shop manager, supervise the profitable operation of all repair activities at the shop. Select, train, supervise shop personnel and maintain training programs for new shop employees. Initiate wage increases, promotions, transfers, disciplinary action, and terminations. Ensure work area is maintained in a clean and orderly manner and that personnel comply with good safety practices and regulations.

Initiate methods of improving efficiency in the shop. Check progress of work performed, resolve problems, and provide technical information and assistance to shop personnel. Make final inspection of completed work. Review serviceability of completed work and ensure completion of all necessary paperwork. Keep shop manager apprised of delays or problems that may prevent meeting work deadlines.

Perform other related duties as required or assigned, and especially with regard to serving the customer.

PHYSICAL/MENTAL REQUIREMENTS: Walking, climbing, stooping, reaching, pushing, talking, depth perception, crawling, crouching, lifting (minimum 50 pounds), handling, hearing, standing, kneeling, carrying, digital dexterity, seeing, working speed, balancing, turning, sitting, throwing, feeling, color vision. Mental requirements include, but are not limited to, the ability to concentrate, take initiative, cope with stress, adapt to and stay alert in a business environment, and to use independent judgment to accomplish results.

Wage and Salary Analyst:_____

Approvals: _____
                    (Name)   (Title)

            _____
                    (Name)   (Title)

Testing the Job Description

The hallmark of a well-analyzed, well-planned, and well-written description is whether a person totally unfamiliar with the job itself could read the job description for the first time and understand in fairly general (if not specific) terms what is expected of the persons classified on this particular job.

Why Job Descriptions Will Remain Necessary

Although job descriptions have been an essential tool of wage administration for quite a few years, modern business practices as well as new governmental rules, laws, and regulations would seem to dictate that they are still vitally necessary and will continue to be a part of the business scene for many years into the future.

Americans with Disabilities Act (ADA)

The Americans with Disabilities Act (ADA), which became effective in 1992, is a prime example of the continuing need for well-written and factual job descriptions. By clearly indicating in the description the duties of the job together with its mental and physical requirements related to lifting, walking, standing, job pressures, and so forth, and by reading or showing the job description to the employment applicant (nondisabled as well as disabled), the employer goes on record as affirming that these standards are an integral part of the requirements of the job being filled. If the applicant maintains that he or she can indeed perform the job as described, the employer is then obliged to include the person in the list or group of potential candidates being considered for the job. If a disabled applicant states that he or she can perform the job duties if some accommodation is made by the employer, and if, as the law states, such accommodation is considered a reasonable one, then the employer is also required under ADA to view the person as a viable job applicant.

In determining just what is a reasonable accommodation, its cost, as well as the inconvenience or disruption to the employer's operation if the disabled person is hired, are both relevant factors. However, as with any new legislation, the matter is subject to various interpretations and will probably only be finally and conclusively settled by precedent court cases or administrative decree. In the meantime, as with so many other business decisions, the more that common sense prevails, and the more that disabled persons are given the opportunity of demonstrating their worth, the sooner they and their new employers will benefit.

In any event, it should be clear that even in this one area of personnel management, companies that do not update their job descriptions to reflect the lifting, walking, standing, reaching, and other physical and mental requirements of each individual job—or that perhaps have no descriptions at all—can look forward to an uphill challenge in defending themselves against charges of discrimination involving disabled job applicants and current employees as well.

Protection Against Other Discrimination Charges

Up-to-date, well-written job descriptions also provide protection against other types of discrimination charges involving sex, age, race, national origin, and religion. For example, it will be clear to government agencies, plaintiffs' lawyers, and the general public that this particular company, in its official documents stating the duties and responsibilities of each job in the company (such as job descriptions), makes no reference whatsoever to any factor relating to discrimination. Properly written job descriptions are sexually neutral, do not speak of age, race, religion, or creed, and speak only to the essential duties inherent in the job. The only stated requirements beside the normal skill and experience qualifications mentioned in job descriptions should be those physical or mental skills that are truly required of *any* person wishing to be considered for employment with the company.

Pay Equity. In today's world we are fortunate to have laws that require equal pay for equal work, regardless of the sex of the worker. In some countries, such as Canada, for example, recent laws and regulations require that workers performing jobs of equal value be paid equally. The Province of Ontario, Canada, has passed laws that require employers with male-dominated and female-dominated jobs to make adjustments to ensure that females and males, respectively, under these circumstances are paid equally, regardless of the type of work they perform. The concept is known as *pay equity* and will undoubtedly become a factor in employee compensation in other countries, including the United States.

Here again, although there can never be a 100 percent guarantee, well-planned and well-written job descriptions are just about the best defense any employer can have against charges of discrimination relating to equal pay, disability, or other forms of employment discrimination. Job descriptions support and back up various point-scoring or other evaluation systems that, in turn, justify different grade levels, with correspondingly different wage- or salary-range guidelines. The case can certainly be made that when the job description makes no reference to gender, men and women alike are eligible and considered for these jobs based on only one criteria, namely their ability to do the job, regardless of being either male or female! The process of determining which job duties and responsibilities are of equal value, as well as who should be involved in this determination, still remains largely unclear.

Don't let anyone convince you that job descriptions are just another example of bureaucratic red tape, or again, merely artistic joy overriding commercial advantage, as we've heard before. To the contrary, you'll find them to be just about the most important weapon in your compensation and human resources arsenal.

The Importance of Updating Job Descriptions

Each job must then be kept up to date as substantive changes, whether additions or deletions of responsibilities or duties, occur. Even if no meaningful changes do happen, for example, within a year, it is still strongly recommended that all jobs be reviewed at least once a year by the compensation department in conjunction with the respective department supervisors or managers involved. By updating the descriptions, including any changes to the original set of duties, and obtaining departmental approval signatures, many problems are thus avoided.

Morale Building

When employees' jobs are systematically and periodically reviewed, their morale will in all likelihood improve when recognition is made of additional or expanded job duties and responsibilities, resulting in possible increases in wage- or salary-grade levels for the incumbents. It should also be recognized, however, that grade-level reductions, together with decreased salary potential, may also occur when significant duties are removed from the scope of any given job. Whether or not labor-grade changes result from the annual or periodic review, the very fact that the company recognized that, for example, duties *were* added to the job and subsequently to the job description, does tend to boost the morale of "our most important asset!"

Protection Against Misunderstandings

An accurate, understandable, and up-to-date job description also lets employees know what is expected of them in terms of their duties and responsibilities, and leaves little room for argument or contention that they were never really aware of what was expected of them. To further insure this knowledge, some companies feel that it's a good idea for all employees to be provided with a copy of their job description, and they require a signed receipt from employees stating they have received, read, and understood the description.

An Aid in Performance Evaluation

A current job description also becomes a valuable tool and aid for supervisors and managers at performance evaluation time. When employees are aware of exactly what is expected of them, supervisors have ready-made and built-in standards against which their people's performance may be measured. When descriptions are confused, hastily prepared, unclear, or not up to date—and certainly if no description exists at all—bosses have an uphill battle explaining and/or defending their evaluation of items in which employees may have fallen short in terms of their performance. So make your managers' collective lives much more pleasant—and your employees' lives as well—by having well-written, easily-understood, and current job and position descriptions for each and every job in your organization.

Please understand the distinction between having a job description for each job in your company, as opposed to having one for each employee. Most companies try to have as few job descriptions as possible. One very effective way of doing this is to use as many generic classifications as possible, such as accounting clerk, receptionist, data entry operator, or administrative assistant. They will have one description (in other words, one piece of paper) for each classification, regardless of how many employees may be classified on them, or the many departments in which they may be used. If the work happens to be organized into different levels or degrees of complexity and grading, you may still have, for example, Accounting Clerk I, Accounting Clerk II, and even Accounting Clerk III jobs with progressively higher grade levels, if the increasing complexity of the work warrants such a distinction. These are still considered to be generic jobs that may be used in all departments.

A Foundation for the Wage and Salary Program

Having a well-written job description for every different job classification in your company should and must be the goal of every compensation manager. Once this feat is accomplished, you have laid the foundation for your wage and salary program.

CHAPTER PERSPECTIVE

This chapter concentrated on several, but not all, areas of responsibility of the compensation function of human resources. It defined the professional tools of the compensation specialists and explained how they are used. It provided an overview of how surveys are conducted and how wage and salary guidelines are constructed. It stressed the importance of having job descriptions to the company and explained how they are written.

Wage and Salary Administration: Job Analysis and Evaluation

INTRODUCTION AND MAIN POINTS

Chapter 6 continues to describe the job analysis and evaluation process that began in Chapter 5. It explains the purposes of a formal wage and salary program and focuses on the weighing and scoring part of the process. A detailed explanation of how to design and construct a formal wage and salary program is presented. Examples of standard factors and degrees help to illustrate the hands-on workings of this important task of compensation.

This chapter also discusses the valuable role of computers, both mainframe and PC networks, in storing and maintaining the data generated in the process of creating a wage and salary program.

After studying the material in this chapter:

■ You will understand what the purposes and advantages of a formal wage and salary program are.

■ You will know what the different steps in the job analysis and evaluation process are.

■ You will be familiar with the basic terminology of the compensation function regarding the job analysis and evaluation process.

■ You will be aware of the important role computers play in compensation's functions, especially in supporting the valuable database for vital statistical information that has been generated as a result of a formal wage and salary program and its maintenance.

THE PURPOSES OF A WAGE AND SALARY PROGRAM

Organizing, developing, and maintaining a sound wage and salary program is by no means an easy task. In case you or your boss, including the CEO of the company, should need convincing as to the useful purposes of all this effort, keep the following advantages in mind.

1) A wage and salary program will help insure your company's wage competitiveness in the geographic area in which your company operates.

2) As a logical, understandable system, a wage and salary program provides management with a means to control wages and salaries.

3) If properly designed, communicated, and maintained, such a program will establish internal equity of pay within your corporation.

4) Supervisors will find they have better knowledge and control of their groups by developing and utilizing written records of duty assignments and responsibilities.

5) Supervisors will find that the wage and salary program will assist them in their hiring, disciplinary action, and performance appraisal functions by allowing them to be much better organized and informed.

6) Management will be better able to detect overlapping job duties as well as unnecessary supervisory levels.

7) Managers and supervisors will come to find that a wage and salary program will result in a uniform, easy-to-maintain job titling system.

8) A wage and salary program becomes an invaluable database for vital statistical information.

THE JOB ANALYSIS AND EVALUATION PROCESS

The basic job evaluation process consists of the following steps.

1) Wage surveys of local companies are conducted in the areas in which your company's facilities are located.

2) Wage and salary range guidelines are built for key or so-called bellwether jobs, based on survey data.

3) A formal wage and salary plan is selected, preferably one with point scoring and factor evaluation systems.

4) Under the guidance of the human resources staff, company managers and supervisors develop organization charts for all departments and divisions within the company, showing the reporting relationships of all jobs involved.

5) Presidents, managers, and supervisors involved are requested to approve and sign each organization chart for which they are responsible.

6) Questionnaires are provided to all incumbents of the jobs being evaluated (and, if possible, also to their respective supervisors), to enable the wage and salary analyst to be aware of the essential aspects of the job or jobs under evaluation.

7) Be absolutely certain that, when at all possible, your wage and salary analysts conduct personal interviews with incumbents (not necessarily all of them; a meaningful sample will do), as well as with the respective supervisors and managers of the jobs under evaluation. No worthwhile job description was ever

written, and no "right-on-the-money" job analysis was ever made from a desk in the compensation department without the analyst having first seen the job being performed, or at least without having discussed it with management when the job or position is new, in the planning stage, or is untenanted.

8) Prepare complete, clear, concise, and straightforward job descriptions to account for each job being performed in your company, from basic operative jobs to the highest echelon of executive management positions.

9) Utilizing all of the aforementioned tools, the analyst is now in a position to appraise and grade the jobs properly, using established wage and salary procedures.

10) Once jobs are evaluated, written, scored, and approved, they must then be maintained (reviewed) on a periodic basis, or whenever there are substantial changes in job duties or responsibilities (either added or taken away). In the interim period after the job is first written, or between normal job description reviews, the job should also be promptly looked at if substantial duties or responsibilities are added to or deleted from it.

APPRAISING AND GRADING THE JOBS

The next and perhaps most subjective step in the process is the analysis, evaluation, weighing, and scoring of the information you've compiled. After you have carefully studied and reviewed your wage surveys, organization charts, questionnaires, and completed job descriptions, and have chosen the appropriate wage and salary plan, you can now begin the process of determining just what value or weight should be placed on each job description that has been written.

As a compensation analyst, you will assign the proper grade level to the job, which in turn determines its appropriate wage or salary range. This scoring and grading process is a very important and key operation in that it may actually determine how effectively your company will be able to attract and to retain competent personnel.

The Design and Construction of a Typical Wage and Salary Program

The design and construction of a typical, formal wage and salary program are explained in detail below. Although there is no perfect way to master this skill and no exact science involved, there is a process to understand. After reading these suggestions, you will have an overview of the process.

The wage and salary plan you've chosen to use may have a number of *factors* relating to the skills or requirements an applicant or employee must possess in order to do the job. Each of these factors will be further broken down into five or six categories known as *degrees*, which indicate whether the necessary job skills for that particular factor are relatively simple or complex. Each degree of every factor will have some sort of assigned point scoring or value placed on it by the plan—the higher the degree, the greater the scoring.

The wage and salary analyst selects and assigns the proper degree of each factor, based on the duties of the job. The combined total point scoring of all the degrees results in a specific grade level. Each grade level in turn has a wage and salary range guideline that you originally developed from your wage survey data (see Surveying and Tables 5-1 and 5-2 in Chapter 5). Incumbents of the job being studied are thus uniformly classified on the resulting grade level.

The following summary may assist the reader in better understanding the job evaluation process.

The wage and salary analyst

1) reviews and analyzes the job duties.
2) selects appropriate degree of each weighted plan factor.
3) adds total resulting point scoring.
4) determines, from the total number of points, the grade level of the job.
5) selects the appropriate wage and salary range guidelines from the previously established plan developed from wage survey data.

FIGURE 6-1
An Example of the Job Evaluation Process

Bob Jones, a wage and salary analyst in the compensation group of the human resources department of Honey Bee Equipment Manufacturing Company, has been requested by Bill Dailey, general manager of the Bee Bonnet division, to evaluate a group of jobs in a newly established department of that division. Mr. Jones has requested and received from Mr. Dailey an approved organization chart showing reporting relationships within the new department, as well as position description questionnaires for the jobs involved.

After reviewing the organization chart and studying the questionnaires, Mr. Jones visits the new department and conducts personal interviews with the job incumbents. Satisfied that he understands the job functions and their reporting relationships, he then proceeds to write accurate job descriptions and submits them to General Manager Dailey for his and other necessary approvals.

When the approved job descriptions are returned, Mr. Jones then begins his evaluation process to determine the exemption status of each job, and to arrive at a grade level by applying the proper point scoring for each

FIGURE 6-1 (continued)

factor (education, experience, job complexity, etc.). One of the particular jobs involved, for example, is titled net sewer. The analyst, based on his understanding and knowledge of the duties of this job, first determines that this is a nonexempt job—in other words, an hourly paid job, not exempt from the overtime and other provisions of the Wage and Hour Law.

He next reviews the different degrees that make up each factor (first degree—5 points, second degree—10 points, and so on), and based on his knowledge of the duties of the job, he then selects the correct degree for each. For example, one specific requirement of the net sewer job might be mechanical knowledge, specifically the ability to operate a professional Model X sewing machine. The applicable factor here would be the experience factor to reflect the amount of time required to professionally operate that machine or an equivalent. If the job required a minimum of two years of such experience, and since the company's wage and salary plan assigns different points to different levels of experience, the job analyst in this case would assign the third degree of the experience factor, which calls for one to three years' experience, and has a point value of 60.

After considering all the factors relating to the net sewer job, he then proceeds to assign the proper degree of each in order to arrive at the total scoring. Mr. Jones' point scoring summary might look like the following:

FACTOR	DEGREE	POINTS
Education	2nd	30
Experience	3rd	60
Job Complexity	2nd	30
Supervision Received	2nd	10
Errors	2nd	10
Contacts	2nd	10
Confidential Data	1st	5
Mental/Visual Demand	2nd	10
Working Conditions	3rd	15

Total Points: 180

FIGURE 6-1 (continued)

Next he refers to the wage and salary point scoring manual, which has a predetermined range of points for each grade level. Table A below might represent a table from a typical scoring manual.

Table A

POINT SCORING RANGE	NONEXEMPT GRADES	EXEMPT GRADES
100 AND UNDER	1	–
105 – 130	2	–
135 – 160	3	–
165 – 190	4	–
195 – 220	5	–
225 – 250	6	21
255 – 280	7	22
285 – 310	8	23
315 – 340	9	24
345 – 370	10	25
375 – 400		26
405 – 430		27
435 – 460		28

Because the analyst has scored the net sewer's job at 180 points, he has determined that his scoring falls in the Labor Grade 4 range, so this job is officially designated as a Labor Grade 4. Because the wage range guidelines for a Grade 4, let us say, have a spread of $6.65 to $10.00 per hour, the net sewer's supervisor may then pay this employee an hourly rate of pay within that particular wage range (see Tables 5-1 and 5-2, Nonexempt Wage Schedule Guidelines and Exempt Salary Schedule Guidelines, in Chapter 5. These are only hypothetical wage and salary range tables, but they show suggested percentage of dollar spreads within each range as well as between ranges.)

FIGURE 6-1 (continued)

The wage and salary analyst then informs the division general manager of the final outcome of the job evaluation project. The analyst also provides copies of all completed job descriptions to authorized managers and supervisors.

PLAN FACTORS

Wage and salary plans normally have several standard factors. Any number of degrees may be included in each factor. In the examples below, five degrees for the education factor are delineated, while only four degrees are given for the errors factor.

Standard Factors

The Education Requirement Factor. One of the most common standard factors is the education requirement factor, which spells out the amount of education an applicant typically should have in order to successfully perform the job.

▬ The *first degree* of the education requirement factor might, for example, call for a high school diploma or GED (high school equivalency program), and this degree of the factor would carry a value, perhaps, of 10 points.

▬ The *second degree* might indicate that high school plus specialized training of some type is required in order to do the job. Let's assume your plan calls for a value of 15 points for this degree.

▬ The *third degree* might specify a requirement for a college degree in a particular field. Let's have your plan assign a value of 25 points to this degree of the factor.

▬ The *fourth degree* of the education requirement might contain a master's degree requirement and have a point value of 40.

▬ The *fifth degree* would normally only apply in the case of a job requiring a Doctor of Philosophy (Ph.D.) degree in some specialized field, assuming that you had such a requirement. The point value here might be 60.

A Sample Evaluation. Focusing upon the education requirement factor, let's do a sample evaluation of a standard accountant-type position, not a bookkeeper or junior accountant, but a basic accountant job. After reviewing the duties and responsibilities of the job, the wage and salary analyst determines that in order for a person to be able to adequately perform the accountant job, the successful applicant would need a bachelor's degree in accounting, or its equivalent in years of experience. Normally, equivalency is determined by equating two years of experience to one year of college.

The education requirement factor may even specify a particular field of accounting (cost accounting, inventory accounting, tax accounting, or other) that the analyst believes is necessary. In any event, in the particular case under discussion the analyst would assign the third degree of the education requirement factor with its 25 points of scoring. In a like manner, the analyst would go through each of the other factors in the plan, assigning the proper degree and corresponding point scoring, exactly as we did with the education factor.

The Errors Factor. In all probability, an errors factor will be included in the wage and salary plan you have chosen. The errors factor addresses the type of error that the incumbent of the job could normally make (that is, has the possibility of making) during the performance of the particular job in question. The reader should clearly understand that this errors factor is not intended to measure that once-in-a-lifetime monumental error that is always possible in the performance of almost any given job, no matter how high or how low its position on the organization chart.

The degrees in the errors factor of your plan might look something like the following:

▬ The *first degree* of the errors factor could provide for the commission of errors that may be of little consequence in the overall job. Such errors require little effort to redo or correct the work. This degree might be assigned 5 points.

▬ Errors in the *second degree* might have an internal effect that would require some corrective measures by others. Let's assign this degree 15 points.

▬ The *third degree* of the errors factor might be considered to be more serious. These are errors that require a great deal of effort by others to correct and/or redo the work. The point value here might be 30 points.

▬ In the *fourth degree*, errors could be considered to be substantial, have an outside effect on the operation of the business, and require a great deal of additional effort to correct. Error in the fourth degree can also result in financial loss since the work normally needs to be redone and corrected. Let's have the plan assign a value of 45 points to this highest degree.

Based solely on the duties described in the job description, the wage and salary analyst now determines that the accountant job under study should carry the fourth degree of the errors factor. The reason is that this degree most nearly represents the typical consequences of any errors that accountants classified on this type of job and performing this set of duties might normally be subject to committing in the course of their work.

Combined Factors. You now have assigned 25 points of scoring based on the education requirement factor and 45 points from the errors factor, for a total of 70 points from these two factors. When you have considered all degrees of each of the remaining factors in your plan in like manner, you then total all the respective scoring points to determine the grade level of the job that, as explained above, gives us the appropriate wage or salary range guidelines to be used to compensate incumbents of the job. We repeat that there are any number of wage and salary evaluation plans that the human resources professional can use, but the scoring procedure just described should be somewhat typical or common to all of them.

STATISTICS, REPORTS, FACTS, AND FIGURES

The heart and lifeblood of any compensation function or department are the meaningful facts, figures, and statistics that group members will compile, collect, and categorize with regard to all phases of employee compensation. As we strive to become more of a paperless society, the more it will require us to mechanize and computerize these data.

Up to this point, data have been maintained on mainframe computers. Now, however, many companies and organizations are turning to personal computers (PCs) linked directly to mainframes or to stand-alone microprocessing platforms utilizing PCs and LANS (local area network systems.) This latter approach normally results in substantial cost savings after the initial investment, as well as practically total freedom and independence from mainframe software and systems. This promises to be a great advantage, both to human resources personnel as well as to compensation department users, whose programs do not always merit top priority in the project request waiting lines of management information systems (MIS) and data processing departments.

PCs

The PC desktop computer and its related programs are the featured sales and marketing products of most hardware and software companies and vendors today. Complete, off-the-shelf PC software is available for just about any business application from fixed assets, accounts receivable, and inventory control, to human resources, compensation, benefits, and payroll functions.

These software programs allow their users nearly total control over their respective reports, surveys, statistics, and other data as they enter, store, and retrieve information that formerly lay exclusively in the domain of the overworked and usually understaffed data processing departments. The microplatform PC software will not solve all your information problems, but it will allow you the luxury of not having to depend exclusively on the availability and priorities of MIS programmers to supply the data you must have on a timely basis in order to do your job—and do it well! (Chapter 5 contains a listing of human resources software vendors with information on their products, services, and contact information.)

CHAPTER PERSPECTIVE

The purposes and advantages of a formal wage and salary program were explained in this chapter. The weighing and scoring part of the job analysis and evaluation process were explained in detail. The basic concepts and terminology of this important compensation process were presented. The chapter also discussed the valuable role of computers in storing and maintaining the data generated in the process of creating a wage and salary program.

Employment Policies and Practices

INTRODUCTION AND MAIN POINTS

This chapter focuses on the employment function of human resources, which is responsible for hiring employees as well as for long-term staffing strategies and programs. The hiring process involves recruiting, interviewing, and screening applicants. The tools and resources of the employment specialists are the application, the interview, preemployment aptitude and personality testing, and substance abuse testing. Practical guidelines on how to hire employees without having your company sued for discrimination are presented. Safeguards of a drug-free work operation are specified. The importance of recruiting personnel for the success of the company's overall performance is emphasized.

This chapter also discusses the unemployment insurance function, which is often advantageously combined with the employment function. The problem of timely responses to claims and suggestions on how to solve this costly problem through centralized processing are presented.

Finally, the need for employment personnel security is explained and several practical recommendations are made.

After reading the material in this chapter:

— You will know what the employment function consists of, whether in a large corporate setting or a small business.

— You will become aware of the importance of recruiting for excellence.

— You will know what the tools of the employment specialist are and how to use them.

— You will know how to avoid discrimination lawsuits against your company while recruiting, interviewing, and screening applicants.

— You will become acquainted with some of the legal ins and outs of drug testing.

— You will know what the unemployment insurance function is and its primary problems in responding to claims.

— You will become aware of the need for security in employment offices and you will learn how to increase security in such settings.

THE EMPLOYMENT FUNCTION

No matter how large or how small, every company has either a highly organized and formal staff of employment interviewers and/or recruiters, or it has as few as one person (often the owner) whose duties include the employment function. Every company, from the Fortune 1000 to the corner independent drugstore or the Little Acorn Family Restaurant at some time or other needs to hire people to help run the business and serve customers. This is the *employment function*, and its importance in any enterprise should never be understated.

In larger companies, the employment function is usually an integral part of the human resources department, and it has the very critical responsibility of recruiting, interviewing, and screening job applicants, either directly or through divisional employment staffs in other geographic locations. In addition, the corporate employment manager normally has the mandate to design and implement the company's long-term strategic staffing plans and programs while, of course, remaining in compliance with state and federal employment laws and regulations.

If its employees are a company's most valuable asset, it follows that the success or failure of the enterprise can be greatly influenced by the quality of the employment group's recruiting and screening efforts. Competent, loyal, hardworking, and productive people, as well as those who lack these particular qualities, all apply at the employment office or answer classified ads. The skill and conscientiousness of the employment staff basically determines which of these two groups will enter your work force, perhaps even to the extent of whether your company succeeds or fails.

Managerial Recruitment

A further refinement of the employment group's hiring responsibility lies in the area of managerial or supervisory recruitment. Many, if not most, companies adopt and adhere to the credo of promotion from within, and in many instances, due to the uniqueness of the company's product or service, promotions are necessarily based on the experience and demonstrated ability of a person within the organization. However, occasions occur in every company when it is practical and necessary to recruit from an outside source, as, for example:

▬ when expanding into a new line of business;

▬ when a particular department or even division is consistently failing to meet profit or other objectives; and

▬ when it is determined, in general, that only an infusion of new blood will correct the problem and put the entity back on the road to profitability.

In such cases, the employment group has the special task of finding and recruiting the particular type of management talent the situation calls for. Depending on the level of the executive or managerial position being sought, the employment department may do any or all of the following.

1) Advertise for the opening in either local or national newspapers, magazines, and trade publications.
2) Participate in job fairs where such candidates may be present.
3) Coordinate their efforts with local employment agencies or executive search firms.

Regardless of the methods used to seek out and attract these managerial candidates, the employment staff must retain complete control of the recruiting effort at all times and must act as the catalyst in making the job search a successful one.

If the opening is for an upper-management position such as a divisional vice president, for example, the board chairman, chief executive officer, or the board of directors itself will normally communicate through the employment manager (or in some cases with the human resources manager or vice president), in order to determine the exact status and progress of the recruiting endeavor.

When a candidate has been selected, or in the event one or more applicants is invited to the company for interviewing and testing, it is often the responsibility of the employment manager to look to all the necessary details of travel, lodging, and interviewing schedules, as well as relocation and housing matters. It is that manager's responsibility to provide whatever assistance it takes to make things as convenient and helpful as possible for the applicants and for their families as well. All of this speaks well for the company regarding its thoughtfulness and concern for its people. Employment applicants—whether or not they are successful—cannot help but be impressed by your courtesy and, either as employees or future customers, they will not forget.

THE HIRING PROCESS

No matter what the size of the particular company involved or the number of job openings being filled, the hiring process is characterized by certain common denominators.

1) A given job opening is advertised in local newspapers, in trade magazines, by posting on company bulletin boards, or by word of mouth.
2) If a person applies for the job, the person is asked to fill out an application-for-employment form and return it to the employ-

ment department. This should apply to former employees as well as previously unknown applicants, so that they can account for their employment experience while away from the company.

3) The employment group then screens the applications to determine whose qualifications most closely fit the requirements of the job in question, calls the applicants in to be interviewed by the employment staff, and from these selects those to be referred to the supervisor or manager of the job being filled for interview and final consideration. Depending on the level of the job opening or the hiring practices of the individual company, the applicant may be interviewed several times before the actual hiring decision is made. This same process may also be used when current employees apply for transfer or promotion to an existing job opening.

4) Once the hiring decision is made, the applicant for our job should be checked for:

Criminal history
Credit history
Employment verification
Education verification
Driving record (including showing valid driver's license)
Personal references

A signed release from the applicant giving the employer permission to check the above items is usually necessary; however, a statement giving such permission may be included on the back of the application form for the applicant's signature. Though sometimes cumbersome and time consuming, checking an applicant's past history to make sure they are who they claim to be is a long-term dividend by keeping problem personnel out of the organization, and protecting the company from employee actions for which it may be legally responsible.

5) Another recommended practice the employment group might follow is that of sending out a thank you letter or card to those who apply for employment, and especially to those who have been interviewed by HR and/or other department or line managers. When an applicant is rejected for a particular job, or the application is put on hold for consideration for other openings, a brief note or even form letter from the company thanking the person for applying is always appreciated. Job applicants are also potential future customers, and they will not forget your courtesy. Unfortunately, many companies today do not follow this simple policy.

TOOLS AND RESOURCES OF THE INTERVIEWER

Some of the key tools and resources that the interviewer needs and uses in the employment operation are

- the employment application.
- the interview.
- preemployment testing.
- substance abuse testing.

These tools and how the employment staff can use them to best advantage are discussed in the sections that follow.

The Employment Application

What May Not Be Asked. The employment application is normally the first step in the employment process. Most, if not all, employers are (or should be) aware of the fact that certain questions and inquiries may not be asked on the employment application, such as questions or items related to an applicant's

- Age,
- Sex,
- Number of children,
- Church attendance/membership,
- Marital status,
- Arrest record,
- Spouse's occupation,
- Applicant's or spouse's pregnancy, or
- Disability or any other health problems.

All such questions may not be asked of the applicant either verbally or on the employment application, or in any other document that the person is required to complete prior to actually being hired.

To say that certain questions may not be asked on the employment application, may be a technicality, in the sense that discrimination laws do not specifically forbid an employer from asking the things stated above, but if a company does decide, for example, to ask for the applicant's date of birth, it had better have an extremely valid reason for doing so. In the event that an age discrimination charge were to be filed against this particular company, its reasons for asking the above question should prove to be very interesting reading, to say the least.

Sources of Application Forms.

Sources of Application Forms. The management services, such as the Bureau of National Affairs and Commerce Clearing House, as well as local stationery supply houses can provide valid, nondiscriminatory employment application forms for your use. Once you have adapted such a form to your own company requirements, you must continue to monitor and maintain it based on current as well as forthcoming employment legislation. (See also suggested Application For Employment form illustrated in Chapter 12.)

A Policy of Accepting All Offered Applications.

Also, for the benefit of less experienced employment personnel, employment managers and supervisors should be certain that their staff is fully aware that they must always accept an employment application from an individual who offers one, regardless of whether or not a job opening currently exists. Failure to do so leaves the company open to charges of discrimination, based on the complaint that "they wouldn't accept my application because I'm minority/female/too old/disabled," and so on. In the personnel/human resources field, the overwhelming majority of managers, directors, and vice presidents in general support civil rights legislation as a matter of justice and fairness, but one will find equally unanimous agreement by these same personnel executives that a certain small percentage of people in legally protected categories sometimes take advantage of these laws and claim discrimination in order to hide their own shortcomings or, in some cases, to perpetrate outright fraud. Being careful about accepting all offered employment applications is just one of the many safeguards human resources professionals should be aware of in protecting their companies against such situations.

A Classification System for Applications.

Once you have gathered a number of employment applications—and they will accumulate in large numbers after a time—you will be faced with the problem of classifying each application based on the skills and qualifications of each individual applicant. It is important to have ready access to the various job specialties and qualifications of applicants as future job openings and opportunities occur.

Fortunately, the employment specialist is now able to review applications and select potential candidates on an office personal computer with comfort, convenience, and a minimum expenditure of time, as it has become standard procedure for a number of human resources software packages to have built-in applicant-tracking functions.

If your own employment operation, however, is a relatively small one and you don't as a rule receive many applications, any clerical or manual filing system will probably suffice. The important thing, of course, is your ability to access and retrieve applications as new job opportunities occur.

Your classification system, whether computerized or manual, will also help you in complying with legal retention requirements of employment applications. They may be safely destroyed in a timely manner, if desired, based on application dates.

The Interview

The employment interview is one of the most essential tools used in the hiring process. Supervisors, managers, and vice presidents, as well as presidents, all have occasion to interview job candidates, whether for new-hire or promotional purposes. And, of course, the employment staff itself interviews job applicants on a daily basis in the course of their work.

More often than not, the interview is probably the primary means of determining whether an offer of employment will be made to the job applicant. It is especially for this reason then that whoever does the interviewing must have a fundamental knowledge of the job requirements, especially the technical qualifications and the necessary personality characteristics.

What May Not Be Asked. Another especially important skill that all interviewers must have, of course, is the knowledge of what can and cannot legally be discussed in the interview. As with the application-for-employment, questions relating to age, disability, marital status, number of children, and dates of graduation from high school or college are just some of the subjects that must not, under any circumstances, be asked of or discussed with an applicant. Since basically all supervisors and managers interview job applicants from time to time, the HR professional should be certain that anyone in a supervisory capacity is informed, by whatever policy bulletins, memos, or counsel are necessary to keep them up to date about what may or may not be said to applicants, promotional candidates, or to any other employee for that matter. The uninformed interviewer risks the possibility of making innocent or offhand comments that might be interpreted as being discriminatory in content.

All supervisors must clearly understand that, regardless of their feelings or well-meaning intentions on the subject of civil rights and discrimination laws, if they ask any of these questions of an applicant, and the person is not hired—for whatever reason—your chances of defeating a discrimination charge or winning a related lawsuit realistically range from poor to none! Therefore, a training program for those who interview applicants and the establishment of good means of communication for keeping personnel up to date on related topics, should be priorities whether you are the employment manager or head of human resources.

The following guidelines illustrate what interviewers may not ask, as well as what they not only may but probably should ask when interviewing job applicants:

TEN QUESTIONS AN INTERVIEWER SHOULD *NEVER* ASK OF AN APPLICANT

1) How old are you?
2) What is your race or nationality?
3) Are you pregnant? (or, Do you have any plans to become so?)
4) Do you have a disability or any other health problem?
5) Are you married, divorced, separated, widowed, or single?
6) Do you have a family? (What are the ages of your children?)
7) Who lives in your household? (disabled or dependent parents, relatives)
8) What is your spouse's occupation?
9) What church, if any, do you attend? (What is your religion?)
10) Have you ever been arrested? (To clarify: Applicants must respond to the question of whether or not they have ever been *convicted* of a crime, but inquiries may not be made about an applicant's arrest record.)

These ten questions, and others asked in different ways on the same subjects, basically have no bearing whatever on whether or not a person is qualified to fill a particular job vacancy, and should not be asked by the interviewer. Prior to federal and state civil rights legislation, employers asked these types of questions (some still do) in an effort to determine how long applicants were likely to work for the company after the expense of training them, or making assumptions that women with families or young children would be likely to need more time off from work (as would also likely be the case if applicants were committed to caring for aging or ill parents and other relatives in their homes.)

Regarding disabled applicants, they held the prevailing viewpoint that they would be unproductive or disrupt the work of other employees. If people acknowledged a history of past or current medical or health problems, they reasoned this might, among other problems, adversely impact the company's medical benefit program costs.

They were also quite certain they could pay a female, for example, a lower wage and provide fewer benefits because her husband was employed. Racial, religious, and sex discrimination usually accounted for the remainder of their misguided inquiries.

TEN EXAMPLES OF QUESTIONS AN INTERVIEWER NOT ONLY *MAY* BUT *SHOULD* ASK A JOB APPLICANT

1) What was the nature of your previous jobs? What kind of work did you do?
2) What were your reasons for leaving your former (or present) job?
3) What did you like best (and least) about former jobs? (This is likely to give insight into one's occupational likes and dislikes.)
4) What are your work/career goals? Immediate? Long-term?

5) What character or personality traits do you like in others? (These may also be the characteristics people like in themselves.)

6) Have you ever supervised or managed others? Did you like it? What was the largest number of people you supervised at any one time?

7) Have you ever had to fire someone? How did you go about it? How did you feel about it? (The answer may reveal something about the applicant's judgment, empathy for others, and the like)

8) What do you already know about ABC Company? (The answers will probably show whether the applicant is interested in the company and has taken the time to research its products or services.)

9) Based on our discussion thus far, in what ways do you feel you could make a contribution to our company?

10) If you did come to work for ABC Company, who do you think will pay your paycheck? (The desired answer, of course, "the customer.")

The interviewer (especially in a retail setting) may be able to tell from applicants' responses whether they really understand the importance to the company of serving and respecting the customer.

Experienced interviewers in human resources and other line or staff departments will find the questions in the guidelines above (often with their own particular modifications), a relaxed yet effective method of sounding out the applicant's personality traits, goals, and general thought processes. Coupled with the more tangible qualities of experience and education, they provide a more complete picture of the individual's ability to do the job while fitting into the corporate culture or mission.

Read the Application Carefully. Another word of advice might be in order for the less experienced employment interviewer, line manager, or supervisor: The employment application should be carefully read and studied by the interviewer. Gaps in dates of employment with previous employers, for example, might signal a problem in the applicant's history that might be worth questioning. It could mean a lengthy period of unexplained unemployment, a long-term serious illness or injury that might adversely affect the person's ability to perform the job in question (even with a reasonable accommodation), and, in a number of cases, further questioning of the applicant may develop that some time had been spent in prison during this period.

Such inquiries of the applicant can and should be handled in a diplomatic and respectful manner, but, again, this is a potential employee, a company's most important asset, and when we make the hiring decision, we must have all the facts because the stakes are always high!

Preemployment Testing

Since the advent of modern civil rights legislation some 30 years ago, much has been written, debated, published, and legislated on the subject of aptitude and personality testing of applicants for employment in the private sector. Subsequent laws have been passed, Equal Employment Opportunity Commission rules and regulations abound, and U.S. Supreme Court precedent cases are handed down. Yet, in some respects, we seem to be no closer to clear and unambiguous guidelines than we were many years ago on this topic.

It is not the intent of this work to debate or even to give an opinion on the merits of this most complex matter of employment testing; the literature is truly saturated already. However, in the hope of focusing a small ray of light on the subject, it is noted that testing, particularly preemployment testing, does have its role in assisting a company supervisor or manager (as well as an employment manager or staff member, of course) to make the all-critical judgment as to whether or not this particular person should really be allowed the opportunity of joining the company as one of its most important assets—an employee. Some companies rightfully insist on calling their people associates, system members, or family members, further emphasizing the company's insistence that these *are* their important assets.

Not the Sole Determining Factor. Preemployment testing is and should be used as just one important item of evidence in considering and making the hiring decision. It cannot be emphasized too strongly that testing should not be the determining factor—nor should it even be a major consideration—for the interviewer. It should, on the other hand, be used to gain some further insight into the applicant's overall qualifications.

A wise move for the HR manager might be to caution all departmental and line managers that they must never be governed by so-called cut-off scores in applicant testing. Some veteran managers believe that they can predict successful job performance on the basis of a specific score on an intelligence or aptitude test. They believe that some specific score, for example, is a predictor of success in the company, whereas a score lower than that is not. In addition to not being a legal test validation, many a good potential employee is probably lost to the company as a result of such a practice.

As an additional tool for the interviewer, testing can often serve as a reliable predictor of successful job performance, and can even be used to validate the interviewer's instinctive feelings about an applicant.

Personality Profile Test. One of the more popular testing or assessment techniques today is the *personality profile test*, which purports to determine various trends or tendencies in an applicant's personality having to do with such issues as loyalty, truthfulness, social values, moral values (as they relate to theft), substance abuse, cheating, and falsifying company documents.

Proponents of these personality profile tests claim validity for them based on the fact that certain given test questions are repeatedly asked from a number of different angles and in various ways, making it almost impossible for applicants to slant their answers based on what they think the company is looking for in the test. Marketers of these tests (at least the more prominent ones) usually claim validation approval by the Equal Employment Opportunity Commission, and as previously mentioned, they are becoming popular with a growing number of employers. These tests should be considered just one more bit of evidence in the employer's overall, total assessment of the applicant's qualifications.

Using Aptitude and Personality Tests Skillfully. Those responsible for the hiring decision should be aware that, although tests can be excellent employment tools, they can also prove to be dangerous if misused, and that skillful administration and interpretation of employment testing can be a very important element in the hiring decision.

Substance Abuse Testing

In Chapter 10, Legal Compliance Role of Human Resources, substance abuse testing laws and regulations will be discussed in detail, with emphasis on the subject of preemployment drug testing policies in industry and business. However, it is appropriate that a preview of the advantages of mandatory preemployment drug testing to the company be presented here, as it relates to the employment function.

A Major Expense. Without a doubt, preemployment drug screening of all applicants is normally a major expense on a company's and human resources' operating budget.

One well-known company had arranged with a national testing laboratory to handle their preemployment drug testing needs for a volume-discounted fee of $30 per test, probably a rock-bottom price so far as these tests are concerned. All applicants for employment, whether full time, part time, or temporary, in this company of over 10,000 employees, were required to pass a drug test between the time a job offer was made and before the person actually began work. Showing a negative drug test result (that is, no drugs are detected) prior to starting work was a hard and fast condition of employment, and there were no exceptions to this policy that also included applicants for top-level executive management vacancies.

The projected cost, or investment, for this drug testing program was budgeted at approximately $350,000 per year. This and all other expenses, including essential drug testing consulting services, were to be paid by the company. Due to unexpectedly heavy turnover experience in the first quarter of the year, requiring additional hiring and testing, costs outran budget projections, and total cost estimates were projected to top $500,000 for the year. Then, as might be predicted, the program was discontinued half-way through the fiscal year.

Nevertheless, the company remained convinced of the value of pre-employment drug testing, and plans were made to resume preemployment testing beginning with the next fiscal year. The only basic difference when the program resumed was that the applicants for employment were now responsible for paying for the drug testing themselves, consistent with state law, rather than the company. Although other companies are also starting to take this approach, it remains to be seen how and if the many foreseeable problems related to applicants paying for their own drug testing will be resolved.

The experience of the company described above can be considered to be typical of the vast majority of employers. Most companies want, if not insist on, having a drug-free environment throughout their organization, but the cost of attaining such an environment in many cases is more than they think they can afford. Fortunately, however, more and more companies, and especially larger companies, are now coming to the conclusion that they can't afford *not* to have a drug-free work environment. Drug testing then becomes a routine step in their hiring procedure.

A Consent and Release Form. If a company decides to include drug testing as part of its hiring procedure, it should also consider using another protection or safeguard: a consent and release form. Applicants sign a consent and release form in which they voluntarily agree to the collection and testing of urine samples, and, at the same time, release and hold the company, its employees, representatives, and agents harmless from any liability whatever arising out of the drug-testing procedure. The form should also contain a statement that applicants authorize the confidential release of drug test results to the company. Legal counsel can prepare an appropriate consent-and-release form containing the above provisions, which is suited to the particular situation.

Other Safeguards of a Drug-Free Operation. In addition to preemployment drug testing, many companies have also set up other safeguards in order to insure a completely drug-free work operation. For example:

1) Postaccident Drug Testing. A company may establish, of course, any type of drug-testing program or procedure it chooses,

consistent with applicable federal, state, and local laws. The following postaccident drug-testing program can work very well and effectively.

Under this program, any company employee reporting a work-related injury, accident, or illness, is required to submit to a substance abuse test within a stated number of hours after the occurrence of the incident. If such substance abuse test reveals a positive result (that is, drugs are detected), the employee is automatically classified as being on an unpaid, substance abuse (SA) leave of absence. The employee must then make arrangements to take another drug test at the original testing facility within 30 days from the date of the first positive drug test result.

If the employee refuses to take this second drug test (that is, within the 30 days), or if the employee tests positive (that is, if drugs are detected) on the retest drug screening, then the employee will be considered as having voluntarily resigned from the company. This latter point is most important in that a dismissal of the employee under these circumstances as opposed to a voluntary resignation could, in some states, be more difficult to defend in any subsequent legal action. While it would be foolhardy to even imply that there can be any such thing as a guarantee of winning a substance abuse or any other kind of lawsuit, your chances of winning your case will be greater if you have a policy similar to the one described above and if you have adhered to the letter of the policy.

If the 30-day retest drug screening in the above example is negative (that is, if drugs are not detected), the employee may be reinstated from the substance abuse leave of absence but would be subject to periodic follow-up drug testing for a period of time, perhaps for one year. A second positive drug test during this 12-month period would be considered a voluntary resignation on the part of the employee. Your policy might also include the provision that while on SA leave of absence, the employee involved would not be eligible for any sort of employee benefit coverage.

The above suggested policy on postaccident drug testing is only one example of policies of this type. Your own company's situation, together with the advice and counsel of your legal advisor, must determine the details of such a program. The policy is presented here so that the human resources manager may have a framework on which to build if it is to be proposed and submitted to company management.

2) Probable cause/safety-sensitive position drug testing. Drug abuse has been recognized for some time as a problem of national proportions, and one that affects almost all businesses. In the interests of protecting its employees, customers, and the general public, many companies have instituted drug-testing safeguards

applying to their current employee population. For example, if a company supervisor or manager has a reasonable suspicion that one or more employees are using, selling, in possession of, or impaired in any way by illegal drugs, alcohol, or abused prescription drugs, the company may request that the person suspected submit to a substance abuse test. As with most situations dealing with this sensitive area of drug testing, however, the supervisor or manager should first contact the company's human resources specialists to discuss the matter and decide on the most appropriate course of action.

In addition, more and more companies are requiring that those of their employees in selected high-risk occupations, such as various vehicle drivers and equipment operators, should be subject to mandatory, random drug testing for as long as they occupy such jobs. Following a series of highly publicized tragic accidents in public transportation in which marijuana and/or cocaine were involved, subsequent congressional action and supporting court decisions have given reassurance to the business community that such testing programs are not only legal but may even be necessary, as well.

3) Random drug testing. In their determination and zeal to maintain a drug-free environment in their workplace, some companies have instituted a system of unannounced, unscheduled random drug testing programs within their various organizations. Normally, the only known or announced element of this testing program is that each employee in the company will be periodically drug-tested on a random basis (perhaps two or three times during the course of a year). An employee selected for such testing is usually given about one-half hour's notice to try to ensure that the employee will be able to provide an adequate urine sample for the test. Employees who refuse to participate in random testing are subject to termination; job applicants are not hired unless they agree to the conditions of such testing.

Random drug testing is the most controversial form of all substance abuse testing. Many employees—as well as nonemployees—staunchly maintain that urinalysis drug testing is an invasion of their privacy, and that any punitive measures their employer takes against them for refusal to be drug-tested constitutes wrongful discharge, intentional infliction of emotional distress, or even breach of contract. Random drug testing is the principal area of testing wherein the courts tend to support the employee rather than the company, especially where the job does not involve high-risk or security issues. Even in the low-risk area, however, several recent court decisions have favored the employer's right to test randomly.

Similar to any other cost/value business decision, the risk versus reward of a random drug-screening program should be carefully weighed and is more open to challenge than other testing programs. Again, this is another facet of personnel relations wherein your legal counsel can play an important role.

APPLICANT RECRUITING

In many companies, particularly larger ones, the employment department includes a group of recruiting personnel. This group regularly visits colleges and universities and sets up and/or attends job fairs with the object of attracting the most qualified candidates for the organization. Large aerospace firms, for example, have historically recruited large numbers of engineers during expansionary periods, but even in lean economic times, they must still recruit a certain amount of new talent in order to keep up with the latest engineering technology and to remain competitive.

Even if yours is a relatively small company and you have no formal employment recruiting staff, you must still be constantly on the alert for the high-tech or highly-skilled superstars who could really be an asset to your company, consistent with budgetary and financial considerations. Classified help wanted ads, job fairs, and membership in various personnel management associations can all be helpful in continually striving to recruit the best talent your company can afford.

It is often the case in business that companies always seem to have the financial means to purchase the latest computer hardware and software (certainly not inexpensive items), as well as the most recent models of production or processing equipment, but, for some strange reason, when the unplanned expenditure involves buying, so to speak, highly skilled personnel talent, there never seems to be enough money in the budget to do so. There are not necessarily a large number of people who need to be recruited; sometimes, even one person can make the difference between black or red ink on the company's profit and loss statement. We normally get what we pay for, regardless of the commodity or resource we're buying.

The simplified model of industrial or corporate organization is a useful concept in understanding the relative importance of business components. A company's organization structure, or table of organization, is normally supported by four separate and distinct columns or legs, the first leg being marketing, the second, manufacturing, the third, money or finance, and the fourth being the personnel leg, or people. Many company CEOs and boards of directors tend to concentrate on and support the first three legs, while deemphasizing or at least giving low priority to the fourth or people leg of the table; in some cases, they even allow the fourth leg to practically atrophy. We all know what happens when one leg of a table is weaker or shorter than the others or, in some cases, missing altogether. The table is seriously unbalanced and may collapse completely, as any number of companies have already experienced to their sorrow and regret.

THE UNEMPLOYMENT INSURANCE FUNCTION

In some companies, the unemployment insurance function may be a separate department, or it may be a section under the employment department and therefore report to the employment manager. A combined employment and unemployment operation is advantageous since there is often a commonality of information and communication in both groups relating to, for example:

- Reasons for termination
- Exit interview programs
- Files and computer data bases
- Contacts with corporate and field managers and supervisors

The joint operation also gives the employment manager a much better grasp and control of the overall employment picture, including having access to reasons for termination of former employees and knowing where more resources and effort must be directed as staffing or turnover problems become apparent in the various company locations.

In Chapter 10, Legal Compliance Role of Human Resources, unemployment compensation laws will be defined, and their role as a form of income insurance protection and how they apply to both employers and employees will be discussed. The value of a conscientious unemployment compensation staff cannot be stressed too strongly. Such a staff continually strives to represent the company's best interests by doing the following:

- Answering unemployment claims promptly and completely
- Strongly contesting frivolous or inaccurate claims
- Protesting and appealing decisions unfavorable to the company by the various state unemployment compensation boards
- Attending and representing the company at state unemployment hearings
- Carefully auditing periodic statements of charges from state agencies

The unemployment compensation group's sole purpose is to decrease the company's unemployment experience rating, as this is the basis upon which states assess charges to the company. Through its efforts, this group can save its employer considerable sums of money, which it would otherwise be legally required to pay.

Responding to Claims

One practical problem that many unemployment compensation groups face is that of responding in a timely manner to employees' unemployment claims received from the state. This is especially true of multistate employers. In most cases, the employer faces a double-edged problem when answers to unemployment claims are not returned to the state on time. First, most states charge the employer a late filing fee, ranging from $15 per claim in Maryland to $50 in the state of New York; second (and most important), a late response is normally considered no response at all, and the exemployee claimant is automatically granted unemployment benefits unless the company can show good cause as to why the response to the claim was late. Examples of good cause might be if the claim was originally sent to the wrong address by the state, or if there was no mail delivery on a certain date that resulted in the claim being received late. If there are other substantive reasons for late claims responses, the unemployment staff should aggressively pursue the matter with the state.

Centralized Processing of Claims

Occasionally, for one reason or another, when the state sends the unemployment claim notice to the local company office or facility, it ends up in a desk drawer or under the counter, and no company response gets sent back to the state. This particular circumstance has prompted employers that operate in various geographic areas to arrange with states to send unemployment claims directly to the corporate human resources (unemployment claims) office. To achieve this, human resources notifies the state unemployment agencies of its intention, and informs the state of the correct corporate address to which all unemployment claims are to be sent in the future.

It is also just as important for all company supervisors and managers to understand that *all* unemployment claims will now be handled by corporate human resources or at other designated locations. With this arrangement, delay is reduced to a minimum since the claims come directly to a central location. The corporate staff then calls the local company or office to determine the circumstances of the employee's leaving the company, and the response is forwarded by corporate unemployment in a timely manner to the appropriate state.

Using this method doesn't mean you'll never have a late unemployment claim response again; however, giving this method a try, you will find that:

- your chances of a timely answer will increase considerably;
- your late charges will drop; and

▬ the percentage of claims you win should show a considerable improvement.

Sometimes, even with this arrangement for central processing and handling, the state may occasionally still send the claim to your local facility, or their new computer may have the wrong corporate address, but, all things considered, centralized processing of unemployment claims works for the company. It will free up local store, shop, or office supervision to concentrate on managing their own marketing, repair, or clerical functions.

EMPLOYMENT PERSONNEL SECURITY

We live in a challenging and, in many respects, a dangerous world. Within any given business organization, the employment personnel staff—the manager, the interviewers, receptionist, or clerical personnel—can be and often are exposed to the same degree of risk as the employees at the company's retail stores, inasmuch as they both deal with and face the general public. In retail situations, it is not uncommon, of course, for an occasional customer to become irate about some facet of a sales or rental transaction, and to vocally express displeasure in no uncertain terms to anyone willing to listen. If the matter is not satisfactorily and quickly resolved, what started as a low-key disagreement could escalate into a full-scale shouting match with the potential for violent and sometimes tragic consequences.

This same type of scenario can also occur in a personnel employment office when, for example, an unsuccessful job applicant (on occasion with a knife strapped on the leg or sporting a gun in a holster!) in no uncertain terms loudly yells to the receptionist something like, "What do you mean I'm not qualified for the job?" and then, "And I want to talk to the idiot who made that decision!"

For those who have been in the trenches of personnel or human resources management for a while, the above example will not appear to be too much of an exaggeration. In those states where carrying an unconcealed weapon is permitted, the possibility becomes anything but remote. It is, therefore, advisable to make sure that your employment group, even if that's only one person, has some means of protecting itself as much as possible from the rare (but real) unbalanced applicant who can cause annoyance, disturbance, and occasionally tragedy in a personnel or human resources employment office.

The human resources employment office or some other area designated to receive applications should be located on the first floor of your building complex for two basic reasons.

1) You don't have to worry about applicants for employment wandering around on other floors of the building.

2) Most important, disgruntled applicants can be quickly ushered out of the building if they become rude or unruly.

Always have a prearranged procedure set up with your security personnel to handle such situations as they arise. Closed-circuit TV cameras or some type of concealed buzzer or alarm system connected to the company's security or building management department, for example, gives a certain amount of protection as well as feeling of security to the employment staff. If such arrangements are not available or practicable, it would certainly be good policy to have other HR staff members alerted to provide assistance when anything out of the ordinary occurs with an applicant. Should an emergency occur (an applicant or other person in your office becoming seriously ill, for example, or suffering some type of seizure) it is important to have at least one HR staff member trained to react quickly to such emergency situations. Once the situation is judged to be serious by a staff member, there should be no hesitation in calling for police or security personnel assistance immediately.

The human resources department, constantly deals with the most complex organism ever invented or discovered—a human being. In our modern society where people seem to be more concerned about rights and privileges than duties and responsibilities, sometimes a termination or the awarding of a job or promotion to someone else—even the slightest perceived offense—can be enough to cause the individual to lose control and the unthinkable happens. News media stories of department managers, supervisors, and personnel staff members being physically attacked or even murdered in a company office, store, or shop are, unfortunately, not uncommon.

While there can be no guarantee of complete protection, it is to the benefit of the management of all companies, large and small, to install the necessary systems and procedures to protect their employees as much as possible. It is an investment, not an expense, in the security of their people as well as that of the company itself.

WEAPONS IN THE WORKPLACE

In addition to a growing host of problems concerning security in the workplace, a new and more serious challenge for human resources managers is the phenomenon of employees, contractors, or visitors of any kind bringing guns, illegal knives, explosives, or any other type of weapon prohibited by law into the workplace. Since no less than 29 states now have laws permitting licensed individuals to carry a concealed handgun, the enormity of the problem of keeping guns out of the office, shop, factory, or other workplace becomes most obvious to security and human resource professionals alike. Similar to the approach to its already full plate of other responsibilities, HR must design a sensible, logical, yet understandable response to this added function of workplace safety and security.

Two specific measures are generally recommended by legal authorities to counter this new challenge.

1) There should be implementation of a workplace safety program, with specific emphasis on the problem of guns in the workplace. Highlighting the program would be the publication and guaranteed enforcement of a no-weapons policy prohibiting weapons anywhere on company premises.

2) Notices prohibiting weapons on company property should be posted at usual building entrances, in parking lots, or wherever the employer desires the policy to be enforced.

A suggested sample no-weapons policy is presented below. The policy should be signed by the company president/CEO, and posted on company bulletin boards and in conspicuous places throughout the property. Some employers may wish to provide a copy of the policy to each employee and request that it be signed, acknowledging receipt.

FIGURE 7-1
ABC Company Policy Regarding Weapons in the Workplace

Discussion: The ABC Company desires to make its employees specifically aware of its position regarding the matter of weapons in the workplace. If, after having read this policy statement, you have any questions, you are urged to refer it to the human resources department.

Policy: All persons entering company premises at any time for any reason, regardless of whether or not the person is licensed to carry a weapon, are prohibited from carrying a handgun, firearm, or prohibited weapon of any kind onto the property. Police officers, security guards, or other persons with written permission by the company to carry a weapon on the property, will be the only exceptions to this policy.

Definitions:
1) Prohibited weapons include any type of weapon or explosive restricted under local, state, or federal regulation, including all firearms, illegal knives, or other weapons covered by law.
2) Company property as stated in this policy includes all company-owned or leased buildings, parking lots, and company vehicles.

Searches: In an effort to maintain a safe and productive work environment for ABC and its employees, ABC reserves the right to conduct searches at the company's discretion. Therefore, every employee will be required, upon the company's request, to submit to a search of any pocket, package, purse, briefcase, toolbox, lunch box, or other container

FIGURE 7-1 (continued)

brought onto company property; to submit to a search of a desk, file, locker, or other container provided by the company; and to submit to a search of any vehicle brought onto company premises. The company reserves the right to conduct searches without the employee being present. By coming onto ABC property, an employee consents to a search; an employee's refusal to consent to such a search can lead to disciplinary measures, up to and including discharge.

Albert B. Collins
President and CEO
ABC International, Inc.

As noted above, posting of notices at all entrances would also notify visitors that weapons of any kind may not be brought onto company property.

Some examples of posted notices might include:

FIGURE 7-2
ABC Company Sample Posted Notices

NO WEAPONS ALLOWED

THIS NOTICE APPLIES TO ALL PROPERTY BEYOND THIS SIGN AND TO LICENSED HANDGUNS

VIOLATORS SUBJECT TO PROSECUTION FOR TRESPASS

NO PRIVATE RESPONSIBILITY FOR ENFORCEMENT

It should be noted that more often than not, the courts support the position of the employer who prohibits employees and others from bringing weapons onto company property. However, because of variations in state laws and other considerations, it is also expedient to consult legal counsel before publishing or attempting to enforce such a policy.

CHAPTER PERSPECTIVE

In this chapter, the employment function and the unemployment insurance function were explained. These functions draw upon much of the same information and are often advantageously combined in one unit. The importance of recruiting to the overall success of a company was emphasized. The procedures of employment's hiring process are detailed, and the tools of the employment specialist are discussed from a legal perspective. How to go about attaining and maintaining a drug-free work operation was described.

The chapter also discussed the primary problem of the unemployment insurance function—responding to claims on time—and offered a proven solution. In addition, this chapter explained the need for security in employment offices and suggested several procedures for increasing it.

Discrimination, Affirmative Action, and Equal Employment Opportunity

INTRODUCTION AND MAIN POINTS

This chapter is concerned with the problems of discrimination in the workplace as well as the development of company strategies for avoiding costly lawsuits. The human resources department has the primary responsibility for protecting and defending the company against charges of violation of discrimination law. Specific strategies include the development of a written policy statement and its communication to management and staff. A sample Equal Employment Opportunity policy statement is presented.

The effects of civil rights legislation on business organizations with 15 or more employees are discussed. Affirmative action plans are defined, and human resources' need to employ an EEO staff member is demonstrated. Reverse discrimination is defined and three landmark U.S. Supreme Court cases are presented as examples of the complexity of this subject.

Finally, sexual harassment in the business environment is defined and discussed. Included are a sample Sexual Harassment Policy Statement and a sample Notice to All Employees.

After reading the material in this chapter:

▬ You will understand what discrimination in the workplace is and why civil rights legislation is necessary.

▬ You will be aware of the importance of developing an Equal Employment Opportunity policy statement and educating management and staff concerning its contents.

▬ You will understand that the primary responsibility for protecting and defending the company against discrimination lawsuits lies with the human resources department.

▬ You will know what reverse discrimination is.

▬ You will know what sexual harassment is and how it can be discouraged.

DISCRIMINATION

Discrimination and its unfair practices have been a part of our existence from the time we first appeared on earth. People who were old, young, disabled, female, or belonged to different races, tribes, nationalities, or religions all undoubtedly experienced some form of discrimination, prejudice, or harassment. In more modern times, working people who wanted to organize into groups to bargain collectively with employers about wages, hours, work rules, and other conditions experienced the same discrimination and resentment.

Although much has been said, many things written, and some progress made in alleviating the causes as well as the effects of discrimination, especially in the latter half of the twentieth century, the substantially discrimination-free society is not yet a reality. Indeed, unless much greater effort at understanding and tolerance is made by all manner of companies, governments, groups, and especially by individual people, it may never become a reality.

Many of the difficulties that arise between nations and individuals today as in the past, can be linked to a misunderstanding of—and often the lack of desire to understand—the motivation and reasons why we human beings act as we do. In other words, *why* did my neighbor do what he or she did, or say what he or she said? Would I have said or done the same thing under similar circumstances? And even more to the point perhaps is, have *I* actually said and/or done the very same thing to my neighbor that I now resent in his or her conduct toward me?

Even as a nation, we might ask the same question when another country acts in any given situation, such as, would my country have done the same thing under the same conditions? And all of this, of course, might lead us to agree that we should certainly "put ourselves in the shoes" of minorities, the disabled, the aged, women, the oppressed, and the homeless, and make an effort to try to understand their point of view as well as their conduct in any given situation or circumstance. Yes, we have heard it all before, but we must continue to remind ourselves that the age of true and absolute nondiscrimination must be preceded by a new and universal age of understanding and reason.

Laws as Interim Need

We in human resources must be pragmatic and practical enough to know and believe that great efforts involving universal understanding and tolerance are still needed before all forms of discrimination cease. In the meantime, assuming this reality may not occur in the near future, governments pass laws in an attempt to make it happen by establishing penalties for those companies and individuals who still choose to discriminate against people in covered classes or groups.

Primary Responsibility

Normally, the corporate guardian, protector, and defender of the company's best interests as they relate to discrimination laws and practices is the human resources department. As discussed in Chapter 2, the successful human resources department creates an environment in which employees consider human resources neutral territory where their concerns are addressed and fairly acted upon, and that by so doing, the human resources department represents even more effectively the best interests of the corporation.

Some people, such as associates in the legal profession, might challenge the previous statement that the human resources department is the focal point in defending the company against charges of violation of discrimination law. Some may feel that the company's in-house legal staff or retained outside counsel should really be the key area and have the primary responsibility of assuring corporate compliance with the myriad of federal, state, and local discrimination laws and regulations.

Where the basic responsibility should lie is governed by the environment or situation. For example, if your company is relatively small and you, with a small staff, handle the human resources function, then you must rely heavily either on qualified company lawyers (if they exist) or on discrimination specialists from local law firms to assist you in representing and defending your company in the event discrimination charges are filed by your employees. Your strategic defense under such circumstances is, as it would be for any other legal charge or suit, essentially in the hands of the lawyers. This by no means implies that you have abdicated your responsibility for handling and defending such charges to your legal counsel; in fact, you may just choose to handle these matters personally, or hire an Equal Employment Opportunity (EEO) coordinator to assist you. If not, then legal counsel must necessarily play a vital and key role in interpreting the law, analyzing the circumstances of the case in question, and advising you as to the wisdom of either fighting or settling the current charge at issue.

Some smaller companies feel it is prudent to rely upon legal advice and assistance when discrimination or other types of charges are filed against the firm. It is, of course, essential to be represented by counsel if a lawsuit involving discrimination or any other charge or complaint is filed by an employee or customer. However, depending on the size of the human resources staff, and its overall experience in handling such matters, discrimination charges may sometimes be investigated, handled, and resolved exclusively by human resources with little, if indeed any, professional legal advice involved. In any event, and under any conditions, where a functional human resources department exists in the company, corporate policy should require that it assume the primary (not to be interpreted to mean exclusive), responsibility of protecting and defending the best interests of the company when charges of discrimination of any kind are filed against it.

STRATEGY FOR FIGHTING DISCRIMINATION

An Official Written Company Policy

The keystone of every company's defense in protecting itself against any type of employee relations law violations, charges, claims, and lawsuits, is a clear, unambiguous, and forthright written company policy signed by the president of the company and stating the company's support of and intention to strictly adhere to the provisions of the particular law in question.

All employees should be provided with a copy of this official policy, which should also inform employees of the procedure to follow and the proper company official or department to contact in the event they have any complaints, problems, questions, or feedback. In addition, employee handbooks, new-hire data packets, supervisors' and managers' personnel policies manuals, and related materials should all contain similar references to the company's position regarding personnel laws, and encouraging employees to advise management if they have questions or encounter problems.

Any number of human resources magazine articles and books, as well as management services of the Bureau of National Affairs (BNA) and the Commerce Clearing House (CCH), contain sample personnel policies. These resources can help the human resources professional in providing at least the framework for developing the company's written position on the policy. In addition, more and more data and assistance regarding HR matters is available through the Internet or so-called Information Highway (see Chapter 16 for more detailed discussion of human resources and the Internet).

The likelihood of a court suit or at least a discrimination charge is very real in most companies today, regardless of size. The courts, the Equal Opportunity Commission, or any other government agency, for that matter, will normally want to see your official company policy on discrimination and equal employment opportunity early on in the proceedings. You will be fortunate, indeed, if you are able to present to the agency in question an up-to-date, well-written company policy that makes it clear that your company not only supports the law in question but also urges its managers and employees to do the same.

Another important point is that company statistics on the numbers of minorities, women, and disabled persons in its work force and in management positions speak much louder than all the protestations the human resources vice president or other company officials may make as to how this particular corporation supports and encourages equal employment opportunity. While it is true that your actions do speak much louder than your words, a strongly worded policy statement directed to each employee indicates your company's official commitment to equal opportunity and becomes a vital element in defending against discrimination claims and charges.

The following is an example of an equal employment opportunity policy statement that has been used and found effective in communicating in simple but direct language the position of the company on this particular subject.

FIGURE 8-1
Sample EEO Policy Statement

ABC Company
Policy Statement
Equal Employment Opportunity Policy

As an equal employment opportunity employer, ABC Company believes in and practices fair and equal employment opportunities for everyone.

Certainly, one of the most complex challenges still confronting our nation in general and industry in particular is to provide full and equal opportunity for all people without regard to sex, age, race, color, national origin, religion, or disability.

While civil rights laws have been enacted for some time to assure such equality, many individuals and institutions continue to be negligent in meeting the requirements of the laws, and to that extent equal opportunity for all is still not a reality.

It is most important, therefore, that we all strive aggressively to assure the entry and growth of minorities, women, and disabled persons in our work force until it is unmistakably clear that equality of opportunity at ABC is a fact as well as an ideal. It is obviously not enough to simply claim that we support equal opportunity; as the law and the courts have stated and continue to state again and again, results count far more than intent. To achieve these results, our efforts toward equal employment opportunity for all our people should go beyond the letter of the law and result in total commitment to this goal on the part of every ABC employee.

Your cooperation and support in this matter are most essential in assuring that true employment opportunities will exist in all ABC entities.

Albert B. Collins
President and CEO
ABC International Inc.

You'll notice that the chairman of the corporation signed this policy statement. It is absolutely essential that no less important an official than the chair of the company sign all policy statements in order to ensure that employees, customers, vendors, suppliers, and others understand that this policy has the backing and total support of the top official of the organization.

CIVIL RIGHTS LEGISLATION

These laws were conceived and created by Congress and/or the presidents of the United States in response to the existing blatant patterns and practices of discrimination against minorities and women in our country, especially in the areas of hiring, promotion, termination, and transfer—in other words, in practically every facet of employment.

The Civil Rights Act of 1964 was the legislative response to the demeaning effects of discrimination, particularly in the workplace. As with the National Labor Relations Act, passed almost 30 years earlier, a specific body or commission was created by the law to enforce and oversee the provisions of the new act. This body, known as the Equal Employment Opportunity Commission, was delegated the power to do the following.

- Receive complaints from employees.
- Mediate and settle disputes related thereto.
- Bring suit against companies for egregious discriminatory conduct or willful disregard of the employment rights of their employees covered by the law.

Generally speaking, any company with 15 or more employees that is engaged in an industry affecting commerce is subject to the Civil Rights Act. Federal, state, local public employers, and educational institutions were added in 1972 to increase the scope of coverage of the law.

AFFIRMATIVE ACTION PLANS AND PROGRAMS

Many companies that are not government contractors voluntarily institute affirmative action plans in order to demonstrate their support of and compliance with civil rights legislation. Such plans generally indicate the company's current minority population and stipulate its future plans and programs for increasing minority as well as female participation in hiring and promotion. The government encourages sincere and realistic voluntary affirmative action plans, and employers will find such plans helpful in preventing as well as defending against future charges of discrimination.

In the event your company is considered to be a government contractor, that is, a business with the federal government in the amount of at least $10,000, you are required to have an affirmative action plan.

Lack of such a plan, or failure to properly maintain or carry out the provisions of it, could result in loss of the current government contract with possible disbarment from future government business for a period of three years.

HUMAN RESOURCES EEO STAFFING

Depending on the size of the company involved, even the most inexperienced human resources managers or professionals will recognize that the complexity and importance of properly handling discrimination charges and dealing with the federal Equal Employment Opportunity Commission, as well as state, county, and municipal civil rights agencies, require at least one full-time staff person. The person in this full-time position would be responsible for the preparation of affirmative action plans and of statements of position, which are written statements to the EEOC or to state or local agencies explaining and defending the company's actions in answer to discrimination charges filed by employees.

If the budget allows, the company might consider hiring an equal employment opportunity coordinator, a position that would report directly to the personnel director or vice president of human resources. Depending on the size of your organization, the coordinator may eventually need an auxiliary staff of one or two part-time or perhaps even full-time people to:

1) Compile related payroll and/or human resources data for affirmation action purposes.
2) Write computer programs.
3) Take statements from witnesses.
4) Handle phone calls, letters, and personal meetings with employees regarding discrimination matters.
5) Draft position statements.
6) Perform the many, many other support services related to defending the corporation when charges are brought, or legal action taken in discrimination matters.

Although the human resources function first and foremost represents the best interests of company management and ownership, HR personnel also assist employees to the best of their ability. Nevertheless, human resources is ethically and morally bound to defend the employer against discrimination charges and court actions—especially the frivolous and vexatious ones—to the best of its collective ability.

REVERSE DISCRIMINATION

If your company hasn't yet experienced reverse discrimination charges, that is, nonminorities or males charging discrimination, you will probably be confronted by such charges sooner or later. The law is very specific in that it prohibits discrimination in any form, against any race, color, creed, sex, national origin, and so forth. It does not state, nor was it ever intended to forbid, discrimination only against a particular race, creed, sex, religion, or anyone who happens to fall in some covered or specified class of persons.

Quotas

The law as written, interpreted, and amended, however, does prohibit the establishment of such things as *quotas*, which dictate that a given company, for example, must strive to employ and promote a specific percentage quota of minority and female employees in order to make amends for the past evils of discrimination. Legislative as well as judicial pronouncements on the subject all stress that such quota systems may not be used, since "the two wrongs can never make it right," nor even adequately begin to atone for the racial sins of the past.

Landmark Cases

The reading of several landmark United States Supreme Court cases that involved reverse discrimination might assist the human resources practitioner in better understanding this concept as well as the court's reasoning in arriving at its decisions. In particular, each of three following Supreme Court cases decided between 1978 and 1980 presented new and different aspects of the reverse discrimination problem to the Court:

- *The Bakke Case*—Bakke, a white student, was rejected for admission to the medical school at Davis. He brought suit, alleging that except for a special minorities admissions program which reserved 16 slots for minority applicants to increase minority representation in the student body, he would have been admitted. He claimed this racial preference violated his constitutional rights under the Equal Protection Clause of the Fourteenth Amendment, as well as Title VI of the Civil Rights Act of 1964, and the California Constitution.

  The Court concluded that Bakke was improperly denied admission to the medical school on racial grounds; but also held that race may be given some consideration in an admissions process in order to create a diverse student body to further the education process. (*Regents of the University of California v. Bakke, 438 U.S. 265, 17 FEP 1000 [1978]*)

- *The Weber Case*—A collective bargaining agreement between Kaiser Aluminum and Chemical Corporation and the United

Steelworkers of America provided for an on-the-job training program to train selected employees in craft skills. One black employee and one white employee were to be alternately selected as training vacancies occurred. The selection process was to be maintained until the percentage of black craft workers at Kaiser approximated the percentage of black employees in the local labor force in each Kaiser plant area. Weber, a white worker, filed suit challenging the program when he was passed over for this training in favor of a less senior black employee.

The Court decided that the training program was valid under Title VII, holding that the law was not intended to prohibit voluntary affirmative action. (*United Steelworkers of America v. Weber, 443 U.S. 193, 20 FEP 1 [1979]*)

- *The Fullilove Case*—A provision was included in the 1977 Public Works Employment Act that required that, absent an administrative waiver, at least 10 percent of federal funds set aside for local public works projects must be used by state or local grantees to procure services or supplies from minority business enterprises [MBE].

  Several contractors sought legal relief from the Court, alleging that the MBE preference was unconstitutional.

  The Court approved the 10 percent MBE set-aside because it was considered to be equitable and reasonably necessary to redress discrimination that had been identified. (*Fullilove v. Klutznick, 448 U.S. 448 [1980]*).

The brief references and discussion of the above three major reverse discrimination cases decided by the U.S. Supreme Court are intended only to acquaint the human resources professional with the basic issues in each. There were a total of 15 separate opinions rendered in these three cases, and the curious reader may wish to review the Court's intricate but rather interesting rationale in these cases.

SEXUAL HARASSMENT

As stated at the beginning of this chapter, sexual harassment is one of those forms of discrimination that began far back in the calendar of our existence. Indeed, it is possible that sexual harassment might perhaps claim the dubious title of the oldest discriminatory practice, first in social, then in business relationships.

The perpetuation of sexual harassment's long history, especially in the business world, is owing to the fact that those being harassed have been coerced into tolerating such behavior under threat of loss of employment or promotion. Many victims of sexual harassment endure a hostile working environment, acquiring an unjust reputation of being a prude, a square, or just a plain weirdo, when they reject the unwelcome sexual advances or refuse to go along with the fun. (For purposes of discussion here, we will assume that the victim of sexual harassment is a female and that the harasser a male, even though the law does not make that distinction, and only addresses the harassment of one sex by a person of the opposite or same sex.)

Sexual harassment is probably one of the most insidious and cruelest forms of discrimination. Although the majority of HR professionals may have no specific admiration or affection for the host of personnel-related laws in our country today, the one exception to this must be that law that prohibits sexual harassment in the workplace in any form. Many strongly feel that it should have been on the books many years before its actual enactment. Harassment on the basis of sex was first mentioned as a violation of Section 703 of Title VII of the 1964 Civil Rights Act. The Equal Employment Opportunity Commission issued the first guidelines on sexual harassment in 1980, and in 1988 the guidelines were supplemented by an EEOC policy statement.

HR support of this particular legislation is probably influenced by the many charges of this nature that HR staff investigates, as well as to some extent by phone calls received. Typically, such calls are from a female employee tearfully relating the usual story of unwelcome sexual advances by her male supervisor or coworker, stressing how badly she needs her job, and in some cases describing the sexual talk, jokes, or pictures at the company facility where she works. Despite repeated entreaties and guarantees of confidentiality, she will often not disclose her name or company location due to her extreme fear of losing her job or incurring the supervisor's wrath if he discovers she has complained to human resources.

The harasser involved is not always but quite often the employee's supervisor or manager who apparently never paid attention to company policy bulletins or manuals regarding discrimination, never read newspapers, books, or magazines, never watched television. Otherwise, he would certainly have known of the literally millions of dollars' liability to which his actions were subjecting his company, for whom he acted and represented. This liability does not even address the issues of moral and ethical behavior that most corporations would encourage in those who supervise their organization's most important asset.

In many companies today, a discussion or even mention of the subject of sexual harassment often brings smiles, sometimes laughter, and frequently humorous remarks. When these elements, together with off-color jokes and remarks, do exist in the workplace, other employees sometimes join in the laughter and go along with this kind of conduct for fear of losing their jobs or being thought of as squares, wet blankets, or of just not possessing a sense of humor. However, the reality of the situation is that when the victim is terminated or demoted, even for legitimate business reasons, or if she perhaps did not receive an anticipated wage increase in a timely manner, the laughter suddenly ceases, a charge of sexual harassment is filed, and the victim's work performance or lack thereof is completely overshadowed by the allegation that an atmosphere of sexual harassment existed at that particular company, and that this was the real reason for her termination, demotion, or failure to receive a wage increase. At this point, the company finds itself with a serious problem involving a possible financial settlement, or facing an expensive court trial and the definite possibility of substantial compensatory and punitive awards to the plaintiff.

Sexual Harassment Defined

It is probably safe to say that the general public, and perhaps even many company managers and supervisors, are in most cases still not clear as to what is actually meant by the term *sexual harassment*. We read quite a bit about it in magazines and newspapers, and probably few people missed at least a part of the Clarence Thomas/Anita Hill televised hearings before a congressional committee in 1991. You will recall that Anita Hill, a former legal associate of Judge Thomas, accused him of sexually harassing her during the time they both worked for the Equal Employment Opportunity Commission in Washington, D.C. To a great extent, the approval or rejection of Judge Thomas' nomination to the U.S. Supreme Court hinged on the committee's decision as to whether or not he was in fact guilty of sexual harassment as alleged by Ms. Hill. These hearings put the rest of the country on the alert that sexual harassment is a reality, and that it is indeed a punishable offense under the law.

Despite the abundance of information on the subject of sexual harassment, most people, including some human resources practitioners, are still confused as to the precise meaning of the term. Therefore, let's look at the EEOC's stated and official definition of just what *sexual harassment* really means. The U.S. Equal Employment Opportunity Commission's definition of sexual harassment follows.

Sexual harassment.
(a) Harassment on the basis of sex is a violation of Sec. 703 of Title VII.[1] Unwelcome sexual advances, requests for sexual favors, and other verbal or physical conduct of a sexual nature

1. The principles involved here continue to apply to race, color, religion or national origin.

---

constitute sexual harassment when (1) submission to such conduct is made either explicitly or implicitly a term or condition of an individual's employment, (2) submission to or rejection of such conduct by an individual is used as the basis for employment decisions affecting such individual, or (3) such conduct has the purpose or effect of unreasonably interfering with an individual's work performance or creating an intimidating, hostile, or offensive working environment.

(b) In determining whether alleged conduct constitutes sexual harassment, the Commission will look at the record as a whole and at the totality of the circumstances, such as the nature of the sexual advances and the context in which the alleged incidents occurred. The determination of the legality of a particular action will be made from the facts, on a case by case basis.

(c) Applying general Title VII principles, an employer, employment agency, joint apprenticeship committee or labor organization (hereinafter collectively referred to as "employer") is responsible for its acts and those of its agents and supervisory employees with respect to sexual harassment regardless of whether the specific acts complained of were authorized or even forbidden by the employer and regardless of whether the employer knew or should have known of their occurrence. The Commission will examine the circumstances of the particular employment relationship and the job functions performed by the individual in determining whether an individual acts in either a supervisory or agency capacity.

(d) With respect to conduct between fellow employees, an employer is responsible for all acts of sexual harassment in the workplace where the employer (or its agents or supervisory employees) knows or should have known of the conduct, unless it can show that it took immediate and appropriate corrective action.

(e) An employer may also be responsible for the acts of non-employees, with respect to sexual harassment of employees in the workplace, where the employer (or its agents or supervisory employees) knows or should have known of the conduct and fails to take immediate and appropriate corrective action. In reviewing these cases the Commission will consider the extent of the employer's control and any other legal responsibility which the employer may have with respect to the conduct of such non-employees.

(f) Prevention is the best tool for the elimination of sexual harassment. An employer should take all steps necessary to prevent sexual harassment from occurring, such as affirmatively raising the subject, expressing strong disapproval, developing appropriate sanctions, informing employees of their right to raise and how to raise the issue of harassment under Title VII, and developing methods to sensitize all concerned.

(g) Other related practices: Where employment opportunities or benefits are granted because of an individual's submission to the employer's sexual advances or requests for sexual favors, the employer may be held liable for unlawful sex discrimination against other persons who were qualified for but denied that employment opportunity or benefit.
(45 Fed.Reg. 74677, 11/10/80.)

What Steps to Take

Heeding the advice of paragraph (f) in the above definition of sexual harassment: "...An employer should take all steps necessary to prevent sexual harassment from occurring, such as affirmatively raising the subject, expressing strong disapproval, developing appropriate sanctions, informing employees of their right to raise and how to raise the issue of harassment under Title VII, and developing methods to sensitize all concerned...," a company needs to promulgate its official feelings via the company policy route and to issue an official statement that might read, for example, something like the following.

FIGURE 8-2.

ABC Company Sexual Harassment Policy Statement

It is ABC Company's policy that sexual harassment of its employees or its customers by company personnel will not be tolerated. All employees, whether supervisors or nonsupervisors, are responsible for ensuring that the workplace is free of sexual harassment. All personnel must avoid any action or conduct that could be in any way viewed as sexual harassment. In addition, any person who has been sexually harassed at work by anyone—including supervisors, coworkers, customers—must promptly bring the problem to the attention of his or her immediate supervisor or an official of the company. In the event that the complaint involves the person's immediate supervisor or someone in the employee's direct line of command, that employee should go to a higher supervisor or manager, or should contact the vice president of human resources.

In order that all company personnel may understand exactly what is meant by the term *sexual harassment*, I have listed below four points that should be helpful in recognizing and defining the subject.

l) Unwelcome advances, requests for sexual favors, and other verbal or physical conduct of a sexual nature that affects employment decisions, interferes with work performance, or creates a hostile work environment.

2) Deliberate or repeated unsolicited verbal comments, gestures, or physical contacts of a sexual nature that are unwelcome or offensive to a reasonably sensitive person. Included in this category are innuendoes, jokes, sexually oriented comments, or any other tasteless action of a sexual nature.

3) Any repeated or unwanted sexual comments, looks, suggestions, or physical contacts that are objectionable or cause an employee discomfort on the job, or the condoning of a working environment in which such actions occur.

4) Any of the above activities between a direct supervisor and subordinates whether you think the activities are welcome or not, or are wanted or not.

It must be also understood that when a company leader, supervisor, manager, vice president—any company official—receives a complaint of sexual harassment, it must be investigated promptly and documentation placed in applicable personnel files. When a manager or supervisor becomes aware of a sexual harassment problem, the following steps are to be taken immediately to resolve it.

1) Interview the person complaining of harassment. Ask the details of the specific instances of harassment, the dates and locations of each incident, and the names of any witnesses.

2) Encourage the complaining person to put the complaint in writing.

3) Make a thorough investigation. Talk to witnesses and other employees. Contact the human resources department for any assistance you may need.

4) Once the details of the complaint have been determined (and within no more than 24 hours, if possible), the person against whom the complaint is being made must be confronted by the supervisor and questioned about the alleged incidents of harassment. The complaining party should also be present at this interview, unless that person specifically requests not to be present.

5) When the entire investigation is complete, take immediate necessary corrective action and apply whatever disciplinary measures may be necessary and appropriate.

Special safeguards should be applied in handling sexual harassment complaints in order to protect the privacy of the complainant as well as the accused party. Discussing the matter with other employees or persons who do not have the need to know (especially coworkers of the complainant), could lead to legal problems relating to embarrassment or even slander of an individual's reputation, and the identity of the party or parties involved should be therefore kept strictly confidential. The charging party should also be reassured by management that there will be no retaliation of any kind by any supervisor or manager for having brought the complaint to the attention of management or the human resources department.

Enclosed with the policy statement is a notice to all ABC employees regarding the company's policy and attitude on sexual harassment. This notice is to be posted on all company bulletin boards throughout the organization so that employees may read it at their place of work.

Albert B. Collins
President and CEO
ABC International Inc.

Mr. Collins, in order to be sure that each and every one of his employees is aware of the company's feelings on sexual harassment, wisely directs that the following notice be displayed in conspicuous places throughout the organization:

FIGURE 8-3

ABC Company Notice to All Employees

ABC Company is an equal opportunity employer. The employment policies and practices of this company are to recruit and hire without discrimination based on race, creed, color, national origin, disability, religion, age, or sex. This policy applies to all terms, conditions, and privileges of employment.

It is ABC policy that sexual harassment of its personnel or customers by company personnel will not be tolerated. All employees—supervisors and nonsupervisors alike—are responsible for insuring that the workplace is free of sexual harassment. All personnel must avoid any action or conduct that could be viewed as sexual harassment. Any person who has been sexually harassed at work by anyone, including supervisors, coworkers, or customers must promptly bring the problem to the attention of his or her immediate supervisor. Sexual harassment can be committed by a coworker as well as by a supervisor or manager. If supervisors or managers are aware of sexual harassment in the workplace and make no effort to stop it, they are subject to immediate termination by their superiors. (If the complaint involves someone in an employee's direct line of command, the employee should go to a higher supervisor or contact a personnel staff member or the vice president of human resources at the corporate office.)

Sexual harassment demeans and offends individuals who are subject to such conduct. It creates unacceptable stress for the entire organization and imposes significant costs including a decline in company morale and work effectiveness. *This company will not tolerate sexual harassment of its employees or customers.*

If you believe you have been sexually harassed, please report any and all incidents to your supervisor immediately. Our company takes these complaints very seriously, and its policy is to take prompt action to resolve the matter. I can assure you it is also company policy that anyone complaining to the company of sexual harassment need have no fear of retaliation either in the form of job security or having to endure a hostile work environment. If it is your supervisor who is harassing you, or if your complaint to your superior does not bring results, please speak with me, the president of the company. If you wish, you may also contact the vice president of human resources at the corporate office.

Remember, sexual harassment disrupts the work environment and is grounds for immediate termination. *There will be no exceptions.* I ask that you please do your part in helping us maintain a positive, healthy, and pleasant work environment.

Albert B. Collins
President and CEO
ABC International Inc.

Despite the fact that sexual harassment does exist in many areas of our society—and probably especially in the business world—there is definitely a growing awareness on the part of the public, and with legislatures in particular, that this is another of the modern-day societal problems and evils that must be controlled and eradicated as much as, and as soon as, possible. Some states also require posting of information specifically indicating that sexual harassment is illegal, and stating the remedies available to its victims. The states of Connecticut, Maine, and Vermont have already passed laws requiring employers to

- set up training programs for managerial and new employees,
- adopt policies against sexual harassment,
- post information on the subject in prominent and accessible workplace locations, and
- provide copies of the policies to all new as well as current employees.

Similar laws requiring these same measures aimed at eliminating and preventing sexual harassment are pending in other states.

From a managerial standpoint, sexual harassment often seems to be an occupational hazard, especially for newly appointed supervisors and managers. In one particular company, no matter what type of company training programs these management trainees attended—including specific, required courses in preventing sexual harassment—within six months to a year after their managerial appointment, a number of male managers of demonstrated ability and great potential were accused of sexual harassment by one or more female staff members at their new locations. Unfortunately, after thorough investigations, the accusations in most cases were determined to be true, and the illustrious but short-lived management careers of these particular managers at this company were ended. They had lost their jobs, the company lost competent, experienced personnel, and employee morale had to be rebuilt. Nobody won. Nobody ever does when sexual harassment infiltrates a company or organization.

It would be somewhat naive to believe that this tendency toward sexual harassment began with these particular managers at the time they assumed their new supervisory duties. Undoubtedly, they had a realization of the status of their new positions and were under the impression they could use their new power with impunity, especially in the area of employee supervision and management. In most cases, it was found that the sexual harassment tendency was present in these people long before they were selected as candidates for any management training program. Intelligence, competency, hard work, and dedication are and should be essential qualifications for promotion. However, company management and those involved in the selection process must be absolutely certain by whatever means available that a sexual harassment tendency is not an element in the candidate's makeup or personality.

The consequences of this cruel form of discrimination in terms of company liability can be financially staggering and could conceivably result in the demise of the company and the loss of employment for many employees, not only those whose actions created the problem in the first place.

The battle against sexual harassment will not be a quick or easy one since, as previously stated, the root causes go far back in our history. But it will eventually be largely eliminated—at least in the workplace—and in all likelihood those most responsible for the victory will be the chief executives of America's business corporations who have the power to require their managers, supervisors, and employees to comply with this as well as all other policies deemed to be primarily in the best interests of the business entity. In truth, however, their customers, employees, and the general public will be the real winners in overcoming this most vicious of discrimination evils.

CHAPTER PERSPECTIVE

This chapter dealt with several types of discrimination in the workplace, and it stressed the need for business organizations to develop written policies regarding discrimination. Sample policy statements on equal employment opportunity and sexual harassment set forth in detail the ground that needs to be covered in such documents. While the existence of the policy statements is a legal protection to the company, the dissemination of their contents to all employees is part of the company's training.

Civil rights legislation and affirmative action were also discussed in this chapter. Reverse discrimination was defined and explored in three U.S. Supreme Court examples. The chapter also presented a thorough discussion of what sexual harassment in the workplace consists of and how it can be discouraged.

Employee Benefits Function

INTRODUCTION AND MAIN POINTS

This chapter discusses the importance of employee benefit programs. It examines the many different types of benefits that a company might offer to its employees in regard both to their effectiveness and their popularity with employees. At the top of the list are medical insurance coverage and other group insurance coverage, employee savings plans, and paid time off, but numerous other benefit programs are evaluated. How legislation affects certain benefit programs is explained. Practical advice on the implementation of several programs is offered.

After you have read the material in this chapter:

▬ You will have a thorough overview of the most important employee benefit programs.

▬ You will understand the relative value of benefit programs during various economic conditions.

▬ You will be aware of which programs are mandated by law and which are voluntary.

▬ You will know which benefit programs work best and why.

▬ You will understand how highly employees value benefit programs and the importance of implementing only those that can be continued.

THE CHANGING PRIORITY OF EMPLOYEE CONCERNS

The three most important aspects of modern-day employees' working relationship with their employers are most likely as follows.

1) Rate of pay
2) Job security
3) Employee benefits

The order of importance of these items to any given employee tends to vary, usually depending on the business and/or economic environment that prevails at the time.

In Boom Times

While rate of pay or salary is never unimportant to an employee, in periods of booming economic expansion values may shift. The inflation during these periods causes merit, promotional, as well as cost-of-living increases, to become a major if not primary concern to employees. Acquiring more liberal and comprehensive employee benefits is normally also considered to be a high-ranking priority so long as boom times continue.

In Times of Recession

When the economy loses its steam and recessionary times follow, personnel layoffs and reductions in force are common and the issue of job security tends to take on a more important meaning for most employees. Once again, their priorities as to pay, security, and benefits are revised and reshuffled.

In the mid-1990s the country emerged from a severe recession, which for the previous four or five years meant massive layoffs in many key industries and the elimination of great numbers of jobs in all sectors of the economy. The loss of thousands of jobs in the defense industry and the closing of many military bases caused by the sudden and complete collapse of the communist system of government in the former Soviet Union, are good examples of the fragile nature of job security even in industries at one time thought to be invincibly secure.

In All Economic Conditions

Whether economic times are good or bad, the subject of employee benefits is always a priority item for a majority of the American work force. At the top of the list of the many different kinds of benefits employees enjoy, you will usually find medical benefits, both for the employee and for his or her spouse and dependents. The ever-increasing costs of health care coverage and the potential for financial ruin as a result of catastrophic illness, accident, or disease are well known to most people who work for a living, and the company that offers the best program of medical coverage and protection at reasonable costs often has the best chance of attracting the most competent and qualified individuals in the job market.

As the country moves from a strictly work-for-a-living culture to a more realistic social and family-values working environment, employee benefits are becoming the centerpiece of employment relationships. Yet, contrary to the opinion of a growing number of consultants in the human resources field, the old adage of "a good day's work for a fair day's pay" is far from obsolete. The employee should certainly have the right, if not the duty, to participate in decisions involving work methods, scheduling, policies, and procedures, and this area has seen more and more good results, especially in the concept of teaming. Nonetheless, this trend is still not inconsistent with employers retaining responsible power and control over their employees' actions, so long as companies are cognizant of modern-day stresses (especially those related to family and dependent-care responsibilities) with which many employees must cope. Regardless of the number of employees, the knowledgeable and caring employer emphasizes and gears the company's benefit program to this need.

THE COST OF EMPLOYEE BENEFITS

When we consider that the volume and scope of employee benefits has greatly increased over the years, it follows, of course, that benefit costs must have increased accordingly. This becomes quite evident when we consider that average benefit costs currently stand at approximately 37 to 40 percent of total payroll expense. In other words, for every dollar a company pays in labor costs, an additional 37 to 40 cents must be added to cover the cost of such benefits. This figure varies from company to company, with some employers paying much less and others much more; however, benefit costs *are* real and they are always an additional cost of doing business. For this reason, the human resources staff must make certain that the company is getting the most mileage for its benefit dollar.

SOME POPULAR EMPLOYEE BENEFITS

Spurred by employee desires as well as union pressures, the importance of benefits to employees continues to be evident as the number and scope of such benefits increases from year to year. The following are some of the more popular, well-known employee benefits:

Medical Insurance Coverage

As indicated above, the single most-valued benefit to the average American worker is, without doubt, medical coverage for the employee and his or her family and dependents.

There have been corporate executives who had accumulated considerable personal wealth over the course of their working careers, and yet whose number one concern (unless previously arranged by agreement or contract) at the time of retirement was that the company provide them and their spouse with sufficient medical coverage to insure that their retirement will be free from the worry of catastrophic, wealth-destroying medical costs. Indeed, medical insurance is a reasonable concern.

Medical care coverage is equally (if not more) important to those not-so-affluent employees who typically are supporting young families, and who have 35 or 40 more years to work before they can even think about retirement. Medical coverage in particular is so important to these latter employees that they sometimes remain with uninteresting, under-paid, and nonchallenging jobs simply because their medical coverage stops on their last day of work. Although former employees may have the option under the Consolidated Omnibus Budget Reconciliation Act (1985), known as COBRA (employee-paid medical insurance), coverage is often unaffordable to the employee out of work.

Most HR professionals today would probably agree that some type of major health care reform is needed in our country. The lack of porta-bility, for example, which would allow continuous and uninterrupted medical coverage to employees changing jobs has always been a problem for employees and businesses alike. *The Wall Street Journal* estimates that 25 million Americans are caught in this so-called *job lock*, a situation in which employees don't change jobs for fear of losing medical coverage due to preexisting conditions. This situation prevailed until the Health Insurance Portability and Accountability Act became law in 1996, and extended new protections for workers, the self-employed, small businesses, and the uninsured.

The expansion of the health care umbrella in this law included the following major provisions.

1) It guarantees that a person who currently has health insurance coverage through work can change jobs without fear of losing coverage, even if that person or a family member has a chronic illness. (Employees with preexisting medical conditions must start a new job within one year in order to obtain insurance coverage.)

2) It prohibits group insurance plans from dropping coverage for a sick employee, or for a business with a sick employee.

3) It sets up some tax-deductible medical savings accounts (MSAs) for small businesses, the self-employed, and the uninsured.

4) It increases tax deductibility for health insurance premiums for the self-employed from 30 percent to 80 percent by the year 2006.

The general feeling also prevails, however, that as needed as the above reforms seem to be, we should never consider dismantling the existing high-quality health care delivery system in the United States today and installing an unaffordable and proven-to-be unworkable socialized medicine approach. The American public made it abun-dantly clear to Congress and others that while we do need health care improvements, it wants no part of national health insurance or socialized medicine—in any form.

Preventive Health Care. Some logical, sound proposals and potential answers are now also coming from prominent physicians and other medical experts who continually crusade for the cause of preventive health care by the individual person rather than the super-expensive corrective and curative measures needed once the person becomes ill. Overcoming bad habits, such as lack of exercise, smoking, eating too much, and improper nutrition is the focus of preventive medicine. These experts are confident that if people kept themselves in better health and adopted sensible lifestyles, the need for hospitals and doctors to acquire expensive and sophisticated medical equipment and technology needed to cure them would decrease, and health care costs would probably plummet accordingly. As an additional benefit, we might even be a healthier and happier society, as well.

In the meantime, until this attitudinal change concerning individual health care does occur, the medical insurance coverage benefit will remain extremely important to all workers and their families.

Although of major importance, health care is only one example on the list of employee benefits. Now let's look at some other benefits and assess their relative importance to employees.

Other Group Insurance Benefit Coverages

These might include the following benefits.

Dental coverage is always important to employees with young families. This benefit normally has a waiting period of one to two years after the start of employment to guard against people getting all of their dental work done (as well as that of their families) when they're first hired and then leaving the company.

Life insurance, of course, gives financial protection to an employee's family in the event of the employee's death. Limited life insurance coverage may also apply to employee's spouse and dependent children. Employee's life coverage is generally based on one, one and one-half, or two times the base salary, up to a maximum of $50,000.

Disability insurance provides salary income protection for employees who are totally disabled from performing their jobs as a result of injury or illness. Disability payments may be provided on a short- and/or long-term basis, and can cover a tax-free percentage of the employee's salary up to a specified maximum monthly limit. For example, disability coverage based on 60 percent of one's salary (tax free), up to a maximum monthly limit of $10,000, often makes the employee whole, and the tax-free disability payment largely offsets the loss of wage or salary income.

Travel/accident insurance provides coverage to employees who travel on company business of a multiple (usually two or three times) of their annual base salary, up to a maximum limit.

Accidental death and dismemberment insurance is designed to provide one-half of an employee's annual base salary up to a specified maximum, for loss of life, limb, or eye, as a result of accidental injury caused directly and exclusively by external, violent, and purely accidental means.

Workers' compensation insurance laws require that every employer carry industrial-accident insurance for all company employees. (Six states have their own state-funded workers' compensation programs to which employers must contribute. These states are Nevada, North Dakota, Ohio, Washington, West Virginia, and Wyoming.) Any injury or illness requiring medical attention that is incurred by an employee, out of and in the course of his or her employment, is covered under workers' compensation insurance, making the employer generally immune from damage suits arising out of occupational injuries.

Employers should make certain that their supervisors and managers understand they may not retaliate in any way against any of their employees for having filed a workers' compensation claim; that is, they may not terminate, harass, or unjustly discipline their employees as a result of having filed a workers' compensation claim.

Employee Savings Plans Benefits

This type of benefit might include any of the following plans.

Employee profit-sharing plans enable employees to share in the company's profits that they help create. Employee sharing may consist of a percentage of the profits based on salary, or on a fixed dollar amount for each eligible participant.

401(k) plans are based upon Section 401(k) of the Internal Revenue Code, which allows eligible employees to contribute a percentage of their salary on a tax-deferred basis into a company-administered investment program. The company may also match employee contributions using a defined formula method in order to increase employee participation in the plan. These types of savings plans are designed to encourage individuals to provide for their own financial needs at retirement through the deferral of taxes on wages and on earned income from company-sponsored investment plans.

Employee stock ownership plans (ESOP) allow an employer to declare a percentage of profits to the ESOP fund and literally give employees an ownership share in the company through company stock. Employees who participate in the ESOP benefit as profits grow and company stock increases in value. They thus become owners of the company, and in some companies the employees literally do own the entire company. Contributions to the ESOP are tax deferred to the individual employee. The tax code also allows favorable tax treatment to companies that borrow money in order to set up such ESOP plans.

Many companies consider an employee stock ownership plan to be the flagship of their entire retirement benefit program. Once an employee passes the required number of years for 100 percent vesting (for example, five to ten years of employment), all monies allocated by the company to that participant become the property of that person. Participating ESOP members who resign or are discharged or laid off prior to being fully vested receive a pro rata share of their ESOP account.

Regardless of what happens to the employee in the future (such as discharge, layoff, or resignation), under the federal Employee Retirement Income Security Act (ERISA), the monies credited to that individual's ESOP are 100 percent his or hers, and are not subject to attachment or garnishment.

As with every aspect of personnel management, it is most important that employees understand and comprehend what an ESOP is and especially how much of a benefit it is now (tax deferral), and can be in the future (secure retirement), for every participant. The human resources benefit group, therefore, has the number one responsibility to communicate with the ESOP participants using every means it can devise in order to get the message across, such as paycheck stuffers, posters, letters to participants' homes (preferably signed by the company president), and any other type of communication human resources can devise to clearly explain the ESOP concept, with special emphasis on two basic precepts:

1) When you are an ESOP participant, you actually do own a portion of the company.

2) By the collective and individual hard work and effort of each ESOP participant, profits can increase and the amount of money contributed by the company to the ESOP therefore can be greater.

With this explanation, it is probably unnecessary to note that an ESOP is strictly a win/win program for everyone!

Paid Time Off

This is one of the more important benefits that modern-day employees enjoy and that, according to most survey results, are so meaningful to them. This trend is likely to continue and expand in the future and employers might be well advised to consider allocating more for this particular benefit, even where the employee-benefit budget dollar is a tight one. Some examples of paid time off include:

Vacations were probably one of the first so-called fringe benefits that employees enjoyed. Vacations are usually based on length of service, with the majority of vacation policies granting two weeks' vacation after one year of service, and three weeks after five years with the company. Vacation allowances of more than three weeks tend to vary with individual employers.

Holidays are usually arranged to coincide with the celebration of national holidays or events. The number of paid holidays varies with individual companies, but common practice is to grant between seven and ten paid holidays annually. In addition, floating holidays, which are used at the discretion of the individual employee or the company, seem to be a popular practice and serve as morale builders and motivators for many employees.

Other examples of paid time off include jury duty, voting time, funeral or bereavement leave, and sick leave (often for nonexempt employees only), as well as serving as a court witness, in military summer camp, and as an election official. (Compensation or fees received by the employee for jury duty, court witnessing, election officiating, and military summer camp are normally coordinated with employees' salaries so they do not lose or gain money as a result of participating in these events.)

Service Awards

This type of benefit is made to company employees, whether full time or part time, upon the completion of specified milestones of company service, normally in increments of 5, 10, 15, 20, 25, 30, and more years. They are normally highly regarded by employees as recognition by the company of their performance and contributions during their years of service. The form of the service award is not of the greatest importance to the employee, but the recognition is.

A number of companies go to great lengths to demonstrate to their employees that management also highly values these awards. In many cases they will provide elaborate, full-color catalogs and/or brochures featuring a large variety of quality gift items from which employees select the service award gift of their own choosing. Other organizations, although still highly valuing the concept of recognition, simply offer a more traditional pin, necklace, bracelet, ring, or watch whose intrinsic value increases in proportion to the number of years of company service or employment.

Severance Pay Program

This benefit is one that most employees hope they never have to use. A severance pay program is set up in most companies to assist employees who, through basically no fault of their own, have lost their jobs and need some financial help to bridge the gap while they are seeking other employment. The company should consider a severance pay company policy normally based on a formula geared to the number of years of service. In the event of a layoff caused by a reduction in work force, organization restructuring, or similar event, the severance policy should be utilized. Also, if an employee's termination results from his or her inability to do the job even though the employee has demonstrated conscientious effort and a generally good attitude, company presidents and managers should be authorized to grant severance pay as provided by company policy.

Although severance is normally not paid when a person resigns voluntarily, the severance policy should not be so rigid and unbending that supervisors and managers do not have the leeway to exercise their own judgment in this regard. They are the people on the spot, and they should know better than anyone else whether or not the person has been a conscientious employee, whether there was any dishonesty or willful misconduct involved, and what the circumstances were in case an individual legal challenge is made.

Regarding severance pay plans, it is important to know that under the federal Employee Retirement Income Security Act (ERISA), a severance pay plan is considered to be a welfare program and, as such, must be reported to the U.S. Department of Labor in the same manner as the retirement plan document, and other employee benefit plans that are defined as welfare programs. Form 5500, "Annual Return/Report of Employee Benefit Plan," must also be prepared and submitted by the company, normally the responsibility of the human resources benefits staff. The company has complete freedom to set up its severance program as a discretionary one, based on whatever provisions it thinks appropriate for its operation. However, the notification and 5500 form must be submitted to the Department of Labor on an annual basis.

Don't let the ERISA reporting requirement stop you from advocating a severance policy. The paperwork, as always, is cumbersome but not excessive. The severance policy will be appreciated by your employees and their families, and though it is a voluntary or nonstatutory benefit (similar to vacations, for example), it can often become meaningful in the competitive market for competent employees.

A severance pay formula might look something like this:

TABLE 9-1
Severance Pay Formula

Years of Service	Severance Pay
After one year of service	1 week
2 but less than 6 years	2 weeks
6 but less than 10 years	3 weeks
10 but less than 15 years	4 weeks
15 but less than 25 years	5 weeks
25 years or more	6 weeks

It should also be noted in your severance policy that, in addition to severance pay, employees discharged or laid off will also be paid for any unused vacation and sick pay for which they are eligible (unless there is evidence of willful misconduct). This makes it clear to employees and supervisors alike that other payments such as vacation and sick pay should not be used as substitutes for, or in lieu of, severance pay.

Educational Assistance Programs

Most companies, recognizing the value of continuing education to the personal development of their work force, will often establish an educational assistance benefit program. Such a program may be designed to assist their employees in becoming better performers on their current job, as well as to prepare them to qualify later for other higher-level jobs within the organization. In addition, educational assistance programs also give the individual employee a better sense of self-esteem and pride in accomplishment—and it certainly is no secret that a company cannot help but benefit from a better-educated work force.

No specific guidelines or standards exist regarding what a company should cover in an educational assistance program. Some companies will pay the entire cost of tuition, books, and other associated fees. Others allow 100 percent reimbursement for college courses that benefit the employee's current position, and 50 percent, perhaps, for those taken for the purpose of preparing for new job responsibilities or advancement within the company. On the other hand, a company may choose to pay for only the employee's tuition, and then not always at the 100 percent rate. Often, a company will require that employees must be approved for the tuition program by their manager; that the employees must attain passing grades, and, to lessen the chances of schoolwork interfering with their job performance, that no more than two courses be taken at any one time. Other provisions or conditions, of course, may be added at the discretion of the individual management.

When we speak about educational assistance benefit programs, we are usually implying a system of reimbursement to the participant: After the tuition is paid at the beginning of the course and the course is completed in accordance with tuition policy provisions, then the employee is repaid by the company.

Some companies that require employees to take certain courses related to their job allow for advance tuition payments whereby the company prepays the cost of the course or courses for those who might not otherwise be able to pay. In addition to the other provisions of the policy, employees given advance tuition must then sign a statement agreeing to reimburse the company from their last paycheck in the event of termination for any reason before courses are completed. Advance tuition reimbursement should be used sparingly as it will otherwise tend to become the rule rather than the exception, and the human resources department runs the risk of becoming a collection agency (along with the related administrative problems and complaints), which it was never designed to be.

Education for the Competition.

One final comment on this particular benefit: A viable, well-administered educational assistance program is an excellent benefit for any company, large or small, to have and to support. The human resources manager, however, must be watchful of the program to be sure that, as sometimes happens, the company is not simply training and educating the work force to qualify for higher-level and better-paying jobs with the XYZ Company located across the street. The XYZ Company may extend open arms to your employees who have completed a portion or even all of their college education through the good offices of your generous educational assistance program sponsored and underwritten by your company.

Of course, a company cannot legally bind its employees to continue employment with it once they have their education behind them, because verbal or even signed agreements are not normally practical or enforceable in situations of this kind. So, how do we cope with such a problem? The old fight-fire-with-fire doctrine might have some application here, in that if the XYZ Company sees value and promise in these people, why can't the ABC Company (your company) do likewise? Because since they are your employees, you certainly have the inside track.

Awarding the Employees' Achievements.

The problems in the ABC Companies of the world on the subject of employee education are more ones of complacency and inattention to the progress of these usually ambitious members of the company. They are determined to get their education and probably just as determined to get ahead in the world of business. In other words, they're good employees! The human resources department can be very effective in making another contribution to the company by, firstly, giving personal recognition to those completing associate's (A.A. or A.S.) and bachelor's (B.A. or B.S.) degrees through the company's educational assistance program. Since human resources administers this program, it knows who the participants are, what courses they're taking, and when they expect to complete their studies. Well-designed and highly embellished Certificates of Achievement, for example, would certainly be in order. Pictures of the graduates in the company newspaper or magazine, and on company bulletin boards, in other words, a little attention, recognition, and publicity is never in bad taste. It might even encourage their fellow workers to also try their hand at this education business.

Second, and probably most important, keep in touch with your employees in the education program, and encourage their supervisors and managers as well to work with them, to notice them, and especially to keep them in mind as new job openings and promotional opportunities arise. After all, you're paying for their education—why not take advantage of your investment? As the complexity of business and technology continues to increase, in coming years the companies with better work force education levels will be the winners as the competition surges. Your educational assistance program may not be the deciding factor, but look at it as one of the more important employee relations investments you will make in your most important asset.

Credit Unions

Although not always considered by employees to be a true benefit, which in fact it is, a credit union is an excellent way for company employees and their families to join together to save at high dividend rates, and to borrow at low interest rates. Credit unions are chartered and regulated by the federal government, and members' savings are insured up to $100,000 by the National Credit Union Administration, an agency of the U. S. Government.

Credit unions also offer the convenience of payroll deductions for both savings and repayment of loans. Special savings plans such as Christmas clubs and vacation clubs can also be included for the convenience of its members. Savings in a credit union are usually known as shares, in that they represent ownership, but unlike stock, because of federal insurance of members' funds, there is no risk. Also, credit union dividends usually exceed interest rates paid by banks on similar demand deposit savings.

For the above reasons, employees in any company, even a relatively small one, will appreciate having a credit union available to them and their families. Company presidents (and human resource managers, in particular), should make certain their business takes advantage of this low-cost, worthwhile employee benefit.

U.S. Savings Bonds

These are another excellent employee benefit that may be offered to employees through the medium of payroll deduction. They provide a systematic savings program for the individual's future needs and goals, and they have distinct advantages in growth, tax exemptions, and security over most other investments. The current Series EE U.S. Savings Bonds allow everyone to receive the competitive market-based interest rates once available only to those with a lot of money to invest. Bond owners also receive a guaranteed minimum rate of interest set at the time of purchase when they hold their bonds at least five years. (They can be redeemed sooner but at reduced yields.)

The interest on savings bonds is exempt from state and local income taxes, and federal tax reporting may be deferred until the bond is cashed or reaches maturity. Federal taxes may be reduced or eliminated when savings bonds proceeds are applied to parents' or children's higher education.

If adequately and properly communicated by human resources, the opportunity of acquiring savings bonds through payroll deduction will be very much appreciated by employees as a worthwhile benefit. And, despite what you may have heard, savings bonds are not normally regarded by business as competition for 401(k) and credit union savings. While benefitting the employee, savings bond purchases also help the country, because they serve to underwrite federal monetary needs and help fight inflation by supplying dollars that might otherwise be borrowed at much higher interest rates. It is officially estimated that one billion dollars in savings bond sales saves the U.S. Treasury (and taxpayers), 70 million dollars.

Direct Deposit

The direct deposit of payroll checks is a benefit that most companies can make available to all of their employees. And for those who do take advantage of it, they will undoubtedly find it a very important as well as convenient one. This program allows employees to authorize automatic deposits from their paychecks directly into their checking and savings accounts, and the only requirement is that the person have or open a checking or savings account with any financial institution.

This is how direct deposit works: Each payday, employees on direct deposit receive a nonnegotiable check as their pay stub, and their deposit is posted to their checking/savings account normally before payday. Direct deposit is convenient and virtually risk free. When employees are on vacation, ill, or just too busy to get to the bank on payday or lunch hour, they have no worries if they have signed up for their company's direct deposit benefit. The company also benefits from this program since employees on direct deposit no longer need to stand in line at their local bank while on short lunch hours, or to frantically run to the bank, perhaps on company time, upon receipt of their paycheck in order to cover some prematurely written personal checks.

There will always be the diehards who will resist the direct deposit program because they "like the feel of the paycheck in their hand," or some other such rationalization. This is one employee benefit that some companies even insist be administered on a mandatory basis for their entire employee population.

Employee Parking

This is probably one of the very few employee benefits more effectively administered outside of the human resources department. If your company provides parking for your employees' vehicles, and especially if it is free of charge to your people, then you, as the human resources manager or director, would be well advised to be sure your building services, security department, or some other authority handles your company's parking program.

Exceptions may exist to this recommendation, particularly if yours is a small company and if parking is not a problem. However, if you have large numbers of employees and parking spaces together with car and van pools, visitor spaces, customer spaces, reserved, covered and uncovered parking, and other variations, you and your human resources staff will spend a good deal of your time immersed in parking problems, a traditional no-win situation. If you have a building management or services group or person, try to include parking as a function in their job description. They are usually much more qualified and equipped to handle it, and you will be doing yourself a favor.

Due to the problems that arise from the parking benefit, it is always wise for the company to charge at least a token amount for employee parking. In this way, people regard the parking space as their personal property as well as responsibility. Pride of ownership usually resolves any number of situations before they become problems or complaints.

Leaves of Absence

When a need arises for employees to be absent from work for a prolonged period of time, most companies will grant them the benefit of a leave of absence, and such leave is normally considered to be a form of employee benefit to the person involved. Employees may request various types of leave such as medical (including maternity), family, personal, and military leave. With the exception of military leaves and those qualifying under the Family and Medical Leave Act (1993), an employer is not required to guarantee reemployment at the time the person is ready and able to return to work. Let's discuss the various kinds of leaves of absence:

Medical leave is normally granted to employees in order to allow them sufficient time to recuperate from a disabling injury or illness incurred on or off the job. The length of the leave is usually based on a physician's recommendation as well as the type of injury or illness involved. It is always advisable to have a company policy that requires that the employee involved must provide the company with a written doctor's release before that employee may return to work from a medical leave of absence. Having such a policy protects the company from the liability associated with the employee returning to work prematurely. Strong Recommendation: Never under any circumstances allow any exceptions to this policy!

Maternity leave is usually considered in the same category as a medical leave of absence. It is designed to allow sufficient time to prepare for and recuperate from childbirth. Most companies permit the employee to continue working up to the date recommended by her doctor, so long as her job performance is satisfactory, but the employee should not be allowed to continue working past the date indicated in her doctor's statement. Again, similar to any other medical leave, no employee should be allowed to return to work from maternity leave without a written doctor's release. The word *written* is an especially important one, both in consideration of the employee's health, and for the protection of the company against lawsuits and legal challenges in the event of serious health problems of the mother before or after childbirth or pregnancy.

Family leave is supported by the Family and Medical Leave Act (1993), which provides for a family leave for employees who wish to take a leave for the following reasons.

- Birth of a child
- Adoption of a child
- Care of a child, spouse, or parent with a serious illness

The length of the leave may not exceed 12 weeks per year, and the employee must have been employed for at least one year, and have worked for a covered employer for at least 1,250 hours over the previous 12 months. The Act also applies if the company has at least 50 employees within a 75-mile radius.

While on family leave, the employee's seniority is protected and that employee must be reinstated in the same (or a similar) job held prior to the leave being granted. In addition, persons on family leave are entitled to the same medical coverage they had prior to the leave.

Executives and others in key positions may be refused family leave under certain specified provisions of the act. As with any personnel legislation, your human resources professionals must be very familiar and conversant with this law in order to answer anticipated questions from supervisors, managers, and employees.

Personal leave is probably the most controversial and misunderstood of all the leaves of absence. Employees as well as supervisors are not always clear on when or even if a personal leave should be granted. In some cases, personal leaves are used as a disciplinary technique and even a device to terminate employees by putting them on a personal leave and then not bringing them back to work on the basis that company policy does not require their reinstatement. This type of usage is highly questionable since it reflects on the judgment, integrity, as well as courage of a manager, supervisor, or even the company itself that resorts to this method of eliminating employees from the work group.

One of the first principles of personnel management is that all managers and supervisors in the company base their disciplinary and termination policies on the truthful reasons for the action involved and not on the easy-way-out method. Examples of the latter might include laying off employees who clearly should have been discharged for nonperformance, misconduct, or insubordination. The long-term consequences of such decisions may come back one day to haunt them, particularly in a court of law.

So long as company policy permits the granting of personal leaves, the granting or denial of such a request should be primarily the decision of the immediate supervisor or even the next level of supervision. The supervisor or manager involved must look at each such request on an individual basis, considering the employee's length of service, performance, attendance, and, of course, the nature and reasons for the request.

Companies may consider granting their people personal leaves of absence for the following reasons.

Death in the immediate family

Settling family estates

Compelling personal matters

Religious needs

Educational purposes

Service in public offices or governmental agencies

Ordinarily, employers should make every effort to grant personal leaves, primarily as a benefit or morale factor, but they should be highly selective on the basis, as stated above, of the individual's performance (including attitude and cooperation), attendance, length of service, and reasons for the request. It will then be recognized by others as a genuine and valued employee benefit.

It is essential that every company establish policies stating the conditions under which a leave of absence will be granted, and what effect a leave will have on the benefits of the employee on leave. It will then be necessary for the human resources department to advise these employees as to what effect their leave will have on their medical and dental coverage, life insurance, retirement savings and pension plans, vacations, sick leave, and any other facet of the employment relationship. As federal laws regulate the conditions under which military as well as family leaves of absence are granted, human resources staffs must be thoroughly familiar with these regulations and how they relate to company policy.

Miscellaneous Employee Benefits

Although the major employee benefits listed previously are the ones that employees as well as employers should be primarily concerned with, some lesser benefits that employees seem to regard highly should also be mentioned. Let's discuss some of these benefits and how they might apply to an individual company and its employees:

Holiday bonuses are a benefit that many companies provide their employees with, in the form of cash bonuses, gifts, or other recognition at holidays and other special times. It is a gesture to their people that they appreciate their hard work and loyalty during the course of the year. Some corporations concentrate on their employees' children, and they put on elaborate holiday parties for them complete with candy, balloons, and decorations, and a substantial toy (reflecting age and gender) presented to each child.

The cost of such an affair, depending upon the size of the company, can be considerable; but the expense is more than justified in terms of employee morale including the involvement of the employee's entire family. Such events often make a lasting good impression on all concerned when they are properly orchestrated and every effort is made for the enjoyment of the children, in particular.

If you as manager, director or vice president of human resources propose such an event to mark the holiday season for your organization's employees and their families, you may get at least one or two objections from upper- or mid-level management that since employee loyalty is currently eroding and will eventually be a thing of the past, why waste money on such an affair? The correct answer to that is a resounding, "Don't you believe it!" Employees are still people, and your company's most important asset.

Despite what you may read or hear, the quality of loyalty remains alive and well in the modern American business community, as those companies with genuine concern for their employees as well as their families have long since discovered and encouraged. Of course, many companies, large or small, downsized or rightsized their work forces during the recessionary years of the early nineties, and some are continuing to do so. Such layoffs are often interpreted by employees as a tangible lack of loyalty on the part of management to its people. While this is probably the case in a number of instances, many other companies who were also forced to cut staff, did so while being as supportive to their employees as possible by job sharing, outplacement, assistance with résumés, as well as job and career counseling. Equally as important, they objectively and effectively communicated to their people the economic or budgetary reasons that made the cutbacks necessary. Most HR managers would perhaps agree that if a company really wants the loyalty of its employees, it will always find a way to earn and deserve it.

Thanksgiving turkeys are simply another means of showing appreciation to employees and their families. Some companies give gift certificates for turkeys, ham, bacon, or other foodstuffs at Thanksgiving, while other companies believe that the actual purchase and distribution of frozen turkeys, to their employees, brings home the message of the company's caring in a more tangible way.

Some human resources personnel may downplay the idea of distributing turkeys to employees at Thanksgiving or during the holiday season, but even in the modern, so-called sophisticated employee environment, people will be just as impressed with the thoughtful employer who takes the time to mark the season with this simple, inexpensive, yet meaningful gesture of appreciation. If this is currently your practice, don't even think of stopping it as a belt-tightening or some other such cost-cutting measure. This type of action often boomerangs on the company that does so, with an offsetting effect of employee ill will and bad morale on the bottom line of the P&L statement. Once again, remember the lesson of never taking away a benefit once given, no matter how small that benefit might be!

Employee discounts usually means giving percentage discounts on company products and services. This benefit has a number of advantages, including feedback from employees as to how they were treated and received as a customer, how the product performed, and other useful data. And, of course, the dollar savings will not be overlooked by your employees as a genuine company benefit.

You will find that extending this privilege to your retired employees also will be much appreciated by them both from a practical as well as goodwill gesture on the part of the company. It also serves to make them feel they are still a part of the organization.

Casual Day. This is one of the less formal yet much appreciated employee benefits on the modern scene. Also called *dress-down* Friday, it is a benefit that a number of companies now use as either an outright benefit or an incentive reward program.

An HR manager of a large corporation was once approached by his staff to discuss the possibility of the office force dressing down and wearing jeans to work every other Friday. Since the manager had for some time been on a low-key crusade to discourage smoking in the office, he not only agreed to jeans every other Friday but, as an incentive, offered dress-down day *every* Friday to everyone, so long as they were nonsmokers. The program worked for a time and a number of staff members did give up smoking, but eventually, the remaining smokers felt the policy was unfair to them and the nonsmoking requirement was dropped. The Friday jeans day remained in effect and was overall regarded as a positive benefit by the HR staff.

Corporate Gym–Wellness Policies. Many corporations now stress the importance of healthy lifestyles of their employees by offering subsidized or discounted memberships in various health and exercise clubs, and providing periodicals, magazines, and posters on healthy foods, diet, exercise, and other information on how to stay healthy. Some large companies are also convinced that building and underwriting their own exercise facilities, gyms, and equipment for employees and their families is a good investment to contain medical care costs while providing employees and families the opportunity of remaining in good health. (See Chapter 13, Lifestyles and Medical Cost Containment, for a further discussion of corporate wellness policies.)

The Company Picnic. Prior to the ever-increasing recognition of the human resources/personnel function over the last five to ten years as an integral part of corporate management and direction, the traditional company picnic was just another of those unimportant, usually overhead items relegated to the personnel department. Over the years, though normally still handled by the human resources department, the company picnic seems to have come into its own as a result of added management emphasis on employee relations, corporate image, and worker morale.

Most employers hold HR responsible to see that employees, their families and guests enjoy the outing, and that the location, food, and other fun activities are up to expectation. Many companies also see the picnic as a good opportunity for employees to meet and socialize in an informal setting with other employees with whom they normally do not have contact in day-to-day business operations.

The company picnic is another of those benefits that, while relatively inexpensive, have real meaning for employees and their families.

THE NEED TO CAREFULLY SELECT BENEFITS

All of us can probably think of many other types of benefits or privileges that employees might appreciate. No matter how incidental a proposal for a new benefit may seem, serious consideration should be given to its implementation provided it fits within the overall company employee benefit strategy and budget. Employees, in many cases, value their benefits as much as they do their paycheck, and in the case of their medical benefits, perhaps even more so.

As benefits are highly regarded by the average employee, companies must make every effort to insure that their benefit program is meaningful, effective, and, not least of all, competitive. This, of course, is all well and good. However, great care must be taken to insure that your benefit program is not too rich or too generous. If a recession or hard times strike the organization and you can no longer afford particular benefits, you will be forced to cut them out or reduce them, thereby creating serious morale problems.

There is a long-standing tenet in the human resources field that you never take away an employee benefit once it has been granted. All human resources managers should consider the consequences of possibly having to rescind a new benefit currently being considered, at some point in the future. As with any other important human resources tool, each employee benefit must be handled in such a manner that both the company and the employee do benefit from its use.

EMPLOYEE ELIGIBILITY

In most companies, employee benefits eligibility is a function of the length of time a person has worked for the company, that is, seniority. The longer service, of course, equates to greater benefits. Though required time periods to qualify for benefits vary with individual corporate policy, the following chart lists typical qualification periods, depending upon the size of the company and whether employment is governmental or private.

TABLE 9-2
Example of Employee Benefits Eligibility Policy

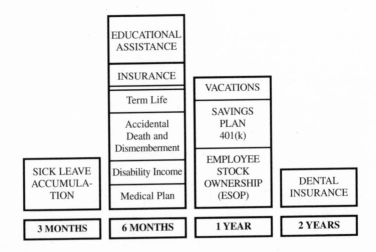

CHAPTER PERSPECTIVE

In this chapter, the importance of employee benefit programs, both to employees and to the companies that wish to attract and retain excellent employees, was discussed. Thirteen of the most popular types of benefit programs were defined and evaluated. Several practical tips on their implementation were offered. The discussion included specific legislation affecting several employee benefit programs. The importance of instituting benefits thoughtfully and carefully was stressed.

Legal Compliance Role of Human Resources

INTRODUCTION AND MAIN POINTS

This chapter summarizes 26 of the most important laws relating to personnel/human resources functions. Federal laws range from the National Labor Relations Act of 1935 to the Health Insurance Portability and Accountability Act of 1996. Topics cover many aspects of the employer-employee relationship from what constitutes overtime to the validity of polygraph testing. State and local laws covering Workers' Compensation, Unemployment Insurance, Health Insurance, and those regulating substance-abuse testing and smoking, are included in the discussion. Relevant concepts, such as exempt status, protected concerted activity, and employment-at-will are explained under the appropriate law.

The necessity for human resources practitioners to become knowledgeable about those laws in order to perform their work well is emphasized. A company's correct compliance with the law not only precludes penalties but often avoids the possibility of lawsuits or strengthens the company's position in the event of a lawsuit. Helpful suggestions concerning timely responses to complaints and disclaimers—how to word them and where to place them for maximum effectiveness—are offered.

After reading the material in this chapter:

■ You will have an overview of the most important laws that impact on the personnel/human resources function.

■ You will understand the concepts upon which many of these federal, state, and local laws are based.

■ You will see the necessity for becoming knowledgeable about these laws in order to correctly comply with them.

■ You will be aware of the importance of formulating written policies and disclaimers in protecting your company from lawsuits.

LEGAL COMPLIANCE

Job evaluation and wage and salary administration form the basis of yet another critical aspect of compensation, namely, compliance with a myriad of federal and state laws dealing with employee compensation and employee relations. A discussion of those laws most frequently encountered by human resources practitioners is important in order to have a general understanding of how they directly or indirectly affect compensation as well as the overall human resources function.

FAIR LABOR STANDARDS ACT (WAGE AND HOUR LAW) OF 1938

The Fair Labor Standards Act of 1938 (FLSA) is the principal federal law relating to overall employee compensation, including the following areas.

- Minimum wage
- Overtime pay requirements
- Exemption status
- Child labor

The FLSA, as amended, and more commonly known as the Wage and Hour Law, is essentially the keystone of employee compensation. Its provisions are relatively clear and generally well known by employers as well as by most employees. The FLSA covers the following employees:

- All engaged in interstate or foreign commerce
- Those producing goods for interstate commerce
- All engaged in commerce or in the production of goods at an enterprise of not less than $500,000 in gross sales

In effect, practically all U.S. workers are covered under the Fair Labor Standards Act.

OVERTIME PAY REQUIREMENTS

In addition to its minimum wage standards and requirements, the overtime feature of the law is the one most generally associated with it and the one most familiar to and understood by employees and employers alike. It provides that all nonexempt employees, such as those who are not exempt from the provisions of the law, must be paid at one and one-half times their base hourly rate of pay (their regular rate of pay), for all hours worked in excess of 40 per week. Paid vacation, sick time, or other compensated hours are not counted in the calculation of overtime. Only hours actually worked in excess of 40 per week are counted in overtime determination.

The law's overtime payment provisions are rigid, and employers must be fully prepared to comply with them, even to the extent of paying time and one-half premium pay if a nonexempt employee takes work home without the knowledge or permission of the supervisor. (When it is discovered that an employee has taken work home without authorization, the supervisor should make it clear to the person involved—preferably in writing—that this must never be repeated without the specific approval of the employee's supervisor. If the situation does occur again, discipline should be assessed up to and including possible termination).

MINIMUM WAGE

At the time of this writing, four states and the District of Columbia had minimum wage requirements that exceeded federal minimum wage standards. (See Table 10-1.) In any of these situations, the higher minimum wage rate will always apply. In most cases of conflict or overlap between state and federal wage laws, the one most benefiting the employee normally prevails.

TABLE 10-1

*States with Minimum Wage Laws Exceeding Federal Minimum Wage
(Based on Federal Minimum Wage of $5.15 per Hour,
Effective September 1997)*

State	Minimum Hourly Wage
Alaska	$ 5.25
District of Columbia	5.75
Hawaii	5.25
Massachusetts	5.25
Oregon	5.50

(Note: Puerto Rico's minimum wage is $6.50 per hour.)

The following graph illustrates the progress of federal minimum wage legislation since its inception in 1938:

FIGURE 10-1

The Federal Hourly Minimum Wage Since Its Inception

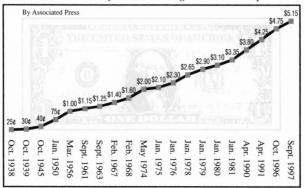

Some states, such as California, also have state wage and hour laws that require the payment of overtime after 12 hours per day, and require that premium time (such as double time or triple time), be paid for Saturday, Sunday, and holiday work. Here again, the employee must be paid the more generous or liberal provisions of either the state or federal law.

EXEMPT STATUS

We have briefly referred to exempt and nonexempt classifications of employees under the federal wage and hour law. The exemption feature of the law basically provides that employees who meet certain compensation or duties standards or tests may be considered exempt from the payment of overtime and from the other provisions of the FLSA. The most common classifications of exemptions (so-called White Collar exemptions), under the wage and hour law are for

Executives
Administrative employees
Professionals
Outside sales employees
Computer-related occupations

The FLSA also provides criteria or tests for each of the above categories in order to determine their exemption validity, and allows for a streamlined test for employees with weekly salaries of at least $250 per week, as well as additional tests for lower-paid employees. Criteria for the five categories are highlighted below. It should be understood that the exemption criteria provided here is not to be relied upon as complete or legally defensible in any exemption question dealing with individual circumstances.

TYPES OF EXEMPTIONS

Executive Exemption
Requirements to meet exemption:

A) The employee in this case must customarily and regularly supervise or manage the work of two or more full-time employees, each working at least 40 hours per week (or supervise or manage the work of sufficient part-time employees whose total hours add up to at least 80 per week).

B) The person's primary duty is the management of a department or subdivision.

C) The employee must have hiring and firing authority, or authority to make effective recommendations to hire, fire, promote, demote, or change the status of employees in other ways.

D) The employee must customarily and regularly exercise discretionary judgment.

E) The employee must not devote more than 20 percent of working time (40 percent in retail business) to nonexempt activities.

The executive exemption is the most common and widely known of all exemptions in that it is probably the most easily understood, and the least subject to interpretation. A supervisor earning a weekly salary of at least $250 per week currently meets the executive exemption if the conditions listed in (A) and (B) are met. This is known as the streamlined exemption test.

Lower-paid employees (those having a weekly salary between $155, and $250 exclusive of board and lodging) may also qualify for the executive exemption by meeting the criteria listed in (A) and (B), but in addition, must also meet (C), (D), and (E), in order to qualify for exemption.

Please note that specific rules apply to owners of businesses regarding this exemption. Further information can be obtained from *Wage and Hour Interpretive Bulletins* for these and other special applications.

Administrative Exemption
Requirements to meet exemption:

A) The primary qualification for this exemption is the performance of office or nonmanual work directly related to management policies or general business operations of the employer or its customers.

B) The duties must require the exercise of discretion and independent judgment.

C) The person must regularly and directly assist a business proprietor, executive, or administrative employee.

D) The person must not devote more than 20 percent of working time (40 percent in retail business) to nonexempt activities.

To apply the streamlined test for the administrative exemption, only tests (A) and (B) are needed to qualify if the person's weekly salary is at least $250 per week. If the weekly salary of the employee is at least $155, and $250, tests (A), (B), (C), and (D) are needed to qualify for the administrative exemption.

Professional Exemption
Requirements to meet exemption:

A) The primary duty is performing work that requires advanced knowledge in a field of science or learning, or if the work is original or creative in a recognized field of artistic endeavor, or if the work imparts knowledge as a certified or recognized teacher.

B) The person must possess a valid license to practice, and practices law or medicine, or has a medical degree and is in an intern or in a residency program, or works as a teacher.

C) The work involved must consistently require the exercise of discretion and independent judgment.

D) The duties must be intellectual and varied.

E) The person may not spend more than 20 percent of his or her time on nonexempt activities.

To apply the streamlined test for the professional exemption, only test (A) is needed to qualify if the weekly salary is at least $250.

If the weekly salary of the employee is at least $170, and less than $250, tests (A), (B), (C), (D), and (E) are needed to qualify.

Outside Sales Exemption

In order to qualify for this exemption, the employee must meet tests (A) and (B), below:

A) The employee customarily and regularly works away from the employer's premises in making sales or obtaining orders or contracts (includes incidental deliveries and collections).

B) The employee may not exceed 20 percent of the work week of the employer's nonexempt workers, doing nonoutside sales work.

Computer-Related Occupation Exemptions

Highly-skilled, computer-related employees who are paid more than six and one-half (6.5) times the current minimum wage are exempt from overtime payments if their primary job duties include:

A) Applying systems analysis techniques and working with users to determine hardware and software specifications.

B) Designing computer systems based on user specifications.

C) Creating or modifying computer programs based on system designs.

D) Creating or modifying computer programs related to machine operating systems.

E) A combination of all of the above duties listed in (A), (B), (C), and (D) above.

Other Exemptions

The Fair Labor Standards Act also contains other exemptions from coverage, including those for nonemployees such as independent contractors, apprentices, and volunteers. In addition, the FLSA, as well as many state laws, prohibits the use of illegal or oppressive child labor, or the hiring of youths to perform certain specified hazardous occupations. As might be expected, a significant body of law and interpretations thereof has developed over the many years of the FLSA's existence, and the compensation practitioner is well advised to consult with the local office of the U.S. Department of Labor when the more difficult problems of exemption, coverage, contract labor, and child labor do occur.

OTHER PERSONNEL-RELATED LEGISLATION

Although extremely important, the Wage and Hour Law is certainly not the only law with which human resources professionals must be well acquainted. Indeed, they must have a working knowledge of a growing list of employee discrimination, privacy, immigration, benefits, and other personnel-related legislation in order to have any hope or possibility of success in this most important but complex profession.

Below are brief summaries of the more important labor legislation with which human resources practitioners must be familiar, and, depending on their particular responsibilities, may be required to thoroughly understand and interpret. Being familiar with these laws may also help the reader to prepare for and understand future people/employee legislation that will undoubtedly affect the human resources function.

National Labor Relations Act (NLRA), 1935

Often known as the Wagner Act, this legislation basically and essentially gave employees the legal right to join a labor organization of their choice. The law also sets up the National Labor Relations Board (NLRB), to coordinate and administer the provisions of this first major piece of labor legislation.

Innumerable books and articles have been written about the profound impact of the NLRA (or Wagner Act, if you prefer), on labor-management relations in the United States. All human resources specialists, whether or not their company is involved in collective bargaining, should have a working knowledge of this landmark law.

Subsequent labor legislation, such as the 1947 Labor-Management Relations Act (more familiarly known as the Taft-Hartley law), and the Labor-Management Reporting and Disclosure Act of 1959 (Landrum-Griffin law) are also on the list of the should-know-and-be-familiar-with legislation for all human resources practitioners, whether their company is union or nonunion.

Protected Concerted Activity—Section 9(a) Many personnel/human resources managers find that one of the Wagner Act's most important but least understood provisions is Section 9(a), Representatives and Elections. Most managers are at least vaguely aware that the Wagner

Act gave employees the legal right to organize a union, as well as to join one of their choice. At any number of personnel and human resources seminars, however, the collective opinion of the conferees always seems to be that as long as there wasn't a union representing the company, Section 9(a) was not something to get overly excited or concerned about.

What, then, is the problem with Section 9(a) and why is it so important? The answer to that question is simply that Section 9(a) basically deals with the subject of protected concerted activity, meaning that any employee or group of employees has the right to present grievances to their employer whether or not that employee or those employees are represented by a union. Let's look at the text of Section 9(a), Representatives and Elections, as it appears in the National Labor Relations Act:[1]

> Sec. 9(a). Representatives designated or selected for the purpose of collective bargaining by the majority of the employees in a unit appropriate for such purposes shall be the exclusive representatives of all the employees in such unit for the purposes of collective bargaining in respect to rates of pay, wages, hours of employment, or other conditions of employment: *Provided*, that any individual employee or a group of employees shall have the right at any time to present grievances to their employer and to have such grievances adjusted, without the intervention of the bargaining representative, as long as the adjustment is not inconsistent with the terms of a collective-bargaining contract or agreement then in effect: *Provided further*, That the bargaining representative has been given opportunity to be present at such adjustment.

What the above Section 9(a) means and why it is so important is made clear in the following example. If any employees (as few as two, and in some cases even a single employee representing a group of other employees) go to their supervisor or employer and complain about some condition of employment not at odds with the rules and regulations of the union contract (if there is a union in the company), those particular employees are protected under the provisions of current labor law just as though they were actually a legal, bona fide labor organization representing the employees of a particular bargaining unit. These employees also enjoy the same degree of protection under

---

1. Section 9(a), Labor-Management Relations Act, 1947, as amended by Public Laws 86-257, 1959, and 93-360, 1974. The Taft-Hartley law amended the National Labor Relations Act, which was subsequently amended by the Labor-Management Reporting and Disclosure Act of 1959, the Landrum-Griffin Act.

labor laws even if there is no union in the company and the complaining employees are not represented by any union. Then, as you might expect, any employer who fires or unjustly disciplines such employees, risks receiving an unfair labor practice charge. Therefore, it is well to remember: Employees always have the right of representation with or without the services or assistance of a labor organization.

Labor Management Relations Act, 1947

This act, more popularly known as the Taft-Hartley law, was passed in 1947 over the veto of President Harry S Truman. While the Wagner Act of 1935 had given employees the right to self-organization and to join a labor union of their choice, this act gave employees the right to not join a labor union. Passed in response to a record number of strikes and labor unrest in 1946, the Taft-Hartley Law (Section 7, Rights of Employees), stated clearly that:

> Employees shall have the right to self-organization, to form, join, or assist labor organizations, to bargain collectively through representatives of their own choosing, and to engage in other concerted activities for the purpose of collective bargaining or other mutual aid or protection, *and shall also have the right to refrain from any or all of such activities* except to the extent that such right may be affected by an agreement requiring membership in a labor organization as a condition of employment as authorized in section 8(a)(3). [Emphasis added.]

The realistic balance of free choice between the Wagner Act's right to join and the Taft-Hartley's right to not join a labor organization had now been struck.

Labor-Management Reporting and Disclosure Act, 1959

The overall purpose and provisions of this law, known popularly as the Landrum-Griffin Act, are to insure that all members of labor unions have the inherent rights of free speech, free assembly, and, perhaps just as important, access to union financial records, which their officers are required to maintain. The law also requires unions to account for all their funds, and sets up rules and regulations for the election and tenure of union officers.

Equal Pay Act, 1963

This act requires that both male and female workers receive equal pay for equal work, that is, for work performed under similar working conditions, and that requires equal skill, effort, and responsibility.

Civil Rights Act, 1964

Title VII of this act, together with Executive Order 11246 forever out-lawed employment discrimination in the United States on the basis of race, color, religion, sex, or national origin.

This prohibition applies to all terms and conditions of employment, including hiring, discharge, and promotion. Unlawful discrimination is defined in the act as

1) the intentional discrimination against any member of a protected class, or
2) when an employer's company policies or practices, though neutral in themselves, have an unintentional adverse impact on a protected group or class of employees.

It is most important for human resources professionals to keep in mind the basic truth well known to all equal employment opportunity coordinators and managers, namely, that proclaiming yourself as a truly equal opportunity employer will avail you little if your work force is lacking in or entirely devoid of minority and female operational and especially managerial personnel. The facts and statistics contained in your company's EEO-1 Report and your affirmative action plan, whether voluntary or mandatory, must support your claim as an enthusiastic equal opportunity supporter.

Civil Rights Act, 1991

In a further strengthening of the country's uncompromising stand on equal opportunity, this latest civil rights legislation permits individuals claiming unlawful, intentional discrimination to bring suit for both compensatory and punitive damages, and may request that their cases be tried before a jury. Also, an employee prevailing on such a discrimination claim may be entitled to back pay, reinstatement to the former job, as well as attorney's fees.

Age Discrimination in Employment Act (ADEA), 1967

This act, passed in 1967 and amended in 1978 and 1986, prohibits employers with over 20 employees from discharging or discriminating in any way against their employees who are 40 or older because of their age. The ADEA does not prohibit early-retirement agreements provided it can be shown that the retirements are totally voluntary and that no form of coercion was used to convince employees to sign early retirement agreements.

AFFIRMATIVE ACTION PLANS AND AGREEMENTS

Three major laws require that employers who have contracts or sub-contracts with the federal government, must take affirmative action and must develop written affirmative action plans whereby the employer commits to employing, training, and advancing individuals in certain protected categories:

1) **Executive Order 11246** requires employers with federal contracts or subcontracts in excess of $10,000 to take affirmative action (using a written plan of action) to hire and promote persons without regard to race, color, religion, sex, or national origin.

2) **The Vocational Rehabilitation Act of 1973** prohibits discrimination by government contractors or subcontractors against handicapped persons. Such contractors are required to take affirmative action to employ and promote the handicapped. Any contractor or subcontractor awarded $2,500 or more in government contracts is subject to this law.

3) **Vietnam Era Veterans' Readjustment Assistance Act of 1974** requires companies holding $10,000 or more in government contracts or subcontracts to take affirmative action to employ and promote qualified, disabled veterans and veterans of the Vietnam era. This law prohibits these employers from discriminating against veterans in all employment matters.

Under all three of the above laws, employers must develop written affirmative action programs if

— their government contracts or subcontracts total $50,000 or more, and
— they employ 50 or more employees.

Failure to comply with any of the provisions of these affirmative action plans or programs could result in

— loss of the government contract, and
— disbarment from bidding on other government contracts for a period of three years.

SEXUAL HARASSMENT

As discussed in Chapter 8, discrimination in what is probably its most insidious form occurs when an employee of either sex is subjected to unwelcome sexual advances, requests for sexual favors, and other conduct of a verbal or physical sexual nature. In addition, such unwelcome advances or requests are often accompanied by threats of job loss, not being promoted, a hostile work environment, or other unpleasant consequences.

To avoid liability or responsibility for such sexual conduct on the part of its employees, including managers and supervisors, the employer must take definite and immediate steps to fully investigate such conduct as soon as it first becomes apparent, or is known by or called to the employer's attention. Such immediate action, together with an impartial and fair investigation, normally assures protection in most cases from legal liability to the employer. Conversely, no investigation at all or even unwarranted delays in beginning an investigation of sexual harassment complaints or charges, practically guarantees the employer an indefensible legal position.

ADDITIONAL LEGISLATION

Americans with Disabilities Act (1992/1994)

This act prohibits discrimination against the disabled by private employers. It became effective on July 26, 1992 for employers with 25 or more employees and effective on July 26, 1994 for employers with 15 or more employees. Employers may not discriminate against individuals with a disability (formerly referred to as handicapped persons), if these individuals are able to perform the essential functions of the specific job held or sought. If the individual's disability impedes or would impede job performance, the employer is required to take steps to reasonably accommodate the individual; however, the employer becomes exempt from this requirement if doing so would impose an undue hardship on the employer.

Congress' intent in this legislation was to set the groundwork for a disabled person and the company working together, rather than creating an adversarial climate as so often happens with many, if not most, other labor-oriented laws. Nevertheless, it is reasonable to anticipate that there will ultimately be numerous court rulings and precedent cases dealing with the interpretation of those highly-interpretable phrases such as reasonable accommodation, undue hardship, and probably many others. Some state legislatures have also passed laws protecting the handicapped and disabled against any form of discrimination.

Occupational Safety and Health Act, 1970

The Occupational Safety and Health Act, also called the Williams-Steiger Act, and more commonly known as OSHA, was designed to promote safety and health in the workplace. This law requires virtually every employer in the United States to furnish its employees with a place of employment literally free from any safety hazards that are likely to cause death or serious injury to them. Under the law, OSHA has the authority to levy fines and assessments on employers who do not maintain an environment of safety and protection at their work sites. The law is administered by the Occupational Safety and Health Administration of the U.S. Department of Labor.

Employee Retirement Income Security Act (ERISA), 1974

The ERISA law is probably the most significant and far-reaching piece of pension legislation ever passed by the U.S. Congress. In one sense, ERISA did for retirees and pensioners what the Wagner Act of 1935 did for employees in the 1930s, that is, it protected their rights to a secure retirement just as the Wagner Act protected their rights to join a labor union for a (perceived) more secure working life.

ERISA protects employees' rights not only with regard to retirement plans, but relating to health and welfare plans as well. This is all accomplished and enforced by the federal government requiring that employers have written plan documents, summary plan descriptions to be distributed to employees, and annual reports to the federal government, and that all plan assets be held in trust together with strict fiduciary responsibilities. Substantial penalties may result from employer violations of ERISA regulations, including loss of deferred tax status of the particular plan involved.

It may be of some historical interest to readers to learn that ERISA legislation faced some formidable opposition when it was first proposed. Because all this occurred more than 20 years ago, most human resources practitioners by this time are probably aware that ERISA opponents had their own version of its acronym—"Every Rotten Idea Since Adam!" Their clever humor, however, was not sufficient to prevent the passage of this landmark personnel legislation.

Immigration Reform and Control Act (IRCA), 1986

This law was passed by Congress to eliminate the illegal practice of employers hiring unauthorized alien workers. Employers are required under this law to verify the identity and work status of every new employee the company hires. All employers, regardless of the size of their company, are subject to the provisions of IRCA.

Employers are required to document all employee verifications, and must maintain files of various documents including copies of Social Security cards, work permits, birth certificates, and other acceptable proofs of nationality and work status. All such documents must be kept ready for examination by immigration authorities and agents at any time. If employers knowingly hire unauthorized aliens, they face significant fines and possible imprisonment. Such fines may also be imposed if the I-9 forms, which specify the particular documents the applicant or employee has submitted to the employer as proof of hiring eligibility, are not well documented or maintained (see I-9, Employment Eligibility Verification form illustrated in Chapter 12).

Consolidated Omnibus Budget Reconciliation Act (COBRA), 1985

Employers with 20 or more employees are legally bound under COBRA to provide their former employees as well as the families of these employees the opportunity to purchase the same health care (medical and dental) group coverage that they had been receiving from their employer and that would normally cease at the time they left the company for any reason, other than misconduct. Such reasons, or qualifying events, as they are known, would include termination of employment, reduction of hours of employment, death or divorce of a covered employee, retirement or disability of a covered employee thus entitling the employee to Medicare, and status change of a dependent child to that of nondependent status.

COBRA coverage is limited to 18 months for employees and 36 months for dependents. Employers must give eligible employees written notice of COBRA rights at the time the qualifying event occurs, that is, termination of employment.

Worker Adjustment and Retraining Notification Act (WARN), 1988

This law in general requires employers of 100 or more employees to provide at least 60 days' advance written notice of layoffs and plant closures to affected employees, their union representatives, and local government officials. The advance-notice requirement also applies if a plant closing will affect 50 or more employees, regardless of company size, or if a layoff affects at least one-third of the employees and at least 50 employees. (If 500 or more employees are affected by the layoffs or plant closure, advance notice is required regardless of the one-third provision.)

If the employer does not give the required notice, it may be held liable for all back pay and benefits for the 60-day notice period for affected employees.

Veterans' Rights and Military Service, 1948

The Selective Service Act of 1948 and subsequent legislation requires companies to reemploy employees who are called to or volunteer for military service, whether active or on reserve duty. The simplest guideline to follow in complying with this law would be that the employer must return military service veterans to the job they would have had if it had not been for their military service. Employers must also grant employees leave time for reserve duty, summer camp, and other training, and they may not require employees to use vacation time for these periods of service.

Although such military leaves may be unpaid, many companies offer to make up the difference between the employee's regular rate of pay, and whatever earnings the employee received from military duty. The U.S. Department of Veterans Affairs offers various manuals and other literature detailing all rights and privileges of returning veterans. Human resource professionals will find these manuals to be handy, understandable references concerning veterans' reemployment rights.

Employee Polygraph Protection Act (EPPA), 1988

Some companies in the past have relied heavily on polygraph or lie detector tests to screen employment applicants, and to test employees where questions of theft, embezzlement, or other wrongdoing were involved. Polygraph tests are generally not permitted to be used as evidence in court, and basically have been found to offer no more than psychological value in assisting employers in hiring or in exposing guilty parties in cases of theft.

In 1988 President Ronald Reagan signed the federal Polygraph Act, which prohibits polygraph testing by employers except under somewhat limited and restricted conditions. The conditions must be carefully monitored and controlled. Under this federal law, lie detector tests may not be given to job applicants for employment; they may be used only where there is clear evidence that a theft involving money or property has taken place on the employer's premises or property. In a number of states, polygraph testing is prohibited altogether.

Workers' Compensation Laws

You will even today still hear many people, including supervisors and managers, refer to this well-known worker-protection program as Workmen's Compensation. So it was called in years past, prior to sexual equality laws and language. The substance of this form of insurance has not basically changed since it was first enacted in Maryland in 1902 (even though it was subsequently declared unconstitutional.) The first Workmen's Compensation laws to be held constitutional were passed in 1911 by four states—California, New Jersey, Washington, and Wisconsin. Since that time, every state has adopted some type of Workmen's/Workers' Compensation act.[2]

Essentially, an employer is required to carry Workers' Compensation insurance for each of its employees, and to pay premiums to either a state fund or to a private carrier to provide its employees compensation for wages lost as a result of an occupational illness or disease, or an injury occurring while on the job. Workers' Compensation laws also protect the company by making it generally immune from lawsuits by

2. Chruden, Herbert J., and Arthur W. Sherman, Jr. *Personnel Management*, 5th ed. Cincinnati, Ohio: South-Western Publishing, 1976, p. 494.

employees for damages resulting from an occupational injury, illness, or disease. Unless the employer's conduct is deemed to be wanton and reckless, even its own negligence is included under the umbrella of Workers' Compensation. Workers' Compensation laws also provide payment for medical treatment, hospitalization, and rehabilitation services for injured or disabled employees.

Unemployment Insurance Laws

This form of insurance protection is a very meaningful program to both employers and employees alike, especially in times of economic recession, consolidations, mergers, and reductions in force. Unemployment insurance laws, governed and controlled by individual state laws, are designed to provide temporary income protection for those workers who find themselves out of work through no fault of their own. However, an employee who quits a job voluntarily and without good cause, who is discharged for misconduct, or who refuses to apply for or accept suitable work may be disqualified by the state from receiving benefits.

Unemployment insurance, contrary to popular notion, is not paid for or provided by the federal or state government; it is paid for by the individual employer on the basis of the company's experience rating, basically determined by the number of unemployment claims paid by the state on behalf of a particular employer during a given period of time.

Currently, unemployment insurance claims costs or taxes to employers (based on their experience ratings) range from a high of $646.40 per employee in Rhode Island, to a low of $98.00 per employee in South Dakota. The U.S. average cost of unemployment insurance to all employers was $232.40 per employee.[3]

Thus, the fewer discharges and layoffs you have in your company, the lower your experience rating, and the greater the savings in unemployment insurance tax dollars will be.

Fair Credit Reporting Act, 1970

Employers who require investigative-type consumer reports on current or prospective employees, must advise these individuals in writing that information about their character, general reputation, or personal characteristics may be disclosed in such reports. An excellent place to inform the job applicant of this fact is in a statement at the end of your employment application, just above the applicant's signature authorizing the company to do so. Such notice is not required, however, if reports are to be used for employment purposes, such as a person being considered for a promotion when the individual has not specifically applied

3. Bureau of National Affairs.

for the position in question.

If an applicant is rejected either wholly or in part due to the information contained in a consumer investigative report, the employer must advise the person of this fact and must also supply the name and address of the consumer reporting agency that made the report.

Willful violations of these provisions of the Fair Credit Reporting Act makes the employer liable for actual damages, punitive damages, and attorney's fees, while negligent failure to comply will result in employer liability for actual damages and attorney's fees.

Family and Medical Leave Act (FMLA), 1993

The FMLA requires covered employers to provide up to 12 weeks of unpaid, job-protected leave to eligible employees for certain family and medical reasons. Employees are considered eligible if they have worked for a covered employer for at least one year, and for 1,250 hours over the previous 12 months, and if there are at least 50 employees within 75 miles of the facility involved. Unpaid leaves of absence must be granted for any of the following reasons:

1) To care for the employee's child after birth, or placement for adoption or foster care.
2) To care for the employee's spouse, son or daughter, or parent, who has a serious health condition.
3) For a serious health condition that makes the employee unable to perform the assigned job.

Other benefits and protection of FMLA include the following.

1) For the duration of FMLA leave, the employer must maintain the employee's current health coverage under any existing group health plan.
2) Upon return from FMLA leave, most employees must be restored to their original or equivalent positions with equivalent pay, benefits, and other terms of employment. (Note: Certain highly paid, designated key employees may be refused reinstatement after FMLA leave if they are informed when they apply for FMLA leave that they *are* key employees, if they are notified as to the reasons for denial of reinstatement, and if they are offered a reasonable opportunity to return to work from FMLA after they receive the no-reinstatement notice. (Key employees are defined as those salaried employees who are among the highest paid 10 percent of employees within 75 miles of the work site.)
3) The use of FMLA leave cannot result in the loss of any employment benefit that accrued prior to the start of an employee's leave.

FMLA does not affect any federal or state law prohibiting discrimination, or supersede any state or local law or collective bargaining agreement that provides greater family or medical leave rights. The U.S. Department of Labor is authorized to investigate and resolve complaints of violations of FMLA, and an eligible employee may bring a civil action against an employer for alleged violations.

Garnishment Laws

Garnishments essentially are court orders requiring an employer to withhold specific amounts of money from an employee's wages for payment of a debt owed by the employee to a third party. The most common garnishment payments involve:

Child support
Bankruptcy proceedings
Unpaid taxes

Garnishment deductions are normally the concern of the payroll department, which in many instances reports to the vice president, director, or manager of human resources. Garnishment orders from courts can become major items of concern for human resources professionals, especially in more difficult economic times. Good times or bad, the volume of such withholding orders continues to grow, especially as more states pass laws to insure stricter enforcement of child support legislation.

The company involved receives no extra compensation or fee for its garnishment work, and in fact, may even be held liable for payment of the subject claim if the garnishment was not legally or properly handled by its employees.

In addition, it is sometimes necessary to assign personnel on a full-time basis to handle just the garnishment work. In spite of these expenses, most human resources professionals would probably agree that these garnishment laws do benefit society in general and taxpayers in particular, and that by and large they do have our support.

EMPLOYMENT-AT-WILL LAWS AND CONCEPTS

The employment-at-will doctrine is basically a carryover from the old English common law that permitted any given employer to discharge an employee at any time, for any reason, or for that matter, for no reason at all. In our modern era, however, this right has been qualified, restricted, limited, and in some instances totally invalidated by the courts, especially state courts. Discharges of employees by companies involving matters of public policy (for instance, employee's refusal to alter company books or records, or to violate other laws or policies affecting the public) are prohibited or ruled against in most courts.

Employment-at-will is a highly complex area of personnel administration. Some courts hold that an employee or supervisory handbook may create an employment contract between employer and employee, and that the employee can only be discharged for violation of the specific reasons listed in the handbook, and for no other reason. Competent labor counsel should be called in to assist the human resources specialist or equal employment opportunity coordinator in adding disclaimer language to personnel handbooks and manuals. The disclaimer should clearly state that the terms and conditions mentioned in such publications are not the only reasons for which an employee may be terminated; and that the handbook or manual involved is not intended to constitute a contract between employer and employee.

Employment Concepts and Noncompetes

It should be clearly understood by the HR professional that simply because we do not acknowledge our personnel policy manuals and employee handbooks to be employment contracts, such contracts are to be considered illegal or unacceptable to management. An employment contract is an HR tool that should be applied and used as circumstances dictate.

Occasionally, a company will have an assignment or project of a limited nature that must be completed within a certain period of time. For example, a company may enter into an employment contract with a college communications or English professor to develop a specific project manual over the three months of summer. The terms of the contract, including compensation, benefits, and other agreed-upon conditions, are all duly spelled out in the employment contract.

Probably the employment contracts most often used are those between companies and executives that are hired by corporations. These contracts normally spell out what is expected of the executive, as well as the perquisites and incentives that may be expected when certain specified goals and objectives are met. Compensation, stock options (where applicable), and medical, retirement, and other employee benefits are included in the contract.

Another type of contract used in business is the traditional non-compete agreement in which employees agree that in the event they leave the company for any reason whatsoever, they will not seek employment with a competitor organization (or start their own competitive company), usually for a specified period of time. Other terms and conditions may also be added to such an agreement, but the non-competitive business restrictions are the essence of the contract.

Attempts to enforce noncompete agreements through the courts have not always been successful, and they are sometimes regarded more as a deterrent in discouraging former employees from joining competitive firms.

At-Will Statement

One of the best and most effective means of insuring the company's employment-at-will status is to include a statement in the employment application itself that the company in question takes the position that any employment relationship is at-will, that it may be terminated by either party (employer or employee) at any time, and that only the president of the company has the right to make any other arrangements to the contrary. By signing the employment application, the applicant is agreeing to accept employment with this particular company under the at-will concept.

Following is a sample statement that might be included on the application for employment form:

FIGURE 10-2

In consideration of my employment, I agree to conform to the rules and regulations of (company name). I understand that any employment relationship is at will and may be terminated at any time, with or without cause, and with or without notice, at the option of either the company or myself. I understand that only the president of (company name,) has any authority to enter into any agreement for employment for any specified period of time, or to make any agreement contrary to the foregoing.

(Applicant's signature) _____

It is also most important that all managers, supervisors, and interviewers in the company understand that they must not make any oral statement guaranteeing the employee permanent employment or job security. An assurance by a manager or supervisor to the applicant or to an employee such as, "Now if you keep your nose clean and do your job, you've got a job here for life" (or some such guarantee in perhaps even more refined language), has spelled defeat for any number of companies in attempting to defend their at-will positions.

SMOKING RULES, ORDINANCES, AND POLICIES

In recent years, to smoke or not to smoke, has become one of those sticky problem situations. Such situations may not have profound consequences for the organization, but they may cause disruption, wasted time, and, in some cases, severely impact employees who are just not able to tolerate cigarette smoke, whether primary or secondary. More and more human resources managers and directors are looking to state or local smoking ordinances as the basis for settling those thorny questions of smoker versus nonsmoker rights within their own organization.

Most smoking ordinances originate with state legislatures, and all tend to be local rather than federal in nature. In many states, smoking in public places is restricted, but private employers have the right to designate smoking and nonsmoking areas within their places of business, or even to prohibit all smoking within their buildings and on their premises, including in company vehicles. Some states protect the rights of smokers to smoke or use tobacco products away from company property during nonworking hours.

A trend is also becoming apparent among some companies to increase medical plan contributions for covered employees and spouses who smoke on or off the job. Skyrocketing group medical costs in the past have prompted some employers to increase fees and deductibles, establish caps or dollar limitations on claims, and in some cases to even completely eliminate medical and dental coverage for those employees whose lifestyle choices such as smoking, nonmedical-related obesity, substance abuse, or failure to wear seat belts account for a greatly disproportionate share of group medical and dental claims dollars paid by employers.[4] On the other hand, some state legislatures are now branding such restrictions and practices as discriminatory. The federal Equal Opportunity Commission (EEOC) seems to be taking the same position, primarily basing its stand on the provisions of the Americans with Disabilities Act of 1992, which the EEOC says forbids such policies and practices.

Future laws and regulations dealing with health-care reform may eventually result in the elimination of such employer practices, medical restrictions, and claims caps, in addition to mandating other totally new concepts of health care financing and delivery.

LAWS AND REGULATIONS REGARDING ACCESS, DISCLOSURE, AND RETENTION OF PERSONNEL FILES AND RECORDS

Whether computerized or manual personnel files are maintained in your company, you should be aware of some of the legal aspects of personnel file maintenance. First, although there are no federal laws that

---

4. An interesting and noteworthy recent study by the Centers for Disease Control and Prevention finds that cigarette smoking costs at least $50 billion per year in direct medical costs (7 percent of *all* U.S. health care expenditures). This staggering figure calculates to $2.00 for each pack of cigarettes sold in direct medical costs. The study did not include indirect results of smoking such as burns or low-birthweight babies. (Courtesy of Mercer Report, August 17, 1994, William M. Mercer, Inc.)

require private employers to grant employees access to their personnel files,[5] there are some state statutes that do allow it (see Table 10-2).

You will note that a number of states do allow current as well as former employees the right, upon request, to inspect and copy their personnel and/or medical file records, and to include their own written rebuttals of any and all matters that they may wish to contest. With the exception of the states listed in Table 10-2, however, employers in other states will find it to their advantage to take the position that personnel files are company property, and as such are not to be copied or privately inspected by employees or former employees.

Instances may occur where employees make what appears to be genuine, good-faith requests to review the contents of their personnel files when, for example, an employee believes it might contain some detrimental item or statement that might be harmful to the individual's progress or advancement within the company. If, after attempting to assure the employee that the human resources department allows only factual documents and material to be placed in these files (and this certainly should be the case), the person still remains unconvinced and wishes to see the file, it is good practice to review each document together, while keeping the file on your side of the table. If the employee objects to some statement or remark in the file for whatever reason, the person should be given the opportunity to submit a written statement of rebuttal concerning the specific matter or episode involved, and have it included in the file. Most people will accept this compromise concerning inspection of their personnel file as it demonstrates that the company is trying to be fair and that it has nothing to hide.

Personnel Work History Documents

If you have a computerized personnel or human resource records system, you will probably have what is known as a Personnel Work History or some other similar feature in your software, which indicates each and every position held by the employee, the departments in which the employee worked, the hourly or salary rates of pay, and a variety of other personnel data items, all of which, of course, can be very helpful if not essential to supervisors and managers of people. The Personnel Work History document is totally factual as to an employee's status and work history with the company, and there is no reason to object to furnishing current (or even former) employees with a copy of this very helpful and complete information. Offering to provide this document, incidentally, will also obviate the need of employees

---

5. Federal Occupational Safety and Health Act regulations, however, do require that employees must have access to their medical and (hazardous) exposure records.

or former employees to peruse their personnel files, for résumé purposes, to see what jobs were held, time on each job, and rates of pay, and the like.

As to the length of time personnel records must be maintained, federal law requires that employment applications and other personnel information be kept for a period of at least 12 months. Longer retention requirements apply to medical and hazardous exposure records.

The human resources manager or director should also be concerned with the kinds of personnel information and data that should or should not be included in the personnel file. In general, any materials having to do with employee hiring, promotion, training, or discipline (employment applications, résumés, performance appraisals, and disciplinary warnings and notices) may be legitimately included in the personnel file. However, any information relating to medical records, garnishments, affirmative action plans, employee charges, lawsuits, and related legal correspondence should all be maintained separately. Separate retention of medical records is required by law.

TABLE 10-2

State Laws Relating to Access to Personnel Files[6]
(Applies to Private and Public Employers Unless Otherwise Indicated)

Employees (normally including former employees) in

Alaska may	inspect and make copies of personnel file.
California may	gain access to personnel files upon request. (Private employers only)
Connecticut may	access, modify, and copy personnel files and medical records. (Private employers only)
Delaware may	access personnel files or medical records on request and at reasonable times.
Illinois may	inspect and copy any personnel records used in making employment decisions.
Iowa may	access and be permitted to obtain, a copy of personnel file maintained by employer.
Maine may	review and copy any personnel file kept by an employer concerning the employee within 10 days of delivering a written request for it. (Private employers only)

6. In most states listed, the express purpose of these laws is to give employees (and former employees) the right to inspect personnel files and records used to determine their qualifications for employment, promotion, pay raises, termination, or other disciplinary action. Employee access and inspection is normally limited to these personnel records.

TABLE 10-2 (continued)

Massachusetts may	inspect, copy, correct, or remove information from personnel file. (Written request to inspect)
Michigan may	review and copy personnel record at reasonable intervals. (Written request to inspect)
Minnesota may	access, correct, and copy personnel records. (Written request to inspect; private employers only)
Nevada may	access and copy personnel file on request.
New Hampshire may	access and copy personnel files, and correct or remove information from such files.
Oregon may	be given reasonable opportunity to inspect all personnel records. (May copy records)
Pennsylvania may	submit written request to inspect personnel file on employee's request and at reasonable times.
Rhode Island may	submit written request to inspect personnel files.
Washington may	access personnel files on request at reasonable times, at least once per year.
Wisconsin may	inspect and copy personnel documents at least twice per calendar year.

It should be noted that at this writing, only the 17 states listed above have enacted legislation with regard to current and/or former employees having access to their personnel files and records.

SUBSTANCE ABUSE TESTING LAWS AND REGULATIONS

Private employers now generally have the legal right to test their employees and job applicants for drugs, alcohol, and other controlled substances. Preemployment drug testing is becoming more and more common in many companies, and testing employees for drugs and alcohol following an industrial accident is also being done by an increasing number of employers. From a legal standpoint, random drug testing is still the riskier aspect of substance abuse screening, although companies in transportation and other safety-critical industries may be required by state or federal law to establish a drug-free environment using such a policy. The bottom line in this complex area of substance abuse testing, however, is that HR professionals must work with their legal department or outside counsel to be aware of the many state laws that deal with substance abuse testing policies and practices in the geographic areas where their companies operate.

Regardless of what other actions you may take in this matter of substance abuse testing, your very first responsibility as the head of the human resources function is to draft a comprehensive yet clear and understandable policy, which must be distributed to every employee in your company. This statement should make it clear to your customers, suppliers, the general public, and especially to your employees, the exact position your company takes on this issue. Your policy should make it crystal clear that the company means what it says: There will be no exceptions to this policy, and an infraction of the rules will bring swift discipline, up to and including termination. Unless your policy is so worded and is in compliance with state and federal law, the policy will not be effective, and your company will be at a great disadvantage in attempting to defend itself against claims and lawsuits from employees, customers, or others alleging violations of civil and constitutional rights. It is strongly recommended, especially in the beginning, to work with qualified legal counsel to draft the necessary policies reflecting your company's approach to this most vital and important subject of substance abuse screening and testing.

THE HUMAN RESOURCES PRACTITIONER AND THE LAW

This is by no means a complete listing of the statutes the human resources professional must be familiar with. Many volumes have been and will yet be written by competent legal experts and others on the various personnel-related statutes and laws. It is merely a brief overview of some of the more important laws one can most often expect to deal with. In reading about the various laws it becomes obvious that not only federal but state laws as well must be a part of the equation in the environment in which the businessperson operates, and the growing list becomes impressive if not awesome.

This comment, of course, is not intended to discourage but simply to impress upon the human resources practitioner the necessity of thoroughly knowing and understanding the basic aspects of personnel law so as to represent the best interests of the employer. And, inasmuch as the foundations of our legal system and social order rest on equity and justice, companies, individual employees, and the public at large, all benefit when our laws are properly interpreted and applied.

CHAPTER PERSPECTIVE

This chapter acquainted the reader with the scope and complexity of federal, state, and local laws that relate to the performance of personnel/human resources functions. The purpose of each law and the relevant concepts were explained in the context of compliance.

Chapter 10 also offered practical advice on how to protect your company from lawsuits in some of the areas covered by these laws. The necessity for the human resources practitioner to gain a thorough knowledge of these laws was stressed.

Wage and Hour Compliance

INTRODUCTION AND MAIN POINTS

Chapter 11 is devoted entirely to the examination of the Fair Labor Standards Act (FLSA), commonly known as the Wage and Hour law, in the context of human resources compliance begun in Chapter 10. The important 80-hours-per-week supervision requirement of the executive exemption category is discussed as it relates to overtime compensation.

While the Wage and Hour law is specific in its requirements and carries economic penalties, it also provides a compromise solution to the problems of excessive overtime through the concept of the Fluctuating Workweek. This option is defined and detailed examples are offered.

The chapter also explores the possible reasons why the Wage and Hour Division of the U.S. Department of Labor, which administers the law, might investigate or audit your company's personnel, wage, and payroll records. Advice on the best response to make to their inquiries and requests is described. Typical Wage and Hour violations, willful violations, Department of Labor enforcement, and proposed FLSA changes and revisions are identified. The special pitfalls and hazards of retail operations regarding compliance with the Wage and Hour law are discussed.

Finally, a Wage and Hour Self-Defense and Preventive Maintenance Program is suggested to avoid many of the aforementioned problems. Five practical preventive measures (PMs) to follow are described.

After reading the material in this chapter:

■ You will understand the importance of complying with the Wage and Hour law.

■ You will be familiar with several of the act's most important provisions and concepts, including overtime, the 80-hours-per-week supervision requirement for executive exempt status, and the Fluctuating Workweek.

■ You will understand why the Department of Labor might investigate or audit your company.

■■ You will understand the problems of retail operations regarding changes in employee exempt/nonexempt status.

■■ You will become familiar with five PMs—preventive measures to avoid serious mishaps in compliance.

THE IMPORTANCE OF KNOWING THE LAW

In Chapter 10, we introduced the basic concepts of the Fair Labor Standards Act of 1938, as amended, commonly referred to as the Wage and Hour law. This chapter is devoted entirely to the understanding of this important law. All human resources specialists should be aware that detailed knowledge of and familiarity with this law is probably the most fundamental prerequisite for performing their job responsibilities—and certainly for performing them well. Compensation analysts, in particular, have a key responsibility to insure that the basic provisions of the Wage and Hour law are being adhered to throughout the organization.

THE OVERTIME PROVISION

In addition to its many other provisions, the main focus of the law's compliance centers on the overtime provisions of the act. It is essential that all personnel classified as exempt from the act's overtime and other provisions actually do meet the qualifications for exemption as spelled out in the law (see Chapter 10 for classification criteria of exemptions covered in the Wage and Hour law).

In most retail organizations, and especially in multifacility retail companies, the executive exemption category requiring the store manager, supervisor, or other entitled executive, to supervise a total of at least 80 hours of work done by others per week, is the most common concern of these organizations. The hours-supervised concept must be thoroughly understood by managers in order for it to be properly applied.

The manager or supervisor must also be perfectly clear on the fact that, in the event that a nonexempt employee (that is, one who is not exempt from the provisions of the law), works beyond 40 hours in any given week, premium dollars must be paid for each hour the person works in excess of 40. Let's look at a simple example:

> If a nonexempt employee works 45 hours in a particular work week, the person is paid *straight time* for all hours worked, (45, for instance), but he or she must also be paid additional *half time* for each and every hour worked over 40 in that work week (such as 5 hours.) For instance, if the employee's base rate is $10 per hour, then that employee would receive $10 times 45 (hours), or $450 for the straight-time hours worked; plus $5 times 5 (hours) for the overtime hours worked, for a total of $25. The employee's

total gross pay for this work week will then be $450 plus $25, or a total of $475 compensation for this particular workweek.

Some employees and employers prefer to think of overtime hours in terms of paying time and one-half for all hours worked over 40 in a given work week. The result, of course, is the same. Using the example quoted in the previous paragraph:

$10 per hour × 40 hours = $400
$15 per hour (time and one-half) × 5 hours = $ 75
Total = $475

This overtime-after-40-hours feature of the Wage and Hour law is perhaps the part of the law that is most understood and, at the same time, most misunderstood both by supervisors and employees alike. Many businesses—and not only smaller ones—will openly complain that they simply cannot afford to pay this premium (penalty) one-half time to their employees. "The cost is too prohibitive." "We'll have to lay off some people in order to be able to pay time and one-half overtime to others." "We may even have to go out of business!" The list goes on and on.

The Need for Compliance

The law is specific, its provisions are clear, and the economic penalties levied against the employer normally serve as effective motivators, as well as tangible reminders as to the wisdom of complying with Wage and Hour law provisions in the future.

The plain facts are that if:

▰ your company or business comes under the scope of the Wage and Hour law as to gross revenue and other provisions as most companies do, and

▰ you do wish to remain in business, and

▰ you do not wish to risk severe penalties for violating the Wage and Hour law, then you do not have a choice—you must comply and pay the premium for the overtime hours.

Typical Wage and Hour Law Violations

Some of the tactics used by employers to unlawfully reduce or entirely avoid the payment of overtime include

1) arbitrarily exempting workers from overtime pay. (In some cases company downsizing pushes authority down through the

ranks, making it harder for employers to know which jobs are exempt and which are not exempt.)

2) pressuring employees to do more work to stay competitive, lengthening the work day and making overtime an even more thorny issue.

3) routinely ignoring overtime rules. Many small companies, especially, to avoid getting caught, do not keep pay records at all or devise false ones.

4) the fact that some larger companies are more likely to issue mandatory overtime pay policies, but then raise productivity targets and look the other way when employees work off the clock to meet those targets.

5) removing substantial duties (purchasing authority, for example) from exempt jobs while still exempting them from overtime.

6) docking exempt salaried workers at any level for missed work time, making those employees ineligible for overtime pay during that particular workweek.

7) simply being ignorant of the law, especially in family or closely held smaller companies.

Willful Violations

The Wage and Hour Division has the authority under the law to require offending employers to go back as many as three years in investigating overtime violations if it is determined that the company deliberately refused to pay the time and one-half rate for overtime hours worked. With the exception of these willful violations, Wage and Hour Division investigations involving two years of checking for overtime violations are more common in cases where employers acknowledge they misinterpreted the law and agree to cooperate fully with the division in resolving the problems involved.

Department of Labor Enforcement

The Wall Street Journal reports that the U.S. Department of Labor's Wage and Hour Division opens about 20,000 cases a year, mostly stemming from employee complaints. The department wins settlements for workers about 90 percent of the time. From October 1991 to June 1995 some 695,280 employees (eight out of every 1,000 workers) were covered by wage and hour settlements. Yet the fact that the number of wage and hour investigators has been reduced by 15 percent to only 800 since 1990 would indicate that many other wage and hour violations are still going undetected.

Proposed FLSA Revisions and Changes

The Fair Labor Standards Act is an all-encompassing, Depression-era federal law that established the foundation for overtime pay. Many employers are not happy with it and would like to see it revised.

Probably the two changes most suggested by companies are

1) to offer workers compensatory time off in lieu of overtime pay, and

2) to extend the period in which overtime is calculated from one to two weeks or even a month, so that, for example, a company could require employees to work overtime in one week and reduce the second work week by a comparable number of hours, thus legally avoiding the need to pay overtime.

Prospects for major revisions to the FLSA, however, appear somewhat dim, and legislation to change it has not been a priority item with Congress. In addition, opposition from unions and sympathetic administrations do not offer much hope for immediate future changes.

LEGAL ALTERNATIVES TO EXCESSIVE OVERTIME

Hiring additional part-time help, restructuring or staggering work schedules, and other innovative time-management measures and scheduling can definitely help to reduce or even eliminate completely the need for working employees overtime.

Compensation department staff should be able to assist management with statistical analyses and studies as to the best methods of controlling overtime expenses, which in some companies are correctly referred to on departmental profit and loss statements (P&Ls) as wasted money! Such remarks on company documents help to serve as effective reminders to supervisors and managers of the need to keep overtime work and hours to an absolute minimum.

Job Sharing

Many companies also have programs that allow two employees to share the same job. This type of situation, for example, is ideal for mothers who can spare only limited amounts of time away from their children. The HR staff works with departmental management to consider possibly dividing an eight-hour job into two four-hour shifts, an ideal arrangement for the two women. On those jobs involving scheduled overtime, such an arrangement could save the company premium wages by splitting the shift between such part-time employees. The resultant overtime savings might then allow the company to offer limited or pro rata benefits to such employees as an incentive to reduce turnover, as well as overtime.

There are many highly qualified and capable people in the job market whose only impediment is that for one valid reason or another, they are just not able to work a full eight-hour job each day of the work week. Any number of smart company CEOs understand this situation well, and they make every effort to arrange hours and shifts to suit the convenience of these part-timers. Far from being considered second-class workers, such companies view them as a valuable and profitable resource, and offer good wages and benefits accordingly.

FLUCTUATING WORKWEEK

One less-well-known provision of the Fair Labor Standards Act, as amended, offers some relief to employers on the overtime pay issue by providing a compromise solution to the need to pay time and one-half for overtime hours. This provision, known as the fluctuating workweek, allows companies to set up a weekly paid, nonexempt salary method of compensation so long as certain conditions of employment exist in the job involved. These conditions include the following.

1) An employee's working hours must be such that they normally vary to the extent the employee can almost never be sure of a specific beginning or ending of the daily work shift due to the requirements and necessities of the work.

2) The employee must be made aware that wages will be paid under the fluctuating workweek method of payment, must fully understand the provisions of the fluctuating workweek, and must agree to compensation under this method of payment.

Although employee hours should still vary in order to use the fluctuating workweek payment method, recent discussions with the U.S. Department of Labor indicate that employers may now use the fluctuating workweek program without strict adherence to the original notification requirements as stated in item 2) above. However, experience tells us that for reasons of proper communication, employee morale, and fairness, employees should certainly be made aware of the system of compensation under which they are working. It is strongly recommended that human resources or compensation managers verify the requirements with the Labor Department before actually installing a fluctuating workweek program in their companies.

The law specifically does require, however, that a person classified on fluctuating workweek must receive a guaranteed weekly salary, which in effect compensates the employee for all straight-time hours that may be called for in a given workweek. Although the person is still a nonexempt employee, any amount of work performed during the week (regardless of how little) guarantees payment of the full week's salary to the employee. In return for this somewhat generous guarantee to the worker, the employer is only required to pay half-time to the employee on fluctuating workweek for overtime work (for example, for all hours worked over 40 during the workweek), rather than the normal time and one-half rate. In addition, the half-time rate under fluctuating workweek decreases progressively as the total number of hours worked during the week increases. It must be kept in mind, however, that regardless of the number of overtime hours worked, the half-time rate may not decrease to less than one-half of the current minimum hourly wage.

The following examples should help clarify this somewhat complex provision of the Wage and Hour law:

Example 1:
■ Weekly guarantee = $300
■ Hours worked this week = 47
■ Hourly wage = (based on number of hours worked this week)
■ $300 (weekly guarantee) ÷ 47 (hours worked) = $6.38/hour (which becomes the base hourly rate for this workweek)
■ 1/2 × $6.38 = $3.19 (the overtime rate for this workweek)
■ $3.19 × 7 (overtime hours) = $22.33 (overtime)
■ $300 (weekly guarantee) + $22.33 (overtime) = $322.33 (total gross pay for this workweek)

Example 2:
■ Weekly guarantee = $375
■ Hours worked this week = 58.5
■ Hourly wage = (based on number of hours worked this week)
■ $375 (weekly guarantee ÷ 58.5 (hours worked) = $6.41 (base hourly rate for this workweek)
■ 1/2 × $6.41 = $3.21 (or, the overtime rate for this workweek)
■ $3.21 × 18.5 overtime hours = $59.39 (overtime).
■ $375 weekly guarantee + $59.39 (overtime) = $434.39 (total gross pay for this workweek.)

Example 3:
■ Weekly guarantee = $250
■ Hours worked this week = 50
■ Hourly wage = (based on number of hours worked this week)
■ $250 (weekly guarantee) ÷ 50 (hours worked) = $5.00/hr (which would normally become the base hourly rate for this workweek. However, since the regular hourly rate falls below the minimum wage of $5.15/hour, the base hourly rate for this week must be increased to and calculated on the basis of $5.15/hour)

> **Example 3 (continued):**
> ▬ $1/2 \times \$5.15$ (minimum wage) = $2.58 (or, the overtime rate for this workweek)
> ▬ $2.58/hour $\times$ 10 (overtime hours) = $25.80 (overtime)
> ▬ $250 (weekly guarantee) + $25.80 (overtime) = $275.80 (total gross pay for this workweek)

The fluctuating workweek might be looked at as a payment method half-way (more or less), between the salary exempt and the hourly nonexempt methods. In retail or service industries where working hours and store coverage are apt to fluctuate on a regular or perhaps seasonal basis, the fluctuating workweek can be an alternative for the employer who currently pays large amounts of overtime based on the expensive time and one-half rate as opposed to using this system of paying only half-time for all hours worked over 40.

If you do happen to decide to bring the fluctuating workweek into your organization, be prepared for possible complaints from employees who will tell anyone who'll listen, "I only get half-time for my overtime hours while my friends and neighbors are all paid time-and-one-half for theirs!" Or perhaps, "My company is really cheap and doesn't care about its employees," and other similarly uncomplimentary remarks. As with most other aspects of business, taking the time to communicate with your employees to explain the pros and cons of the fluctuating workweek is vital, and would certainly be in your best interests to do so.

One company's unique experience with the fluctuating workweek involved installing a pilot program in one of its largest field districts. After careful monitoring of the program, the company discovered that many of their field service representatives who had been on a standard 60-hour workweek for quite some time and were thus paid time-and-one-half for 20 overtime hours each week, were now beginning to report an average of some 45 hours worked each week. The astonishing thing was that they were actually accomplishing all or most of their regular work in 45 hours instead of their former standard 60-hour workweek. This indicated that, at least in part, the knowledge that they were receiving only half-time instead of their former time-and-one-half rate for overtime hours convinced them to get their work done as soon as possible. They were also acutely aware that working the additional overtime hours decreased their basic hourly as well as overtime rate of pay. The additional 15 hours of free time for themselves and their families was undoubtedly their main incentive.

Whatever their individual motivation, the fact remained that these employees were getting more (or at least as much) work done in 45 hours on fluctuating workweek as they had formerly done in 60 hours.

In this situation, the employee as well as the company benefited. Under the proper conditions, you might try this program at your company on an experimental basis, always with the option of returning to more conventional compensation methods if, for whatever reason, the trial run does not prove successful.

In some states such as California (as well as Canada), the fluctuating workweek method of payment may not legally be used due to preempting state (or provincial) legislation. In most states, however, it can be and is used, and though you may run the risk of employee displeasure and grumbling, it is in the long run a most economical way for the company to keep the number one expense item—personnel costs—under control.

DEPARTMENT OF LABOR INVESTIGATIONS AND AUDITS

Don't be shocked or surprised if you receive a call one day from one of your field offices or retail stores that an investigator from the U.S. Department of Labor (DOL) is there asking to see personnel records, pay logs, time cards, and other such data. The DOL has probably called upon you for one of two reasons: Either this is simply a routine, unscheduled wage and hour compliance audit, or, as is more likely the case, the DOL received a complaint that one of your employees was classified in the company's records as an exempt employee when actually the individual believed this not to be the case due to the preponderance of nonexempt work done in the normal course of the job. Because, in all likelihood, this person had worked a considerable number of overtime hours without additional compensation and this practice had allegedly been going on for some time, the DOL was informed of these facts, and the department's Wage and Hour Division is now asking the employer involved the very same questions.

If the claimant was an exempt manager or supervisor, that person may even be claiming that at least 80 hours of work by their subordinates had not been supervised by the claimant, and that the claimant should have indeed been properly classified as nonexempt. Therefore, all hours worked over 40 in each work week should be paid as overtime hours.

There are other reasons, such as methods and timeliness of wage payments, that employees contact the Department of Labor, but statistics show that exempt/nonexempt questions, especially those related to the payment of overtime, are the main reasons for a visit to your company by a wage and hour representative. In any event, you are now involved in a full-scale wage and hour investigation.

Cooperation

Your course at this point is clear: You have absolutely no choice; you must cooperate fully (we might as well add cheerfully and without hesitation) in providing the DOL agent with the information, records, files, logs, or whatever other data the investigator requests. The above approach is highly recommended since you will probably fare better by demonstrating an attitude of cooperation and cheerfulness in providing whatever data or documents the DOL requests. Also remember that, regardless of your attitude, it is usually not wise to volunteer any documents or items of information that are not officially requested. Neither you nor any member of your staff are legally obligated to volunteer information or to guide the investigator in any way.

If the DOL agent asks that you arrange interviews with current employees, provide names and last-known addresses and perhaps phone numbers of former employees, by all means do so. The DOL has the legal right to talk with your current and former personnel to determine if they perhaps have now or have had in the past the same type of complaints as those presently under investigation by the DOL. Also be aware that the Department of Labor has the right to subpoena whatever records and information are relevant to the investigation.

The importance of cooperation on the part of the employer with the DOL cannot be stressed too strongly. This is a most essential element in dealing with them, as it is with any federal, state, or local enforcement or regulatory agency. Whether the subject is discrimination, compensation, or any other area of personnel relations, cooperation eventually wins the day. Government employees have a job to do just as you have in the private sector. If you interact willingly with them and help make their investigation as professional and orderly as possible, you will be the winner in the end, whether or not wage and hour violations have occurred.

Keep in mind that you and your local manager or supervisor represent your company or organization, and your job is to do whatever is legally and ethically permissible to successfully defend your employer and to effectively and economically resolve the issues under investigation. Don't forget that if you sincerely believe the information requested is not relevant to the case or situation in question, then by all means politely but firmly make the point in writing to the agent or agency involved. You may want to consult with your legal advisor for a second opinion on this point, but in any event, stand your ground when you're convinced your position is sound.

On the other side of the coin, if a mistake has been made by a supervisor or someone in a management capacity regarding how an employee was compensated under the Wage and Hour law, have it resolved as quickly as possible and try to negotiate the best deal you can. This is where your cooperation and positive attitude toward the investigation will normally work to your advantage. Make sure that whatever dollar settlements are agreed upon for the employee (or former employee) involved are made promptly, and that proper releases are signed by them. It is also the responsibility of the human resources department to make certain that supervisors and managers who were the focus of the wage and hour investigation fully understand the problems that may have surfaced, the seriousness of any errors made, and, most important, that they learn from their experience.

The Department of Labor can be a most helpful source of guidance and counsel before problem situations are officially brought to their attention, and their staff in any local or regional office is neither unreasonable nor hostile either when seeking their advice or in the course of an investigation. They do their job thoroughly and objectively as the law requires, but they are generally understanding, cooperative, and fair.

RETAIL OPERATION PITFALLS AND HAZARDS

One of the key requirements for supervisors and managers to meet the executive exemption test under the Wage and Hour law (see Chapter 10 for criteria) is that they must supervise the work of two or more full-time employees, each working a total of at least 40 hours per week, or supervise or direct any number of part-time employees (or a combination of both full-time and part-time people) whose combined hours total at least 80 per week. Simply stated, in order for supervisory employees to qualify for the executive exemption, they must supervise or direct a total of at least 80 hours of time worked by their employees in a given workweek.

If they do not supervise at least 80 hours of work on a regular week-by-week basis, the employer has no choice but to classify these supervisory employees to nonexempt status and must pay them on an hourly rate basis, with time and one-half for all hours they work over 40 in any work week. (The only other choice the employer has is to use the fluctuating workweek method of payment described earlier in this chapter, assuming the supervisor's or manager's hours of work are subject to daily fluctuation.)

In the retail business especially, it is certainly to the company's advantage to have store managers, for example, paid as exempt employees, thus eliminating the necessity of paying premium overtime dollars for the long hours usually associated with these kinds of occupations. In economic hard times, we normally find an increase in wage and hour claims due to companies cutting back on numbers of employees and asking (read *requiring*) exempt managers and supervisors to put in additional hours to make up for the reduction in nonexempt personnel hours. Often, no corresponding increase in salary is made for these individuals and, all things considered, the likelihood increases of their claiming to be in a nonexempt status and thereby entitled to overtime after 40 hours.

If a number of supervisors make this claim, and they are successful in convincing the U.S. Department of Labor that such practices are widespread throughout the organization, the company could be facing a massive, full-scale wage and hour investigation in a given district or even in the entire company. Size does not matter in these cases; the economic consequences are potentially most unpleasant if your company is found to be guilty of such violations.

WAGE AND HOUR SELF-DEFENSE AND PREVENTIVE MAINTENANCE PROGRAM

No guarantee exists that you will always receive a clean bill of wage and hour health throughout your company even if you make the most conscientious efforts to insure compliance. The larger your company, and the more outlets or facilities you have, the greater the possibility of wage and hour problems occurring. Some defenses, however, can at least insure against some possibly widespread, undetected, serious violations. These defenses are called preventive measures (PMs) and it is suggested that you consider having your human resources compensation group initiate these PMs with your field, office, and headquarters groups as applicable. For example, you could establish one or more of the following preventive measures.

PM-1: Company Internal Audit (CIA) Checkups

This CIA PM would require the help and assistance of the company's own internal audit department to check on the validity of the exempt status (in particular, the executive exemption) of the various store managers in the field. While it is certainly true that the internal audit department has its hands full with its own responsibility of checking financial and cash management methods and procedures at company retail stores and locations, internal auditors can be of tremendous help to human resources as they travel from company location to location keeping a watchful eye out for potential wage and hour problems. Even if they only observed and raised questions when exempt salary managers seem to have no other subordinate help in their stores, for example, such information would surely be of interest to the compensation staff of human resources.

Another CIA PM in which internal audit can be helpful would be in noting whether or not minimum wage, disability, discrimination, and other legally required posters or notices are displayed on the bulletin boards of company stores and branch locations they routinely visit. In addition to checking for these government notices, internal auditors can provide invaluable help to the HR staff by checking on the prominent display of company policy bulletins and statements dealing with sexual harassment, substance abuse, drug testing, and, assuming you are a nonunion company, the president's statement with respect to your reasons for not turning to an outside party (such as a union) to help management run its organization.

As mentioned previously, the internal audit staff may have about all it can handle in traveling long distances and performing its normal auditing functions on a close time schedule without the added responsibility of performing some human resources work as well. Nevertheless, the staff will normally cooperate and make the effort to spend the few extra minutes to check bulletin boards for posting of appropriate notices and documents. Think about the strategy best suited to your company in handling these challenging opportunities, and work with the internal audit manager to obtain his or her cooperation.

While the name internal audit manager may evoke an image of a large company, no company is too small to have an internal audit function, even if it is simply an added responsibility of a staff member who handles a variety of other duties. An investment in self-audit and policing practices in any company usually pays off handsomely in long-term dividends, regardless of the type of operation being audited.

PM-2: Human Resources Department Random Checkups

This preventive-measure procedure could be a random check of selected stores' or other locations' payroll logs and records, personnel status reports, and other personnel data by the human resources compensation group to detect possible minimum wage, overtime, exemption, and wage payment method violations. This PM-2, while similar to the PM-1, would entail a more in-depth check and analysis of wage and hour compliance and could pay valuable dividends in terms of uncovering violations while still in the early stages. The fact that branch and store managers know they are under such random surveillance also goes a long way toward keeping major infractions to a minimum.

PM-2s could be conducted by wage analysts over the phone, by computer network, in writing, or in person, or a combination of these things, depending on the size of your company and the geographic dispersion of your various facilities. A good computer network with proper software should enable the analyst to monitor these activities for each company department or entity. All things considered, nothing works better than a regular or occasional personal visit (or the prospect thereof) to the store or other company facility to keep these critical wage and hour elements under control and in balance.

Many companies find, to their later financial sorrow and loss, that if employee records, especially those dealing with time worked, are not kept accurately and up to date, the Department of Labor will rely on the employee's own records, estimates, or even memory of overtime hours worked and not paid for, as well as for other types of wage and hour violations. Back pay assessments and penalties against the company could be made for the last two or even three years, depending on how willful or deliberate the DOL determines the company has been in evading the law and attempting to avoid these legally required payments. This is why, as in the case of diseases of the human body, good preventive maintenance and early detection of problems can prevent major difficulties, work disruptions, and serious monetary losses at some future date.

PM-3: Human Resources Department Regular Audits

Even the most basic personal computer software available today has the ability to provide a printout or table (or both), showing the employment status of each employee in the company by department, shop, store, or other facility grouping. This tool, sometimes referred to among other titles as a Personnel Status Report (PSR), should include:

Employee's name

Hire date

Company identification or Social Security number

Job title

Job code number

Rate of pay

Whether salary (exempt) or hourly (nonexempt)

Whether full time, part time, or temporary

Date and amount of last wage or salary increase

The PSR should be run and issued to supervisors and managers either weekly or monthly (the latter reduces paperwork and seems to work out better), and chances are they will find it a great help in administering the compensation, promotion, appraisal, and other employee personnel functions as well. With this information at hand, and being provided to them on a regular basis, managers will have little need or occasion to maintain their own unofficial personnel files on their employees, a practice that could sometimes be quite embarrassing if not actually dangerous when damaging handwritten remarks or notes are made a part of field or noncentralized personnel files.

One unique advantage the Personnel Status Report has for human resources compensation professionals from a wage and hour exemption standpoint is that it gives them an overall, always up-to-date means of identifying and monitoring the number of employees each manager supervises at each company location. The PSR is normally sorted in company and/or location order, and it then becomes a simple matter of scanning the PSR and noting those locations where exempt supervisors or managers appear to not be supervising a sufficient number of subordinate working hours to justify the Fair Labor Standards Act executive exemption.

If an exempt supervisor or manager supervises other exempt personnel, a credit of 40 hours per week is given for each exempt subordinate (as well as for each full-time hourly (nonexempt) person working at least 40 hours per week). In addition, as covered earlier, if a particular location also has part-time, hourly paid employees, the exempt manager or supervisor may take credit for supervising whatever hours these part-time employees work. In other words, if the exempt supervisor or manager supervises any combination of hours of exempt, full-time hourly, or part-time hourly jobs that results in a total of at least 80 hours supervised per week, then for each such week, the manager in question meets the 80 hours of supervision per week wage and hour test and may be considered to have met the executive exemption. If the manager's salary also meets the wage and hour salary test, the manager would then be considered exempt.

When the human resources compensation staff reviews the PSR on a consistent basis, it will be able to easily recognize the first warning signs that an exempt manager has dropped below the 80 hours of supervision required for exemption. The manager's supervisor must then be immediately contacted and instructed to change the status of the manager to either nonexempt (hourly) or to fluctuating workweek (weekly paid) for that particular week, and continuing until such time as the manager is again supervising any combination of 80 hours of work in a given workweek. It must be emphasized that the 80 hours of supervision requirement for exemption applies week by week only. We may not take a monthly, annual, or other time-frame average, as the law is quite specific in requiring 80 hours of supervision each and every week to meet the exemption test.

With the understanding and cooperation of higher level management to whom exempt supervisors and managers report, the human resources compensation analyst can almost guarantee immunity from wage and hour violations regarding the amount of hours supervised by exempt managers simply by doing the following:

▬ conscientiously auditing each current Personnel Status Report (PSR), showing all personnel the manager supervises;

▬ spot checking these employees' time logs; and

▬ alerting the proper officials when exempt managers' status must be changed to nonexempt in order to conform to the law.

This is truly preventive maintenance in action, and is well worth whatever resources must be allocated or redirected from other areas within the human resources department in order to accomplish this objective.

PM-4: Child Labor Violations Checkups

The Wage and Hour law also provides penalties for modern-day abuses of child labor, a practice extremely prevalent in the early part of this century and before. The law establishes minimum hiring ages, maximum number of hours that may be worked, and also when hours may be worked by children when school is in session. Also specified in the law are the types of hazardous tools and equipment children are prohibited from using or operating, as well as the type of hazardous operations around which they may not work.

The human resources professional must be especially mindful of and pay close attention to a child-labor PM program. It may be the one about which the practitioner may mistakenly feel the most confident, while in reality it may be the very program in need of attention. Without a planned (manual or computerized) applicant tracking system, and frankly a visual spot check every now and then as well, minors will slip by and be hired under legal age limits, or, if legally hired, may be working around hazardous equipment, materials, or operations, working too many hours when school is in session, or other potential child labor violations.

These days, with sophisticated computers and software, we should have no trouble whatever monitoring PM-4. However, other responsibilities abound and it may at times be rather easy to convince one's self that this aspect of the complex human resources job is being looked after by your competent supervisors and managers who interview, hire, and/or supervise people—including minors—at the various office and field locations. You must also remember that although this is normally the case, human resources staff personnel are ultimately responsible for protecting the corporation from this and other serious and potentially costly employee relations problems by being alert and sounding the alarm as soon as they first develop.

In addition to your more standard safeguards, make an occasional spot check a normal part of your Child Labor PM-4. You may be pleasantly (or unpleasantly) surprised at the results of such an inspection. In any event, current problems will be easier to correct, and you will come to learn through habit and practice that there is no substitute for early detection as the secret to a healthy, thriving personnel relations program.

PM-5: Personnel Action Changes Monitoring and Checkups

When the status of an employee changes for any reason, the document used to make such a change may be called an Employee Status Change Form, a Personnel Action Form, or some other such title. Whatever you choose to call it, you will want to complete a status change for each of the following events.

New hire
Termination
Promotion
Demotion
Transfer
Disciplinary action
Change of marital status
Address change
Phone number change
Leave of absence
Return from leave of absence

Include any other event that may, and likely will, occur to your personnel at some point in time. Whether you use the latest computer network software to input these status changes, or whether you operate with manual forms and input as some companies still do, you once again have a golden opportunity to utilize your preventive-measure techniques by having your compensation group monitor all such changes, and especially all proposed changes.

Probably the most effective way of monitoring personnel actions and changes is to assign the function to a central location such as the corporate or divisional human resources staff, thus insuring compliance with state and federal wage and hour laws, and other regulations relating to personnel matters. The responsibility of the human resources central staff would be to check such employee status changes for

1) validity of proposed administrative, executive, or professional exemptions.
2) possible child labor violations relating to age, hours of work, and working conditions.
3) the purpose of ensuring payment of minimum hourly and salary wages.
4) any other aspects of Fair Labor Standards Act compliance.

THE AUDIT FUNCTION

The audit function that is normally the responsibility of the human resources compensation professionals can also be useful in detecting other potential HR problems such as compliance with the Immigration Reform and Control Act of 1986 (IRCA). Compensation staff must insure that the proper I-9 paperwork is complete and that the forms are kept in separate file locations (not in the personnel files) and organized so that Immigration and Naturalization agents may conveniently inspect them. Compensation can also check for equality of pay rates for male and female workers doing the same jobs, assuming equality of job performance. For that matter, such an audit can be of invaluable help to human resources in monitoring the provisions of all personnel-related laws and regulations summarized in Chapter 10 of this book.

Occasionally, these PM audits of personnel files will reveal comments on the Personnel Action Form from a manager or supervisor such as:

This employee is being terminated (or demoted, transferred, or other) due to a physical disability that prevents this employee from performing all aspects of the job.

Or:

This employee is being terminated (or demoted, transferred, disciplined, or other) on suspicion of having stolen XX dollars (or items of company equipment) from the employer.

To the more-experienced personnel or human resources professional, these two examples of remarks found on Personnel Action Forms may seem a bit bizarre if not unbelievable. However, these well-intentioned supervisors and managers thought they were doing the right thing but did not realize the problems they were creating by such wording, and the position in which they placed their company from the standpoint of legal liability.

Other examples of dangerous remarks on the Personnel Action Form consist of references to race, sex, or age, character assassination, and unsupported accusations of all sorts that, if entered as a permanent record in the individual's personnel file, could be most detrimental to the company's position in the event of discrimination charges or other legal action taken against the company. It must be remembered that anything that becomes a permanent part of an employee's written work record or history will probably be subject to being subpoenaed by the courts in any future legal proceedings.

Another benefit of the compensation audit is that it permits the auditing or checking for required approval signatures on forms or paperwork relating to hiring, discharge, promotions, wage changes, leaves of absence, severance pay allowances, and discretionary bonus payments. If your company is using or planning to use a computer network in the future, it is also important for compensation analysts to monitor personnel action changes coming in over the network to insure the integrity and validity of signatures and assigned security codes authorized for processing such actions. Those companies currently employing manual methods and systems must, of course, still check for authorized approval signatures, as well as for accuracy and completeness before entering them into their official human resources files and systems.

Sometimes it is recommended to human resources that in order to facilitate the processing of these Personnel Action (Change of Status) Forms, it might be well to forego the auditing procedure on these recommended actions. This same argument is also made regarding the checking of employment applications, W-4 withholding forms, I-9 immigration forms, and a variety of other new-hire paperwork that cannot be sent over a computer network and must therefore be manually forwarded to human resources for handling. When such paperwork is incomplete, illegible, or in some cases, missing altogether, it is literally the duty of the human resources' staff to follow up with company presidents and managers to correct such problems and counsel them on proper data-handling methods in the future.

Although these audit functions sometimes can be time consuming and tedious, they are absolutely vital to a well-organized, efficient personnel records system that will stand you in good stead, especially when the U.S. Department of Labor, immigration compliance officers, and possibly other government investigators come to call. The audit function, including the review and checking of exemptions, proposed wages, job titles, written comments, and other information on the Personnel Action Form, is a most important ingredient of the compensation analyst's job, and can be effectively done only by and in the human resources department.

PAYROLL FUNCTION

The basic audit function is not the responsibility of the payroll department staff, for example, as their function is one of production (of paychecks) rather than analysis, and they are charged with implementing the wage policies and procedures as established by the human resources compensation group. A timely, correct paycheck is the all-important end result of a cooperative effort between payroll and the human resources compensation staff. Probably nothing can be more traumatic or cause more confusion and complaint than a paycheck error, with the possible exception of a misdirected or missing paycheck, or one that is delayed beyond the normal distribution or delivery date. Thus, payroll department personnel do have a critical responsibility to ensure that payroll and paycheck problems are held to an absolute minimum. However, human resources and payroll people must also understand the need for mutual cooperation while attending to their own individual responsibilities. New businesses as well as companies that have been around for many years all understand the importance of producing balance sheets, profit-and-loss statements, annual reports, and similar items, but they must also be keenly aware that the company's most important, most untouchable document it produces is the weekly, biweekly, or monthly employee paycheck. Incidentally, in order to avoid some of the occasional conflicts between human resources and payroll, and for general efficiency purposes, many companies combine these two functions under the manager, director, or vice president of human resources in order to assure the smooth coordination and operation of these most vital areas.

CHAPTER PERSPECTIVE

This chapter examined the Wage and Hour law and the problems that can arise out of improper compliance or noncompliance with its specific provisions. Typical wage and hour violations, willful violations, Department of Labor enforcement, and proposed FLSA changes and revisions were all discussed in some detail. Special attention was given to the problems of retail operations. It focused on the overtime compensation provision, the necessity for correctly categorizing exempt executive employees, and the fluctuating workweek concept. How best to respond to Department of Labor investigations or audits was discussed. Several practical preventive measures (PMs) to monitor possible problem areas were prescribed.

Personnel Policies and the Personnel Policies Manual (PPM)

INTRODUCTION AND MAIN POINTS

This chapter is about formalizing personnel policies and compiling them into a Personnel Policies Manual (PPM). First, the need for formalizing such policies is discussed. Second, guidelines for constructing a PPM for your company are given, with special attention to the table of contents, the subject index, and the cover. The inclusion of important personnel policy statements in the introductory part of the manual is recommended. These position statements are on the topics of:

Individual department policies
Corporate commitment
Employment-at-will
Equal employment opportunity
Unions
Substance abuse

Sample personnel forms most often used in the human resources function should also be included in your personnel policies manual. This chapter gives 12 examples of customized forms, statements, and agreements, and why and how to use them. These forms cover the following topics:

Application for employment
Confidential reference inquiry
Educational reference inquiry
I-9 (Immigration forms)
Employment eligibility verification
Personal progress interview, appearance, and property return
Warning notice
Voluntary resignation
Exit interview
No solicitation, No distribution, Posting rules
Gambling on company property
Letters of recommendation or reference letters

After reading the material in this chapter:

▬ You will understand why it is important to formalize your person-nel policies in writing and to compile a Personnel Policies Manual.

▬ You will have a good idea of how to go about constructing your Personnel Policies Manual.

▬ You will be aware of the importance of including a position state-ment in the introduction.

▬ You will know which sample forms should be included so that managers, supervisors, and HR practitioners will have them as handy reference tools.

THE NEED FOR FORMALIZING PERSONNEL POLICIES

Regardless of the size of your company, one of the principal and key duties of the human resources department (or the person who handles the human resources function) has to be the origination, development, main-tenance, and ultimately the publication of all of your approved and official personnel policies. Smaller firms might sometimes feel that the formalizing and publication of their personnel policies is not absolutely necessary inasmuch as their employees already know these policies in a general way, and their supervisors and managers don't want to be fenced in by formal policy statements and inflexible work rules. Some companies might even take the position that if they have no Personnel Policies Manual, no employee handbook, and no published individual personnel policies of any kind, their employees will be unable to chal-lenge the actions or decisions of management or supervisors by pointing out the written provisions of any given personnel policy.

Unfortunately, this head-in-the-sand attitude will create far more problems than it avoids—for companies of any size. In this current era of discrimination complaints and governmental laws, rules, and regula-tions, the very nature and complexity of operating a modern business enterprise makes it absolutely necessary that every company have a set of specific, clearly written and understandable personnel policies detail-ing exactly what the company's stand is on any given personnel matter.

If your organization is currently relatively small, you will probably find that, as your company expands and your population grows, your supervisors and managers will soon be requesting, if not insisting, that management establish formal personnel policies where none now exist, and that such policies be written and published, preferably in manual form. Most experienced managers seem to instinctively know that a clear, well-written, and complete PPM, when properly followed and applied, can be one of the most important tools that makes their primary responsibility of getting work done through people much easier.

The lack of a published PPM does not, of course, result in chaos or inertia within a company. However, it could also be argued that the company does not necessarily need a marketing plan, an advertising budget, or viable computer software and hardware, unless the life expectancy of your company is not important to you and your company's stockholders. An effective PPM falls into this order of importance.

In the fortunate circumstance that you have been able to convince your management that putting together a PPM is a wise thing to do, you might ask:

■ Where do you start?
■ How specifically do you go about creating such a document?

You may or may not be aware that there are many consulting firms, lawyers, and others who will provide you with professional advice and counsel about what such a manual should contain. Many will also offer examples as well as samples of the ideal policies manual for your use in constructing your own. While a number of these services do have merit, you should always keep in mind that you and your associates in ABC Company can normally produce a more-than-adequate PPM simply by compiling all your existing personnel policies into one written format. Then it is highly recommended that you include some very specific statements or disclaimers in your manual in order to protect your company as much as possible against certain charges or complaints such as discrimination or wrongful termination. These measures can also serve to alert everyone inside as well as outside the organization that your company is a nonunion one, assuming that is the case, and that you intend to remain so.

HOW TO CONSTRUCT A PERSONNEL POLICIES MANUAL

You can and should construct your policies manual in the format that best fits your organization's needs and that will be relatively effective in explaining company policy and withstanding employee complaints and the legal challenges that most HR practitioners must inevitably face. The occasion could be an attorney demand letter on behalf of one of your employees (or former employees), or perhaps having to read one of the policies in your manual to a jury when you are defending your position in the courtroom.

While formalizing a policies manual along the following guidelines is no warranty or guarantee of immunity, it will help you to understand what normally goes into the making of a good PPM.

1) Whether you have few or many personnel policies in your company, be sure each of them is included in your manual, which should be revised as policies are added or changed. If each of your policies is spelled out in clear, concise language, there

will be no excuse for supervisors and managers to make up their own policies, regardless of their personal feelings or opinions to the contrary.

2) Establish a table of contents and group your personnel policies under general headings for related policies. For example, you might show a general category of EMPLOYEE BENEFITS. Under this title, you would list all of the various benefits your company offers, benefit eligibility rules, dates of eligibility, and all information related to your company's benefits. Then, once your pagination was final, you would add the page numbers where these items are located in the manual.

A TABLE OF CONTENTS

Examples of other possible general categories in a PPM's table of contents are set forth in Figure 12-1.

FIGURE 12-1

The Figure 12-1 example is only a partial listing of what you might want to include in your PPM's table of contents. Depending on the number of policies in the manual, you will want to build on your original listing and amend the table from time to time, as policies are added or changed.

A SUBJECT INDEX

In the back of your policies manual, you will want to include a detailed subject index in alphabetical order indicating the subjects covered and the corresponding page number locations. If in doubt, you will find that over-indexing your subjects is far better than too few subject listings. Your supervisors and managers will thank you if you break your subjects down into as many subcategories as possible.

THE PPM COVER

One word on the overall appearance of your PPM: For aesthetic purposes as well as for readiness of identification and reference, you may want your art department or an outside illustrator to design an attractive cover for it. The cover design may incorporate a picture or drawing of your principal products, or, because it is essentially a human resource product, you may want some design relating to the people perspective as you may envision it, keeping in mind that human resources professionals serve and give helping hands to employees, customers, and others. Whatever your situation, when you have a published, well-written PPM, you have the opportunity of using your talents and imagination as well as those of your staff to create an appropriate and meaningful cover design related to the HR mission statement. Don't attempt a work of art, but have fun and take pride in creating an attractive yet very necessary publication.

POSITION STATEMENTS

Another real advantage of publishing a PPM is that it gives the company an excellent forum for stating its views, philosophies, and objectives in writing, so that everyone (including the courts and plaintiffs' lawyers) may know its official position on a variety of personnel relations subjects. The following possible topics for official position statements do not necessarily appear in the sequence you may choose for your own PPM.

1) On an introductory page of the manual, you might wish to make it very clear that, on occasion, various divisions or departments of your company might find it necessary to issue individual personnel rules or procedures relating to, for example, dress code, personal appearance, tardiness, unexcused absences, or payroll

deductions for cash shortages or missing goods or equipment. These separate local policies or procedures may be necessary, as situations can vary from facility to facility. For example, some employees may deal directly with retail customers, while others will work entirely in office, shop, or warehouse areas, with little if any contact with the customer.

However, your introductory statement might also caution supervisors and managers that, due to the sensitive and potentially discriminatory nature of these individual rules, they should first be referred to the human resources staff before they are published or actually put into effect.

2) Many companies and businesses have a long-standing corporate culture or objective that might also be given prominence on an introductory page of the manual. Your statement might read, for example:

FIGURE 12-2

ABC COMPANY
Our Sales and Service Commitment to Our Customers
ABC Company was founded on a commitment to always provide the best quality product and service to its customers at the lowest possible cost. This original commitment has become a part of ABC's corporate culture, and will continue to be, so long as our customers permit us to serve them.

Although such a company statement of purpose may seem innocuous and even unnecessary, it could serve as a general guideline or Rosetta Stone, if you will, for all of your supervisors in dealing with customers, as well as in managing their employees.

3) It is also very important that your policy manual (as well as any type of employee handbook) contain an at-will employment statement. Such a statement should be placed either on the inside front cover or the first page of your manual, and to be sure of getting the necessary attention, it should be printed in bold or all capital type. Displaying your at-will statement in this conspicuous manner helps to strengthen the company's position that it does not hire prospective employees under any contract of employment. You should also be sure that your statement makes it clear that the personnel policies listed in the manual are to be used only as guidelines by company supervisors and managers who handle personnel matters.

A sample at-will statement is presented in Figure 12-3.

FIGURE 12-3

ABC COMPANY
AT-WILL/PERSONNEL POLICY STATEMENT

The contents of this manual set forth general statements of policy that are to be used as guidelines by management when handling personnel matters. As such, these policy statements do not constitute promises of specific treatment to employees and, depending upon the circumstances of a given situation, management's actions may vary from the written policies. THE CONTENTS OF THIS MANUAL DO NOT CONSTITUTE THE TERMS OF A CONTRACT OF EMPLOYMENT.

This manual shall not be construed as a guarantee of continued employment, but rather employment with ABC Company is on an at-will basis. This means that the employment relationship may be terminated at any time, with or without cause, with or without notice, by either the employee or the ABC Company for any reason not expressly prohibited by law. Any oral or written representations to the contrary are invalid and shall not be relied upon by any prospective, past, or present employee.

The personnel policies contained in this manual were written by ABC Company. The manual itself replaces all previous manuals, directives, bulletins, newsletters, pamphlets, and other corporate materials containing statements of personnel policies by ABC Company or its affiliated companies. These policies may be changed and others may be added from time to time.

Albert B. Collins
President and CEO
ABC International Inc.

You will notice that the president and chief executive officer of the company is signing this statement, inasmuch as it serves as the primary shield in protecting and defending the entire company against charges of wrongful termination, especially those based on claims of implied contract and employment guarantees.

4) It would probably be prudent to have another page of your introduction devoted to an equal employment opportunity policy statement, such as the one shown in Chapter 8 of this book.

The importance of this policy statement also requires that it too be signed by the president and chief executive officer of the company.

5) Assuming you are a nonunion company and you have a strong commitment to remaining that way, you would be well advised to publish your company's position on the subject of unionization in order to make sure your employees know exactly where your company does stand. Again, you will find no better place to take your stand and make your statement than in the front or introductory section of your PPM.

The following suggested statement is not designed nor intended to be antiunion; it simply communicates the concept that, since in the past, the ABC Company and its employees have always been able to deal with each other on a reasonable and respectful basis, the company sees no reason now to change that relationship by having an outside third party allegedly help run their business. With that thought in mind, we might word our statement something similar to Figure 12-4.

FIGURE 12-4

ABC COMPANY
WHAT ABOUT UNIONS?

ABC Company attempts to provide a good environment for all our employees both as to working conditions and in the personal team relationships between management and all of our people. In other words, you can talk to us, we can talk to you, and with your help, we hope to keep it that way. Each employee is treated as an individual and is an important participant in the operation of our company

In today's uncertain world, there are many pressures and anxieties. We strive to keep our company free from any artificially created tensions and work interruptions that often arise when a union is on the scene. Indeed, there are many other companies where employees have chosen not to have a union and we think it a commendable choice.

ABC strongly believes that individual consideration in employee-supervisor relationships provides the best climate for maximum development, teamwork, and the attainment of employee goals and those of the company. We absolutely do not believe that union representation of our employees would be in the best interests of either the employee or the company.

FIGURE 12-4 (continued)

We believe that a union would be of no advantage to any of us here, nor to our customers, nor to the business growth that we all depend on for our livelihood. We sincerely believe that any outside third party could seriously impair the relationship between the company and the employees, and that it could retard the growth of our company and the progress of ABC employees.

We also believe that we have enthusiastically accepted our responsibility to provide our employees with good working conditions, good wages, good benefits, fair treatment, and the personal respect that rightfully belongs to our people. All these things are already a part of our employees' jobs with ABC and certainly do not need to be purchased from an outside third party.

We are fully aware that all ABC employees want to express their problems, comments, and suggestions to us so that we can all better understand each other. Our employees already have that opportunity here at ABC. This can be and has been done without having a union involved in the communication between the employee and the company. Here you, as an employee, speak up for yourself at all levels of management. We will continue to listen, and to do our best to give you a responsible reply. You should understand that if your supervisor cannot resolve your problems, you are expected to see me!

Albert B. Collins
President and CEO
ABC International Inc.

In addition to including this policy statement on unions in your PPM, it would also be an excellent idea to have it posted at all company locations and facilities in a conspicuous place so that there can be absolutely no doubt about the position your company takes on unionization.

Similarly, the union policy statement belongs in any sort of employee handbook or manual you might publish and distribute to new and current employees as well, so that the new employee, in particular, will find it unnecessary to ask about a union.

6) You may wish to include one other general aspect of personnel and employment relations in the introductory portion of your manual—the matter of substance abuse and the company's attitude toward it. It is, of course, impractical to try to highlight

each of your personnel policies in the introduction, especially when the policy itself is spelled out in detail in the text of your manual. There are, however, certain policies that are and can be so vital to the company's operation that it is probably prudent and wise to emphasize and highlight them in the beginning of the manual, as well. The subject of substance abuse is one of these. Figure 12-5 is a suggested statement, again signed by the company president.

FIGURE 12-5

ABC COMPANY
SUBSTANCE ABUSE POLICY STATEMENT

Contained in this PPM is a clear, comprehensive, and unequivocal policy and program for dealing with the subject of illegal drugs and alcohol in the work environment. Although the specifics of our program are quite well documented herein, I believe it is my responsibility to officially state the company's overall position regarding this critical matter:

It is certainly no secret that substance abuse, which includes the use of illegal drugs and the abuse of alcohol and prescription drugs, is one of our nation's most serious problems. Substance abuse reduces productivity, increases accident and illness rates, and is a main cause of embezzlement and theft. It increases medical and hospitalization costs, and is often a crime. We at ABC Company are quite proud of the fact that we owe our success to safety-conscious, clear-thinking, innovative, and productive employees—and we intend to keep it that way! We also take the position that our customers and employees, as well as ABC shareholders, are entitled to protection from the high costs of lost productivity, increased medical expenses, and unsafe conditions caused by the influence of illegal drugs and the abuse of alcohol and prescription drugs.

Our substance abuse policy makes it very clear that the possession, sale, or use of illegal drugs, alcohol, or the abuse of prescription drugs by our employees in the work environment is unacceptable and against corporate policy. Likewise, the impairment of employees caused by the possession, sale, or use of illegal drugs, alcohol, or abused prescription drugs is also unacceptable and against corporate policy. In the work environment, as a condition of continued employment, our employees are required to be free of any measurable amounts of illegal drugs, alcohol, or abused prescription drugs. If any

FIGURE 12-5 (continued)

supervisor or manager has an employee with a problem with drugs or alcohol—or if an employee requests help in this regard—the supervisor or manager is urged to contact our human resources department so the person may be referred to an outside agency for professional help. All inquiries or requests will be kept confidential to the utmost extent possible, with the understanding that drug-screening lab reports and other related documents may be used as admissible evidence in unemployment and workers' compensation benefit determinations, administrative hearings, civil actions, or other legal proceedings.

Our company policy regarding substance abuse is intended to be supportive rather than punitive. We are concerned about coworkers who abuse drugs or alcohol, and we hope that we do not lose a single person as a result of this program. Every one of us is an important member of the team, and the successful implementation of our substance abuse program will guarantee a safe and drug-free environment for us all.

Albert B. Collins
President and CEO
ABC International Inc.

PERSONNEL/EMPLOYMENT FORMS, STATEMENTS, AGREEMENTS

For the convenience of your managers and supervisors, who will hopefully refer to their policies manual at all times when necessary, it is expedient to include in the manual references to (and reproductions of) some of the personnel forms they will more frequently be apt to use. The Bureau of National Affairs, Inc. offers a wide variety of sample forms, notices, and posters covering practically any procedural or policy phase of personnel management, based on the actual policies of many companies, plants, and businesses. These can all be very helpful to a start-up as well as existing human resources department, and I recommend a careful examination of them by any interested human resources manager.

As you can imagine, it would be impractical and unwise to try to include each and every such form or statement in your PPM; however, a few of the most essential and commonly used ones should be considered for inclusion. Figure 12-6 to 12-10 are examples of the forms you might find most helpful in human resources management.

FIGURE 12-6
Application For Employment Form

ABC CO. APPLICATION FOR EMPLOYMENT   ❑ FULL-TIME   ❑ PART-TIME   ❑ TEMPORARY

ABC IS AN EQUAL OPPORTUNITY EMPLOYER. ALL QUALIFIED APPLICANTS WILL BE CONSIDERED WITHOUT REGARD TO RACE, RELIGION, COLOR, SEX, NATIONAL ORIGIN, AGE OR DISABILITY.

IMPORTANT: THIS APPLICATION **MUST BE FILLED OUT COMPLETELY**, EVEN IF YOU HAVE SUPPLIED A RESUME. PLEASE PRINT LEGIBLY.

DATE	POSITION DESIRED					PHONE NO. (AREA CODE)
LAST NAME	FIRST	MIDDLE		SOCIAL SECURITY NUMBER	MESSAGE PHONE	
PRESENT ADDRESS		CITY, STATE, ZIP				HOW LONG?
PREVIOUS ADDRESS		CITY, STATE, ZIP				HOW LONG?

POSITION DESIRED	DATE YOU CAN START	SALARY REQUIREMENTS

ARE YOU EMPLOYED NOW?   ❑ YES ❑ NO   IF SO MAY WE INQUIRE OF YOUR PRESENT EMPLOYER?   ❑ YES   ❑ NO

EVER APPLIED TO THIS COMPANY BEFORE? ❑ YES ❑ NO	WHERE?	WHEN?
EVER WORKED FOR THIS COMPANY BEFORE? ❑ YES ❑ NO	WHERE?	WHEN?

REASON FOR LEAVING

NAME OF LAST SUPERVISOR AT THIS COMPANY

WHO REFERRED YOU TO THIS COMPANY?
     ❑ EMPLOYMENT AGENCY   ❑ NEWSPAPER ADVERTISING   ❑ FRIEND
     ❑ STATE EMPLOYMENT OFFICE   ❑ COLLEGE PLACEMENT SERVICE   ❑ WALK IN   ❑ OTHER

COLLEGE OR UNIVERSITY

EDUCATIONAL INFORMATION

CIRCLE LAST GRADE COMPLETED IN ELEMENTARY OR HIGH SCHOOL
1 2 3 4 5 6 7 8 9 10 11 12   ❑ GED

NAME AND LOCATION (CITY AND STATE) OF LAST HIGH SCHOOL

NAME AND ADDRESS OF SCHOOL	GRAD-UATED	TYPE OF DEGREE	CURRICULUM	GRADE AVERAGE
COLLEGE OR UNIVERSITY	❑ YES		MAJOR	
ADDRESS, CITY, STATE	❑ NO		MINOR	
COLLEGE OR UNIVERSITY	❑ YES		MAJOR	
ADDRESS, CITY, STATE	❑ NO		MINOR	
GRADUATE SCHOOL	❑ YES		MAJOR	
ADDRESS, CITY, STATE	❑ NO		MINOR	
OTHER TRAINING (TRADE, BUSINESS OR CORRESPONDENCE SCHOOL)	❑ YES ❑ NO			

SECURITY INFORMATION

IF YOU ARE OFFERED EMPLOYMENT, CAN YOU SUBMIT VERIFICATION OF YOUR LEGAL RIGHT TO WORK IN THE UNITED STATES?
     ❑ YES   ❑ NO

HAVE YOU EVER BEEN CONVICTED—OTHER THAN MINOR TRAFFIC VIOLATIONS, FOR WHICH A PARDON WAS NOT GRANTED?
IF YES, EXPLAIN. (CONVICTION WILL NOT AUTOMATICALLY BAR EMPLOYMENT.)
     ❑ YES   ❑ NO

CLERICAL/SHOP SKILLS

SHORTHAND	TYPING	10-KEY		NAME OFFICE MACHINES AND/OR SHOP MACHINES YOU CAN SET UP AND OPERATE
		BY SIGHT	BY TOUCH	
WPM	WPM			

PC SKILLS AND WORD PROCESSING EXPERIENCE (LIST SOFTWARE YOU ARE SKILLED ON)

REFERENCES

YOU MUST GIVE THE NAMES OF THREE PERSONS WHOM YOU HAVE KNOWN AT LEAST ONE YEAR. PLEASE EXCLUDE RELATIVES AND FORMER EMPLOYERS.

NAME	ADDRESS	PHONE	OCCUPATION	YRS. KNOWN
NAME	ADDRESS	PHONE	OCCUPATION	YRS. KNOWN
NAME	ADDRESS	PHONE	OCCUPATION	YRS. KNOWN

SEE REVERSE

FIGURE 12-6 (continued)

U.S. MILITARY STATUS	
BRANCH	RANK

DESCRIPTION OF RELEVANT SKILLS ACQUIRED DURING U.S. MILITARY SERVICE:

WHAT SPECIAL OR PERSONAL FACTS SHOULD THE COMPANY KNOW ABOUT YOU?
(exclude any that would indicate race, color, religion, national origin, sex, age or disability & ancestry)

SPECIAL TRAINING

SPECIAL SKILLS

RECORD OF EMPLOYMENT: FILL IN COMPLETELY, BEGINNING WITH PRESENT OR LAST POSITION.

NAME OF PRESENT OR LAST EMPLOYER		TYPE OF BUSINESS OR COMPANY PRODUCT	
COMPLETE ADDRESS (INCLUDE STREET, CITY, STATE, ZIP)	PHONE NO. ( )	STARTING DATE (MO/YR)	LEAVING DATE (MO/YR)
NAME OF SUPERVISOR	SUPERVISOR'S TITLE	STARTING PAY	FINAL PAY
YOUR JOB TITLE (PRESENT OR LAST)	REASON FOR LEAVING		

DESCRIPTION OF WORK AND RESPONSIBILITIES

NAME OF NEXT PREVIOUS EMPLOYER		TYPE OF BUSINESS OR COMPANY PRODUCT	
COMPLETE ADDRESS (INCLUDE STREET, CITY, STATE, ZIP)	PHONE NO. ( )	STARTING DATE (MO/YR)	LEAVING DATE (MO/YR)
NAME OF SUPERVISOR	SUPERVISOR'S TITLE	STARTING PAY	FINAL PAY
YOUR JOB TITLE	REASON FOR LEAVING		

DESCRIPTION OF WORK AND RESPONSIBILITIES

NAME OF NEXT PREVIOUS EMPLOYER		TYPE OF BUSINESS OR COMPANY PRODUCT	
COMPLETE ADDRESS (INCLUDE STREET, CITY, STATE, ZIP)	PHONE NO. ( )	STARTING DATE (MO/YR)	LEAVING DATE (MO/YR)
NAME OF SUPERVISOR	SUPERVISOR'S TITLE	STARTING PAY	FINAL PAY
YOUR JOB TITLE	REASON FOR LEAVING		

DESCRIPTION OF WORK AND RESPONSIBILITIES

PLEASE EXPLAIN ANY EXTENDED PERIOD OF UNEMPLOYMENT

CONDITIONS OF EMPLOYMENT: I understand that false statements or omissions on this application or resume may result in dismissal at any time. **I agree to a urinalysis drug screening, if required.** I understand and agree that all information furnished on this application may be verified by ABC or its authorized representative. I hereby authorize all individuals and organizations named or referred to in this application and any law enforcement organization or credit bureau to give ABC all information, relative to such verification and hereby release such individuals, organizations, and ABC from any and all liability for any claim or damage resulting therefrom.

In consideration of my employment, I agree to conform to the rules and regulations of ABC. I understand that any employment relationship is at will and may be terminated at any time, with or without cause, and with or without notice, at the option of either the Company or myself. I understand that only the President of ABC has any authority to enter into any agreement for employment for any specified period of time, or to make any agreement contrary to the foregoing.

APPLICANT'S SIGNATURE: **X**_____

NOTE: If the job you are hired for requires a driver's license, you must furnish a copy of your driving record from the State Motor Vehicle Department.

Interviewer's Notes:

FIGURE 12-7

ABC COMPANY
CONFIDENTIAL REFERENCE INQUIRY

(Employee Please Complete This Section)

Dear Sir or Madam:

I have made application to ABC Company for employment. I request and authorize you to release all information requested below by ABC, including that concerning my employment record, character, habits and abilities, and reasons for leaving your employment. The following data may help in identifying me and my employment record:

Name While in Your Employment_____
Social Security No. _____
Dates of Employment: From _____To _____
Position Held   _____
Department   _____
Immediate Supervisor _____
Rate of Pay: $ _____ Per _____
Reason for Leaving:

_____
_____
_____
_____

Signature _____ Date _____

(Past Employer Please Complete This Section)

Dear Sir or Madam:

We are asking your assistance in making an employment decision and would like to reassure you that all information provided on the form will be held in strictest confidence. An immediate reply will be appreciated. Please don't hesitate to contact me if I can reciprocate in providing you with information regarding former ABC employees.

Thank You,

_____
Mary Cameron
Human Resources Manager

FIGURE 12-7 (continued)

Dates of Employment: From _____ To _____
Rate of Pay: $ _____ Per _____
Position Held _____
Department _____

	EXCELLENT	GOOD	FAIR	POOR	COMMENTS
Quality of Work					
Dependability					
Cooperation					
Attitude					
Attendance					

Reason For Leaving:

_____

Would You Reemploy?
Other Remarks:

_____

_____

_____

_____

Signature: _____ Title: _____
Phone No.: _____ Date: _____

FIGURE 12-8

ABC COMPANY
EDUCATIONAL REFERENCE INQUIRY

(Employee Please Complete This Section)

Dear Sir or Madam:

I have applied for employment with ABC Company. I hereby authorize all individuals and organizations named or referred to in this request to give ABC all information relative to such verification and hereby release such individuals or organizations and ABC from any and all liability for any claim or damage resulting therefrom.

Applicant's Signature _____ Date _____

FIGURE 12-8 (continued)

The following information has been provided by the above-signed applicant. Would you please verify this data by a check mark in the boxes provided, and indicate any discrepancies in the comments section below. Please sign the completed form in the space provided. We sincerely thank you in advance for your cooperation.

Sincerely,

_____

Mary Cameron
Human Resources Manager

Applicant's Name: _____

VERIFY(✓)

Social Security Number: _____

Date of Birth: _____

College or University: _____

Graduate School: _____

Other (Vocational, Trade or Correspondence): _____

Dates of Attendance: From _____ To _____

Degree or Courses Completed: _____

Major: _____

Minor _____

Credits Completed: _____ Grade Point Avg.: _____

College or University Official: _____

(Signature)

Date: _____

Comments: _____

_____

_____

_____

FIGURE 12-9
Employment Eligibility Verification Form

U.S. Department of Justice
Immigration and Naturalization Service

OMB No. 1115-0136
Employment Eligibility Verification

Please read instructions carefully before completing this form. The instructions must be available during completion of this form. ANTI-DISCRIMINATION NOTICE. It is illegal to discriminate against work eligible individuals. Employers CANNOT specify which document(s) they will accept from an employee. The refusal to hire an individual because of a future expiration date may also constitute illegal discrimination.

Section 1. Employee Information and Verification. To be completed and signed by employee at the time employment begins

Print Name: Last	First	Middle Initial	Maiden Name
Address *(Street Name and Number)*		Apt. #	Date of Birth *(month/day/year)*
City	State	Zip Code	Social Security #

I am aware that federal law provides for imprisonment and/or fines for false statements or use of false documents in connection with the completion of this form.	I attest, under penalty of perjury, that I am (check one of the following): ❏ A citizen or national of the United States ❏ A Lawful Permanent Resident (Alien # A_____) ❏ An alien authorized to work until ____/____/____ ❏ Alien # or Admission # _____

Employee's Signature	Date *(month/date/year)*

Preparer and/or Translator Certification. (To be completed and signed if Section 1 is prepared by a person other than the employee.) I attest, under penalty of perjury, that I have assisted in the colpetion of this form and that to the best of my knowledge the information is true and correct.

Preparer's/Translator's Signature	Print Name
Address *(Street Name and Number, City, State, Zip Code)*	Date *(month/day/year)*

Section 2. Employer Review and Verification. To be completed and signed by the employer. Examine one document from List A OR examine one document from List B **and** one from List C as listed on the reverse of this form and record the title, number and expiration date, if any, of the document(s)

List A	OR	List B	AND	List C
Document title: _____		_____		_____
Issuing authority: _____		_____		_____
Document #: _____		_____		_____
Expiration Date *(if any)*: ___/___/___		___/___/___		___/___/___
Document #: _____				
Expiration Date *(if any)*: ___/___/___				

CERTIFICATION: - I attest under penalty of perjury, that I have examined the document(s) presented by the above-named employee, that the above-listed document(s) appear to be genuine and to relate to the employee named, that the employee began employment on *(month/day/year)* ___/___/___ **and that to the best of my knowledge the employee is eligible to work in the United States. (State employment agencies may omit the date the employee began employment).**

Signature of Employer or Authorized Representative	Print Name	Title
Business or Organization Name	Address *(Street Name and Number, City, State, Zip Code)*	Date (month/day/year)

Section 3. Updating and Reverification. To be completed and signed by employer

A. New Name *(if applicable)*	B. Date of rehire *(month/day/year) (if applicable)*

C. If employee's previous grant of work authorization has expired, provide the information below for the document that establishes current employment eligibility.
Document Title: _____   Document #: _____   Expiration Date *(if any)*: ____/____/____

I attest, under penalty of perjury, that to the best of my knowledge, this employee is eligible to work in the United States, and if the employee presented document(s), the document(s) I have examined appear to be genuine and to relate to the individual.

Signature of Employer or Authorized Representative	Date *(month/day/year)*

Form I-9 (Rev. 11-21-91) N

FIGURE 12-10

ABC COMPANY
PERSONAL PROGRESS INTERVIEW

This form is to be completed by company managers and supervisors together with each full-time, part-time and temporary member of their organization. THE PRIMARY PURPOSE OF THIS INTERVIEW IS TO ESTABLISH OPEN COMMUNICATION BETWEEN MANAGERS OR SUPERVISORS AND THEIR EMPLOYEES. A completed copy of this form should be sent to the human resources department for the employee's personnel file.

Employee Name: _____

Employee No. _____

Job Title: _____

Company/Dept. Name: _____

Company/Dept. No.: _____ Time on Job _____

Hire Date _____

We need and would appreciate your comments on the following: (Please tell it in your own words as you see it).

What do you like most about your job?

_____
_____
_____
_____

What do you like least about your job?

_____
_____
_____
_____

What changes, in areas outside of your control, could be made to improve your job?

_____
_____
_____
_____

FIGURE 12-10 (continued)

How would YOU rate your own overall job performance in the following areas:

(Check one: 5 = most effective; 1 = least effective)

	1	2	3	4	5
INITIATIVE					
PRODUCTIVITY					
JUDGMENT					
EFFORT					
TEAMWORK					
SAFETY					
JOB KNOWLEDGE					
FOLLOWS DIRECTIONS					
CUSTOMER SERVICE					
TELEPHONE SKILLS					
ATTENDANCE					

Do you feel ready for more responsibility? If so, what type?

_____

_____

_____

Where do you see yourself in 1, 5, or 10 years? (Answer as you wish).

_____

_____

_____

Have you successfully met your job-related goals over the past 6 months?

Yes: _____ No: _____

Specifically, what have you done?

_____

_____

Let's set some goals for your job for the next 6 months:

_____

_____

_____

FIGURE 12-10 (continued)

What changes would you suggest to help make our crew function better overall?

_____

_____

_____

Is there any way that I, personally, can help you to be more productive?

_____

_____

_____

Any additional comments?

_____

_____

_____

Manager/Supervisor's Signature _____

Title _____Date _____

The Personal Progress Interview

The personal progress interview form (PPI) is one of the more important tools in the overall human resources inventory. The personal progress interview serves as a half-way or balance point between the use of complex performance appraisal systems (sometimes stereotyped and time consuming), and having no appraisal program at all. Used conscientiously at regular, predetermined intervals, this PPI form creates an environment of what might be called comfortable communication between supervisors and employees. It asks employees what they like most as well as least about the job, what improvements and changes could we (you and I) make to it, and if the employees are ready for more responsibility. Supervisors and employees then together set goals and review progress on the job-related goals previously set six months (or other period of time) ago. In order to completely avoid eliminating the appraisal function, employees are asked to rate their own overall job performance in specific areas.

You may find that the use of this form can result in some surprising and valuable information about which the supervisor was totally unaware. Many if not most employees will often not confide in their boss, or let them know when something important is bothering them. The PPI interview process sets the stage for some amazing discoveries by simply asking employees in so many words, "say, Mary (or Dave), how's everything going, and just what do you think about your job?"

You may learn that morale in the department, shop, or plant is not quite as good as you thought it was. Or, as a nonunion employer, you might also hear that one or more people are occasionally making comments in the lunchroom about "how great this place would be if we just had a union around here!"

One of the best motivators in personnel relations is recognition or attention to employees, even if it's just taking the time to ask them what they think. Use of the personal progress interview process fills this need, while at the same time demonstrating to employees that perhaps the company does genuinely value the opinion of their most important asset. Once again, it follows the general theme of this book that if you value your employees and help them to be more productive and successful, you yourself will become successful. The employee, you, and the company will all be winners. To do this, supervisors, managers, and the human resources department *must communicate* with employees. HR professionals must know employees' needs, wants, and desires, and help them attain their goals. The personal progress interview is an effective way of helping them to do this.

Proper and conscientious use of this personal progress interview form will replace the drudgery, procrastination, and general unpopularity of filling out performance appraisal forms (whether supervisory or self-appraisal) with an enthusiastic and positive response from both the employee and the supervisor/manager.

Other Forms

FIGURE 12-11

ABC COMPANY
APPEARANCE AND PROPERTY RETURN AGREEMENT

I understand that it is my responsibility to, at all times, keep my personal appearance at a level that is acceptable to our ABC Company customers. And I also understand that appearance standards are determined by the company on the basis of its public image and customer reaction. If a uniform is required to be worn at the company facility at which I work, I agree to appear in that uniform during all working hours. The company will provide me with whatever uniform is to be worn, and I will be responsible for the cleaning, pressing, and maintaining of those items furnished by the company as well as any furnished by myself. All items of uniform furnished by the company are the property of ABC, and must be returned if I leave the company. If I do not return any uniform items, I authorize my employer

FIGURE 12-11 (continued)

to deduct their replacement cost from my final paycheck, where permitted by state law.

I further agree that, if I leave the company, I will return all equipment, keys, tools, ID cards, manuals, etc., which are the property of ABC. If I do not return ALL items that are the property of the ABC Company, I authorize my employer to deduct the replacement cost of said items from my final paycheck, where permitted by state law.

Number of Uniforms Returned: _____

Employee's Signature: _____Date: _____

Number of Uniforms Returned: _____

Supervisor's Signature _____Date: _____

FIGURE 12-12

ABC COMPANY
WARNING NOTICE

Name of Employee Receiving Warning: _____

Job Title:_____ Employee No.: _____

Date Warning Issued to Employee: _____

Name of Supervisor Issuing Warning: _____

Job Title: _____

Department Number and Name: _____

THE INTENT OF THIS NOTICE IS TO INFORM YOU THAT YOUR PERFORMANCE HAS NOT BEEN SATISFACTORY FOR THE REASONS INDICATED BELOW, AND TO PRO-VIDE YOU WITH AN OPPORTUNITY TO COOPERATE WITH YOUR SUPERVISOR IN ATTEMPTING TO CORRECT THIS SITUATION. HOWEVER, IF THIS MATTER IS NOT CORRECTED WITHIN (30, 60, 90 DAYS OR specify), YOU WILL BE SUBJECT TO FURTHER DISCIPLINARY ACTION, UP TO AND INCLUDING TERMINATION.

Details of Situation (Be sure to include dates of specific incidents):

_____

_____

_____

_____

_____

FIGURE 12-12 (continued)

X_____   _____
  Employee's Signature   Supervisor's Signature
Date: _____   Date: _____

Note To Employee:
Signing this form does not indicate agreement with the above
statements. It simply verifies that you have been informed of
the above action, and that you have received a copy of this
warning notice.

Names of Witnesses, if any:
Witness #1: _____
Job Title: _____
Witness #2: _____
Job Title: _____

FIGURE 12-13

ABC COMPANY
VOLUNTARY RESIGNATION

This completed form should be attached to the final paperwork
for an employee who resigns voluntarily, and should be then
forwarded to the human resources department for processing.

I, _____, SSN _____,
hereby resign my position as _____
                                             (Job Title)
from _____ Effective _____
    (Company/Dept. No.)

My reason(s) for voluntarily resigning my job is (are):
(Please check all reasons that apply):
_____ Relocation
_____ Illness
_____ To seek other employment
_____ Have obtained other employment
_____ To return to school
_____ Personal/family business
_____ Dissatisfied with pay, hours of work, working conditions,
      type of work, (Please comment briefly in comments
      section below.)
_____ Retiring
_____ Other reasons

FIGURE 12-13 (continued)

Comments: _____

_____

_____

_____

Amount of notice being given:

_____ days   _____ weeks   _____ none

Signature: _____

Date Signed: _____

Where at all possible, it is always a good idea to have terminating employees sign this voluntary resignation form when they leave the company of their own accord. In a subsequent charge, complaint, or court action, it may be your primary defense in showing that employees did leave voluntarily, and that they voluntarily signed a resignation form on the date indicated.

Another excellent tool of personnel management and one that supplements the Voluntary Resignation form is the exit interview process, including the exit interview form, an example of which is given in Figure 12-14. The exit interview process assists the human resources practitioner in determining patterns or trends of events occurring within a company or department, and will often reveal critical problems with supervision, or with work rules, wages, or working conditions that do not surface while the person is still employed.

It is also important that the respective supervisor and manager of the terminating employee be provided with a copy of the exit interview form in order to offer an opportunity to correct some particular condition or situation about which they may not have been aware.

Exit Interview

A personal exit interview between the terminating employee and the supervisor and/or manager, or with a member of the human resources staff is usually the most productive method of obtaining information from the employee. Many times, employees will tell you more than you ask if they feel the interviewer is a good listener and is genuinely interested in what they have to say.

Where the personal interview procedure is not practicable, the next best method is to mail an exit interview form to all employees who leave your organization—full-time, part-time, and even temporary—and ask if they would take the time to complete and return the form. You might be surprised at the percentage of returns you can get for your efforts. To insure a maximum response, set up the form in a folded card format with postage prepaid, and preaddressed to your human resources department. Most people will find this method convenient. Others will wish to say more and will return the form in a separate envelope, sometimes with attachments and occasionally even photographs of company property or equipment if related to their discharge or resignation.

At the same time, the reader should also be cautioned about drawing hasty conclusions or opinions based solely on exit interview statements. Occasionally, the information or feedback from the terminating employee is inaccurate, sometimes exaggerated, or just plain wrong, due to the person's lack of experience or time on the job, or failure to see the total picture.

Nevertheless, your employment relations manager, EEO coordinator or some personnel staff member should take the time to carefully read each of the exit forms. Your HR department will then have taken the first steps toward monitoring employee morale, and be in a better position to anticipate, correct, and prevent problems before they become serious. In addition, every now and then someone will return a form that has some good things to say about the company and its supervisors. That's good information, too, and you wouldn't want to miss it.

FIGURE 12-14

ABC COMPANY
EXIT INTERVIEW FORM

Name _____

Social Security Number_____

Co./Dept. No. _____ Department Name _____

Job Title _____

Length of Service: Years _____ Months _____

Employment Status: ❑ Full-Time   ❑ Part-Time   ❑ Temp.

Paid By: ❑ Hour   ❑ Weekly   ❑ Monthly

What Was Your Main Reason(s) for Leaving ABC?
(Check all that apply.)

❑ Relocation   ❑ Benefits

❑ Working Environment   ❑ Supervision

❑ Layoff   ❑ Terminated for Cause

❑ Training   ❑ Pay

❑ Return to School   ❑ Hours

❑ Career Change   ❑ No Advancement

Other Reason(s) (please specify):

_____

_____

_____

FIGURE 12-14 (continued)

How would you rate ABC on the following items?
(Check one box for each item)

	EXCELLENT	GOOD	FAIR	POOR	COMMENTS
Supervision	❏	❏	❏	❏	
Training	❏	❏	❏	❏	
Advancement Opportunities	❏	❏	❏	❏	
Communication/ Feedback	❏	❏	❏	❏	
Your Treatment as an Individual	❏	❏	❏	❏	
Company Benefits	❏	❏	❏	❏	
Rate of Pay	❏	❏	❏	❏	

Was there anything in particular you especially liked about
your work experience at ABC?

_____

_____

_____

Was there anything in particular you especially did not like
about your work experience at ABC?

_____

_____

_____

How could your own job have been improved upon?

_____

_____

_____

Additional Comments:

_____

_____

_____

Signature_____ Date _____

We sincerely thank you for taking the time to complete this exit
interview form. We will do our best to see that your thoughts
and observations are put to use by the ABC organization.
Once again, thank you very much.

ABC Human Resources Department

In the event yours happens to be a nonunion company, you might find the following form or statement to be a valuable tool in helping you to remain that way. In actuality, the form has a two-fold purpose, in that it creates a workable system for internal posting, and it prevents your being deluged with requests to post notices of outside meetings, social events, and charitable causes on your bulletin boards. The wording of the statement also has the general approval of the National Labor Relations Board as it relates to the posting of (or refusal by the company to post) union organizing information and material. The statement follows.

FIGURE 12-15

ABC COMPANY
NO SOLICITATION—NO DISTRIBUTION—POSTING RULES

In order to prevent disruption of operations, interferences with work, as well as inconvenience to employees, the following policies apply to all facilities of the ABC Company:

1. Solicitation by employees for any purpose is not permitted during working hours.

2. Distribution of literature of any kind by employees (other than company literature) is not permitted in working areas at any time.

3. Distribution of literature and/or solicitation for any purpose by nonemployees on company premises is not permitted at any time.

Posting on Company Bulletin Boards

All materials for posting on company bulletin boards or on company property will be screened and must be approved for posting by the store manager, or by the general manager or plant manager of the facility involved. At company headquarters, the ABC human resources department must approve all materials for posting on ABC Company bulletin boards. All materials will be initialed and dated, and will be posted for a period not to exceed two weeks, with the exception of job postings.

Materials advertising non-ABC Company products or services will not be posted. Sideline business advertisements for household cleaning or personal care products (perfumes and toiletries, dinner and tableware items, for example) will be denied posting rights. Solicitation by employees or outside persons for these and other similar products is also prohibited.

All company presidents and managers should see that NO SOLICITATION—NO DISTRIBUTION signs are posted at all entrances to each company facility.

In addition to the aforementioned items that should not be allowed or permitted on company property, it would probably be well to include a specific notice or statement in the PPM dealing with the subject of gambling.

FIGURE 12-16

ABC COMPANY
GAMBLING ON COMPANY PROPERTY

Gambling in any form on company property is strictly prohibited. All forms of betting, including lotteries, football, baseball, and other types of sports pools, card playing for money, or any other type of gaming activity in which money is involved, are not appropriate in a business environment, and are not permitted on company time and on company premises.

Many times, in a well-meaning attempt to help a terminated employee secure work in another organization, company presidents, managers, or supervisors will write glowing letters of recommendation or reference relating to the person's employment with their company. If it should so happen that the terminated employee later decides to bring charges or suit against the former employer for discrimination or wrongful termination, the company finds itself in the somewhat embarrassing position of having highly recommended and praised—in writing—the abilities and talents of someone who had perhaps been previously fired from the job due to incompetency or other problems. Legal counsel generally recommends the wiser course to be for the company to have a policy that no such letters of praise be written, using the suggested language in Figure 12-17.

FIGURE 12-17

ABC COMPANY
POLICY STATEMENT REGARDING REQUESTS FOR
LETTERS OF RECOMMENDATION/REFERENCE LETTERS

ABC Company does not provide letters of recommendation; however, if requested in writing, ABC will provide a statement outlining dates of employment and positions held by former employees.

This is the only information that will be provided in response to reference requests from prospective employers.

FIGURE 12-17 (continued)

All requests for information on past employees should be directed to the ABC human resources department. Managers and supervisors are especially cautioned not to provide letters of recommendation or to give out any information whatever, either in person or over the telephone, regarding the employment of former employees. Refer all such requests to human resources.

The forms and statements shown above in their entirety may be thought of as customized forms to be used by the individual employer as necessary. Their suggested content should be especially helpful to supervisors and managers, as well as to the human resources staff. Keep in mind also, that if you do choose to follow their format in your company, you should regularly review and make changes in them from time to time as business conditions change or new labor laws are passed.

There is available a vast number of other personnel forms that most businesses and employers will have occasion to use at some time or other. Basically these others are all standard forms, that may be obtained through various management services companies or stationery suppliers.

CHAPTER PERSPECTIVE

In this chapter the importance of formalizing personnel policies and compiling them into a Personnel Policies Manual (PPM) was discussed. Guidelines for constructing a PPM for your company were given. The important personnel policy statements that should appear in the introductory part of the manual were delineated. Also highly recommended was the inclusion of sample personnel forms to be used as reference tools by managers, supervisors, and HR staff. Examples of customized forms were presented and their use explained.

Lifestyles and Medical Cost Containment

INTRODUCTION AND MAIN POINTS

This chapter highlights the problems surrounding the rising cost of group medical insurance coverage to business. The effect of lifestyles on employees' health has brought several issues under scrutiny by employers. These issues include:

Substance abuse

Failure to wear seat belts

Smoking or other use of tobacco

Body weight

Aerobic exercise

Cholesterol levels

Physical examinations

Participation in high-risk sports

The rising costs of insuring those persons with unhealthy or high-risk lifestyles has caused many employers to limit or deny employees group medical insurance to them or to require that they pay higher premiums for same. These measures have been unpopular, and many people oppose them. Other problems of the current system such as preexisting conditions and the ineffectiveness of COBRA, a stop-gap program, are also discussed.

In this important arena of health care, the human resources department must heed the call to contain costs from the management of the company and communicate changes in plan coverage to employees.

The need for changes to the system is demonstrated, but the wholesale dismantling of our current high-quality health care delivery system is viewed as the wrong direction for the country to follow.

After you have read the materials in this chapter:

▬ You will be aware that the problems surrounding the rising costs for group medical insurance coverage are serious ones.

▬ You will know what several of the lifestyle issues are as they relate to health insurance coverage of employees.

■ You will know about several plans of employers who wish to contain the costs of their medical insurance coverage by limiting or denying coverage to those with unhealthy or high-risk lifestyles.

■ You will be aware of other health care system problems such as preexisting conditions and the inadequacy of COBRA.

■ You will know why the current system is in need of change, but not of dismantling.

THE RISING COSTS OF GROUP MEDICAL INSURANCE

As discussed in a previous chapter on employee benefits (Chapter 9), medical care insurance coverage is probably the most important of all employee benefits from the employee's point of view. The rising costs of medical insurance and claims paid by employers, even though currently rising at a slower pace, all give rise to justifiable concern among business and government leaders, and the general public as well. Solutions and ideas are being offered from many sources, including both state and federal agencies, but medical costs continue to edge upward in company benefits budgets.

LIMITING OR DENYING COVERAGE

One step more and more companies are taking in their continuing battle against ever-escalating medical costs is to limit or even deny altogether group medical coverage to employees who choose to follow unhealthy or riskier lifestyles than those of their fellow employees. For example, in some companies, covered employees and their spouses and dependents who are proven guilty of alcohol, drug, or controlled substance (prescription drug) abuse when involved in a motor vehicle accident in which a covered person was the driver are also denied coverage. In other instances, employees, covered spouses, and dependents involved in motor vehicle accidents while not wearing an available seat belt are also not eligible for company medical benefits coverage.

Companies are also beginning to examine other areas of lifestyle selection that impact on the health of employees and their spouses and, therefore, affect group coverage rates. Interest has been focused on:

■ employees who smoke or use tobacco in any form;

■ employees whose body weight is not within specified weight tables;

■ employees who do no aerobic exercise, such as walking at least 30 minutes a day, three days a week;

■ employees whose blood cholesterol levels substantially exceed recommended limits;

■ employees who do not receive periodic physical examinations;

■ employees who engage in other high-risk lifestyles or activities, such as:

Sky diving
Motorcycling
Mountain climbing
Auto and boat racing
Piloting private airplanes
Bungee cord jumping.

To encourage the practice of regular physical examinations, some companies pay the full cost of exams for employee and spouse without the necessity of meeting annual deductibles.

RESTRICTED LIFESTYLE VERSUS HIGH MEDICAL COSTS

The clamor persists, and will probably become more and more vocal, that companies do not have the right to restrict, control, or interfere with an individual citizen's lifestyle, either on, or (especially) off, the job. However, more employers seem to be accepting the challenge and will continue to run the risk of bad publicity, irate stockholders, legal challenges, or threatened boycotts, in order to keep medical cost increases in line. It is hoped that, in the long run, such measures will help the company avoid benefit cutbacks, at best, and bankruptcy, at worst. You can expect to see more and more managements insisting that if their employees and their spouses choose riskier or, at least, unhealthy lifestyles, these people will be required to pay an increasing amount of corporate health care costs.

Human resources directors and managers continually find themselves solidly in the center of the fray: On the one hand their top management or board of directors insists they control medical costs, and on the other, company employees or union representatives point to the continual erosion of employee benefits as their members share more of the medical plan costs, or benefits are reduced or selectively eliminated.

LEGISLATION ON HEALTH CARE

Corporations are currently hearing from state and federal regulators and particularly the U.S. Congress on the subject of health care. At this writing, a number of states have already instituted measures to make health care available, through employers, to more of their citizens. In addition, the Health Care Portability and Accountability Act of 1996 resolves the problem of employees being forced to remain with their present employer simply because of preexisting health conditions that would defer or preclude medical coverage with a new company.

Even though in the early 1990s a universal health care bill was abandoned in Congress, modified legislation in this regard is likely to be passed eventually, providing adequate health care coverage to most, if not all, Americans. The cost of such socialized health care as originally proposed would probably have bankrupted a large segment of U.S. industry, particularly small businesses. In addition, the experience of Canada and several European nations with national health insurance was anything but encouraging. The United States has the finest health care delivery system in the world, and opting for logical, common sense adjustments rather than its complete destruction would seem to be the will of the American public.

Most human resources executives will probably agree that the health care problem is a staggering one, that certain changes are needed, and that all of our citizens are entitled to the opportunity of acquiring some form of health care protection. They also believe that, however well-intentioned, government intervention and control of such a program is definitely not the answer.

Some recently published surveys show that in many cases, people with little or no medical coverage are in this situation because they choose to be; that is, they can well afford medical coverage but, for one personal reason or another, they choose not to be covered, or perhaps just haven't gotten around to it yet! The problem is not dissimilar to that of motor vehicle insurance coverage: If there were no state laws mandating some form of liability insurance coverage on the family car, how many insured drivers might we expect to see on the highway? Auto insurance is generally required of all motorists, and yet we don't hear of that many cases of inability to afford auto insurance premiums as we do health insurance, even though auto insurance is not inexpensive.

COBRA
While the Consolidated Omnibus Budget Reconciliation Act (COBRA) allows former employees to purchase medical insurance from their employers for up to 18 months (36 months for dependents), the cost of such coverage can often be too prohibitive for persons who have lost their job, their sole source of income. For those who can afford the coverage, after 18 months they again find themselves without insurance protection.

THE FUTURE OF HEALTH CARE
Despite the fact that the quality of U.S. health care is unexcelled in any other country, no logical or caring person will dispute the fact that problems do exist within our health care system. Problems such as health care costs, availability, and a number of others must and are being addressed. Nevertheless, any experienced human resources professional, as well as a logical and caring public, would probably agree that we absolutely should amend, adjust, or change the things that need changing, but not tear down the entire program. Neither does it

seem viable to adopt one of the more grandiose and unaffordable schemes of national health care that some other countries have at one time installed and invariably later discarded.

CHAPTER PERSPECTIVE

This chapter focused on the problems of continuing to provide employees with their number one benefit—health insurance coverage. In an effort to contain the rising costs of insurance, employers have had to limit or deny group medical insurance to employees with unhealthy or high-risk lifestyles, or require them to pay higher premiums. Lifestyle issues discussed included substance abuse, failure to wear seat belts, smoking or other use of tobacco, body weight, aerobic exercise, cholesterol levels, physical examinations, and participation in high-risk sports. Controversy has arisen over these unpopular measures.

The role of the human resources department in managing this most important employee benefit program is discussed.

The chapter also dealt with other problems of the current health insurance system. The need for changes was demonstrated, but the excellent quality of the health care itself in our country advocated that a moderate approach would be best.

Diversity in the Work Force

INTRODUCTION AND MAIN POINTS

This chapter tackles the meaning of one famous buzzword—diversity—and what its implementation in the work force can mean to human resources professionals, management, supervision, and the community. Diversity is defined, and specific examples of diversity in the workplace are discussed.

An historical perspective on diversity in America's cultural and political roots, as well as diversity's impact after the initial Civil Rights Act, is offered.

What attitude and steps human resources professionals should take to accommodate these changes is discussed.

After you have read the material in this chapter:

__ You will understand what diversity means as applied to the work force.

__ You will know that diversity is not something new to this country.

__ You will know how human resources professionals should best respond to increased diversity in the work force.

BUZZWORDS

Buzzwords are those catchy words and clever-sounding phrases that often seem to spring literally from nowhere, capture the attention of human resources managers and management consultants, and, as a result of constant repetition, eventually become a part of our everyday business management vocabulary. (Note: Definitions will be found in the Glossary at the end of this book.) Some familiar examples will serve to illustrate the point.

Management by Objectives (MBO)
Total Quality Management (TQM)
Management by Walking Around (MBWA)
Employee Empowerment
Reengineering
Benchmarking

Broadbanding
Teaming
Downsizing
Rightsizing
Outsourcing
Restructuring
Multiculturalism
Information Superhighway
Globalization
Managing Diversity

Such words normally have a rather limited life span due to the fact that their exact meaning is sometimes unclear, ill-defined, or at best, debatable. Sooner or later, it no longer appears in management memos, college textbooks, or graduation speeches, and is eventually replaced by one or more newly created terms patiently awaiting their own introduction into management books, tapes, and seminars.

DIVERSITY DEFINED

There is one such word, however, that will probably outlast the rest of its listed colleagues by many years. That item is the last one mentioned, *Managing Diversity*. Let's officially define this particular term:

Merriam-Webster's Collegiate Dictionary (10th edition) defines the word *diverse* as

"**1.** differing from one another: UNLIKE

"**2.** composed of distinct or unlike elements or qualities..."

We can all probably agree that the definition of diverse describes the human condition very well. The diversity in races, colors, creeds, religious preferences, national origins, and a host of other differences and diversities the world over is self-evident.

DIVERSITY LEGISLATED

With the advent of a multitude of local, state, and federal laws protecting the rights of peoples and groups, the business community (voluntarily or otherwise) now employs literally millions of women and minorities. Thus, American industry has become the microcosm or empirical laboratory where diversity will be tested to see if it will work; that is, to determine if this diversity of colors, feelings, opinions, and choices can work together permanently, progressively, productively, and, ultimately, profitably. Eventually, it might even prove to be the experimental evidence we've been looking for to determine just how we can and must all work together as human beings on a universal or global basis. A simpler way of saying it might be that business and industry will now be the proving ground to demonstrate just how we can work together as employees, neighbors, and perhaps even as nations.

AN HISTORICAL PERSPECTIVE ON DIVERSITY IN THE UNITED STATES

Many historians, observers, and other students of history who study the American experiment of government going back some 200 and more years ago, conclude that the political success of the early colonies rested largely on the fact that these early citizens had come to the new world specifically hoping to find a land where diversity of opinion and interest, as well as of nationality and culture, were tolerated. As described in their political documents, this new country would be a place where they could enjoy the freedom and the right to be able to say, do, write, and think as they wished, within a government of laws that they themselves chose to establish. They knew that if they were not able to manage this diversity of interests, their experiment would fail—and they were not about to let that happen. Freedom was the bottom line of their great experiment, and the return on their investment and sacrifice has prospered ever since.

AN ANALOGY WITH BUSINESS TODAY

We are all flooded with expert opinions that, as more and more women, minorities, and people with different lifestyles and sexual preferences enter our work force, the diversity of their viewpoints, interests, needs, and cultures will create monumental complexities for supervisors and managers, the likes of which we have never seen.

If the statistics are correct on the continuing rate of increase of women and minorities in the work force, by the year 2000 the company that has not prepared for this event may very well find itself included in those other statistical data showing the numbers of businesses, large and small, that for one reason or another, failed to survive.

Similar to professionals in other disciplines, most human resources professionals wonder and speculate about what the business environment will really be in the future if, as predicted, minority employment continues to increase while fewer nonminorities enter the work force. The answer to this is simply that there will be a need for substantive changes in some company policies, programs, and procedures to accommodate this influx. However, there should really be no reason for major readjustments or for reengineering (see the buzzword list on page 223) the total infrastructure of the business to the point that it will be unrecognizable from the way business was formerly conducted.

The Civil Rights Act of 1964, together with succeeding amendments and other new civil rights legislation, set the stage and established the blueprint to guide employers in the hiring and promotion of minorities and women in the workplace. It can be no coincidence that those business organizations that cooperated and complied with civil rights laws should discover the many advantages of employing these groups, and that they were by and large successful. Similarly, there is no reason now to believe that those organizations that accept the principles of diversity management will not be equally successful.

From a practical and realistic view, most company presidents and managers have had the challenge of managing diverse groups of employees for a number of years. For instance, homosexuals have been acknowledged as comprising a certain percentage of the work force in the past, and from this point on into the future it will become a matter of reality and fact that these and others we may think of as belonging to diverse groups will be entering American business in ever-increasing numbers. We may speculate as to what the exact percentage of increase may be, but the projected demographic statistics of U.S. population figures should provide us with some reliable evidence as to the mathematical probabilities of diversity employment.

Whatever the exact percentages may be, it is certain that supervisors will be required to devote an increasing amount of their time to the management and direction of these diverse newcomers. Individual opinions notwithstanding, the point must be acknowledged and understood by every supervisor and manager, and particularly every human resources manager—that full-scale diversity management is already here today, and that it will not go away! These changes will not take place without a challenge; however, the companies that are prepared to step up to the challenge and look at it as an opportunity, will be the winners from a competitive as well as a societal standpoint. In any event, companies will need all the help they can get in order to prepare their own supervisors, managers, and general employee population to properly play their individual roles.

DIVERSITY AND THE HR FUNCTION

The stage is now set for human resources specialists and professionals, who had better be prepared to add another key function to their job description: namely, advising and counseling line managers, office and staff supervisors, and probably most of all, the top management of the organization, about the proper, the legal, and the best way of coping with this new challenge of managing diversity.

For the experienced human resources professional, it should not really be necessary to retrain or go back to school in order to successfully handle this subject. Savvy and competent human resources practitioners will take the pragmatic approach to the matter by
- displaying a large amount of patience;
- proactively implementing meaningful orientation and training classes for members of these diverse groups;

▬ providing whatever other assistance may be necessary to make them productive; and,

▬ from a moral as well as good-business point of view, by making them feel welcome and wanted.

DIVERSITY AND SUPERVISION

It will be supervision's most important responsibility to make it clear to all current employees (both nondiverse and diverse) that everyone without exception will work together cooperatively and productively. Worker harmony and teamwork are absolute essentials for successful diversity management, and hostile personal feelings toward other workers must be left outside before employees (and especially supervisors and managers) come into their office, store, shop, factory, warehouse, or laboratory. Failure to do so must be dealt with in the same way as any other disciplinary problem.

One of the cardinal principles of personnel management is that nothing must be permitted to disrupt or adversely affect the operation of the work group. Management and supervision have not only the right, but the duty, to resolve the matter and restore harmony, even if that means the termination of the employee creating the problem. For example, there have been cases where employees have complained to their bosses about the personal appearance or personal hygiene (such as failure to bathe regularly) of another employee. Since these lifestyles were sufficiently offensive to disrupt the operation of the work group, the offenders were advised by supervision to either change their personal habits or seek employment elsewhere. Such disciplinary measures under these circumstances are generally supported by the courts.

DIVERSITY AND THE ROLE OF THE HUMAN RESOURCES EXECUTIVE

Although the tone must be unmistakably set by the CEO of the company, diversity management and its successful implementation throughout the corporation should generally be the direct responsibility of the head human resources professional. The wise and perceptive human resources manager, director, or vice president will readily understand how diverse populations can present not only meaningful challenges but also major opportunities—realistically, even profitable opportunities—for bringing new ideas and viewpoints into the company. In addition, the company will be thought of in the community and by the public in general, as one of those good neighbors we spoke of earlier.

There can be no better advertising campaign for an organization than the reputation of being a company that willingly, even enthusiastically, hires, trains, and promotes minorities, women, and all other members of diverse groups into its work force. All progressive and proactive companies know that the age of diversity has already arrived—that the future is not just coming, but the future is *now*!

HOW CORPORATE AMERICA VIEWS DIVERSITY

A number of Fortune 1000 companies and other farsighted employers have already acknowledged and implemented diversity-oriented policies. Among these are Rockwell, Chase Manhattan Bank, the National Football League, the National Football League Players' Association, State Farm Insurance Companies, Merrill Lynch, Nissan, and Chrysler, to name but a few.

The attitude and approach to diversity of these organizations is probably best typified by the following statement (quoted in part) by Bob Eaton, Chairman and CEO of the Chrysler Corporation:

> Diversity in the workplace is not like clothing, something to be worn and removed to fit the occasion. Nor is it a prize to be sought for its own sake.

> At Chrysler Corporation we believe that diversity in the workplace is a competitive advantage and that our success as a global company depends less on raw materials, technology, and processes than on making full use of the wealth of backgrounds, skills, and opinions that a diverse environment offers...

> Chrysler is a company of inclusion, one that fully values and utilizes the unique characteristics and abilities of every employee.

The *diversity* buzzword has already become a meaningful and permanent part of our business vocabulary. As the human resources general, rapid implementation of the diversity concept in your own organization should be one of your prime targets and strategies.

CHAPTER PERSPECTIVE

This chapter discussed the meaning of *diversity* in the work force and its implications for the business world. Diversity was defined, and an historical perspective on diversity in America, both at its inception as a nation and after the first Civil Rights Act, was presented. Guidance for human resources, as well as other areas of a business organization, was provided regarding the best attitude and appropriate steps to be taken to accommodate these changes. Finally, a positive statement on diversity from the Chairman and CEO of Chrysler Corporation was quoted in part as representative of the attitude of a number of Fortune 1000 companies and other employers toward this critical issue.

Other Issues and Challenges in Human Resources

INTRODUCTION AND MAIN POINTS

This chapter deals with some specific issues and challenges in the area of human resources for which no clear-cut solutions have yet been found. The HR practitioner is being alerted to the fact that these are some of the issues for which there is probably no consensus about the ideal way in which they should be handled. They are examples of problems that fall into the general category of consideration on a case-by-case basis. The pros and cons of each issue are explored. Issues include:

Smoking in the workplace
Hiring smokers
HR systems of software and hardware
Merit pay versus new pay methods
Preemployment testing
Personnel policy exceptions
Attitude surveys
Liability for employees driving company vehicles
After you read the material in the chapter:

■■■ You will know that there is no consensus about smoking, as various laws prohibit smoking and others protect the rights of the smoker.

■■■ You will know that there are four approaches to dealing with HR data management: manually, mainframe computer systems, personal computer systems, or outsourcing.

■■■ You will have an overview of various compensation arrangements: automatic progression pay system, merit pay and pay-for-performance systems, and new pay methods.

■■■ You will have insight into the application of preemployment testing criteria after having read an excerpt from the *Griggs v. Duke Power* decision (see page 234).

■■■ You will understand the importance of adhering to personnel policies and not making exceptions, to safeguard the company as well as your own credibility.

▬ You will understand the value of attitude testing but realize that such testing should not be used casually.

▬ You will learn how to protect the company from liability suits arising out of employees driving company vehicles.

▬ You will have a better insight about whether to disclose problems of former employees relating to violence, dishonesty, and performance when job reference inquiries are received from other companies.

SMOKING IN THE WORKPLACE

As discussed in Chapter 10, the subject of smoking in the workplace is still controversial and will probably continue to be for some time. Keeping in mind the health, comfort, and safety of the company's most important asset as well as those other valuable people, your customers, you might think about recommending to your top management that all company facilities, including stores and all customer areas, be smoke-free, and that employees be allowed to smoke outside of company premises if desired. This type of a smoking policy is already in effect in many companies, and all indications are that others are preparing to follow suit.

Recent survey data on the harmful effects of even secondary smoke should also alert companies without smoking policies about the potential liabilities of not addressing this very critical personnel issue. Look for the federal government, based on recommendations by the surgeon general, to come out with increasing legislation designed to curb the use of cigarettes and tobacco in any form in private business as well as in public places. In a number of city councils and state legislatures as well, smokers are finding less and less support. Effective in 1995, for example, California passed legislation that imposed a virtual statewide ban on smoking in the workplace.

HIRING SMOKERS

The subject of hiring smokers, of course, then becomes an integral part of the overall smoking question, and it too is anything but clear-cut. The human resources employment staff, as well as operating supervisors and managers, are all well aware that many highly-qualified and capable applicants are smokers, and that by having a no-smoker hiring policy, you are probably passing up a certain amount of talent that your company might happen to need at the time. It becomes difficult, if not impossible, however, to explain that we support a smoke-free environment for our company (assuming that is the case) while we hire smokers because of their special talents.

Eight states—Alabama, Georgia, Kentucky, Mississippi, North Carolina, Texas, West Virginia, and Wyoming—have no state laws regarding smoking in the workplace. The other 42 states and the District of Columbia all have passed laws relating to workplace smoking.

Some of the provisions of these workplace smoking laws include
- written and/or posted smoking policy or rules;
- posting of signs;
- specifying smoke-free and smoking-permitted areas;
- reasonable accommodation for smokers;
- penalties and/or civil remedies for noncompliance;
- requiring the control of smoke with existing physical barriers and ventilation systems.

Some states, on the other hand, continue to pass smoking legislation protecting the rights of smokers. Smokers' rights laws (often included in a state's fair employment practice statute) generally prohibit employers from discriminating against workers on the basis of use or nonuse of tobacco, and, at this writing, the following 27 states and the District of Columbia prohibit discrimination based solely on a person's smoking habits: Arizona, Colorado, Connecticut, Illinois, Indiana, Kentucky, Louisiana, Maine, Minnesota, Mississippi, Missouri, Montana, Nevada, New Hampshire, New Jersey, New Mexico, North Carolina, North Dakota, Oklahoma, Oregon, Rhode Island, South Carolina, South Dakota, Tennessee, West Virginia, Wisconsin, and Wyoming.

It is suggested that you work closely with your legal department or local counsel to assist you in coping with this vexing personnel challenge of smoking in the workplace.

SYSTEMS SOFTWARE AND HARDWARE, MAINFRAME, MICROPROCESSOR, OR OUTSOURCING

It is strongly recommended that your department have state-of-the-art information systems software and hardware that allow for current operations as well as future growth. Smaller companies and those with limited resources may find they cannot afford the cost of these computer installations, and that is understandable. However, as we enter the age of information superhighways (see Chapter 16, Human Resources and the Internet) and the ever more rapid gathering, processing, and analysis of data, these are among the most necessary costs of doing business, and employers must recognize them as such. A listing of human resources system software vendors along with their products and services can be found in Chapter 5.

Personal computers (PCs) are by far the first choice of a majority of organizations for almost all their business applications. In some cases, huge sums of money are being spent on converting to personal computers as companies rely on the perceived long-term, economic advantages of abandoning slower and more expensive mainframe operations. Should you decide to change, however, don't make the switch to total PC applications too quickly; if you are experiencing no major problems, mainframe processing may be more than adequate for your company at the present time. Have your information systems experts and others analyze your needs from a cost/value perspective, then make your decision. The decision as to the adequacy—current and future—of your human resources information system must be a priority.

Outsourcing should be investigated as an alternative. Many companies have decided that outsourcing some or much of their human resources electronic recordkeeping functions (benefits, retirement plans, and others) to outside professional companies, reduces or completely eliminates the need for high-powered and expensive HR information systems. It might be the smart way to handle your processing needs, as more and more corporations are doing. Others, for various reasons, prefer the do-it-yourself, in-house system, but outsourcing should at least be kept in mind as another option.

MERIT PAY VERSUS NEW PAY

If you have attended any of the recent national conferences of the major personnel associations, you have probably been exposed to various statements and speeches by personnel consultants and other experts urging you to consider abandoning the traditional merit pay and pay-for-performance systems in favor of the so-called new pay methods of compensating employees.

Such new pay methods may include:

■ *Team-based pay strategies*, wherein all team members share in increased compensation rewards based on achievements of the team rather than individual goals.

■ *Annual or one-time bonus awards* that are proposed on the theory that a bonus for achievement rewards the employee with the whole loaf rather than getting only a slice of the total annual increase amount each payday. The larger reward on a one-time basis theoretically is more meaningful and increases employee motivation for improved job performance.

■ *Competency-based reward systems*, which recommend that the competency requirements of either the person or the job be used as the fundamental basis for defining value. The knowledge, skills, and abilities of the individual, regardless of job or position assignment, it is claimed, will determine the pay decision. Alternatively, the competency requirements for the successful performance of the individual job or position itself might be used in setting up a competency-based pay system.

However, it should be noted that not many companies currently use competency exclusively in making pay decisions, because other factors (such as job performance and results) are also taken into consideration.

A number of these different compensation arrangements have existed and been advocated for a number of years. While some companies have tried new pay, it has not yet exactly revolutionized the payment of wages and salaries in the business community, and it does not appear to be doing so any time in the near future.

Any number of meaningful improvements in our compensation systems have been proposed and adopted in recent years, and the change/improvement process should continue. However, there should be tangible, demonstrable improvements when proposed changes directly and radically affect an employee's paycheck, even those concerning the method of wage payments. There are few items in the business world that are as highly sensitive and jealously guarded as the American worker's paycheck.

Over the past five to ten years, merit pay itself has been making inroads in the compensation structures of many large as well as small companies. The old automatic progression pay systems, often the favorite of the unions, seems to have lost much of its luster and steam as employers increasingly look more for performance results than length of service. If your organization still has any vestige of automatic wage increases in your compensation program, do whatever you can to change it to a merit structure. Merit pay is here to stay!

PREEMPLOYMENT TESTING

Even among people not associated with the human resources field, the subject of preemployment testing can usually generate a good deal of interest and discussion, at times including heated debate. The testing controversy is not new; it has been going on for many years.

Legal Points

Preemployment testing has been the target of civil rights legislation almost since the enactment of Title VII in 1964, and it probably reached its apex with the precedent *Griggs v. Duke Power Company* decision by the U.S. Supreme Court in 1971 (401 U.S. 424, 3 FEP 175). In this case, the company had established requirements that, as a condition of employment in or transfer to certain operating departments in which only whites were employed, a high school education and passing of two general intelligence/aptitude tests, were required. The question at issue was whether an employer is prohibited by the Civil Rights Act of 1964, Title VII from instituting these requirements when neither one is shown to be significantly related to successful job performance. Both requirements operate to disqualify black applicants at a substantially higher rate than white applicants, and the jobs in question formerly had been filled only by white employees as part of a long-standing practice of giving hiring preference to whites.

A company official testified that the high school diploma and intelligence test requirements were established by the company with the intent of generally improving the overall quality of the work force. The evidence, however, showed that employees who had not completed high school or taken the tests continued to perform satisfactorily and make progress in the departments where high school and test requirements existed.

In reversing the judgment of the Court of Appeals, Mr. Chief Justice Burger, who delivered the opinion of the Supreme Court, held that

> Good intent or absence of discriminatory intent does not redeem employment procedures or testing mechanisms that operate as 'built-in headwinds' for minority groups and are unrelated to measuring job capability...

and that

> Nothing in the (Civil Rights) Act precludes the use of testing or measuring procedures; obviously they are useful. What Congress has forbidden is giving these devices and mechanisms controlling force unless they are demonstrably a reasonable measure of job performance. Congress has not commanded that the less qualified be preferred over the better qualified simply because of minority origins. Far from disparaging job qualifications as such, Congress has made such qualifications the controlling factor, so that race, religion, nationality, and sex become irrelevant. What Congress has commanded is that any test used must measure the person for the job and not the person in the abstract...

The Griggs case is now well over 25 years old, but even today you will probably not find many human resources professionals or any other informed persons, for that matter, who would not agree that, in general, preemployment testing absolutely can have a disparate impact on disadvantaged minority versus nonminority job applicants.

Practical Points

In addition to its legal aspects, let's discuss some of the practical or objective points of preemployment testing. From the standpoint of using employment tests as a means of selecting the best applicant for a job opening, such tests are not the key predictors of success in hiring that some interviewers may claim them to be. The subject of testing is broad enough in its own right that numerous books have been written, seminars held, judicial rulings made, and courses offered, thus, it will not be our purpose here to try and convince anyone one way or the other. If you have been in the personnel or human resources field for any length of time, you've probably already formed your own opinion about the value of testing.

Certain types of testing, including clerical, typing, mechanical aptitude, and basic mathematics can be useful to the interviewer when hiring for jobs in which these particular skills are required. However, these or any of the many other employment tests currently in use are simply more evidence that may indicate whether or not this candidate should be offered the opportunity to join the company. You would, of course, be remiss if you did not take into consideration the applicant's experience, education, personality, appearance, interview results, previous track record with other companies, and a host of other (including legal) factors that must necessarily play a part in the overall selection process. To ignore any of these latter qualities and to base one's hiring decision simply on test cut-off scores (whether validated or not) does a grave injustice to the applicant, and can involve the company in serious legal problems, as well.

There are certain promising assessment and profile testing programs on the market today that appear to have merit, especially for those companies in retail sales. Once again, they should be given their proper weight and not looked at as the *magic bullet* that could revolutionize the entire hiring and selection process.

PERSONNEL POLICY EXCEPTIONS

Chapter 12 dealt with the subject of personnel policies and the policy manual, and you were urged to have specific, written, and well-communicated personnel policies in your organization. Recalling the old adage that "rules were made to be broken," you will inevitably, sooner or later, face the situation where a manager, supervisor, foreman, or even employees themselves, will request that for a good and sufficient reason, an exception should be made for a particular employee with regard to some specific personnel policy. You will probably be told that Mary White or Jim Smith is one of the best workers this manager or supervisor has ever had, who never misses or is late for work, and is really very deserving of being granted an exception to policy.

It is not the intent here to belittle such a request, for in many cases it is most natural, even recommended, that the personnel manager fully appreciate an employee's plight and have empathy for his or her problem.

This is especially true when the policy exception involves some aspect of medical plan coverage where denial of the request could possibly result in severe financial hardship to the employee and his or her family. It would probably be the most natural thing in the world for the personnel manager to be inclined to approve the exception request in an effort to help a loyal, deserving, and perhaps long-service employee. Even though it would be a nice gesture and undoubtedly very much appreciated by the employee and his or her family, there are also good business reasons why approving the exception might not be the right decision:

1) Any policy exception you make or are contemplating making must be done with the full realization that, even though you will benefit this particular deserving employee, you are in all probability being unfair to other employees who may be in a similar situation, and for whom no exception request was made or even considered. If granted, you may be establishing a very embarrassing precedent when someone wants to know why you made the exception for Sally or Bill "...and you won't do the same for me!"

2) If the exception request involves the company's medical or retirement benefits policies, you might want to check to be sure that its approval would not be considered a violation of the Employee Retirement Income Security Act (ERISA), to which most companies are subject. If it can be shown that there was indeed some violation of ERISA laws, the entire qualification status of your retirement benefit plan, for example, could be in jeopardy, with the possible loss of its pre-tax-deferred contribution feature that participants enjoy.

Therefore, be very careful of the normal inclination to help a deserving employee by approving an exception to a company policy. In the long run, you will make your own job a lot easier while at the same time protecting the company by not granting such policy exception requests. Making your calls or decisions in this manner is not the way personnel or human resources managers win popularity contests, but it is a way of living up to the responsibilities of the job, while making it just that much easier to not grant future exception requests.

ATTITUDE SURVEYS

For any number of years, managers have been advised by consultants and other experts that, if they want to get in touch with the true feelings of their employees, they should send out attitude surveys so the employees can tell you how they really feel on any number of work-related issues. Quite often we think we know the likes and dislikes of employees, but just as often are surprised when we don't. The attitude survey, frequently done anonymously in order to encourage participation, can be very effective in discovering what people really want, or what they like or dislike.

However, it is well to exercise some caution in using this tool. When you ask employees to tell you candidly just how they believe a particular problem can be corrected, what new or revised procedure they'd like to see in place, or what new benefit they think should be added to the benefit program, you'd better be prepared to do (or at least come close to) what they are asking you to do! If they recommend or ask for something via the attitude survey—and for whatever reason (often financial) you are not in a position to grant it—you've then got a bigger problem than if you had never asked people what they liked or disliked, or wanted or didn't want, in the first place. Attitude surveys can be effective, provided you limit them to those particular benefits or problems that, if necessary, you are prepared to grant or resolve, respectively.

LIABILITY

Employees Driving Company Vehicles

If your company happens to be one in which your employees are required to drive company cars, trucks, or any other type of vehicle requiring a current, valid driver's license, you will want to install a fail-safe system to ensure that none of your employees will ever step into a company vehicle without being in possession of that current, valid driver's license.

When these employees are first hired, their job offer should be contingent on their presenting you with an up-to-date motor vehicle driving record report, and a current, valid driver's license for the state in which the person will be (or may be) driving. The new hire would then be required to fill out a standard driver questionnaire form, which should include questions such as:

■ Has your operator's license/registration ever been suspended or revoked?

■ Have you ever had a conviction involving drugs, alcohol, reckless driving, homicide, manslaughter, or assault arising out of the operation of a motor vehicle?

■ Have you been involved in any motor vehicle accidents in the last five years?

■ Have you received any driving citations (other than parking or those listed above) in the past five years?

In addition to the above questions, applicants should agree to sign a statement included as part of the driver questionnaire that they will only operate company vehicles:

- when in full possession of their faculties;
- when the vehicle is in safe mechanical condition;
- in accordance with all traffic laws, signals, and markings; and
- in a courteous manner at all times.

An additional statement on the questionnaire authorizes any state motor vehicle department to disclose information regarding the applicant's driving record. The applicant certifies that the answers given are true and further agrees that any falsification of information requested on the questionnaire form is cause for dismissal. The applicant then signs the questionnaire, which is subsequently included in the individual's personnel file.

It is also very important to establish a procedure whereby, on at least an annual basis, (or perhaps even every six months), each employee updates and signs another driver questionnaire form. In this way, the driving records of all employees are monitored, preferably by human resources, on a continuing basis for serious traffic violations—including DWIs—and especially for suspended or revoked licenses.

By setting up this type of driver questionnaire program, your company may be protecting itself from the liability of millions of dollars in jury verdicts in the event one of your employees with a suspended or revoked driver's license is involved in a serious or fatal traffic accident. Whatever the cost of administration, such a program is probably one of the best investments your company can make.

JOB REFERENCES

Perhaps one of the most problematic issues personnel and HR managers face today is the almost no-win situation of giving job references to other companies that are considering their former employees for hire. A 1995 survey by the Society for Human Resource Management revealed that fully 63 percent of HR managers, convinced of the possibility of lawsuits or other legal actions against their company, refuse to provide information about former employees. These and most other HR professionals still abide by the safe approach of disclosing only name, rank and serial number information when asked about the performance, reliability, character, honesty, and such, of an exemployee who was perhaps discharged three weeks previously for theft, or an act of violence against a fellow employee.

Despite these majority feelings against full disclosure of problems involving a former employee, however, the tide of opinion, both managerial as well as legal, does seem to be turning. This change of attitude or policy is coming about as more companies are finding that in the process of not disclosing a more serious character or personality flaw of one of their former employees, the boomerang effect takes over, and the company is now being sued for what the employee did not disclose to the new employer. Once again, HR faces the typical no-win situation, with possible defamation lawsuits if you do disclose, and negligence or other types of lawsuits if you don't.

Employment lawyers are now beginning to advise more of their corporate HR clients to change the no-comment approach to reference inquiries to one of objective disclosure of violent behavior incidents or other safety-sensitive problems of those they formerly employed. If, in the opinion of the HR manager, the incident or problem is of a sufficiently serious nature, the wiser course would be to provide detailed disclosure to the prospective employer. As with all important matters handled in the HR function, the unbiased facts and reasons for disclosure should be documented to protect the company against potential defamation lawsuits from the exemployee.

In support of this legal advice, HR managers argue that when the situation is reversed and they are attempting to hire a former employee of another company, it's logical for them to also want to know everything they can about the person under consideration. They also contend that from the employees' standpoint, full disclosure is always welcomed by those who want their new employer to be aware of their prior good performance and track record.

Release Forms

Another way companies can further protect themselves from liability is to have departing employees sign release forms stating that they will not sue their former employers over job reference inquiries. On the premise that people (and especially exemployees) are not always inclined to do or give something for nothing, some companies now offer employees who resign or are terminated a stipulated amount of severance allowance, ranging from an extra two weeks' to a month's pay, for example, if, without coercion, they will sign an agreement that they will not bring job-reference or wrongful termination litigation against their former company. Although the validity of these release agreements has been upheld in some courts, there is, as yet, no specific blanket form that might guarantee immunity in each case in question.

State Laws

In addition, a number of states have passed laws protecting employers who provide truthful information from defamation and other claims. However, even though these laws do not provide complete protection to

employers, and some require job applicants to sign statements authorizing reference requires, some observers worry that companies may
take advantage of the opportunity to retaliate against former personnel,
especially when they leave for a better job opportunity.

From this discussion, one may conclude that the little-or-no-infor-
mation job reference policy is changing slowly, but that the dilemma
will probably persist for quite some time.

CHAPTER PERSPECTIVE

This chapter discussed the intricacies of several controversial issues
or unresolved problems in the area of human resources. Readers are
made aware of the following issues or problem areas and gained some
perspective on possible resolutions.

▬ Where should your HR department stand on smoking and hiring
smokers?

▬ Should your department continue to handle its data management
manually, with mainframe systems or PC systems, or outsource the task?

▬ Should your compensation group modify its pay arrangements to
new pay methods?

▬ Would your proposed preemployment test pass muster under the
law?

▬ Should you make an exception to the personnel policies spelled
out in the PPM to a deserving employee, especially one having to do
with health care?

▬ Should you take an attitude survey and then file the results away
indefinitely for lack of funds?

▬ Can you find a way to not only hire good, qualified drivers to
drive company vehicles, but to monitor any changes in their status?

▬ Should you disclose instances of violence, theft, poor performance, or other problems of former employees applying for jobs with
other companies?

Human Resources and the Internet

INTRODUCTION AND MAIN POINTS

Chapter 14 illustrated some sixteen different examples of familiar buzzwords that catch the attention and fancy of business professionals, including personnel/HR managers and management consultants. One word purposely omitted from this buzzword list of business vocabulary is Internet, which, in its meteoric rise in general popularity and acceptance, did not even pause long enough at the buzzword category to be considered a serious contender for mention or inclusion on that list. The Internet, with its universal interest, value, affordability, and appeal for all types of businesses, groups, and individuals, has almost reached the point of induction into the Business and Personal Essentials Hall of Fame. Other inductees that you will recognize as already enjoying this honor include the computer, the copier, the stapler, and—who could ever forget?—the familiar paper clip that first appeared on the office desk about 1919. Since data gathering and disseminating responsibilities are hallmarks of the human resources profession, each practitioner should be on the cutting edge of utilizing this most powerful business tool to its full advantage.

After studying the material in this chapter:

■■■ You will learn the background of the Internet itself. This history is included here in order to give you a better understanding of the potential of this powerful new tool.

■■■ You will understand the relationship and value of the Internet to the human resources operation.

■■■ You will be shown how the Internet can operate as an essential tool in the retrieval and distribution of information and data used in the day-to-day HR function.

■■■ You will be pointed in the right direction toward exploring on your own the almost endless possibilities of discovering personnel/human resources information that might be exactly suited to your own company's needs and requirements.

▬ You will learn what search engines are and will be given well-known examples.

▬ You will be shown and most likely convinced of the unbelievable potential for companies large and small that advertise their products and services on the Internet. Human resources practitioners can play a key role in convincing top management of the wisdom of using this medium to advertise employment opportunities and to recruit for their greatest asset: employees, system members, associates—in other words, people.

WHAT IS THIS PHENOMENON KNOWN AS THE INTERNET?

For those not totally familiar (or perhaps not at all familiar) with the Internet, some introductory background remarks are in order:

1) The Internet can be thought of as an electronic pipeline or information superhighway made up of millions of so-called *nodes*, a node being defined as an individual computer, personal or otherwise, which is connected to a network.

2) The Internet as an entity is really thousands of networks connected to a vast global network. This Internet pipeline/superhighway circles the earth, with data and information of practically every kind flowing through it (or on it), picking up and dispensing its informational contents to corporations, universities, government agencies, and individuals in almost every location on earth.

3) In addition to being a practically unlimited yet easily accessible source of knowledge and information, the Internet is still one thing more. It is the means or the vehicle by which people can communicate with other people at any time, about any subject, anywhere on the face of the earth. Probably never since the invention of the printing press has there been such a revolution in the way that people are able to communicate with each other. Through its unique characteristics and availability to practically everyone, thoughts and ideas constantly flow back and forth over the Internet between individuals and groups of people in all walks of life. The Internet potential for problem solving, peaceful dispute resolutions, scientific advancement, and especially for understanding among and between persons, communities, and nations would seem to be unlimited.

These comments are not meant to be predictive since any number of other proposals or ideas related to the welfare and benefit of human beings have in the past proven unsuccessful, and in many instances can now only be classified as fads, their good intentions notwithstanding. Indeed, many people today are of the opinion that the Internet will also turn out to be such a fad; however, with the growing enthusiasm of people and organizations everywhere and the unique history of its phenomenal growth and development, the Internet appears today to be more than a passing fancy and the future seems bright and brilliant. As always, time will be the judge.

A better understanding of the background and history of the Internet might help us make our own judgments as to its viability and survival.

INTERNET BACKGROUND AND HISTORY

Perhaps the last object or force one might associate with the origin of the Internet would be nuclear energy, and although this network is powered by electronic rather than nuclear power, there is a historical relationship between the Internet and the atom that makes for one of those serendipitous incidents so common in the history of scientific invention and discovery.

Need for Maintaining Communication

Since the inception of the Cold War with the Soviet Union, the Pentagon in Washington had initiated every manner of contingency they felt could occur in the event of an all-out nuclear war with Russia. One concern (if not the primary concern) of the Pentagon, was the necessity for somehow maintaining military as well as civilian communication facilities in the event the nation was bombarded with awesome atomic or hydrogen weapons that would certainly destroy existing hardware and equipment, military command centers, and switching stations and related wiring, no matter how well-armored or protected, not to mention the fact that central communication nerve centers would be primary targets for incoming ballistic missiles.

The assignment of finding an answer to this seemingly impossible problem was turned over to the Rand Corporation, at that time probably the most prestigious think tank of the scientific community. Rand understood that despite the certainty of a post-attack, science-fiction landscape of radioactive rubble, the country would still have to have some form of intact network linking cities, states, and military facilities.

As analytical studies, reports, and experiments progressed, it became increasingly clear to Rand that the answer to the problem had to be rooted in a totally decentralized network, with each station (or node, as referred to previously), completely autonomous in its own right, with no central control, operating under the worst of conditions, and with the whole country and its normal communication facilities in shambles. With all of these negative contingencies in mind, in 1964 the Rand people—with particular credit to their Paul Baran—not only built answers to these questions into their conclusions, but in fact designed the program specifically to operate when the whole communications system was in chaos, unlike other analytical studies of military, scientific, or commercial origins whose results and reports assumed ideal conditions for their theoretical conclusions.

Packet Switching. The unique but somewhat simple principle in the Rand solution was the fact that each node in the communications network would be equal in rank to every other node with its own capability of sending, receiving, and passing on messages. Data could then be moved around on this internet via so-called packet switching, in which all data coming out of an individual computer is broken up into chunks, each chunk having the address of where it came from and where it was headed. This enables data from a variety of different sources to commingle on the same lines and be sorted and directed to different routes by special machines along the way; thus, many people can use the same lines at the same time. Even if a large portion of the network were to be destroyed, the packets would still be airborne and propelled across and around the system by whatever nodes happened to survive. The delivery system itself, while not exactly neat, would be practically indestructible.

ARPANET. In the late 1960s the Pentagon's Advanced Research Projects Agency (ARPA) funded a larger refined network project to assist scientists and researchers in performing and sharing long-distance computing operations. Within a year or two of its inception, however, it became abundantly clear that the ARPANET (named after the project's sponsor) was being utilized more and more for nonscientific communications, including personal messages, addresses, and electronic mail. Next, a tide of unbridled enthusiasm sprang up for this interesting and fun person-to-person communication technique that has been gaining exponential momentum ever since. Other networks later linked up with ARPANET, eventually outdistancing it.

An Expanded Network. As general interest grew, many organizations tried but were not able to tap into ARPANET. The government's National Science Foundation (NSF) then decided it would construct a new network that would accommodate everyone's demand and valiantly attempted to get colleges and universities to also take advantage of this expanded network. Standards were developed to allow all computers involved to talk to each other and a network of networks was created—an Inter-network that ultimately became known as the Internet—and the rest, as they say, is history. Over the years, other governmental agencies such as the National Aeronautics and Space Administration, National Institutes of Health, and the Department of Energy have also joined the Internet club as newer, faster computers and links were developed.

As with other great inventions and discoveries of worldwide impact, following on the heels of those governmental, military, and educational pioneers, marketing and commercial interests have arrived on the Internet where the home pages of countless organizations and companies, large and small, are to be found. With as much public interest and attention as the Internet is generating—10 million subscribers (and still counting)—there is money to be made in Internet sales and marketing, with apparently still plenty of opportunity for all interested commercial players. (And what company would *not* be interested?)

Fueled by the prospect of freedom to access almost unlimited knowledge and to speak and contribute one's own thoughts and ideas freely and with little restraint, the Internet's pace of growth into the year 2000 and beyond can only be described as a spectacular feeding frenzy, and so long as the Internet continues to belong to everyone and to no one at the same time, there is literally no end in sight!

ACCESSING THE INTERNET

How do you as a company president/owner—or even as a private individual—get to join in and become a member of this worldwide knowledge college?

Hookups. Actually, it's relatively simple, and though there is some expense involved, as you might expect, all you basically need is a computer capable of handling Internet software, a telephone line, and a MODEM (acronym for MOdulator, DEModulator), a device that connects your computer to your phone line, thus allowing your computer to talk to other computers through the phone system. (Another way to think of it: Modems enable computers to talk to other computers in the same way telephones allow humans to talk to each other.) Work and studies are currently going on to develop computers dedicated specifically to Internet access, and priced at a fraction of the cost of a PC. When these become reality, Internet access may be as easy as turning on your television set and it may even be that phone lines will be replaced by cable television pipelines or via satellite. But the equipment described above is the only technology existing today.

Service Providers. Assuming you now have the necessary equipment and phone hookup installed, you may tap into this Internet pipeline by contacting a service provider, one of a number of companies that own and control the doorways to the Internet, to request admittance and membership. Just as you might expect to pay your money at the subway turnstile, you are required to pay a relatively modest installation and monthly usage-related fee in order to enter this bright, new world teeming with information and knowledge.

You should also be aware that there are two categories of service providers from which to choose:

1) commercial on-line service providers, and

2) Internet service providers, either national or local.

Each category of service provider has its upside as well as downside and you can always switch to another provider if you choose, but whichever system you choose, you eventually come to that interesting, fascinating, and almost unbelievable world of cyberspace, and whether you use it for personal or business reasons (in most cases for both), you will have the pleasure of looking forward to an incredible journey!

In exploring the differences between the two services, you will find that commercial on-line service providers such as America On-Line and CompuServe are privately-owned companies with central computers that house all the information they offer in one place, and once you dial into their central computer, you can access all the services you need without leaving the site. The Internet is actually located anywhere on earth. With an Internet provider, it is necessary to go to different computer systems (addresses) to access the services you want; however, one of the most important advantages of Internet service providers is that they offer subscribers direct access to the World Wide Web (the Web), a term that will be discussed later in this chapter.

SEARCH ENGINES

If you have no original address for your subject, you have the option of searching the World Wide Web with a search engine. A search engine is simply a computer program that searches through large amounts of text or other data to find material on the World Wide Web. Examples of some of the better-known search engines used to find material on the Web include Yahoo, Magellan, Infoseek, Lycos, Web Crawler, and Alta Vista. To search, you enter your topic of interest or a key word, and the search engine creates an index page of links (hypertext linkages) that match or satisfy your request. This process may take some time, depending on the scope of the search requested and the current Internet traffic. Your web browser (software used to explore the Web) should have a feature that points you to your search engine.

The hypertext linkages referred to above and offered by Internet service providers, are highlighted words, phrases, or pictures in the text that the user simply points to or clicks on with the PC mouse in order to jump automatically to another related area in the same document, to another document at the same site, or to another site altogether. Thus, no additional addresses are necessary in searching for a particular subject once the viewer has arrived at the first port of call.

On-line companies represent a typical business organization with a CEO, board of directors, and stockholders. They are subject to all established laws and regulations and have their privately-owned physical plants or infrastructures. The Internet itself is not in a specific location and no one really owns it. Internet providers simply provide doorways that give organizations and people access to dedicated phone lines used to transmit data.

Charges

On-line providers generally charge a monthly subscription fee that entitles one to a limited number of hours' usage, after which additional hours are charged for the use of their resources. Competition, however, is now causing some on-line providers (such as America On-Line) to rethink their pricing structure, and they are now offering flat monthly rates to their customers, similar to those of Internet service providers. With the latter, one pays a flat monthly fee entitling one to an unlimited or a specific number of hours per day or per month. This rate is normally much less than the on-line provider's hourly rate, although the monthly fee may be more.

Once inside the system, the user is free to request or contribute data on just about any subject, from apple pie and brownie recipes to nuclear physics, all types of personnel/human resources subjects and information (as discussed below), and much more! As with any organization, company, or group, certain reasonable rules and regulations must be followed, violations of which—including attempted illegal activities—can result in loss of Internet service or even prosecution, depending on the seriousness of the offense. Because more than 10 million individuals and businesses in the United States alone subscribe to on-line services, a completely new body of law has evolved, one that will undoubtedly continue to grow and develop as Internet technology develops.

HUMAN RESOURCES PROFESSIONALS AND THE INTERNET

One of the more challenging problems in writing about how human resources professionals can use this almost limitless knowledge found in the universe of the Internet is the fact that, just like the universe, the world of the Internet is also constantly changing. If the author points out some specific locations (addresses) where helpful personnel or human resources data are to be found on the Internet, it is not only possible but likely that before this information even reaches the reader, things will have changed, and what was unheard of today, may be valid tomorrow. It has been said of the development of the Internet that because it is created by people, it has all the characteristics of a living organism.

Each day something new is born. Each day something grows. And each day some part of the Internet dies.

Therefore, in the interests of keeping its readers as up-to-date as possible, this book will concentrate on the more established organizations and institutions where such human resources information resides and can be accessed by the user. The assumption may then be made that the continued existence of these organizations on the Internet and for some time into the future will likely be more assured. You will be given as much detail as possible, including the addresses and home pages of these sources, so you can obtain the particular type of information and answers you may need to do your HR job.

PARTS OF THE INTERNET

The Home Page
You will see the term *home page* referred to frequently in this chapter, and you should know that a home page is simply the first or primary screen (page) of that particular organization's total presence on the Internet. It may consist of, for example, the company's logo, mission statement, general information about the company, and listings of everything it offers to Internet browsers, surfers, or just plain viewers.

Each company, individual, corporation, college, government bureau, or any other organization you will find on the Internet has a home page, and each home page will be the same size as your PC screen, regardless of whether you are as large as IBM or as small as The Little Acorn restaurant. In addition, by advertising on the Internet, and using a bit of creative artistry and imagination, the home pages of many thousands of small companies can be considered their storefront as seen by viewers literally worldwide. This exposure results in an incredible bargain to the advertiser, especially considering that the cost of setting up a business home page is relatively modest.

The World Wide Web
Before launching into the more likely organizations and sites that will provide valuable input for human resources professionals, we must spend a few minutes identifying and defining one of the most vital terms and functions on the Internet. You will constantly read and hear it referred to in the Internet community as the Web, short for the World Wide Web.

You will probably hear this name identified in a number of ways, including

■ the graphical and interactive area of the Internet;

■■■ the whole gamut of resources that can be accessed using the various related computer tools provided;

■■■ the universe of hypertext servers (computers or software packages) that allow text, graphics, sound files, and other Internet elements to be mixed together. These hypertext servers provide and serve the hypertext linkages described earlier in this chapter.

As you begin your Internet journey and eventually become a more experienced (as well as convinced) client, the Web will be a most familiar term to you, and you may well want to add your own definition of the World Wide Web to those listed above.

RECRUITING SOURCES

It is no great secret to most HR managers and professionals (and especially to employment managers and recruiters) that the cost of newspaper, magazine, and trade journal advertising can range anywhere from expensive to outrageous! At the same time, the mandate from their own managers (and/or CEOs) is always to find well-qualified applicants in the least amount of time and at the lowest possible cost.

Well, HR employment and other practitioners take heart. Help is not only on the way; it has arrived. Job recruiting is experiencing an absolute boom on the Internet and the Web, and the number of people logging onto the Internet to list or find jobs is expected to increase 100 percent within the next year or so. Employers are posting job and position openings on their own home pages or with one of the many job-posting sites currently available. Job seekers can also post their own résumés on Web sites such as The Monster Board in order to assure a wide coverage of employers looking to fill available job openings.

Many companies are now beginning to feel that, from the standpoint of economy and effectiveness, posting job openings on their own home page results in an added benefit of product promotion and company awareness by those reading and/or responding to their listings of job opportunities. Many organizations, however, in addition to or in lieu of home page recruiting, still prefer to list their job openings with commercial job-posting sites. The best of both worlds resides with those employers who list their job opportunities with these job-posting sites and, in addition, have hotlinks back to their own Web sites or home pages.

There are literally hundreds of employment-related sites on the World Wide Web, among which The Monster Board, E-Span's Interactive Employment Network, Career Mosaic, On-line Career Center, Career Path, Career Web, and Job Web (not necessarily in that order) are probably among the best known. It is also generally felt that since attrition is known to be somewhat high among these hundreds of sites, the individual corporation's own Web site will always be a viable as well as reliable option.

Software programs currently exist and are constantly being further refined and developed to enable companies to track applicants, organize data, and transfer information from résumés into an applicant data base file, using e-mail, fax, or scanning. Any local Internet access provider will be able to assist a company or individual job applicant by answering questions and providing information about the services of employment-related sites on the World Wide Web.

Notwithstanding the vast scope, interest, utility, and magic of the Internet and World Wide Web that already exist today, HR professionals and others must realize that this electronic marvel is only in its infancy, and that changes and innovations are taking place at breathtaking speed! Personal computers dedicated strictly to Internet access and costing less than current PCs, modems that hook up to the Internet without requiring a telephone line, cable companies researching the possibility of Internet access via cable pipelines—these and many other improvements and capabilities are on the drawing boards of hundreds of enterprising companies.

The long-discussed one world and global community concepts now appear to be at least one step closer to reality, thanks to the Internet and the Web. It is conceivable that in the not-so-distant future, human resource staffs may have to be as familiar with the Internet and all its capabilities as they are today with, for example, wage and hour laws and regulations. Among other advantages, the ability to post job openings at any hour of the day or night, and to browse through résumés at work or after hours at home via a modem linked to the Internet could forever change the way HR (or at least the employment function) currently operates. Companies have the ability to scan résumés from all parts of the country—indeed, from all over the world—in order to fill specialized or executive job openings formerly requiring many weeks or even months of advertising, planning, and traveling. A word of caution is in order, however: Once you experience the power, capabilities, and magic of the Internet, you'll never be the same HR person you once were!

Note: For your interest, following are the Internet addresses of the employment-related Web sites mentioned above (all sites use the prefix of *http://www*):

- Monster Board: *monster.com*
- E-SPAN's Interactive Employment Network: *espan.com*
- Career Mosaic: *careermosaic.com*
- Online Career Center: *occ.com*
- Career Path: *careerpath.com*

- Career Web: *cweb.com*
- Job Web: *jobweb.com*

WEB SITES FOR HUMAN RESOURCES PROFESSIONALS

The Society for Human Resource Management (SHRM)
(Home Page address and Web site: *http://www.shrm.org*)

There are probably few, if any practitioners in the personnel profession today who have not heard of (or do not belong to) the Society for Human Resource Management, more familiarly known as SHRM. The society was formerly known as The American Society for Personnel Administration (ASPA), but changed its name to more properly reflect the profession's increasing emphasis on human resources as opposed to personnel.

The Society for Human Resource Management acts as the leading voice of the human resource profession, and represents the interests of approximately 75,000 professional and student members around the world. SHRM offers its members information and education services, conferences and seminars, government and media representation, and publications to support the advancement of human resources professionals as leaders within their own organizations.

SHRM also makes available to members, through its affiliate, the Human Resource Certification Institute, various levels of human resources certification to those individuals who qualify through examination and experience in the HR field. Such certifications in the HR profession are becoming increasingly important to practitioners, and employers are more and more interested in finding such certifications on HR applicant résumés.

For HR generalists or professionals (or for small business owners seeking answers to their personnel problems or questions), the SHRM/Human Resource Information Network (SHRM/HRIN) offers a huge body of human resources information on-line. Through this network, HR professionals can search a vast library of HR management information, reference works, periodicals, and daily news covering every facet of HR management. The system includes over 70 databases to search for information on:

- Diversity in the workplace
- Total quality management
- How to draft effective job and position descriptions
- Affirmative action regulations
- Labor/management relations
- Benefits and compensation
- Training and development

▬ Employment and recruiting

▬ Just about any other HR question, problem, statistic, rumor, etc., with which the HR practitioner grapples almost daily.

The SHRM/HRIN on-line service is available to SHRM members at discounted prices, and the ability to search multiple databases from multiple suppliers brings prices for any HR practitioner well within the realm of a positive cost/value decision, similar to any other necessary item in the human resource budget.

SHRM has also added a new on-line feature known as HR Talk, which are interactive bulletin boards that allow users to write and read messages from constituents about new and previous human resources topics. HR members receive this service free of charge, and are able to discuss and compare notes with their peers around the country without having to wait for seminars or the annual HR conference. HR Talk is available seven days a week, 24 hours a day.

For anyone interested in knowing more about the SHRM/HRIN on-line service, SHRM membership, certification, or other information, call up the SHRM home page address and web site listed on the previous page. There certainly are many other valuable personnel information avenues open to the Internet searcher, and we will explore a number of these below in this chapter; but the Society for Human Resource Management is in many respects a good starting point.

Incidentally, there are other non-Internet services of SHRM that HR professionals should not overlook. SHRM membership includes:

▬ *HR MAGAZINE on Human Resource Management*—Issued monthly and covering a wide variety of current HR topics and issues; also contains columns, departments, and special features by HR practitioners, consultants, and educators in the field.

▬ *HR NEWS*—Monthly newspaper to HR members featuring articles on current and proposed HR legislation, listings on HR jobs available, and positions wanted.

▬ Other SHRM members publications include *Workplace Visions*, a bimonthly report on workplace issues; *HR Legal Report*, containing latest HR legal issues; and *One Step Ahead*, a quarterly volunteer leaders newsletter.

SHRM also sponsors an annual conference and exhibit, legislative and leadership conferences, state conference, and national seminars. It also offers learning systems for certification preparation.

Bureau of National Affairs, Inc. (BNA)
(Home Page address and Web site: *http://www@bna.com*)

The Bureau of National Affairs, Inc. is a leading publisher of print and electronic news and information services covering the legal, business, tax, labor, environment, health, and safety fields. Headquartered in Washington, D.C. since its founding in 1929, BNA is uniquely qualified to understand and interpret the ever-dynamic legislative climate and the forces behind it.

In addition to its coverage of human resources, health care, labor relations, public policy, environment, and safety, banking, legal and tax systems, BNA offers books, training programs, customized research, surveys, and indexing services. Its products are delivered in periodical, CD-ROM, on-line, book, video, or reference binder form to its many business subscribers and others.

Following is a listing of human resources information products available through BNA.
- Newsletters
- Personnel management
- Compensation
- Labor relations
- Fair employment practices
- Wages and hours
- Government forms, notices, and posters
- Sample policies and forms

In addition to the above, BNA offers information on benefits, employment, work force strategies, payroll, workers' compensation, EEOC compliance, and many other important and timely topics of interest to HR managers and professionals in manual, CD, newsletter, report, or book format.

CCH, Inc. (CCH)
(Home Page address and Web site: *http://www.cch.com*)

CCH is a large, Fortune 1000 publisher headquartered in Riverwoods, Illinois. For the small office or home office, CCH offers the CCH Business Owner's Toolkit, the Premier Internet Guide for Small Business. CCH's Business Tools also features model letters, contracts, policies, forms, and financial templates ready to customize for the business owner.

Available Business Tool categories include:
- Business finance
- Compensation and benefits
- Employee management
- Firing and termination
- Marketing
- Recruiting and hiring
- Starting your business
- Vehicles and equipment
- Worker safety

Federal Government Information Sources

In addition to all of the available commercial resources, including those listed here, HR professionals should also be aware that the Internet provides them with a vast storehouse of information from the federal government. As an added advantage, much of the material may be accessed without cost and, since it resides in the public domain, may be freely used and quoted, so long as users credit the source appropriately. In addition, due to the rapid development and expansion of the World Wide Web, navigating it to obtain the desired information becomes ever easier.

Some of the primary federal government sources of Internet HR information are given below:

United States Department of Labor (DOL)

(Home Page and Web site: *http://www.dol.gov/*)

The home page of the U.S. Department of Labor contains a great deal of data on the department itself, including its history and mission, how it is organized, portraits of the secretaries of labor, major statutes, and links to other data sources, including a link for regulatory and statutory information. From there, you can determine the laws and regulations administered by the DOL, text of some of the statutes and executive orders, proposed regulations, and compliance assistance information.

Another interesting feature you will find in the DOL Internet data is a reference to the Economics and Statistics Administration (ESA), whose key responsibilities include the compilation of all statistical, economic, and demographic information collected by the federal government. These data are then made available to the public through the bureaus and offices of the Department of Commerce, known collectively as the Economics and Statistics Administration.

The various ESA departments and work groups, include:

- The Bureau of the Census—the nation's factfinder
- The Bureau of Economic Analysis—the nation's accountant, gathering and interpreting voluminous data to draw a complete and consistent picture of the U.S. economy
- STAT-USA—a giant information service providing economic, business, and social/environmental program data produced by more than 50 federal sources
- ESA reports and working papers

The Wage and Hour Division of the DOL's Employment Standards Administration provides compliance assistance materials on the Internet in the form of handy reference guides, as well as Fact Sheets on a wide variety of topics, all under the Fair Labor Standards Act (FLSA). These

subjects, among many others, include:
- Retail industry
- Manufacturing establishments
- Exemption for executives, administrative, professional, and outside sales employees
- Recordkeeping requirements
- Overtime pay requirements
- Section H-2A of the Immigration Reform and Control Act
- New businesses under the FLSA
- Family and Medical Leave Act of 1993

The DOL also displays a Corporate Citizenship Resource Center on the Web that emphasizes the wisdom of employers treating employees as important assets to be developed and as partners on the road to profitability. DOL maintains this resource center to enhance public access to information on workplace practices that embody a commitment to the principles of corporate citizenship that include a family-friendly workplace, economic security of employees, investment in and partnership with employees, greater worker involvement in the work process and product, and a safe and secure workplace.

The DOL considers the information currently available at this resource center as a starting point, and asks the assistance of the public in helping it to continually revise, update, and improve the service. Businesses, workers, unions, researchers, and public officials are urged to let the DOL know about companies that practice this employee-oriented philosophy, or a business committed to corporate citizenship in principle but worried about the cost, perhaps a union contract negotiator who wishes to improve the work life of the members involved, or the results of researchers' innovative workplace practices studies. Send all such comments to: *Webmaster@ttrc.doleta.gov.*

The DOL offers a wide variety of products to help businesses attain these corporate-citizenship goals, including profiles of companies that demonstrate a commitment to one or more of these principles; and a list of not-for-profit service provider organizations that offer related assistance and resources.

AJB. Finally, the Department of Labor sponsors America's Job Bank (AJB), in cooperation with the various state employment services. Through AJB, any U.S. employer or any foreign company legally authorized to operate a business in the United States, may list its job openings with this public employment service. Employers also have the option of having the service provide screening/referral control of candidates or receiving referrals directly from job seekers. No charges or fees are involved with using this service. If a company already posts job openings on the Web, a link may be made to them from America's Job Bank.

U.S. Bureau of Labor Statistics (BLS)

(Home Page and Web site: *http://stats.bls.gov:80*)

This federal government agency is the source of survey, statistical, and other data frequently used in the human resource function, including:
- Surveys and programs
- BLS information
- Economy at a glance
- Publications
- Research papers
- Regional information
- Feedback
- Keyword search of BLS Web pages

By entering desired searches on subjects such as employee benefits, compensation, turnover, health and safety standards, or whatever HR subject you may be interested in, you follow the links on the screen that guide you sequentially from the general to the specific topic you are seeking. Experienced human resources professionals are already aware of the traditional gold mine of information contained in the Bureau of Labor Statistics. BLS access via the Internet will now make the mining process easier and more productive.

Occupational Safety and Health Administration (OSHA)

(Home Page and Web site: *http://www.osha.gov/*)

Aoubt 100 million working men and women in the United States together with their six and a half million employers are covered by the Occupational Safety and Health Act of 1970 (OSHA). This law is administered by the U.S. Department of Labor's Occupational Safety and Health Administration in partnership with the federal and state governments. OSHA's mission is to save lives, prevent injuries, and protect the health of America's workers. OSHA and its state partners currently consist of approximately 2,100 inspectors, plus discrimination complaint investigators, engineers, physicians, educators, standards writers, and other technical and support staff in more than 200 offices throughout the country.

A listing of the various services OSHA offers on its Internet home page include:
- Information about OSHA
- Directories
- Media releases
- Publications

- Programs and services
- Compliance assistance
- Federal register notices
- Frequently asked questions
- Statistics and data
- Standards
- Safety and health Internet sites

Similar to other divisions of the U.S. Department of Labor, OSHA is continually seeking feedback from employee surveys, in meetings with employee and employer groups, and from focus group discussions with workers from many plants and industries around the country, in efforts to upgrade and improve the quality of performance in delivering services.

Academic Information Sources

Various colleges and universities across the nation are also involved in providing management and human resource information to Internet users. As previously mentioned in this chapter, the difficulty in assessing the value of these and other sources is the uncertainty of not knowing whether such entities will continue to be viable and have Web sites in the future; however, shown below are two academic sources that will probably have Internet sites for some time to come.

Cornell University School of Industrial and Labor Relations (ILR)

(Home Page and Web site: *http://www.ilr.cornell.edu/othersites/ index.html*)

Cornell's ILR's Virtual Library on the Internet displays the following partial subject index that would be of interest to unionized companies, although a number of subjects would apply to the nonunion business, as well.

- Behavior at Work—Psychology; sociology; communication
- Compensation and Fringe Benefits—Compensation management, policies, and theories; wage systems; enterprise, government, and labor union benefit plans
- Current Contracts—Negotiations in progress between specific companies and unions; strikes over contracts; collective agreements reached and evaluated
- Economics and Business—Enterprise, government, and labor union policies; economic conditions; cost of living; productivity statistics
- Education and Training—Enterprise, government, and labor union programs; scholarships; vocational rehabilitation
- Employee Representation—Labor union organizing activities; unionization and representation elections; labor union memberships statistics and trends

▬ Human Resource Management—Employment procedures; absenteeism; employment discrimination and fair employment practices; office procedures, retirement policies; placement; performance appraisal

▬ Industrial Engineering—Data processing technology; human factors engineering; time and motion studies; production standards; work measurement; data security; manufacturing technology; technology transfer; technological development

▬ International Relations and Governments

▬ Labor and Industrial History—Development and evolution of workers' movements and labor unions; labor union structure, legal status; industrial development

▬ Labor Force and Labor Market—Enterprise, government, and labor union manpower policies; employment and unemployment; labor force statistics

▬ Labor-Management Relations—Industrial relations; labor-management cooperation; participative management; antiunionism

▬ Negotiation Process and Dispute Settlement—Collective bargaining theory and statistics; labor disputes; strikes over grievances; arbitration, mediation, grievance procedures

▬ Research Institutes and Academic Programs

▬ Safety and Health—Enterprise, government, and labor union programs; government safety and health standards; hazardous substances and occupations; accident, sickness, and mortality statistics; industrial and transportation security

▬ Socioeconomic, Political, and Ethical Issues—Position of enterprise, labor unions, and professional groups; enterprise and labor union community activities; ethical issues and behavior in society

University of Southern California (USC), Department of Government Documents

(Home Page and Web site: *http://www.usc.edu/Library/GovDocs/index.html*)

USC's Government Documents Department is an excellent depository for federal, state of California, and Canadian documents. In particular, the federal government web sites allow human resources surfers to explore many locations that should be of more than casual interest to them. These sites include:

▬ Administration on Aging

▬ Code of Federal Regulations—Allows the viewer to search the complete CFR

▬ Environmental Protection Agency

▬ Federal Grant Information

▬ Government Printing Office

- Superintendent of Documents Home Page
- Health and Human Services Department
- Health Care Financing Administration
- Labor Department—Including America's Job Bank, (listing job opportunities that can be searched by job category), and Bureau of Labor Statistics
- Library of Congress
- National Institutes of Health
- National Performance Review
- Social Security Administration
- Supreme Court—Searchable Supreme Court decisions, 1990 to present
- Veterans Affairs

At other sites, full text is included of the *Congressional Record* for recent sessions of Congress, NASA, and the White House.

The Library of Congress

One particular web site in the above listing merits special attention and mention. The Library of Congress, probably the most voluminous and prestigious library in the world, offers to the Internet citizen expansive data on research and reference, data bases and resources; acquisitions, cataloging, preservation, special programs and services, publications, and historical collections—much of which, though not directly related to human resource endeavors, is noteworthy if only for the fact that from our offices at home or work, at any time of the day or night, we have the opportunity to access one of the premier information sources on earth..

FINAL THOUGHTS ON THE INTERNET

The versatility of this new medium of global communication seems to be endless. With many new potentials and possibilities still to come, the Internet even now permits its cybercitizens to:

- access literally a world of information from a wide variety of companies and institutions, universities, and government agencies, some by subscription and some for free, but all of great value to the human resource practitioner and other professionals;
- send and receive messages via electronic mail (e-mail), and communicate with other citizens at work, in professional, family, or social groups, or anywhere on earth;
- join in one of the thousands of electronic discussion groups with persons of similar interest—such as human resources personnel—throughout the world;

▬ view artists' works and tour museums in all the major capitals of the world;

▬ purchase books, cars, or any number of other products and services offered by the currently 10,000 or so advertisers on the Internet;

▬ post job openings on Web sites.

▬ check résumés posted on the Web for that ideal candidate for the management slot you've been trying to fill.

Intranets

Organizations are beginning to create Intranets, which may be thought of as miniature Internets offering the business organization all the qualities and features of the Internet, but on a corporate rather than global scale. The Intranet is also a developing entity and we can look for continuing progress in its usage, especially among larger corporations.

Webmasters

Large and small companies are recognizing the need for a new job function to handle the coordination, management, marketing, and all other aspects—technical as well as nontechnical—of the Internet.

As might be expected, the title and function of such a job will vary from company to company, but a key point to be considered is that even though the Webmaster is responsible for the overall Internet operation, including the company's Home Page and Web sites, we should probably think in terms of function rather than as a full-time job in itself. In most cases, the Webmaster will have other duties and should therefore be the type of individual who thrives on a full plate of job responsibilities.

Employee Abuses of the Internet

As noted in the introduction of other new products or services into the business world, employers are now showing increasing concern about losses in productivity among workers who abuse the Internet by exploring nonbusiness-related topics on the World Wide Web.

While there are software programs available to restrict access to Internet sites, the wise employer simply makes it known to employees that such conduct is unacceptable and will be dealt with and discipline assessed in the same manner as for any other infraction of company rules or regulations.

Employees should also be cautioned about the misuse of e-mail privileges and that the Internet and corporate e-mail systems are not private. In most companies, messages sent by e-mail are usually stored on hard disks or tapes in company historical archives. Even if sender and receiver delete e-mail messages in their mailboxes, such messages can still be saved in company backup files. Legal problems could result for both employee and the company if Internet and e-mail policies are not followed and monitored.

CHAPTER PERSPECTIVE

In this chapter the phenomenal, worldwide communications system known as the Internet was discussed. We examined the origin, history, and development of this revolutionary communications network and its effect on the millions of people all over the world who now make up this incredible scientific achievement. We discussed the hardware and software necessary in order to gain access to the Internet. A definition and explanation of service providers was given, and the advantages, disadvantages, and basic differences between commercial on-line service providers and Internet service providers was discussed. It was then pointed out how human resources managers and professionals can and should take advantage of the almost limitless knowledge and information that the Internet represents.

The home page and World Wide Web features of the Internet were explained, and a number of reliable and respected information sources for human resources practitioners on the World Wide Web was described in detail.

The types of human resources/personnel information available from all of these various sources was listed and described in some detail, and the Home Page or Web site address to access each of them was provided.

Descriptions were also given of restricted company communications systems—Intranets—and the advisability of appointing one individual to coordinate and manage an organization's Internet operations (known as a Webmaster), was also discussed. Advice was given to organizations about the proper means of dealing with employees who explore Internet non-business-related topics on company time with resulting losses in productivity.

Disciplinary policies were also discussed in relation to problems of employees misusing e-mail communications at work, together with possible legal liabilities for the company as well as the employees involved.

The Evolving and Future Role of Human Resources

CHAPTER 17

INTRODUCTION AND MAIN POINTS

This chapter focuses on the expanded role and responsibilities of the human resources function. The strategic, as opposed to the traditional bureaucratic, role of human resources is gaining recognition in the modern business world, as human resources becomes the leader in areas such as manpower planning, diversity programs, community programs, and management training. Company priorities determine how the People department is valued, and whether or not HR executives will represent this important function at Board of Directors meetings.

Human resources is viewed as an excellent background for a CEO position, or as a prerequisite for managers and other positions. A vital and critical function that reaches into every aspect of the employer-employee relationship, human resources is seen as an area of growth and an excellent career path.

After you read the material in this chapter:

■ You will understand how the human resources function is involved in all aspects of the employer-employee relationship.

■ You will see that the complexity of the modern world, with its legislation and other new cultural needs, has expanded the role of the human resources function.

■ You will recognize the critical need for human resources representation on the Board of Directors.

■ You will see human resources as an appropriate background for the CEO and other positions.

■ You will understand that human resources is a growing area and a viable career path.

AN EXPANDING ROLE

Much has been said and written in recent years concerning the increasingly important role the human resources or personnel function plays in the infrastructure of the modern business organization. As has been demonstrated in preceding chapters, the HR department is very much involved, sometimes in great detail, with practically every phase of an employee's life and service with a business. Should we be doing anything less for the company's most important asset?

The human resources department has the awesome responsibility at all times of dealing with and overseeing this most important, complex, and valuable commodity or resource any company can have—its people. As this key responsibility of this most vital department begins to be more recognized and better understood by top company managements, the *strategic*, as opposed to the stereotypical *bureaucratic* role of human resources is being acknowledged in ever-increasing numbers of company boardrooms and CEO offices within industry and throughout the business community.

If we look at HR's role as a profit center—even if it is sometimes an indirect one—it begins to become even more apparent as human resources departments lead the way in

1) corporate manpower planning.
2) designing and developing present and future work force diversity programs.
3) creating and maintaining a positive company image in training and counseling services for disadvantaged youths, and other local community action programs.
4) successful negotiation and dealings with unions, where applicable.
5) education and training of company supervisors and managers in the proper handling of discrimination and wrongful termination charges in order to protect the company against potential monumental punitive and/or compensatory damages and other awards in jury trials.
6) researching, analyzing, and recommending new employee involvement programs dealing with assessment, empowerment, reengineering, and team-building concepts.

And all of these activities, whether the company is an established Fortune 1000 one or a fledgling five-employee operation, are essential and important to the success of the company now, and to its survival in the future.

Community Consciousness

Just as society's economic and social views of the world are fast changing to a one-world concept, so the successful business organization must understand that it can no longer operate in a vacuum of self-interest and isolation from the problems and concerns of the community in which it is located. A former CEO communicated to his executives, managers, and operative people that business organizations in the United States operate only with the permission and tolerance of the American public, and that, therefore, business had the obligation to act at all times in a responsible manner to the people it served, whether in the quality and pricing of its products, compliance with federal, state, and local laws and ordinances, maintaining appearance standards, obeying local zoning regulations, having genuine concern for environmental matters, and so forth.

Good Neighbor Policy

More and more U.S. companies are realizing and acting on the premise that just as good residential neighborhoods depend upon the goodwill, cooperation, and sharing of the individual neighbors involved, these same attitudes apply equally as well to a corporate neighbor. In a rather strict sense, the corporation is accepted and permitted to operate in the neighborhood in which its office, plant, building, etc. is located, and it should reciprocate and recognize its obligation of being a really good neighbor!

While there is no question that being a corporate good neighbor may be equated by some as simply a matter of good business (and who can deny that it is), nevertheless, the increasing involvement of shareholders, the media, environmentalists, and other groups makes it imperative that companies be aware of and constantly strive to improve their corporate as well as public image.

Executives from companies both large and small are permitted and encouraged to volunteer hours, days, or are even loaned out for periods of time to organizations such as United Way, Junior Achievement, Big Brothers and Sisters, and other forms of charitable and public service. AT&T has recently made a public commitment to provide employees with a paid day off for volunteering or performing a public service. American Express, Xerox, The Gap, and other civic-minded organizations make every effort to teach, train, and work with disadvantaged youth and adults to help prepare them to enter the work force, or to change occupations when downsizing or layoffs result in calamitous family and financial situations.

There are many serious problems in our world that require much thought and attention, but as more and more companies provide for these types of commitments in their operating budgets, the lot of many potential workers will improve, society will benefit, and the reputation of big (as well as small) business cannot help but improve.

Whatever the issue, charitable, civic, or social, the corporation has the obligation to act as a good neighbor in the community in which it operates. The company's human resources staff can and should be instrumental in making sure this good neighbor policy is in operation at all company locations.

PRIORITIES WITHIN A COMPANY

Based on the major obligations and responsibilities of the human resources function, it becomes apparent that because people are the most important asset of any organization, the people department must necessarily command a prominent place in the company leadership hierarchy. As indicated above, this is beginning to happen in some companies, while, in others, top management has no idea what projects or activities the human resources department handles, and, in some cases, it literally does not even know on what floor its people department is located and sometimes make little effort to find out. This is a sad commentary, since it says so much about the value such companies place on their most important asset!

Recognition of the importance of the human resources function in the business community has been gradual and slow, but it is beginning to happen. In the typical large corporation, particularly, the marketing, finance, engineering, and production areas still continue to receive priority emphasis and attention, with the exception perhaps being those occasions when, for example, major discrimination or wage and hour problems arise and the human resources head is asked to give a full accounting to top management as to the causes and circumstances of the matter. It is undeniable that these above-named functions are vital to the success of any organization, no matter how large or small; but in many instances, practically the only time full attention is focused on the people aspect of the business is when sales are off, inventories up, or profits down, and the rumors begin to circulate throughout the plant that layoffs and a reduction in force are imminent. Our most important asset now commands attention simply because, as usually happens in difficult times, it once again becomes the most expendable asset.

On the other hand, there still are companies that guarantee employment to their people after a specified number of years of service. (three years at Lincoln Electric, for example). Although employees on the production line may suddenly find themselves in the sales department, or salesmen on the assembly floor, they all appreciate the fact that they are still employed. They will doubtless give 100 percent effort regardless of the task to which they are assigned.

THE HUMAN RESOURCES MANAGER, THE BOARD OF DIRECTORS, AND THE CEO

With all of the key responsibilities and duties of the human resources function, it follows with some logic that the head of that department merits a seat on the company or corporate board of directors alongside the representatives of the legal, finance, manufacturing, accounting, and other departments or divisions. There is no one more qualified than the manager, director, or vice president of human resources to best represent the interests of the employees of the enterprise, and to provide information and guidance to the board concerning personnel policies, practices, and procedures. The one area in which confusion often reigns supreme in these meetings is on the very subject of personnel or human resources (in other words, people matters). As a board member, the human resources executive can literally function as a gyroscope to add balance to the proceedings and enable the board to deliberate on important matters on the basis of fact and truth rather than on guesswork and those ever-popular glittering generalities. The overwhelming personalities on the board will continue to quote those impressive-sounding but often erroneous statistics relating to people, employment, and other HR matters of concern, but the capable human resources member who has the real, unvarnished facts, and doesn't hesitate to make the rest of the board aware of them, can be of invaluable assistance in helping the other members distinguish between perception and reality.

In the future, human resources executives will represent the company's most important asset on company boards. Today, union leaders, clergy members, and dissident shareholders are often appointed to the boards of major corporations. Tomorrow, human resource directors or vice presidents will be recognized to be in the best position within a corporation to speak for the men and women of the company. Human resources executives know the most about the opinions and attitudes of the company's employees, about personnel law, company personnel policies, compensation, benefits, diversity, and other employee issues. A board of directors should include representation from each of the major operational elements of the organization, including one of the most important elements, the personnel or human resources function.

In order to fulfill such a role, of course, the human resources executive must be one who

- demonstrates outstanding leadership and competency;
- is admired as a genuine people person; and
- consistently relates to the needs, concerns, problems, and potential of the employees of the enterprise.

While ideal people executives maximize these qualities partially from a sense of social or community responsibility, they are also well aware that, in a very real sense, it's just plain good business practice to do so. If the emphasis is on people, all other advantages follow, and there can be no limit to the company's potential progress and success.

What better candidate for the CEO job than a human resources executive to whom the emphasis on people is simply second nature?

Of course, this person must also have a grasp of finance and marketing principles, legal matters, and computer technology, combined with a certain amount of that intangible charisma that every good leader must possess. Insofar as surrounding himself or herself with capable if not outstanding executives, who should have more ability to recruit and select people than the head of human resources? Where better to expect to find that most necessary CEO quality of good interpersonal skills than in this particular executive?

There should be no doubt in anyone's mind that such human resources executives exist today, and that they become more and more qualified for top executive echelon positions as they continue to meet and resolve the same kind of complex people-related problems that modern CEOs must cope with and that increasingly demand more of their time and attention. Aspiring human resources executives must, of course, work diligently to increase their expertise in the many other required aspects of corporate leadership, but as the era of individual and employee rights continues to expand, qualified human resources practitioners will find their corporate ladder of success reaching ever closer to the top level of the organization.

LEARNING ABOUT THE HUMAN RESOURCES PROFESSION

Experienced practitioners in the personnel or human resources field must understand their responsibility to encourage and inform their own staffs, personnel trainees and interns, as well as interested college students and recent graduates, about overall potential of the human resources profession. It should be stressed that a career in human resources can be the beginning of a promising business career, and that it can lead to the top job in the company. They must understand that knowledge of other business disciplines, such as marketing, finance, sales, and manufacturing, are also necessary qualifications for those interested in making it all the way to the top.

As it becomes known that such upward job potential exists in the human resources profession more highly qualified candidates should be encouraged to consider a career move or change to the human resources field. Regardless of a person's ultimate career choice, experience in human resources can give a good, basic grounding in people relationships, company policies and organization, and a firsthand exposure to the philosophy and culture of the organization. For those whose goals involve supervisory or management responsibilities, there is no better training ground anywhere in the company than in the human resources function.

Although even today applications for the human resources department exceed the number of openings, in the future it will be one of the most popular and sought-after professions. Experience in human resources will be a prerequisite training stop on all executive management career paths. The problem might be, however, that once they experience human resources, aspiring managers and executives might discover that this is really the career they have been seeking.

CHAPTER PERSPECTIVE

This chapter examined how human resources responsibilities have grown and how the role of human resources in the business world has gradually become more important in modern times. HR was viewed as being involved in every stage of an employee's career with a company, including retirement and beyond. As the People department, human resources was seen as the most appropriate representative of a company's most important asset at board of directors meetings. As a discipline, human resources was seen as an excellent background or prerequisite for the CEO, managerial, and other positions. It was also seen as a currently growing employment area and an excellent career path.

Glossary

ADEA (Age Discrimination in Employment Act) act passed in 1967 and amended in 1978 and 1986 that prohibits employers with over 20 employees from discharging or discriminating in any way against their employees who are age 40 or older, because of their age.

AAP (Affirmative Action Plan) plan or program originated by an employer to demonstrate support of and compliance with civil rights legislation. Such plans generally indicate the company's current minority population and stipulate its future plans and programs for increasing minority as well as female participation in hiring and promotion. For all practical purposes, government contractors are required to have and comply with affirmative action plans.

ADA (Americans with Disabilities Act) 1992 law prohibiting discrimination in employment due to an individual's physical or mental disability; requires reasonable accommodation on the part of the company to assist the disabled person in performing the job.

Bargaining unit employee unit appropriate for collective bargaining (especially in representation elections) between employers and unions, as determined by the National Labor Relations Board. The commonality of interests among employees is one of the primary criteria in the Board's bargaining unit decisions.

Benchmarking program in which businesses send their employees to visit other firms to discover new ways of running a company and handling its problems.

Blind ad newspaper or magazine advertisement for employment, requesting replies to a post office box number rather than listing the company name, address, or phone number.

BLS (U.S. Bureau of Labor Statistics) federal government agency that is the source of survey, statistical, and other data frequently used in the human resources function, business groups, personnel associations, and a variety of other sources.

Broadbanding a wage system that eliminates multiple salary grades and replaces them with a few in order to encourage more movement among jobs.

Chain of command managerial or supervisory reporting function within any organization or company.

Civil Rights Act, 1964 act that contains Title VII, which, together with Executive Order 11246, forever outlawed discrimination in the United States on the basis of race, color, religion, sex, or national origin. This prohibition against unlawful discrimination applies to all terms and conditions of employment, including hiring, discharge, and promotion.

COBRA (Consolidated Omnibus Budget Reconciliation Act, 1985) act that states employers with 20 or more employees are legally bound under COBRA to provide their former employees (as well as the families of these employees) the opportunity to purchase the same health care (medical and dental) group coverage that they had been receiving from their employer and that would normally cease at the time they left the company for any reason, other than gross misconduct.

Direct deposit program that allows employees to authorize their employer to make automatic deposits from their paychecks directly into their checking and/or savings accounts in any financial institution.

Diversity overall process of assimilation, training, promotion, management, and implementation of ever-increasing numbers of minority personnel into the industrial work force. Human resource leaders must consider rapid implementation of the diversity concept a prime target and priority within their own organizations.

Downsizing scaling back of numbers of employees in order for a company to become more efficient and profitable.

Drug-free environment policy determination made and communicated by a company that it will make every reasonable effort (including applicant and employee drug testing) to create and maintain a working environment free from illegal drug use, possession, or sale within its organization.

EEOC (Equal Employment Opportunity Commission) a specific federal body created by the Civil Rights Act of 1964 to oversee and enforce the provisions of this law banning discrimination, especially in the workplace.

Employment-at-will concept maintained by most employers that any employment relationship is *at will*, that it may be terminated by either party—employer or employee—at any time, and that only the president of the company has the right to make any other arrangements to the contrary. Various court cases, decisions, and opinions may be found upholding or rejecting the at-will doctrine.

Empowerment act of giving workers more power and authority to make decisions that affect their own jobs.

EPPA (Employee Polygraph Protection Act, 1988) law that prohibits polygraph testing by employers except under somewhat limited and restricted conditions. Lie detector tests may not be given to job applicants and may be used only when there is clear evidence a theft of money or property has occurred on employer's premises. Some states prohibit polygraph testing altogether.

ERISA (Employee Retirement Income Security Act, 1974) law administered by U.S. Department of Labor that protects retirees' and employees' rights regarding retirement, health, and welfare plans. Employers are held to rigid accountability standards including provision that all retirement plan assets be held in trust, together with strict fiduciary responsibilities.

ESOP (Employee Stock Ownership Plan) a type of profit-sharing program in which an employer allocates shares of company stock to eligible employees, based on a percentage formula relating to annual company profitability. Employee eligibility is normally based on the individual's length of service, with the actual number of shares awarded each person determined by a ratio of his or her annual wage or salary.

Exemption status classification of each job in an organization to determine whether or not it is exempt from the provisions of the Fair Labor Standards Act, especially the overtime provision of the act. Specific salary and other criteria tests must be applied (normally by company compensation personnel) to determine eligibility for executive, administrative, professional, outside sales, and computer-related occupation exemptions.

Fluctuating workweek provision of the Fair Labor Standards Act that allows companies to set up a weekly paid, nonexempt, guaranteed salary method of compensation without the need to pay time and one-half for overtime hours. If employees' working hours vary such that they can never be sure of specific beginning or ending of daily work shift duties, employees may be classified on fluctuating workweek and paid half-time for all overtime hours; however, if employees work any amount of time during the workweek, the employer must pay them the weekly salary guarantee.

FMLA (Family and Medical Leave Act, 1993) law requiring covered employers to provide up to 12 weeks of unpaid, job-protected leave to eligible employees for certain family and medical reasons. The employer must maintain employees' current health coverage under any existing group health plan during FMLA leave.

Globalization operation of a company or business without regard to international borders. Instead of operating from their home country, companies go where their customers and clients are, and using foreign nationals, they establish manufacturing and service facilities in order to serve those customers.

Home page first or primary screen (page) of a particular organization's total presence on the Internet; used by advertisers, in particular, to display company's logo, mission statement, general company information, and listings of what it offers to viewers.

Human resources function that deals with all aspects of a company's employees; usually administered by a human resources (or personnel) department responsible for employment, compensation, benefits, equal employment opportunity, employee counseling, personnel software and hardware systems, retirement matters—and all other phases of employer-employee relationships.

Information superhighway Internet, the World Wide Web, linking together people of all nations through electronic communication.

Internet huge collection of interconnected electronic networks spanning the globe. An electronic pipeline or information superhighway made up of millions of individual computers (nodes) connected to a network, with data and information of practically every kind flowing through and on it; an outgrowth of military and scientific computing networks developed by Rand Corporation and the Pentagon.

Intranets networks that may be thought of as miniature Internets offering the business organization all the qualities and features of the Internet, but on a corporate rather than global scale.

IRCA (Immigration Reform and Control Act, 1986) attempt by Congress to eliminate the illegal practice of employers hiring unauthorized alien workers for their companies. All employers, regardless of size, are subject to the provisions of IRCA.

Job description written description of the duties and responsibilities of a particular job function in an organization or company, prepared by the wage and salary analysts of the human resources department. The job description should begin with an initial summary paragraph indicating the job's general duties and responsibilities, followed by subsequent paragraphs describing in some detail the general duties referred to in the summary paragraph. The job description should relate only to the required duties of the position and never to the qualifications of the current or prospective incumbent. It should be written clearly and succinctly. Seldom recommended to exceed one page in length, it must give a reader unfamiliar with the job a clear understanding of what the job entails.

Job evaluation formal system of analyzing and evaluating jobs based on the duties and responsibilities of the individual job. Job evaluation attempts through a given rating plan to determine the relative weight of the function, and its overall importance to the company. The wage and salary analysts of the human resources department normally have the responsibility of performing the job evaluation process.

Job questionnaire form document used by human resources wage and salary personnel to gather data from job incumbents and/or managers in preparation for job evaluation projects. The questionnaire asks incumbents about day-to-day duties and responsibilities, including type and nature of work performed, frequency and level of contacts, difficulty of the work, decisions made, etc. The questionnaire is used as a supplement to personal interviews with job incumbents.

LAN (Local Area Network) network of computers linked together in a restricted or local area, most often in a single building or adjacent group of buildings, in a specific department or floor of a building, etc.

Management by Objectives (MBO) top down sequential, formal, and cooperative method of setting and developing organizational goals and their supporting objectives at each level of the organization. MBO addresses key result areas such as profitability, productivity, market share, customer service, and satisfaction, employee training, career development and performance, corporate image, conservation of resources, public responsibility, and ethics. MBO's five procedural steps include: identification of key result areas, setting performance standards, creating objective measures of performance, appraising performance, and mutually determining ways to improve performance.

Management by Walking Around (MBWA) theory that managers cannot possibly do an effective job of supervising others unless they leave their office or desk to observe and collect data and impressions by informal visits to work sites and areas.

Merit pay method of compensating employees based on established company standards of performance. More and more companies are now installing merit pay systems and eliminating automatic wage increases based on time on the job or overall seniority.

MODEM acronym for MOdulator, DEModulator, a device connecting a computer to a phone line allowing computers to talk to each other over the phone system, thus providing access to the Internet.

Multiculturalism political or social philosophy promoting cultural diversity. This philosophy is supported by many educators in the United States who favor the teaching of different cultures so that they may be understood and appreciated. This teaching, known as multicultural education, especially relates to the contribution of women, non-Europeans, and people of Hispanic ancestry to our society.

Organization chart graphic representation of jobs or positions within a company, department, or other unit. Chart depicts jobs and job titles, reporting relationships, and the number of current or authorized incumbents on each job; used by wage and salary analysts as an important tool in job evaluation.

OSHA (Occupational Safety and Health Act, 1970) act, also known as the Williams-Steiger Act, which requires virtually every employer in the United States to furnish its employees with a place of employment literally free from any safety hazards likely to cause death or serious injuries to them. OSHA has authority to levy fines and assessments on employers who do not maintain an environment of safety and protection at work sites.

Outsourcing practice of hiring vendors or other outside companies to perform work previously done within a given company. Such decisions by corporations to farm out work to other organizations are normally based on cost/value judgments considering both economy and effectiveness.

People principle principle practiced by a company when it shows genuine respect for its employees (whether union or nonunion), and recognizes the dignity of work as well as the dignity of the individual. Employees, even in our modern era of eroding employee loyalty, will still respond favorably to a management that demonstrates sincere concern for their welfare.

Performance appraisal periodic supervisory evaluation of an employee's job performance; Process should include discussion of areas in need of improvement, as well as praise for improvements made. Goal setting, sincere compliments on work well done, and genuine supervisory interest in the employee's comments or complaints, are all essential elements of the performance appraisal.

Piecework rates method of compensating workers based on number of items or parts produced per given time period. Consideration is made for accuracy, complexity, and other factors involved in the production of individual units.

Protected concerted activity section 9(a) of the National Labor Relations Act that provides that any employee or group of employees has the right to present grievances to the employer whether or not that employee is represented by a labor union.

Reengineering procedure whereby a company reorganizes its work process to more effectively create its product or service for the customer. Reengineering often eliminates layers of jobs.

Restructuring process of reorganizing businesses and/or getting rid of unnecessary operations.

Representation election election by eligible employees of a company to determine whether a particular labor union will represent the employees of the company, department, or unit involved. The election is conducted by the National Labor Relations Board by secret ballot. A simple majority of those voting determines the winner of the election.

Rightsizing eliminating or scaling back unnecessary or outdated jobs to achieve more efficient operations.

Search engine electronic Internet information searching device that allows the user to access predetermined multiple networks or categories of information or data, without having to enter individual addresses or locations for each specific item of information desired. Examples of well-known search engines include InfoSeek, Lycos, and Yahoo.

Sexual harassment "...unwelcome sexual advances, requests for sexual favors, and other verbal or physical conduct of a sexual nature constitute sexual harassment when (1) submission to such conduct is made either explicitly or implicitly a term or condition of an individual's employment, (2) submission to or rejection of such conduct by an individual is used as the basis for employment decisions affecting such individual, or (3) such conduct has the purpose or effect of unreasonably interfering with an individual's work performance or creating an intimidating, hostile, or offensive working environment..." (U.S. Equal Employment Opportunity Commission)

SHRM (Society for Human Resource Management) leading association and voice of the human resources profession; offers its approximately 75,000 members around the world information and education services, conferences and seminars, government and media representation, and publications to support the advancement of human resources professionals as leaders within their own organizations.

Substance abuse testing drug testing by employers, the major areas of which include: employment testing of newly-hired job applicants, post-accident testing of employees following industrial accidents, probable-cause testing of employees, based on reasonable suspicion of impaired performance, random testing, which refers to a company policy of unscheduled, unannounced random drug testing of employees within the organization and safety-sensitive position testing of employees in selected high-risk occupations such as vehicle drivers and equipment operators.

Taft-Hartley Law (Labor Management Relations Act, 1947) law passed as a balance to the 1935 National Labor Relations Act giving employees the legal right to join a labor organization, Taft-Hartley essentially gave employees the legal right to not join a union.

Teaming process of organizing teams of employees at all levels of an organization to discuss and make decisions or effective recommendations about how work operations should be organized or structured, work assignments for team members, and other operational matters or problems. Teaming objectives are based on the premise of greater work efficiency.

Total Quality Management (TOM) attempt by employee teams to find ways of improving their own productivity and the quality of their product or service.

Unemployment insurance laws laws governed and controlled by individual state laws, designed to provide temporary income protection for those workers who find themselves out of work through no fault of their own. Unemployment insurance is paid for by the individual employer to the respective state, based on volume of unemployment claims payments made by the state on behalf of a particular employer.

Validations statistical programs used by employers and outside professional groups designed to serve as reliable predictors of successful job performance. Validation methods are commonly used in determining the value as well as legality of employment tests used in industry.

Vesting process whereby an employee is required to remain with a given employer a specific amount of time in order to be eligible to share partially or totally in company contributions to an employee pension, profit-sharing or retirement-savings plan.

Wage and Hour Law (Fair Labor Standards Act) 1938 law (as amended) that is the principal federal law relating to overall employee compensation, including minimum wage, overtime pay requirements, and child labor; the keystone of employee compensation.

Wage surveys tool used by compensation analysts to determine wage and salary rates and ranges offered by other companies in a geographic area. Survey methods include letters, phone calls, and personal visits to companies, local chambers of commerce, libraries, and local businesspeople and merchants' associations.

Wagner Act (National Labor Relations Act, 1935) legislation that essentially gave employees the legal right to join a labor organization of their choice. The law also established the National Labor Relations Board to coordinate and administer the provisions of this first major piece of labor legislation.

WARN (Worker Adjustment and Retraining Notification Act, 1988) law that in general requires employers of 100 or more employees to provide at least 60 days' written advance notice of layoffs and plant closures to affected employees, their union representatives, and local government officials. If employer does not give required notice, it may be held liable for all back pay and benefits for the 60-day notice period.

Web browser a software program used to research a wide variety of Internet resources and to explore the World Wide Web (WWW).

Webmaster individual or function designated by a company or organization to handle the coordination, management, marketing, and all other aspects—technical and nontechnical—of the Internet.

Workers' compensation insurance insurance that covers any injury or illness requiring medical attention that is incurred by an employee, out of or in the course of his or her employment, making the employer generally immune from damage suits arising out of occupational injuries. Every employer is required to carry this insurance for all company employees. Six states have their own state-funded workers' compensation programs to which employers must contribute.

WWW (World Wide Web) graphical and interactive area of the Internet; the whole gamut of resources that can be accessed using the various related computer tools provided to the Internet user.

401(k) plans savings plans based upon Section 401(k) of the Internal Revenue Code, which allows eligible employees to contribute a percentage of their salary on a tax-deferred basis into a company-administered investment plan.

Bibliography

Arthur, Diane. *Managing Human Resources In Small and Mid-Sized Companies*, 2nd Edition. New York: AMACOM, 1995.

Badgett, Tom and Corey Sandler. *Welcome to Internet: From Mystery to Mastery*, 2nd Edition. New York: MIS Press, 1995.

Bangs, David H., Jr. *The Personnel Planning Guide: Successful Management of Your Most Important Asset*, 2nd Edition. Dover, NH: Upstart Publishing, 1989.

Bardwick, J. et al. *Change as the Status Quo: Implications for HR Professionals*. New York: Human Resource Planning, 1993.

Baytos, Lawrence M. *Designing and Implementing Successful Diversity Programs*. Englewood Cliffs, NJ: Prentice Hall, 1994.

Beach, Dale S. *Personnel: The Management of People at Work*, 6th Revised Edition. Old Tappan, NJ: Macmillan, 1994.

Business and Legal Reports Staff. *How to Analyze Jobs: A Step by Step Approach*, Madison, CT: Business and Legal Reports, 1982.

Comer, Douglas. *The Internet Book: Everything You Need to Know about Computer Networking and How the Internet Works*. Englewood Cliffs, NJ: Prentice Hall, 1994.

Compensation and Benefits Alerts. Boston, MA: Warren, Gorham & Lamont, 1993.

Fishman, Daniel B. and Cary Cherniss, Editors. *The Human Side of Corporate Competitiveness*, Thousand Oaks, CA: Sage, 1990.

Foulkes, Fred K. and E. Robert Livernash. *Human Resources Management: Cases and Text*, 2nd Edition. Englewood Cliffs, NJ: Prentice Hall, 1989.

Garfield, Charles. *Second to None: How Our Smartest Companies Put People First*. Burr Ridge, IL: Irwin Professional Publishing, 1991.

Gomez-Mejia, Luis R. *Compensation and Benefits*, (SHRM-BNA Ser: Vol. 3). Washington, DC: Bureau of National Affairs, 1989.

Grant, Philip C. *Multiple Use Job Descriptions: A Guide to Analysis, Preparation, and Applications for Human Resources Managers.* Westport, CT: Greenwood, 1989.

Hall, Jay and Susan M. Donnell. *Nice Guys Finish First.* Woodlands, TX: The Woodstead Press, 1988.

Jelepis, Chris T. *The Human Factor: Managing People,* 2nd Edition. Dubuque, IA: Kendall-Hunt, 1991.

Kelly, Barbara. *HR Training.* Madison, CT: Business and Legal Reports, Inc., 1996.

Kolker, Linda. *HR Manager's Guide to the Internet.* Madison, CT: Business and Legal Reports, Inc., 1996.

Leveque, Joseph D. *Manual of Personnel Policies, Procedures and Operations,* 2nd Edition. Englewood Cliffs, NJ: Prentice Hall, 1993.

Lutz, Carl F. *How to Develop, Conduct and Use Pay-Benefits Surveys.* Crete, IL: Abbott Langer Associates, 1986.

Maitland, Iain. *The Barclay's Guide To Managing Staff for the Small Business.* Cambridge, MA: Blackwell Publishers, 1991.

Mercer, Michael W. *Turning Your Human Resources Department into a Profit Center.* New York: AMACOM, 1989.

Neusch, Donna R. and Alan F. Siebnaler. *The High Performance Enterprise: Reinventing the People Side of Your Business,* 2nd Edition. New York: Wiley, 1995.

The Personnel Department: The Complete Do-It-Yourself Kit for the Growing Company, Englewood Cliffs, NJ: Ring Binder, Prentice Hall, 1991.

Traynor, William J. and J. Steven McKenzie. *Opportunities in Human Resource Management Careers.* Lincolnwood, IL: NTC Publishing Group, 1994.

INDEX